DEADLY UNTRUTHS

P.J. Allen

CyPress Publications

Tallahassee, Florida

Inquiries should be addressed to:
CyPress Publications
P.O. Box 2636
Tallahassee, Florida 32316-2636
http://cypresspublications.com
lraymond@nettally.com

Library of Congress Cataloging-in-Publication Data

Allen, Pamela J., 1955—
  Deadly untruths / Pamela J. Allen. — 1st ed.
    p. cm.
  ISBN 978-1-935083-01-6 (trade paper)
  1. Women journalists—Fiction. 2. Women journalists—Crimes against—Fiction.
3. Investigative reporting—Fiction. 4. Iraq War, 2003—–Atrocities—Fiction.
5. Political fiction. I. Title.
  PS3601.L4338D43 2008
  813'.6—dc22

                    2008027694

ISBN: 978-1-935083-01-6
First Edition

Dedication

To C.H.W.

Prologue

The two men, one short and stubby, one tall, hovered over the handsome but meek man sitting at the aristocratic desk. The room was rich, masculine. The dark mahogany bookshelves, matching the desk, were filled with volumes of history and other non-fiction. The paintings on the walls were oils, portraits and scenes of people and places from long ago. The old Persian rug remained remarkably thick and plush, resilient and robust. As the day waned, the lighting was subtle, adding to the false atmosphere of coziness, warmth, and general sense of well-being. Ghosts, victims of previous wars unable to find rest, thus attaching themselves to items of familiarity that allowed them a sense of belonging, lurked among the ancient artifacts comprising the room and watched with apprehension.

"You'll have to sign. We can't move forward without it. It will be missed if we do," the pudgy man said, gently but authoritatively.

"I'm not sure what it's suggesting. What does 'consequences' mean?"

The tall man sighed, slightly.

"There will be consequences. It's not complicated," the short man said, holding out the pen.

The other man, the one who sighed, subtly looked at his watch. "I remember hearing your discussion with each other, the other day, about annihilation."

"Shhhh . . . that word must never, ever, be mentioned by any of us. Can you imagine what kind of reaction that will elicit? Please, don't say that again."

"So . . . once I sign, we can move on, things will get better? They're pretty bad right now. Even I know that. I can tell by the way the staff looks at me, the way you look at me," he said, rather apprehensively.

"It's going to get a whole lot better. Trust us." The short man jabbed the pen at the hesitant man once again.

This time, he took it. He looked up at them both and quickly scratched his signature.

The Ghosts recoiled.

The tall man looked at his watch again.

At that moment, on the other side of the world, bombs began raining down on a town in the Middle East. Buildings crashed, people—men, women, children, the elderly—all ran. But there was no place to run. The bombardment was fierce and abundant. It lasted for hours. Once it stopped, not even a barking dog could be heard. While few had escaped, many had left earlier, suspecting they were going to be a target. They would all come back soon, to bury the dead and to try to start over. When they did, they would be confronted with the collection of tens of thousands of small, missile-like objects, some of them still not activated. But accidental activation would be the least of their problems. Their nightmare had just begun.

The Ghosts wept.

1

"Hello?" she inquired breathlessly, quickly clicking on the cell, hoping the caller had not hung up. The time was 3:40 a.m.

"Andie? It's Deidre."

"Who?"

"I feel trapped. I don't know how I got here." The woman's crackly voice sounded muted and distant. "Andie, I'm in a cement room, alone. I don't know why."

Andie felt the hairs on the back of her neck stand up. She began walking through the den, toward the sliding glass doors to her balcony, as she tightened the robe's belt around her body. Later, she thought it must have been intuitive. She thought she needed to hear Deidre's voice more clearly. What she was being told didn't make sense.

"What can you remember?" Andie asked, innocently enough. "Who put you there?"

"I couldn't tell. I don't know," Deidre responded, a little more frantically. "I don't think I'm going to make it, Andie."

"How long have you been there?" was Andie's next question, and a logical one.

"Hello?" she asked. "Hello?" The phone had gone dead, but not before she heard a truly mournful sob.

Andie hadn't realized it, but she was now standing on the balcony, staring into the night lights of the city as the snowflakes floated silently through the air all around her. Her feet were bare, but she didn't notice that they were also freezing. She sat down on the cold, hard, metal chair. *Well, that was bizarre.*

Andie didn't know a Deidre.

3

2

The newsroom was chaotic as usual. Though she tried to concentrate, she had never been able to get back to sleep after the phone call the night before, so Andie couldn't think clearly now. Tired, grouchy, hungry, and a bit on edge, she was dreading her upcoming meeting with someone she'd never met, only to verify a source. Why he couldn't give it over the phone she didn't understand. If she didn't have the two o'clock deadline, she would have gone to the gym and then home. Instead she was gulping cold coffee. Ugh. She couldn't even remember when she had prepared it. She kept thinking back to the incident that had occurred earlier, the phone call from Deidre. Christ, now she was actually attaching the name to the voice, as though she knew her. But then, how had Deidre known her? Perhaps it was a fluke, a one in a million chance that it was a coincidental mistaken identity. *That could be,* Andie mused. *A freaky coincidence.*

"Andie!" Andie jumped as her thoughts were harshly interrupted by her boss, Simon Feldman. Jeez, he was practically standing on top of her. "Are you deaf? I've been calling you for the past twenty minutes," he barked.

"Oh, sorry. I didn't hear you," she stated, wondering how she could have been that engrossed; but noting how noisy it was with the constant buzzing of cell phones and the accompanying loud conversations, she guessed it hadn't been that hard. This floor alone contained over thirty cubicles. There were at least as many employees working the phones, their cell phones, and faxes throughout the day. It was the busiest floor of the entire company, which consisted of six floors altogether. The building also housed a real estate office, two law firms, and a dingy coffee shop. It was relatively low rent for the D.C. area, and it was obvious why. The building had not been updated over the past twenty years. Hence, there were window unit air conditioners and wall heating radiators, fluorescent lighting, no carpet, dark halls, a really pathetic basement that had low-water-pressure showers for the exercise buffs and the oldest, most rickety elevators in the entire town. Every year, when they received a clean bill of health from the building code authority, Andie figured someone must have taken a bribe. It's why she always took the stairs.

"Yeah, you better be sorry. I had to get out of my chair, get on the elevator, and walk all the way over here. It's not easy, you know." Andie did feel badly that he had to go to such trouble. Simon had been in a bad accident as a teenager, and the vertebrae in his lower back were permanently damaged to the degree that he could not walk fully upright. His walk accentuated what had become over time a rather contorted body. Without proper exercise and rehab, he had learned to swing his legs from side to side as he progressed forward. The effect on his physique was to create huge shoulders which provided an umbrella for the rest of his body. His neck was almost non-existent. A few months ago he grew his thinning hair out to cover this flaw, or because he wanted to appear younger; Andie didn't know which reason was the major impetus, but in either case she felt it had failed. Add about thirty extra pounds to a man who measured only five feet, ten inches tall, and he was not all that attractive. "I'm really sorry, Simon," Andie said sincerely.

"I know you are. Forget it. I needed to get some exercise. But where have you been? Did you confirm that source? It's almost 11:00."

"Oh my God," Andie exclaimed, realizing that she'd lost all sense of time. "I've got to go, Simon. I'll have the piece completed by deadline. I promise."

"But . . . I thought you . . ."

"No . . . I'm going now," she interrupted, and with that she threw her cape over her shoulders, shaking her long black hair out from under it, and ran for the stairs. She had an appointment, and she was going to be late. "Go, go, go,'" she muttered under her breath, skipping every other step down the three flights to the ground level, where she made a beeline for the bar several blocks away. Well, if he wanted to meet in a bar, he must be busy having a drink, she reasoned. *Don't worry. Just get there,* she told herself, barely avoiding a collision with an elderly man rounding the corner at the Farragut North Metro entrance. *Just get there.*

The snow was melted and the sky was overcast, making the slush look more dismal than usual. Andie dodged the puddles and the occasional ice patch, in between the other pedestrians. As she approached the bar, *Norman's 18th Hole,* a man was exiting. She hoped it wasn't her guy. She greeted him with a smile as she was entering, but he didn't even make eye contact. *Guess not.*

Wow! Even with overcast sky outside, Andie's eyes could not adjust to the darkness fast enough. She was literally blinded for several seconds after entering. Once she could make out her surroundings, she realized there were only three people in the establishment: the barkeeper and a man at the bar, and another man sitting in a booth smoking a cigarette. She noticed he had what looked to be tomato juice. He was reading a newspaper. She decided to hedge her bet on the guy with the newspaper. She hung up her cape on a loose hook by the door and walked across the very worn wooden floor to him. He glanced up. She smiled, trying to gauge whether he was irritated that she was late.

"Hi, Elliot," she started. "I'm Andie."

The man glared. "Do I look like an Elliot?" he inquired rudely. Andie wondered how she was supposed to know what an Elliot should or shouldn't look like, but that was beside the point. "Listen, Andie, beat it. I've got a hell of a hangover," he said, as he inhaled deeply on the cigarette and resumed reading the paper. Andie glanced over her shoulder. The customer at the bar was grinning at her. He motioned for her to join him there.

Andie didn't consider this to be funny. She walked over as the man was pulling out the rickety stool next to him. "Hi, Andie," he said, as she reached the bar. "I'm Elliot," he gestured by offering to shake her hand. She took it, grudgingly, and squeezed hard. He grinned slightly when she did so. She decided to ignore it, knowing it was her own fault for guessing, but more importantly, she had to get this guy to talk so she could meet her deadline. "Do you want to sit in a booth?" he asked, still grinning.

"No, this is fine," Andie laughed slightly, appreciating the irony in the offer.

"What do you want?" the bartender muttered, without taking his eyes from the talk show on the TV above the bar.

"I'll have coffee," Andie said.

"Fresh out." he replied, still not looking at her.

"I'll have a Coke," she responded. He moved like a robot, reaching for the glass, scooping the ice, and depressing the nozzle on the soda machine; all the while his head was cocked up, apparently in total rapture with the shouting audience and pitiful person being jeered at by the very unsympathetic TV audience. He set it down with a thump, turned on his heel, and went back to watch, leaning against the prep counter.

Andie picked up the drink and for the first time turned to look at Elliot.

He was a nice looking guy from what she could see in the dreary lighting. Sandy hair, nice countenance. Nice enough build. She guessed he was in his early forties, but who knew these days?

"You called to say you had some information for me?"

"That's why you're here, right?" he said, smiling slightly.

"Yeah, that's right."

"Well, ask away."

Andie looked over at the bartender, concerned about eavesdropping. She didn't need to worry, apparently; he was literally glued to the raunchy show. She could see him grinning and shaking his head in agreement with the crowd. Nonetheless, she felt extremely uncomfortable talking within range of his hearing.

"Let's move over to the window," she suggested. "I'd like a little more light."

"Sure," he agreed.

They both took their drinks and walked over to the small café table next to the only window in the place. He actually pulled the chair out for Andie. Once they were seated, they both found themselves looking out the window at the passersby. Virtually everyone was walking briskly, head down, and weaving in and out of the pedestrian traffic. Cars appeared stalled.

"It's supposed to be a harsh winter," Andie said, as she turned to begin their conversation again.

Elliot was still staring out the window. It looked like he was a million miles away. She had a chance to observe him more closely now. He was really very nice looking. He looked like he worked out, or ran, or did something to keep trim. He suddenly turned, seemingly returning to the present. "Go ahead," he said. "You were going to ask me some questions."

Andie took a deep breath and began. "You said over the phone you had some very interesting information about a leak from the White House."

"Well, actually I said from this administration, which could be from any department."

"Oh. Well then, from this administration. Can you tell me the nature of the leak?"

"The nature of the leak is the leak itself."

Andie was irritated by this response. "I don't understand. Am I missing something here?"

"The leak is a plant, and it's intentional."

"Leaks are usually intentional."

"True, but this plant is physical, in a passive way."

"This administration? The most hawkish administration in the history of this nation?" Andie admonished, sarcastically incredulous. Elliot said nothing. He simply continued to look at her, nodding his head in agreement, ever so slightly.

Andie looked back out the window, barely noticing that it was sleeting now. She began to think that her "source" was a nut. She decided to speak her mind. She had nothing to lose. The story she thought she was going to submit today hinged on a name, which she thought she was going to get from this guy. In fact, she had been sure she was going to get the name of a White House staff member who was deliberately feeding untruths to a complacent media outlet, calling itself a news station. But instead she was getting . . . perhaps the runaround? Perhaps her story about bad reporting would have to be scrapped, at least for the foreseeable future.

"Do I have to continue to guess, or will you tell me what you mean? This is not helpful. It's just frustrating. Why'd you call me?" she added, not being able to control her irritation.

"I can't tell you more. It would be unwise. If you really are interested in pursuing a career in investigative journalism, I suggest you start your research today." He smiled wanly and stood up. "I promise you, you do not want to learn what I know through me. It won't be safe. You've already been given three clues; you are on your own now," he said quietly, as he held out his hand to shake hers. Andie looked up and saw that the expression on his face was one of great concern.

"Will I hear from you again?"

"Maybe. It all depends on you."

She reached out and shook his hand. They exited the bar together, after Elliot paid for the drinks. He was going in the opposite direction, so they said another good-bye. "Elliot," Andie spoke just as he was about to walk off.

"Yes?"

"How *did* you get my name?"

"One of your colleagues told me to contact you; a good friend to both you and me," was all he said as he pulled up his collar and headed off.

Andie walked slowly back to the newsroom. The sleet was heavy, just hard ice pouring down on her.

She felt let down and depressed. No story for now. No winning article. No exposure of the yellow journalism practiced more and more boldly by the "RW&B," short for the Red, White and Blue news agency. Damn. Sometimes she wished she had pursued a different career. At one point, in fact, she had thought about being an entomologist. Then, however, she realized she liked studying people more than bugs. Bugs were just too predictable. But now, looking at the breeding practices of butterflies seemed to be a more rewarding endeavor than trying to figure out some cryptic comment from a person with no last name. "Three clues, give me a break," she muttered to herself. A gust of wind blew just as she reached the door to her building, momentarily preventing her from opening it. As she struggled to do so nonetheless, she saw a man in the reflection staring at her from across the street. She turned to look at him, but at that moment someone came out, causing her to turn back to avoid being hit by the door. Once the person exited she turned to look again, but the man was gone. She quickly entered the building to get out of the storm and looked back once again, just in case. No one.

Now, for the big problem. She headed up the stairs to talk with Simon.

3

Reflecting later upon that scene, now several hours past, she had to admit it had not been a pleasant one. She still could hear Simon yelling at her. "Where am I supposed to get an article in less than an hour?" "What the hell were you thinking, not having more than a first name?" "I asked you: Are you sure?" "Do you have this nailed down?" "Why would he call you?" "What is his angle?" Blah, blah, blah. Simon's scolding had lasted for at least five minutes. She had just stood there. She knew she deserved the dressing down. It was so embarrassing. At least she felt better that he might have felt better, and at least he had not used the word *fired*.

She actually wasn't really afraid of him firing her. Their relationship was too intertwined to allow for that, although she made sure she never exploited it. It so happened that Simon and her mother had been dating when he had the accident that had crippled him. They were both only sixteen, so it wasn't a serious relationship at the time, but nonetheless, her mother had stuck by him during the long healing process and had remained his friend when others had distanced themselves because they felt uncomfortable. Coincidentally, Simon and his mother also had attended the same college. Their friendship was firmly cemented by the time they graduated. They remained very close as time passed, and her mom had asked Simon to be her daughter's godfather when the time came.

Yes, it was true. She had gotten the job with a little help from their relationship, but Andie believed she was an even better employee because of it—although sometimes she wondered if that was just a rationalization on her part because she hated any kind of cronyism. But she and Simon had never really discussed it. Andie liked it best this way and had decided that he must, too.

Returning to the present, Andie heard herself promising Simon that she would make up for it, although in fact, she didn't have any idea how she was going to do it. Simon had countered that hesitancy or delays on their part just gave the bloggers scoops as gifts and built their growing credibility. But tomorrow was another day. She needed to get some sleep.

As she prepared for bed, Andie thought again about her meeting with Elliot. How strange. What was it he said? A leak, but not just any leak, a physical leak, in fact he had used the word plant to be more specific. What was all of that about? It really made her angry. Why wouldn't the guy just tell her what he meant? What was that nonsense about *three* clues? So what? He'd given her two . . . an intentional leak that was a physical plant. Why couldn't he have given her the third one? She shook her head as she picked up her book to read, hoping that she would fall asleep quickly. She did. She was dead tired.

4

The bunker was not so much unknown as known not to be in use. At least that is what Agent Ingram had been told. He knew that the fewer questions he asked and the less he knew, the happier and perhaps safer he would be. *The activities occurring down here are not legal,* he thought.

The woman with the hypodermic and stethoscope, the small rooms, and the immense silence unnerved him. Again, he told himself, *it's none of my business.* He had prepared the "conference room" as requested, and now he stood outside waiting, for what he did not know. Suddenly, his cell phone began to ring. *Oh my God,* he thought. He shut it off, but not before noticing that the call was from his buddy, who was definitely not in the bunker. *Wow,* he thought, *I had no idea that they would work down here.* He made sure he switched it to vibrate so it would not happen again.

An hour and a half later he began to hear voices. Male voices. The footsteps that matched the voices now rounded the brightly lit hall. Three men. Agent Ingram tried not to gasp. The Vice President was in the middle. His Chief of Staff was next to him. He didn't recognize the third man. He opened the door as they approached. No one even acknowledged him. The door shut and locked automatically after they entered. Agent Ingram had been ordered to stand guard until "the persons attending the meeting departed."

Once inside and seated at the table, the pasty-faced VP gave a barely perceptible nod to the third man, known simply as Jones. Jones cleared his throat and began. "It's true we've had a few hiccups, and admittedly it's been a tough ride."

The VP said in an even, but obviously menacing tone, "What do you mean a few hiccups? They have been monumental failures."

"With all due respect, sir, I believe that's an exaggeration," Jones said as a matter of fact. The VP said nothing. Instead he held out his hand to his Chief of Staff, who responded by immediately handing him a folder. The VP nodded for the third man to continue, as he began flipping through the folder. "We believe we have ironed out all the wrinkles and are now on schedule."

The VP's face started to turn a darker shade of putty as he raised his hand with the folder in it and slammed it down on the table. "Cut the crap. You know it's been a miserable performance. Now, what are you going to do about it?" he shouted, noting the diamond earring in the man's ear with disgust. *Pussy,* he thought.

If Jones was intimidated or frightened by this behavior, he didn't show it. He didn't even flinch. Actually, he could not help being distracted by the very unattractiveness of the VP. It was no accident that this public servant was shown on TV as rarely as possible. He was downright ugly.

But it didn't matter because he was so indispensable to the administration. He could have been a green being from the bowels of the sea, for all this government cared. His institutional memory was known to be idolized by his followers. Christ, it seemed as though he'd been around for most of the Twentieth Century. And ruthless, Jones thought. But he could care less, which is why he hadn't flinched. He, Jones, had something this man needed. "We have infiltrated two of the three departments. Our mistake was the prioritization. We have reversed our emphasis at this point in order to address this oversight. The problem is now being addressed with a two-pronged approach so we can change and eliminate targets, if necessary. And I would like to gently remind you that this prioritization was determined by consensus, so the 'failure,' as you refer to it, is shared."

At this point the VP stood up and leaned toward Jones, so as to physically intimidate him this time around. "Don't you ever contradict me again. The fault lies with you and your stupid, third-rate minions. If you can't get this on track within the week, you're toast, and that's not a euphemism," he growled, as perspiration gathered at his temple.

"Sir, we'll do our best, but if you continue to threaten me or if you fulfill your threat, then you'll be nowhere," Jones said confidently.

"You make me sick," the VP growled. "I'll expect an update within forty-eight hours and a demonstration. Now get out!"

Jones simply stood up and walked out.

Agent Ingram was startled when the door opened, noting that only the third man was leaving. He watched him as he ambled away, whistling of all things. The tune was familiar, but he couldn't place it. The lanky man appeared to be in his late thirties or early forties. Not a word had been exchanged between them.

Inside the room, the VP said, "Get someone to watch him as best you can, and make sure the Secretary of Defense doesn't find out. He still considers him to be a loyal servant."

"You don't think he is?" the Chief of Staff asked, surprised.

"Are you kidding?" the VP scoffed. "I don't trust anyone, including you. Now, let's get out of here."

After the two left, Agent Ingram exhaled a sigh of relief. He went into the room and looked around. Nothing. He turned off the light and exited. Just when the door slammed behind him, Agent Ingram recalled the tune the thin man was whistling. It was *Brown Eyed Girl*.

Though Agent Ingram felt better having remembered the tune, Andie was not having similar luck discerning the third clue. And besides, she thought as she jogged, once she had figured it out, then what? Elliot had acted so mysteriously, as though he knew of some nefarious action taking place. Would the third clue allow her into his world? Her ringing cell phone brought her out of her reverie. She slowed to a little more than a walk to answer.

"Andie, I'm still here," a crackly voice indicated. Andie stopped cold. *No! It couldn't be. It just couldn't.* She looked for the number on the cell. It just showed "01." Just like last time.

"No one has visited me. It's dark and it's cold. Andie?"

"Deidre?"

"Yes, I'm still here. Can you help me?"

"Deidre, you must have the wrong number. I don't know you."

"Yes. You must. You're on the List."

"What list? What are you talking about?"

"The J . . . ist." The connection was beginning to break up.

"What list?" Andie shouted, as though the problem was simply a matter of raising her voice.

Then, it was gone. Andie stood for a few more moments, staring intently at the phone as if it was supposed to provide her with information. "Damn!" She was so mad she hurled it through the trees, barely missing a young man walking. He turned to look at her and then walked gingerly in his good dress shoes onto the damp, muddy ground, picked up the phone and walked back to hand it to her. "I think this belongs to you," he said politely, handing it to her. "If I can make a suggestion," he continued, "it's not good to blame the messenger." Andie nodded, knowing that she was turning red, as she took back the phone. "Thank you," was all she could think to say. That was when it dawned on her . . . the third clue. It had to be.

Andie half loped and half jogged to the basement showers. She continued to muse about the events that had just transpired as she waited for the hot water to kick in. What the hell was going on? If she was right, what did it mean? Why did Deidre continue to call her? Who was she? What was the reason for her distress? What was the woman trying to say to her? She said Andie was on some kind of list? What list? Was it a hoax? Andie began to think about her contacts over the past six months.

Had she pissed anyone off? Was it supposed to be a joke? Whatever the cause for the phone calls, the spooky factor had clearly just been ratcheted up a notch. Finally, the water temperature was good enough. She showered quickly and dressed even faster, shivering due to the dribbling water and the cold basement.

Climbing the stairs to the newsroom, feeling very melancholy about her screw-up from the day before but somewhat encouraged that she might have a handle on the third clue, Andie noticed a fellow newspaper colleague coming toward her who was clearly upset.

"What's wrong? Jane, what's wrong?" Andie inquired with concern. Jane just shook her tear-stained face and kept going down the stairs.

Andie picked up her step, quickly reaching the entrance to the newsroom's hallway. Now she heard sobbing. A couple of women were hugging each other as they entered the bathroom, holding onto each other. Andie entered the large newsroom only to see that everyone, absolutely everyone, was crying or looking teary-eyed. She rushed over to Simon, who was holding a piece of paper and looking out over the room. "What's wrong, Simon?"

"Oh, Andie," he said, obviously choked up, "I just announced the heartbreaking news. Claire was killed a couple of hours ago. We just received the information by fax. I don't even know if her family has been notified; and so soon after Michael's death. I don't think anyone is going to be able to take this, it's too much," he added, looking out over the room at the weeping staff. Michael had been a stellar investigative journalist working for WSSN, too. He had died in Iraq, just over three months ago.

"Oh my God." Andie sat down on the nearest chair. "How did it happen?"

"I spoke briefly with Nathan. He said she was shot. He was standing right in front of her." Nathan McCabe was the cameraman.

"Where was she?" Andie could not believe this had happened.

Simon tossed the fax to her and slowly made his way over to console Ellen, or Miss Ellie as she was commonly called, who was the oldest person working at WSSN and assumed the mother role for almost anyone under the age of sixty. She was unable to sustain that role at the moment however. Andie saw that she could not contain her grief as her shoulders shook beneath Simon's hug.

The fax was notably uninformative and rather crass, Andie imme-diately observed.

FACSIMILE

U.S. Department of Defense

TO: WSSN

FROM: PENTAGON

DATE: DECEMBER 2005

RE: Claire Thompson, accidental death

Claire Thompson, age 32, investigative re-porter for World Space Satellite News, WSSN, was killed accidentally when a random bullet from an as yet unknown source struck her. It appeared that she was in the process of pre-paring to deliver her daily report from the front of the hotel in Baghdad where she and other reporters are staying. Ms. Thompson was not embedded, which leads to the speculation that she or her company have accepted undue risk and hence the occasional fatality that occurs without having previously accepted military protection.

Andie read it again, becoming increasingly angry with the content and tone. No one had even had the decency to put his or her name on it. The "Pentagon" was not a sufficient contact for follow-up questions. And wait a second. What daily report? That was an obvious contradic-tion to the investigative reporter title, which had been stated correctly. Claire never provided daily reports. She "sleuthed," as she referred to her working technique. Sometimes, Andie thought, Claire fancied herself more of a PI than a reporter. She even dressed the part, wearing black everything. In fact, she had eagerly adopted the burka dress in Iraq for that very reason. It was black and kept her "sleuthing" image current, and in this case, culturally fitting.

Andie looked around at the room and decided she was going to pur-sue this faxed notice. This is exactly what happened when Michael died, Andie recalled, but no one had any experience with it so, somehow, with all of the grief and sadness experienced by the newspaper and its close-knit staff, it had just been accepted. *Not this time, though,* she thought determinedly. This time, someone was going to have to provide a better explanation than accidental death by bullet.

As she slipped out of the room, she thought about the paper's position in terms of its relationship to the government. WSSN was not their favorite news agency—in fact, quite the contrary. Of the dozen or so US global news agencies, Andie was proud that she worked for the only one not beholden to the government for funding in any form, be it corporate or the supposed public broadcast. All the rest of the news agencies had become businesses first, and responsible journalism second. It was the main reason for her interest in implicating RW&B through her informant. RW&B was the most egregious of them all. People not swept over by their faux homey-like discussions and quick news bites called the station Racist, Whacko, and Biased. In reality, however, the name originated from the owner's initials: Richard Wilson Bozman, a very big contributor to the administration's political machine. His total MO was to support the powers that be and their agendas. WSSN, on the other hand, was proudly a pain in the ass to this administration. Many a journalist had desired working for it before they realized they would not get the glamorized treatment the government afforded those who kowtowed. At WSSN, the pay was minimal and the roadblocks to visibility numerous. It was only from a sense of intense public service that people worked here. Nonetheless, most of the Pulitzer prizes for informative journalism were still awarded to the hardworking, dedicated WSSN staff. It was what kept Andie going, as well as most of her colleagues.

She climbed determinedly up the stairs to Simon's floor where she could concentrate. She suspected no one would be here. She was right, she thought, as she sat down at Simon's old, beat-up desk, noting the disgusting array of fast food containers, some empty, some not. *Hmmm, looks like he likes Chic-Fil-A best,* she surmised, counting six of those snack boxes. *Oh well, everyone had their vices,* she thought. She decided she would start by trying to contact Nathan. *Poor Nathan. He had been there when Michael was killed, too. What an unlucky coincidence,* Andie reflected.

As she tried to contact Nathan, Andie began to feel guilty. She hadn't thought about Michael at all this week. And yet, for the past several weeks, since his untimely death, she had awakened every morning feeling sad that she would not be receiving his reports. He had been providing a touching insight into the people of Iraq. He had been fortunate enough to speak the languages, so his reports were speedier and more factual than had he been using a translator. And, more importantly, he had been able to live with families there, getting to know them, their celebrations, the nuances of their religions, their wants and needs, and their struggles and pain both under Saddam and now under the US led occupation. What a tragic loss Michael's death had been.

She could hear Nathan clearly when he answered. WSSN might have shabby environs, but its technology was state-of-the-art. It was as if Nathan was standing right next to her.

"Nathan, this is Andie."

"Andie, hello. I guess you've heard the news."

"Yes, that's why I'm calling. How are you doing?"

"As good as can be expected, I guess. First Michael and now Claire. Jesus." Andie thought she could detect his voice catching in his throat. She was surprised he wasn't bawling, actually. He was only twenty-one.

"Nathan, where are you now?"

"Back in Baghdad now, back at the hotel. Drinking. Jack and Sam are with me."

Good, thought Andie, *at least he's not alone and drinking,* although she didn't know who Jack and Sam were.

"Okay, Nathan. Listen, can you describe what happened? I think Simon couldn't concentrate. You know how sensitive he can be and now he's trying to console the entire press corps, and the fax we received doesn't shed any light on the event, either. Just tell me where you were in proximity to Claire and what you saw and heard."

"Oh, Andie, it was so awful," Nathan started. "We were standing about two hundred yards from where a blast had occurred, just five minutes before. Our troops were there already, they were shooting at Iraqis in a blazing car, as they were trying to get out of it, and then the helicopter showed up. It started to buzz the crowd. I was filming Claire, who was standing in front of the scene, so I could get both her and the bomb blast in, which is what she asked me to do. I swear she asked me to, Andie, she wanted to be in the scene."

"I'm sure she did," Andie said soothingly. She was so shaken by what she was hearing, but she didn't want him to freak out because of her shock. She needed time with him to find out more. "Then what happened?"

"Andie, I swear to God, the next thing I knew, her head had been blown clear off. Then her body just collapsed. I ran toward her, and at the same time two or three contractors rushed toward me waving their guns, yelling at me. One of them got right in my face, grabbed my camera, and threw it to the ground, shouting 'Get out of here,' saliva was spewing from his mouth. He acted like he was rabid."

Andie grimaced as she heard Nathan's description of the rapidly unfolding events that had just taken place not even ten hours ago. She looked around for a remote control to check the TV news channels. Every office in the agency had at least one TV monitor attached to the wall. She aimed it and started channel surfing. Nothing. No bad Baghdad blast, no military scuffle, no dead female reporter; just news as usual. Today, the news amounted to a scene where police cars were chasing an apparent felon along a freeway in San Francisco. The ticker tape reported to all those who could read fast enough, "We don't know what this means, we are waiting for additional information." The two news "personalities" were grinning as they, too, were shown to be observing the scene on the ground through the same helicopter webcam as the viewers; other webcams were capturing the same scene, unbeknownst to most. It was simply disgusting. The dumbing down of American news coverage was truly startling. Andie shook her head, quickly returning to the conversation at hand.

"Nathan, How are you holding up? I have just a couple of more questions. Are you still there?" She knew she should let him go, but she needed to know. "Nathan, was Claire wearing the burka?"

"Yeah, of course. I think she really liked them. She said she felt like she blended with them on."

"Okay, Nathan. Was the mike on her, or was she holding it? How was she standing?"

"Naw, the mike was clipped to her. She was just standing there talking. There was so much chaos. Fallujah is in ruins. You'd think they'd just abandon it."

"You and Claire were in Fallujah?" Andie asked, confused, as she suddenly recalled that Nathan had said "Back in Baghdad." "The fax indicated that she was accidentally killed in Baghdad."

"No. Not true," Nathan replied. "We were in Fallujah."

"But, Nathan, you know you're not supposed to be there, why would you go there? Did Claire insist on it?"

"Very funny, Andie." Nathan was sounding pissed off. "WSSN ordered us to go there."

"What? Who?"

"I don't know. Claire took the call. I remember when she told me that she was very excited. She said she'd gotten a driver, and we needed to get to Fallujah, ASAP, the newspaper said there was a story there."

Andie couldn't believe what Nathan was telling her. Whenever there was danger, Simon, in particular, told his staff not to take chances. And besides, Fallujah, like so many other parts of Iraq, had simply become off limits to non-military until things cooled down. She knew it to be policy.

"Nathan, when did Claire get the call?" Andie was trying to backtrack to find out how this tragic miscommunication had occurred.

She could hear him take a gulp, and then she heard a man's voice say, "Just hang up."

"I gotta go, Andie, I need to quit talking. I'm feeling sick. Call me later." And then he was gone.

Andie clicked off the phone and just sat there staring. He hadn't said it, but Nathan had seen it. She knew he knew that Claire's death might not have been purely accidental. But why would anyone want Claire dead? Was it really possible? She felt concerned for Nathan suddenly. Was he in danger? She tried calling back, but he must have turned off his phone. There was no response.

Considering what she had just learned, Andie tried to think back to Michael's death and how it had been reported. "Accidental," that was for sure. *But what were the extenuating circumstances? No one knew except Nathan, and who had he talked to? No one,* Andie figured. No one had followed up. The death was so shocking, no one had any desire to take a hard look at the circumstances. It had all been an experience in shock and sadness. But now this. *How bad had it gotten there?* she wondered. "Who is doing this to us?" she asked out loud. What she really needed to find out though, and she knew it, was *who was making these decisions? Who was wiping out their reporters, and why? That was the question du jour.* Andie had a sneaking suspicion, but needed some evidence.

Just as she was standing up to leave, Andie noticed the address of a thick letter in Simon's OUT box. It was to the DoD. *Why would he be writing to the Department of Defense?* Andie wondered. She looked around, suddenly nervous that she may not be alone, although she knew most assuredly that she was. Nonetheless, she couldn't bring herself to even touch it. She had been taught by well respecting parents that mail was private. Still . . . and then she figured it out. Of course, Michael had been KIA, so it was understandable that Simon would still be communicating with them about it. It probably was information needed to provide full disclosure so his widow could claim compensation, if that was ever possible, she thought glumly. Killed in Action was difficult to document when the country was so hostile.

With that, she walked out, noting that no one had returned to the floor yet. Given that it was for the executives' offices and their secretaries, and conference rooms, it wasn't so surprising. Simon was the only one who showed up regularly. He was the Chief Operating Officer. The others on this floor were primarily board members.

As the staff moped about the rest of the day, many of them leaving early, Andie sat at her computer and reread Michael's stories from Iraq. He had been everywhere. He did not mention the specifics of the violence, however, so it was unclear what kind of take he had on who was doing what to whom. He concentrated on the effect it had on the families and family members. *Boy, he was good,* Andie thought, sadly. She had tried Nathan again, but to no avail. She was worried about him, and wanted to warn him not to discuss what he'd seen with anyone else. *He must know it,* she thought. News folks, like those in the hotel, were okay, but not outsiders, not news folks from unknown agencies. It just wasn't safe.

Finally, as the afternoon started to move into evening, she decided she'd had enough as well. She thought about going to the gym, then reversed her thinking totally and thought about going for a drink. Maybe Craig, her buddy from Commerce, was in the same mood. He usually was. She gave him a call, and yes, indeed, he was ready.

"What have you been up to?" he asked. Andie could tell he was smiling.

When she told him what had happened to Claire, deciding not to mention the Fallujah connection over the phone, he was crestfallen. Craig had met her a couple of times. "That lady was crazy, but in a good way," he said. "What a senseless waste. Yes, let's definitely go for a drink. We need to toast one to her for sure."

Andie had known Craig since college. They had both attended the University of Virginia and had stayed in touch throughout the years, given that they both worked in D.C. Craig had been engaged at one point, Andie recalled, but the woman was an IT specialist and had wanted to transfer to the West Coast. Since Craig was brought up on the East Coast, the idea of moving to the other side of the country was too troubling. Plus, he had moved up quite nicely in the Department of Commerce and enjoyed his work.

They agreed to meet around the corner from Craig's office, on 12th Street, around 6:00. She arrived late because of a Metro delay. She knew better, she thought, entering the establishment. She should have walked. It would have been faster.

Except for Craig, the bar was empty. There were a lot more people sitting in the booths, Andie noticed. The background music was Steely Dan, and the two TVs were airing sports programs. *No war going on here,* she thought cynically. Craig was already nursing a beer as she approached. She immediately recognized the sporty outdoor clothes he liked to wear, including the longish brown hair he wore in a pony tail. He gave her a peck on her cheek when she reached him. "How are you holding up, sport?" he asked.

"Okay, I guess. It's nice to see you, Craig," she said, and it was. He looked at her intently and gave her a big hug. She could feel his strong arms even beneath the bulky ski sweater.

"I'm so sorry. First Michael and now Claire. Reporting is definitely one of those dangerous jobs that doesn't get the full recognition it deserves," Craig noted somberly.

Andie could only shake her head in agreement. She could feel the tears welling up in her eyes. "Oh, Craig," she said softly, "you have no idea. I can't believe this is happening."

"Well, they are in war zones. It's not like it's just Michael and Claire. It is truly dangerous."

Again, Andie shook her head in agreement. She looked around to see who else was sitting near them. No one.

"Yeah, but it just seems so unfair. Something's not right," she whispered.

Craig simply raised an eyebrow in response.

"Yeah, strange things are going on."

Craig looked up and motioned to the bartender. "Could we get another draft?" he asked. The bartender who was quite busy rushed to provide it and returned to what appeared to be an order for a batch of mixed drinks. The waiter paced anxiously as he waited for them, at the other end of the bar.

Andie held up her beer and Craig did the same. "To Claire," they said in unison. For a few minutes they just sat there. Silence had overtaken their discussion.

Craig finally broke the stillness. "Now, what do you mean 'strange'?" he asked with a concerned look.

"Just not right. Too many fishy things are happening. There are strange phone calls and strange contacts, and well, it's fishy, it's the only way I know to describe it."

Craig sighed and faced the bar, looking down at his beer as if it were a magic witch's ball. "Andie, I know you have a lot going on and you're privy to a lot of information, but I just want to mention that you do have an obsessive compulsive tendency. I mean . . ."

"Craig, please don't start," Andie interrupted. "Let's not even go there, and besides, you should use the past tense, *had,* not *have,*" she said, emphasizing the two words to make the distinction. "Besides, this is nothing like that. You know I haven't been behaving like that since, well, since college."

"Yeah, but I thought you said that your shrink said it could crop up anytime."

"Jesus, it's not like I was hitting the light switch forty times before I could leave a room. I just had a bit of a crazed desire to be perfect. It led to over-studying and a few other things."

"Yeah, like trying to make sure you aced all tests, exercised every day, and ate exactly correctly, based on some metabolism assessment you paid big bucks for."

"Okay, okay," Andie was getting exasperated. "That was over ten years ago. I'm finished with all that nonsense. I'm not OC. It's not in my repertoire, believe me. This is different."

"What then, tell me all that's been happening," Craig insisted. Andie could tell he was not totally convinced.

Andie looked around the bar. "I actually don't feel good talking about it here," she said. "Let's change the subject."

Craig took another drink, finishing off his beer. "I've got an idea," he said suddenly. "After you finish your beer, lets get a six pack and go to my office. We can talk there."

"No . . . that's okay," Andie replied, hesitating ever so slightly.

"No, it's not okay. Come on, finish it and let's go," Craig said as he stood up, putting money on the bar.

Andie downed her beer and they left.

After walking a few blocks, Craig and Andie entered the RRB. "No one is supposed to be here after hours," Craig told Andie over his shoulder, "but that just applies to the majority below a certain GS level, the ones in the cubicles. Those below it don't know about this privilege, and those above it don't tell."

"Why is it called the RRB?" Andie asked, obviously not knowing the origination of the building.

"As in the Ronald Reagan Building," was all Craig said.

"Oh."

He opened his office door with a swipe of a card that hung from his lanyard. Andie entered, gazing around the spacious office. Craig pulled out a plush chair for her to sit in, across from his executive's desk. He sat on the other side, in a large, leather-upholstered, high-back office chair. "Boy, what did you do to deserve such fancy digs?" she asked, after putting her feet up on the other side of his desk, trying to get a rise out of him. "So, do you have important people come in here to sit and talk to you to get your advice?" she asked mockingly.

"Sometimes," Craig replied, as he sat down again. He had just walked over to open his closet door in order to expose a basketball hoop. He threw a miniature basketball into it just then. "Sometimes they just want to be close and marvel at the great ideas that come out of my mouth."

"Ha ha," Andie said, laughing for the first time all day. "Very funny." *Craig was a good guy,* she thought. *Decent, smart, and funny. Funny was important.*

"So, Andie, what's up really," Craig asked, as he turned around to look at her while his ball bounced off the rim and then hit the window, landing in the chair opposite Andie.

The look on her face made him follow her gaze. She was staring at what appeared to be an electronic white board where a light orange iridescent diagram was presented. In a couple of places blue dots were moving, in many places green dots were rapidly blinking. "What is that?" Andie asked, rather apprehensively.

"Oh, it's there from a three-day conference we've had about GPS guidelines. It's not a big deal."

"How does it work? I must be way ignorant, but I haven't ever seen GPS being used. What's it stand for?"

"You're not alone," Craig said, as he made his way to the six pack. "Hold on to your seat. You're in for a quick GPS 101 lesson that will be enough for you to talk as if you invented it."

Craig popped a beer, leaned back in his chair with his feet on his desk, like Andie was doing, and grinned before beginning his short dissertation. "GPS or Global Positioning System is not new. It's based on a constellation of twenty-four solar-powered orbital satellites about twelve thousand miles above the Earth. A GPS receiver on the ground looks for tracking signals from at least three satellites, then interpolates the data to establish latitude and longitude. If a device can pick up four or more signals, it can also determine a user's altitude, for whatever that's worth. The first satellite was launched in 1974. Users can get accurate location information across the globe, and most equipment can interpret it to provide speed, distance to a destination, and even exact local sunrise and sunset times. The FAA uses it for obvious reasons, drivers can get it installed on their cars, which is becoming pretty standard in a lot of models, and there are handheld devices for hikers. Some cell phones are adding them to the package, for a price. Of course, the military uses it for a number of purposes. For example, it's adapted bombs with GPS receivers that can guide the weapons to targets."

"Wow," Andie exclaimed.

"Yeah, wow. It's pretty nifty," Craig replied. "This one is a new application. It's state-of-the-art. It's used to track business activity. We're working with DOT to assess where the Christmas and Chanukah holiday spending is occurring. This map here is a four-block quadrant in Bethesda. The blue spots indicate department store activity. Most of them are closed, or are closing, so there's not much movement. The green spots show restaurants. You can see there's a lot of activity."

"What are the red squiggly lines?" Andie asked curiously.

"It's airwave interference. Most of these are cell phones."

"Craig, I didn't know you were so knowledgeable about this technology and its use. You're in charge?" Andie asked suddenly.

Craig looked both proud and hurt. "Andie, I'm not twenty-one anymore. It's been over ten years for me, too, you know. This is my area of specialty. I was promoted because of it. So . . . yes, to answer your question, I am in charge. I do have higher-ups that I report to, but they mostly leave me alone since they don't know anything about technology. They always just want the bottom line, or should I say in this department, the bottom dollar. And . . . I must say with this new administration, their egos are so big, they don't want to be reminded that they don't understand it, so there's a lot less to answer for than in the previous administration. I'm my own boss in other words."

"I didn't mean to minimize your responsibilities," Andie protested. "Actually, just the opposite. I'm very impressed. It's just that you never mentioned exactly what you do, so I'm a bit taken aback, that's all. It's very interesting. It's almost like spying."

Craig laughed. "It's not *almost like spying*," he stated emphatically. "*It is spying*. We know a lot about people's movements, even though they have no idea we're around. But we gather information on people, not on one person, so there is a big difference."

"Craig, how far out can you go? I mean, what's your radius?" Andie asked tentatively.

"Well, as I said, it's GPS, G as in Global. It's available anywhere, if you have the right technology. Theoretically, we here at Commerce could observe certain types of activity anywhere in the world."

Andie looked thoughtfully at the screen. "Could you find someone in Iraq? I mean someone I haven't been able to reach by cell?" Andie was thinking of Nathan and the fact that he appeared to have disappeared.

"I don't know, I'd have to think about it. Is that what you've been concerned about and what's got you spooked?" Craig asked sincerely.

"It's part of it," she responded, and it was. Over the last two days, strange things had occurred. Claire's death (or murder?) was the latest in a string of events, all of which could be purely coincidental and totally ordinary. But the GPS opened up a new avenue, and she didn't want to complicate her request to Craig by conveying all of these strange happenings that were, by most standards, seemingly unrelated *at least on the surface,* she thought. "I really need to try to communicate with the cameraman who was present when Claire was shot."

"Oh, of course," Craig said. "I can understand how that is a priority. Of course. I guess the questions I have to ask in answer to your question is, Can I do it? and Can I do it legally? Give me a couple of days if you don't mind."

"Well, Craig, it's a bit of an emergency. Can you let me know by tomorrow?"

Craig hesitated but then, looking at Andie's wishful eyes, responded in the affirmative, "Yeah, I think I can. What's the number so I have something to work with, *if* I can." Craig was already thinking ahead, knowing that it was technically a piece of cake. But it was not legal. He was trying to rationalize how he might justify it if it was detected. Not that he thought it would be. As he had said to Andie, no one was interested in being reminded that he or she was, well, basically technologically challenged. He'd never seen so many people with so little desire to learn or be informed. Good for him.

"Now, let's go get some dinner," Craig suggested after jotting down the number. Andie agreed wholeheartedly.

Andie entered her apartment building following dinner and a cab ride home. She was feeling better than she had earlier in the day. Her remorse for Claire's senseless death was still lingering, but now she had a new mission. She was going to find out what the hell was going on with her colleagues and their ability to report the news. Before she could get through her door, her cell phone began to ring, startling her. She checked the number, again "01." A sinking feeling came over her. She clicked it on and answered apprehensively, "Hello?"

"Andie? It's Deidre."

"Ohhhhhhh," Andie shivered when she heard the voice.

"Andie, don't worry. I won't be bothering you after this call. I'm not feeling so bad anymore. Andie are you there?"

"Yes, I'm here, Deidre," she said hesitantly. "You're feeling better, you said?"

"Yes. I'm not afraid anymore."

"That's good," Andie said, as though to a child. "Deidre, how did you get my number? What list am I on?"

"The List is in my head. I still remember a few names and numbers, but you are the only one I could get through to. So, thank you for being there."

"Does it have a title, the List?"

"It's just a list of journalists, you were first."

The phone went dead.

5

While Andie was trying to cope with a phantom, Jones was on the other side of town, sitting alone in the bunker, awaiting the VP and congratulating himself in advance. The results the VP wanted were going to be spectacular, he had decided. He was prepared to show him the before and after tapes that would knock the repulsive man's socks off. Secretly, Jones hoped that someday he could be one hundred percent personally responsible for the asshole's death, regardless of how it might take place. Hell, he'd love to see him drop dead from an embolism that occurred due to rage induced by yours truly, Jones. The guy was a walking nightmare . . . a real SOB. Their history went way back, further than the VP could ever admit to. He glanced at his watch. They'd be here momentarily.

After the VP and his Chief of Staff were seated, Jones clicked on the DVD player. "This is the before disc, made two days ago."

The VP leaned back in his chair, hands behind his head, appearing to be bored and resigned to disappointment. The Chief of Staff sat stonily.

The woman in the video appeared to be in the process of being interviewed. She wore denim jeans and a loose, albeit low-cut, knit sweater, to which was attached a clip-on mike. Her boots were shiny. She wore her thick, brown hair tied up with a clip, which accentuated her high cheek bones and prominent eyes. She appeared to be about twenty-five. The person asking the questions could only be heard, not seen.

". . . What do you think is the basic premise for the attacks against the troops?"

"It's not for me to say at this point. We need to talk with the Iraqis, the American soldiers, and the various leaders, both religious and secular."

"You don't have an opinion?"

"Well, I'm a journalist, so I will stay as objective as possible until I can get at the truth, or at least as close to it as possible."

"Do you think you are being inhibited from getting at 'the truth,' as you put it?"

"By whom?"

"I don't know, I'm just asking if you think you're able to do your job effectively, or if you feel there are impediments."

"There are impediments to our objectivity, yes. The US government will not allow us to present all of the facts all of the time."

"How do you feel about that, can it be justified due to the fact that we're at war?"

"No, I believe any impediment represents an infringement on the First Amendment."

"Even at a time of war?"

"Especially at a time of war!"

"Jesus!" the VP exclaimed.

"Thank you for your time."

"My pleasure," the woman responded, her brown eyes glittering.

"I'll say it again. Jesus!" the VP growled incredulously. "Where did you find that nitwit? Are there really Americans who believe that nonsense? 'Especially at a time of war,' " he repeated, mimicking the woman's tone. "So now what, she's been rehabilitated? By you? Let's see it," the VP demanded of Jones with shaking jowls.

Jones simply exchanged discs and hit play.

The same young woman was again being interviewed, although she wore a loose blouse over the jeans instead of the sweater. Her hair was down, but brushed back into a ponytail. The interviewer's voice suggested it was a different person. The interviewer asked the woman the same questions, with certain modifications.

". . . What do you think is the basic premise for the attacks against the troops?"

"It's hatred of freedom and democracy," she said with conviction.

"That's your opinion?"

"Well, I'm a journalist, which allows me to know why there's so much carnage. What I see is hatred against America and Americans. It's so obvious. Once there is freedom, the attacks will end."

"Do you think you are being inhibited from getting at the truth?"

"By whom?"

"I don't know, I'm just asking if you think you're able to do your job effectively, or if you feel there are impediments."

"The only impediment to our objectivity is that we're afraid for our lives. It's dangerous out there. Thankfully, the US government has offered for us to be embedded, which has helped a lot in getting us as close as possible to the war at the ground level. We, that is, journalists, are extremely grateful for this support and protection."

By now, the VP and his Chief of Staff, a wiry man named Lowell, were straining forward in their seats to make sure they were hearing every word.

"So there are no impediments that you see to covering your stories?"

"Absolutely not. We can fully do our duty as journalists with the government's help. The First Amendment is alive and well in my book."

"Even at a time of war?"

"Especially at a time of war. It's important for the American people to get and continue to get the truth through the American news."

"Thank you for your time."

"My pleasure," the woman responded, her big brown eyes smiling brightly.

"My God, hallelujah!" the VP screeched, as spittle sprayed from his mouth. "Is that really the same women? Hallelujah! How the hell did that metamorphosis take place? Hallelujah!"

Jones gritted his teeth and mentally prepared for battle, while the VP whispered to his Chief of Staff. Jones knew that he was willing to help the cause, but he would not give away his secrets.

While Jones awaited this little showdown over techniques, Andie was sitting in the newsroom mulling over the most recent transcripts from Claire's reports. She looked at the number when her cell phone rang. It was Craig. "Andie, you want to get together tonight? I have something I need to discuss with you," he said, in what Andie construed as a comically cryptic, hushed voice.

"Yes, of course," Andie said, wondering why he was whispering, as though it were a secret. "Where and when."

"How about The Brewing Pub in Bethesda?"

"Bethesda, why there? Because of your map?"

"What?" Craig at first didn't understand the reference and then realized she was talking about the GPS map of Bethesda that he had pointed out. "Oh, no, not at all. It's just less congested."

Oh, more cryptic talk, Andie thought. "Okay. It will take me a while to get there. Let's say 7:00."

"See ya then." Craig hung up.

Andie shrugged to herself and then tried Nathan's phone again, to no avail. She buzzed Simon and asked if she could talk with him. Based on her cursory research about Claire this morning, she was in the process of developing a plan. Last night's phone call from Deidre had added another item to the list of things she wanted to discuss.

"Come on up."

As she entered his office, she noticed he had cleaned it up considerably since yesterday. No trash, no Chic-Fil-A, no nothing. More remarkably, there were no papers or letters in either his IN or OUT box. "Wow, you've been up to some serious cleaning," she said smiling.

"Why would you say that?" he asked, almost aggressively.

"No, I just meant that it was, I, oh, never mind. Your office looks nice," Andie replied, not knowing why she was lying about having been here yesterday.

"Oh . . . well, thanks," was all he said, pausing. Then he seemed to be glad to have her here. He needed advice. "I've asked Miss Ellie to make arrangements for a funeral memorial for Claire for next Friday. Do you think that timing will work? I mean, it's right before Christmas, but I don't want to do it between Christmas and New Years, given that some folks will be gone."

"I think it will be fine," Andie said with conviction. She could tell he was very distraught and apparently hadn't showered this morning. His longish hair was hanging in clumps, and a lot of bald places could easily be spotted. It was obvious that he was very, very, sad about Claire's death.

"Simon, maybe you should take some time off," she suggested.

"*No.* I need to stay busy."

"Okay," Andie said. "I understand."

"What's up with you?" he asked.

"A few things, Simon. Actually, I would like to do a piece on Claire. I think she deserves recognition, even if it is posthumous. People, Americans, need to see how she contributed to ensuring that we have an informed populace and the sacrifice she made to do it. I think we should showcase her ideals alongside her thoughtful, comprehensive work. She's a hero, too." Andie had practiced this little speech on her way to work. It had fortunately dovetailed nicely with his discussion about her memorial.

Simon perked up with this proposal. He leaned back in his oversized but unattractive chair that was built ergonomically to accommodate his condition. "What kind of piece, more than an article?"

"A long, in-depth, above-the-fold article that contains photos. I have a storyboard planned in my head that I can draw up for you by the end of the day," she said, hoping she was exuding confidence.

Simon tapped his fingers on his desk, looking at her intently. "What about the other story? Are you just going to abandon it?"

"Nooooooo. Not in the least. I'm still eager to do that, too. It's just that it will take more homework. This article on Claire could be out by the first of the year."

Simon started to nod, and Andie knew she had him hooked. *Thank God,* she thought. Now she could justify all of the research she needed to find out what really happened over there, starting with finding Nathan.

"Okay," Simon said. "But I want to see that storyboard on my desk before you leave this evening. This is important," he added, "and deserved, as you said."

"*Thank you,* Simon, you won't regret it."

"Okay, okay." He acted as though he was going to dismiss her, so she quickly added, "Do you know how I can get hold of Nathan?"

"Try his cell," he said, as though she hadn't thought of that.

"I mean, is there any other way? I've had trouble connecting."

"I don't think so. Maybe you ought to have your cell checked. You know they're the most powerful available. There shouldn't be a problem."

"Okay, thanks. And, Simon?"

"What is it?"

"Just one more thing," Andie added quickly. "Do you know of the existence of a list of journalists?"

"A list of journalists? I haven't a clue, who mentioned that?" he said. But he seemed a bit startled by the question.

"No one you know. I was just curious," she added.

"Nope, don't know about a list, never heard of it," he stated again.

"Okay, thanks, Simon."

Andie excused herself and headed back to her desk, where she spent the rest of the day designing the most impressive plans for highlighting Claire's work and life. She made numerous phone calls asking folks for interviews, including Claire's mother. She had no siblings, which made talking with the mother even more important. Andie dreaded that interview the most. It was interesting, or should she say surprising, but many of the people she'd contacted didn't know that Claire had perished. Aside from being the bearer of terrible news, the fact that so few were aware of it really upset Andie. She had been so busy lately that she had not been checking other news sources, but apparently no one besides WSSN had mentioned her death. Christ. Phony news coverage had become the death knell of journalistic integrity. In reality, you were rewarded for the inside spinning of leaked stories, i.e., Reliable Sources *Not* Wanted. Anything that got close to exposing the government's lies or misinformation was snubbed out faster than it could be written, read, and digested. The death of a journalist in Iraq for doing her job was not marketable news.

She finished her storyboard and quickly transferred it to Simon via email. She also placed a hard copy in his IN box, just in case. She wanted to make up for her earlier foul-up. Which reminded her, she had some unfinished business with Elliot, including several follow-up questions. She needed to pursue her other story just as diligently as she was going after Claire's. Andie found out a long time ago that there was no room in this business for shyness. You had to keep after your sources once they were identified. They would eventually "tell all," *or at least most of them would,* she mused. Elliot might just be the exception.

6

"It's too complicated to even begin to understand," Jones explained to the VP. He always ignored his Chief of Staff, simply by avoiding eye contact with him. The three were back in the bunker's conference room. The VP wanted to know the plan and the timeline, as he had insisted earlier. Jones liked to make him sweat. *I'm not planning on laying out everything. I'm not relinquishing the secret nor its "application," as I like to call it.*

The VP scowled. "You don't think I can understand a bit of science? A bit of mind manipulation or whatever you were able to do to her?"

"It's not that. If you know everything I know, you won't need me anymore. This way, I maintain some collateral," he stated bluntly.

"You are dispensable, don't kid yourself," the VP stated matter-of-factly.

"Huh?" Jones sniped, "I don't think so. This will revolutionize the party for decades to come. Hell, you guys are almost a one-party system as it is. This will put you over the top, and you know it. You need me more than ever."

The VP looked over at his Chief of Staff. "Leave us for moment," he ordered.

The Chief of Staff jumped up and left the room to share the outside corridor with Agent Ingram.

"Jones, you're right. I can't fight you. I can't kill you, and I can't ignore you. So . . . I am ready to make you an offer you can't resist," whereupon he proceeded to outline what he expected. Jones listened carefully, noting the VP's twitchy eyes as he proceeded to deliver an offer so full of holes even a fourth grader would have laughed. When he finished, he smiled insincerely. Jones noticed the sweat on his upper lip.

"That's not a deal. At best, it's a merger where I lose everything," Jones admonished. "The answer is an unequivocal no. Now, here's my offer," he continued. "As you know, we're pilot testing the 'show,' so to speak, with staff from the different departments, as I like to refer to them. You'll be able to see how effective and successful we can be, within days. As you also know, I will not tell you what is in the formula, but I will be happy to orchestrate the full-blown campaign. Take it or leave it. I could care less. But, if you decide to take it, I want a slice of the pie."

"What's that supposed to mean?" the VP growled.

"You know what it means. I want in on the decision-making process from here on, a silent seat at the table, if you will. I want a percentage of the profits from the mercenary companies' contracts, a percentage from the political contributors, and a percentage of the direct war profits, meaning, of course, proceeds from the wholesale profits of the oil confiscated, and all operations involved in doing so, including security."

"You're out of your pea-sized mind."

"Perhaps," Jones replied nonchalantly. "But it's no skin off my back if you don't get these staff corralled, undetected. We can go our separate ways right now. In fact, I'm ready to split, literally. Others would pay appropriately for this tool. You'll never see me again," he concluded smugly, leaning comfortably back in the conference chair, hands clasped behind his head.

"You *traitor!*" the VP exclaimed vehemently, starting to stand, but he sat back down when the chair didn't slide easily due to the bulk of his frame. The pressure on his knees was God-awful painful.

Jones shrugged, noting the VP's physical vulnerabilities. "It takes one to know one," he said evenly.

Internally, the VP was furious. He could actually feel his blood pulsating through his veins. He tried to calm down, but as he looked at his adversary, he could only hear ringing in his ears. *He* was in charge, not this *asshole*. Outwardly, he simply glanced down at the folder his Chief of Staff had left. He calmly looked up and said only, "Very well. This meeting is over. We will meet again when . . ." but he stopped as he saw Jones remove an envelope from his blazer's inside pocket. With the VP watching his every move, Jones proceeded to slowly remove the contents of the envelope and carefully unfold it. Then, he slapped it down in front of the ugly man, who had begun to look, for the first time Jones could ever remember, compromised.

7

The Brewing Pub was a lively place tonight Andie thought, as she wove her way through the throng of suits and their loud, supportive shouts for the sports TV and music. Craig must have arrived much earlier because he already was seated at a hightop by the window. "Hey, you," she said. "When'd you get here?"

"A while back. How are you doing?" he said as he greeted her.

"Okay. Boy, it's busy tonight."

"Yeah, everyone's getting ready to take off for the holidays, I suppose."

"Yep, no war here," Andie responded sarcastically, noting the TV sports, loud music, and loud people. Only one channel had the news on. Craig was staring at it intently.

"Something interesting?" Andie inquired.

Craig glanced over. "Oh, sorry," he turned to face her. "Yeah, you could say so. The President just appointed Bobby Puckit as FCC Chairman."

"Oh, no. That slimy, fake, good ol' boy got it?"

"Yeah, he sucks big time," Craig said in disgust.

Bobby Puckit was a buddy of thirty years from the President's pre-government days. He was about the same age but did not inherit his money. He actually had swindled his way to the top, and everyone knew it, but no one had been able to do anything about it while it was occurring. Construction was his gold mine. After college, he had noted the fast growth in the New Orleans area and was able to save enough money by holding down two jobs and living with his mother, who survived, in part, on food stamps, to buy several acres for dirt cheap way outside the city limits. Soon, however, the area had been incorporated, and it screamed for development. After selling a couple of the acres for good profits, he took the money and put up cheap, matchstick homes, before the days of any seriously enforced regulations. His fortune was launched. The rest was history. Once regulations, such as they were, came into being, Bobby was able to buy off the enforcers. His houses were crap, but for thousands of families, it was the only affordable option. On top of these corner-cuttings, he began to capitalize on an advertising campaign that was parallel to none at the time. He bought up radio and TV time, and space in newspapers, to herald his "success" and go after anyone who tried to out-build or out-sell him. The attacks were carefully subtle, and contesting them took more money than was potentially to be made. Hence, he had no serious competitors for at least two decades. Ironically, it was this "experience" with the media that was used to qualify him for the FCC position.

"So, get ready for the funny business to begin," Craig stated, shaking his head. "He's already talking about curtailing beeped-out foul language."

"It's beeped, that's the point," Andie argued.

"He said 'same difference as saying it' since everyone knows what is meant by the beep."

"What a joke."

"Yep. Bobby Puckit, crony number five hundred joins the team."

The waitress approached their table. "I'll have another one," Craig said, downing what was left of his pint.

Andie wanted to find out what Craig had discovered. Puckit could wait another day. "So, why so secretive?" she asked, deliberately changing the subject.

"I just prefer a crowd when I'm discussing illicit actions I've committed. Call me paranoid," Craig responded wryly, before following this comment with a matter-of-fact statement. "I found him."

"What?" Andie couldn't believe it. "Did you make contact with Nathan then?"

"No. Sorry. I mean I can't get a response, just like you. But it gets more strange. His phone is in Sadr City."

"What?" Andie almost fell off her stool as she leaned toward Craig. "It's in Sadr City? But no one is supposed to be in Sadr City. I mean, no media. Anyway, we wouldn't have sent him there." This seemed to be a disturbing rerun of Nathan and Claire being in Fallujah.

"Yeah, that's what I figured."

"Oh, no, what's happened to him? Oh, Craig. The guy's such a rookie. He's only twenty-one. He begged for the job. He told Simon he looked forward to the adventure and challenge. But he confided in me that he really needed the money to pay off his school loan and thought that six months or more there would put a big dent in it. I mean, when I spoke with him, he was in Baghdad. What took him to Sadr City? It looks so ominous."

"I know. I don't think it looks good either. No response, but sure enough I pinpointed it this morning. There's no mistaking its location."

"Craig, this is the kind of stuff that I've been alluding to. The people from WSSN are dying or disappearing at an alarming rate."

"Andie, let's not jump the gun. Like I said, it's dangerous business. Accidental deaths are bound to happen. It's unfortunate, but reporters are going to be killed or wounded."

"There are others, true, but, well, you don't see anyone from RW&B dying."

"So what are you suggesting?" Craig asked challengingly. More shouts and cheers from the bar area drowned out Andie's next comment. She waited a moment and then repeated it, cautiously.

"To be honest, Craig," she said quietly, "I think Claire was murdered." There, now she had said it.

"Murdered! Jesus, Andie, you mean you think it was intentional?"

"Not so loud," she said, looking around. With the sounds of the TVs, music, and chatter, she hardly had to worry. No one even knew they existed.

"Yes, I do," she whispered. She then relayed what Nathan had told her, emphasizing the fact that Nathan and Claire were not where they were reported as being. "But I need more information. That's one of the reasons I need to talk with Nathan again. Now I'm worried that I can't reach him, and yet we just spoke yesterday afternoon."

"Did he say what he was going to do next?"

"No. He was drinking with some buddies. He sounded like he was in shock."

"But who do you think murdered her? Why would Iraqis want her dead? She was trying to provide an objective assessment of activities there, wasn't she?" Andie nodded yes, and kept staring at Craig. "So. . . . Oh, no, oh, no, Andie," Craig protested, as he began to understand Andie's inference, "Oh, no . . ."

Again, Andie just nodded.

"Well, I don't want to believe that."

"Me neither, Craig, but from what Nathan told me, I think it's the only conclusion. And as a fellow journalist, I think it's my responsibility to check it out. I mean it might be true in Michael's case, too. So that's why I'm asking about reaching Iraq through your GPS. If we can map out where our folks are and track them, especially if we can't get through, which seems to be the case, then we can know where they are or were if something happens to them."

"Well, yeah, I see your logic, and all journalists are listed, so we know where they're supposed to be."

"What do you mean all journalists are listed?" Andie asked quizzically.

"There's a list that includes all media personnel. It's been in effect since, oh, I guess maybe the 1970s. Now it includes contact information, which of course is much more relevant, given the advent of the cell phone. I think the FCC maintains it."

"Then why did you ask me for Nathan's number?"

"It was easier than looking it up, and frankly, I didn't want to make a formal inquiry," Craig said, shrugging. "Jeez, don't be so paranoid."

"Yeah, okay," Andie said. "I'm just wondering why I didn't know about this list. How do you access it?" she asked.

"It was just given to me," Craig said, shrugging. "I don't know how well known it is that the List has been compiled. But I have one."

Andie was simply dumbfounded. "Craig, there's another strange occurrence that I've been confronted with over the past two days, that I haven't mentioned. "

Craig raised that familiar eyebrow again. "I don't know how much more I can take, Andie," he joked.

She smiled wryly. "It's not that easy to describe, because it may make me sound insane, or at least on my way to being insane."

"Well, a shrink I'm not, so go ahead and spit it out, I won't be able to tell."

Andie relayed in minute details her interactions with Deidre, or the woman who called herself Deidre.

Craig sat quietly, listening. When she finished, he ordered another round of beers. After the waitress had served them, he held his up for a toast. Andie, who was totally perplexed by this action, did the same, whereupon Craig exclaimed, "Congratulations, you're certifiable."

"Well, screw you, Craig," Andie said angrily, as she stood up and began gathering her belongings.

"I'm joking, Andie, please, it's a joke, I'm kidding." Craig was begging her now to stay.

Andie calmed down a bit and sat back down. She stared at him and said very quietly and in an even tone, "Craig, I'm not kidding."

"Okay, okay. That was in poor taste. My apologies. It's just that you seemed so serious about it, and while I believe you, I think it's a mistake. I was trying to diffuse your anxiety. I don't think there's anything to it. It could be a hoax, as you even suggested, or a case of mistaken identity, again as you suggested."

Andie said nothing.

"Okay, what do you think is really going on? If it's not any of the above, what is it? "

"Well, don't you think the reference to the *List* is pretty peculiar? I mean, what is that related to? You don't think, not even for a moment, that she could have gotten my number through the *List*?" Andie asked with a concerned tone.

"So? What if she did? What does it mean?"

"Well, for starters, you just said that it's not a well-known list, but here it's being referred to as though I should know about it. It's just another link in the chain of weird, very weird, events that have come about."

Craig sighed. "Let's suppose there is something to this, that perhaps there is a connection between your phantom caller and the List. What's it supposed to mean?"

"That's exactly what I need to find out or, at the very least, rule out anything peculiar. I'm telling you about this, confiding in you, because I need another set of eyes and ears. Maybe you can find out who maintains the List. Who updates it and who has the responsibility for distributing it, or deciding who gets it and how. I mean, when you think about it, a list of this nature, if it's totally comprehensive, would be enormous. There are subsidiary media conduits all over the world. We have three reporters in Iraq from our office here, but we have maybe another dozen from outlets throughout the US, and then there are the foreign reporters hired by us as well. And it's not all about Iraq, they're not all there."

Craig began to sense how big this was indeed. He'd had no idea. "I do apologize for making light of this now," he said, a bit chagrined. "You're right. That's a lot of information about an industry."

"No kidding," Andie whispered, as she leaned toward Craig. "It's more than any other industry would ever have made available to, well, to anyone except those at the top. Can you imagine Holyruse listing who works for them and where?" Holyruse was the contractor winning the largest no-bid contracts in Iraq, and apparently other places in the Middle East, although that was always hushed up, since some of the countries were supposed to be off limits for US dealings due to their "terroristic" behavior. It was well known that the company was based in the state most staunchly supportive of the current administration. Craig nodded as his comprehension caught up with the implications.

"Yeah, no kidding," he somberly agreed, nodding again. He looked around the bar and sighed. "Let's get out of here."

The two of them bundled up against the cold night air before leaving the bar. If anything, Andie noticed, the noise level had increased twofold with the games coming to an end, and even louder, drunker customers who seemed to need to shout lest they think they couldn't be heard. As Andie pulled her hair out of her coat before wrapping a scarf around her neck, she noticed a man in the far corner staring at her. Just staring. He was virtually bald, wearing the usual suit, and holding a large, brown envelope. Actually, he didn't look like he belonged in this sort of establishment, which is one of the reasons she had noticed him. Too staid. Too unenthusiastic. She turned to reach for her backpack, and when she looked again, he was gone. She glanced around the bar area, but didn't see him.

"Did you see that guy?"

"What guy?"

"Never mind."

"Let's go."

A biting wind hit them as they exited.

"God! It's cold," Andie exclaimed. "Which way?"

"Well, according to my GPS map, which I study endlessly every day," Craig joked, "I'd say it's faster the back way to the Metro." It was about four blocks south on Wisconsin Avenue, or half the distance with a little bit of weaving in and out of short streets, angling toward the station. He intertwined his arm in Andie's, which was already deeply buried in her pocket, despite her thickly lined gloves. He did the same. They started walking fast.

"Wow, Craig. You didn't say there was a hike involved," Andie said, laughing but breathing hard.

"But my GPS says it's faster . . . I think," Craig responded, with the same shortness of breath.

Suddenly, out of the corner of her eye, Andie saw a shadow approaching, with lightning speed. It appeared to be aggressive. And so was the human being that was making it. Given the direction of the lighting, it was hard to tell how far away the person was.

"Craig, run," Andie whispered.

"Yeah, I see him, too. The lights from the Metro are right around the corner. Go . . . but don't run."

"How can we beat him if we don't run?"

"Okay. . . . *Run!*" The two of them took off, continuing uphill. They could hear the person behind them now.

Andie couldn't believe this. She was shaking, and not from the cold. They weren't going to make it.

"Andie," a voice gruffly called out from behind. "Andie, stop running."

Andie and Craig stopped on the spot and turned.

The person standing in front of them now was hatless, the light shining off his bald head. He held out the large envelope she had seen earlier. "This is for you."

Andie felt like crying, both from anger and relief. "Who the hell are you?" she practically screamed. "How do you know who I am? Why didn't you give that to me when we were in the bar?"

"Too many eyes. Be careful." He turned and walked off in the direction from which they had all just run.

"Dammit," Andie exclaimed, stamping her foot.

Craig was silent. Stupefied might be a better description. "You don't know who he is?"

"No. I just saw him in the bar. Let's get to the Metro."

They found a relatively empty car. "Hurry and open it," Craig urged.

Andie was trying to do just that. The damn envelope had been glued and taped. She finally ripped it open across the top.

A 3x5 card dropped out.

$$^{238}\text{U}$$

"What's that mean?" Craig inquired, asking the obvious.

"I have no idea," was the obvious reply.

8

The man called simply Jones was relaying the latest meeting with the VP to one of his two "deputies," Maria Stone, as he liked to refer to them. Dr. Veritos, the other "deputy," was not present, as he worked from another location. Jones tried to remain objective, but it was hard. Maria was still laughing at the description of the "compromised" VP.

"I bet that sentiment was a new one for 'his majesty,' " she snorted. She knew the two men's history, and knew that the sparring rarely resulted in a conclusive win. This time, however, might be the exception. Jones had definitely put the big man, 'the *grand fromage*,' in a compromising position. What he would do, they both could only guess. "You think he's going to kill you?" Maria asked suddenly. The two of them were working in a modestly sized office located in Silver Spring, Maryland.

"Does the Iraq war provide for war profiteering?" Jones asked rhetorically. "I'm sure he has certainly thought of it, unequivocally. He would do anything to write me out of the equation."

"Very funny," Maria said, glancing at the dozen computers whizzing away, creating pictorial and verbal psychological storyboards by which Jones had developed his hypotheses and resulting coup that was continuing to play out. "I'm serious, Jonesy," a nickname Maria had begun using years ago when they actually had had a brief relationship.

Jones looked over at her concerned expression. He still cared very much for her. He did then. It was just bad timing. In the meantime, during a downtime for Jones, the provocative woman from Venezuela had met a perfectly stable bureaucrat from Virginia, and they had married. She now had two beautiful children, a decent husband, and a rather unremarkable life, at least not including this little aspect of it. "I know you're serious," Jones said, as he looked out the window at the street below. There were several cars parked along both sides, presumably residents of the old townhomes that existed in and among the various shops serving this lower-income neighborhood. "I know," he continued. "Let's put it this way. He can't possibly proceed without me. He doesn't know who, if anyone, knows what I know, so he's stuck. He can spend a lot of his resources tracking down relevant information, but he can't possibly be sure that it would lead to what I know. And there's the time factor. He wants everything yesterday. No doubt about it, he's stuck. He has as much as acknowledged it by the expression on his face. But I never underestimate my enemies. Believe me, we need to be more careful than ever."

"Why don't you just do everything now?" Maria entreated. "Give him the plan, the means to achieve it," Jones frowned at this comment, "I mean everything except the formula, of course, and get lost. I mean, I will miss you, and so will Dr. Veritos, but at least you'll be alive, safe, and rich. Isn't that what you've always dreamed of? What did you tell me when we first met? Life is all about options, and if a person doesn't have them, then he's just like a prisoner. I mean, those are enough options, aren't they?"

Jones nodded slightly. "They're certainly a lot of options, you're right. But I've added one more criterion."

"What?"

"Options need to include the ability to come to closure."

Maria sighed, knowing exactly where he was going with this statement. "Well, Jonesy, that may be the toughest criterion yet."

"Hey, I haven't found a challenge I couldn't meet, at least not yet," he added, smiling smugly.

As usual, Maria found that smug smile so endearing. "You're right," she said. "You are right."

9

Andie was busily identifying all of the places Claire had been working since joining WSSN when Simon came into the noisy, cell-phone-riddled newsroom. A young, comely, waif-like woman was at his side. Andie thought for some reason, although she didn't know exactly why, that she looked like a deer, no, more like a doe. "Everyone," he called, clapping his hands, "everyone, may I have your attention?" No one really paid much attention at all. He picked up a coffee cup from Joel's desk and began tapping it with his pen. Joel looked ticked off and got up, leaving the room, still carrying on his conversation through his cell, held closely to his ear. The noise subsided somewhat, but the remaining phone users, and they made up the majority, were still busy doing business. *"Everyone!"* Simon shouted. Some folks got up and followed Joel out, nodding at Simon and pointing helplessly to their phones. The room had quieted down considerably, with just the normal below-the-radar rumble. Simon proceeded.

"Folks, I would like to introduce DeeDee Morgan. She will be joining us beginning, well, beginning today," he stated matter-of-factly, but beaming as though he'd just introduced a famous person. Later, Andie would question whether that might have been the case. DeeDee, on the other hand, looked a bit shy and reticent. Simon proceeded. "DeeDee will be conducting investigative reporting from Iraq." Suddenly the room went totally dead. Simon definitely had their undivided attention now, Andie quickly surmised. *Christ,* she thought, *we haven't even attended Claire's memorial, and Simon has replaced her.* This sentiment was obviously shared, Andie could tell. By looking around, it was clear that her colleagues were upset by this revelation. Simon, however, didn't skip a beat. "I have broadcast an email bio about DeeDee, so we can all get to know her as quickly as possible. In brief, she has lived for many years in the Middle East, as her parents were in the foreign service there. She is cognizant, therefore, of the cultural history, nuances, mores, current changes, and so forth of the region, and . . ." he said proudly, almost as though he was referring to himself, "DeeDee speaks fluent Arabic, among other relevant languages. Suffice it to say that we, I, consider ourselves to be extremely fortunate to have DeeDee join our team and provide an added dimension to our portfolio. Everyone, let's give DeeDee a warm hand and welcome," Simon said in conclusion, shaking her hand.

DeeDee had stood quietly by during the entire announcement, staring out at the room of people and, frankly, looking very uncomfortable. Andie didn't want to prejudge, but she just couldn't imagine this woman out and about in Iraq, as Claire had done. Now, Simon was escorting her to a desk that Miss Ellie must have cleared just this morning. *Thank God it wasn't Claire's desk,* Andie thought. Miss Ellie obviously had shifted someone instead. Not surprisingly, the press room remained silent, visually following Simon and DeeDee as they moved across the room. *The beauty and the beast,* Andie thought rather cruelly. This was so unlike Simon. He had committed a really callous act that would definitely negatively affect the morale of his whole crew, who were already deeply depressed. *What was he thinking?*

She got up and left, needing some fresh air. Within a few minutes, as she rounded the block for the first time, she began to reflect back to last night and how she had revealed her suspicions to Craig, finally. It had been a relief, actually, to finally confess and, no, she did not think she was crazy, much less paranoid.

After exiting the Metro station in D.C., they picked up Chinese takeout and went to their respective apartments. Craig lived only a few blocks from hers, near Adams-Morgan. She had left most of her meal uneaten, too tired and uninterested to bother with it. She remembered wondering what the media folks were eating in Iraq. What were they getting that was totally new, and what were they missing? What had Claire been surviving on? Was it mostly western food, given the hotels? She had gone to bed thinking again about how sad things had become of late, with the war that was going nowhere except down, the folks that were being sucked in by it, for good or for worse, the money being expended, stolen, and wasted, and the overall tragedy of addressing change with fear. *It was the end of our nation state* she had thought pessimistically and remained of the same mind-set this morning. And now, Simon uncharacteristically was hiring a replacement for someone who had not yet been formally mourned. *Damn him.*

10

After Simon escorted her to her desk and had departed, DeeDee took a deep breath and clicked on her computer, as a distraction. She could tell from the murmuring that the people in the room, her new colleagues, were debating how to judge this new turn of events. Most of them, she rightly assessed, were uncomfortable with her hiring, perhaps not her personally, hopefully, but uncomfortable because it brought back all of the pain of losing their colleague. Simon had explained that it would be a bit awkward at first, but that it would be best if she could get to Baghdad as quickly as possible so the vacuum created by Claire's death could be filled, thereby ensuring full coverage by a WSSN point person. DeeDee had agreed that representation was necessary sooner than later, but argued that it would be best if she was introduced in absentia.

"No, no, no," Simon had countered. "They'll be seeing your reports within days. Then they'll give me hell for not introducing you. It's a lose-lose situation for me. I'll take care of it. You need to be introduced and then get on the next plane to Baghdad. Tonight, if at all possible."

That was yesterday, and no, tonight was not possible. She was departing tomorrow afternoon, prior to the memorial for Claire, and just before Christmas. What a life. Things had been happening at such a whirlwind pace lately. Joining WSSN was definitely a sudden move for her, and one that had never even remotely occurred to her. She had been enjoying her previous job, but the headhunters had come at her so convincingly that she had finally accepted this new position. She was flattered, but she didn't really think she had warranted this kind of status. Yes, she was fluent in Middle Eastern languages, and, yes, she knew their histories, but being tasked with investigative reporting sounded so technical. She just felt so miserably unqualified and, yes, confused. If truth be told, in fact, lately she felt that she was living a perpetual déjà vu. On a regular basis, as in every hour or so, she felt she recognized someone, some event, or some professional experience, but in fact was unable to put it into any context. Suffice it to say it was extremely disconcerting. DeeDee Morgan was hoping that a change of landscape would end the occurrences, or at least mute them. In that regard, even though it was dangerous, she was glad she was leaving. At the same time, it was unfortunate for her, she thought, that she would not be able to attend the memorial for Claire. Simon had insisted that she leave ASAP, though. DeeDee felt badly for the deceased woman. Then, uncharacteristically, she muttered to no one but herself, "Well, it was her own goddamn fault for not being embedded with the US military." She stopped and looked around, hoping no one had heard her. Where did *that* come from, she wondered. She felt ashamed, but only for a second. "Oh, well, too bad for the bitch."

11

Craig had culled all of his resources in order to backtrack to his receipt of the Journalist List. For the life of him, he could not recall when he had received it. Suddenly, he had an idea. He hit the intercom button on his desk phone. "Doris, could you get me that Journalist List I received a while back?"

"Sure, give me a few minutes," she responded. God, he loved the little perks that came with this job. Who'd of thunk ten years ago he'd have a corner office in the US Department of Commerce, with one of the few existing windows, and a personal secretary? *Who wudda thunk indeed?* He picked up his basketball and made a rimless shot. A few seconds later, she knocked. *Ha!* he thought. *That was easier than I could have imagined.*

"Craig, this is very strange." Doris, a skinny, red-headed, freckled, and very myopic woman of about forty-five, was holding an intergovernmental envelope in her hand along with her trusty personal, leather-bound tracking notebook, and most importantly, the List. She was a great administrative assistant, as they were required to be called, but she was extremely compulsive, which could drive someone crazy. One time, when Craig had first started working in his current capacity and hadn't realized what kind of gem he had working for him, as he had inherited Doris from his predecessor, he had asked for an explanation of the phone system. Two hours and three cups of coffee later, he had politely escorted her out, thanking her profusely and reassuring her that he "got it." It was strange, he had remarked only to himself, she didn't even know she was over the top. She didn't understand that no one needed that much of an explanation unless they were blind and spoke English as a second language. He had learned from that instance coupled with a few more that this was the way it was going to be. Funny, if you really listened to her, instead of just waiting for the answer to your question, you often learned a few things that you had not even considered. In other words, Doris was worth every bit of aggravation due to her compulsive nature; she covered his butt, kept his very busy schedule organized and prioritized, and loved him like, well, a brother.

"What is strange?"

"Welllll . . . I'm a bit surprised, because normally I'd have caught a mistake like this, and I really don't know how or why I did not, although this is definitely my signature, but I honestly cannot tell you that I actually remember signing for this, although I know that does not excuse me from taking responsibility for the mist . . . error, although as I've said it just is not like me to have . . ."

"Doris, what is it? It can't be that bad. Just tell me," Craig interrupted.

"The Journalist List was supposed to go to a Craig Hagan, not Craig Harkan. It was accidentally misrouted, and I didn't catch it." She sounded almost tearful.

Craig, on the other hand, was grateful and curious. "Where is Craig Hagan, here in the Commerce Department?"

"No. He's at State. I knew you were going to ask me that, so I already looked him up."

"Big guy?" he asked as he reached for the List, which she handed to him with both hands, as it was quite hefty.

"Very big. I can't believe I let this happen," Doris continued.

"Oh, don't be so hard on yourself," Craig said reassuringly. "It's obviously an easy mistake to overlook. You didn't send it to the wrong department." Deep down, he was again very grateful for this human error. "So, where was it routed from?" Craig continued, assuming it originated at State, since that seemed most logical.

"Oh," Doris said indifferently, "DoD. I thought you knew that?"

"DoD?" Craig stifled his surprise, for no other reason than to diffuse what was becoming a complicated discussion with Doris, which he did not need right now. Especially given this latest information. *Jesus,* Craig thought, *the DoD?* Andie was not going to like this one bit. He didn't like it, but she was going to flip.

"Thanks, Doris, I guess I just forgot," he responded. "No harm done. I think we should just put this issue to rest for now. I'll call you if I have any more questions about it."

"Oh, Craig, don't you think I should contact the other Craig, or at least his office? I mean, he doesn't know that he didn't receive this, and he may need it."

"You know what, Doris?" Craig inquired, in a very soothing but non-condescending tone. "If we had discovered this mistake a couple of days after it was sent here," and he was careful to include the *we* so as to reiterate that he did not blame her for the oversight, "I would agree with you. But I'm sure he already has another copy. It's basically a contact list, like a phone book. It was sent to a lot of folks. Others in his department have most assuredly sent it to him. So it's really too late to correct it now. I mean, how long has it been? At least three or four weeks. Let's just let it go."

"But, Craig, I . . ."

"No, I'm serious, Doris; I don't want to draw any attention to this. Believe me, it's not worth it," he said as he subtly escorted her out, as he often did.

"Okay," she agreed reluctantly. "As long as you don't want me to follow up . . ."

Craig interrupted again, "No. No follow-up, Doris, no need. Also, I think since we're not following up, let's not mention this to anyone. You know how people can turn little things into big things all throughout this town. Let's let sleeping dogs lie, in other words." She nodded her acceptance of this agreement. "Again, Doris, thanks so much. You're really great." She turned and smiled. "You really are, Doris, I mean it." Her grin increased twofold, but it was still dwarfed by her glass-framed magnified eyes.

12

Andie was reading the bio on DeeDee. She didn't want to look at it, she had told herself as she rounded the block for the sixth time, but her curiosity had gotten the better of her. The minute she got back to the press room she had clicked it on, but not before noticing that many of her colleagues were doing the same thing as they multi-tasked their other work assignments. Some were talking with each other in what could only be described as hushed tones, compared to the usual cacophony.

Well, Andie thought, as she leaned back in her chair reviewing the highlights. DeeDee Morgan had been born in Morocco. There were several photos of the "precocious only child of a foreign service couple living primarily in the Middle East for the past twenty years." She had attended American schools up until tenth grade and then had been sent off to prep school in Switzerland, "her first non Middle East locale."

Big deal, Andie thought. *Those American schools were just that. Everything American. They probably even got macaroni and cheese for lunch, for God's sake.*

After prep school she attended an unidentified "liberal arts college in New England, majoring in communication and debate. . . . By her sophomore year, she was selected president of the debate team." Wow, Andie mused, she sure didn't seem like a debater standing up there with Simon. She seemed, well, rather self-conscious and shy. The bio continued, "Because of her debating skills, she switched to journalism in her senior year, recognizing that the ability to go after a story included being able to debate a source to reveal all." *Christ,* Andie thought, *who the hell had written this nonsense?*

Uh, oh, Andie thought as she continued. This next part was not as Rockwellian as the previous storybook tale. Her parents had been killed in the bombings in Tanzania in 1998. "Fortunately, of course, DeeDee was in the States at college." *Fortunately?* What the hell, she had lost her parents. They were dead. . . . Again Andie thought, *who put this bio together?*

"DeeDee had understandably been devastated by the tragedy. She graduated early, magna cum laude, and spent the next two years investigating the bombings and the communication failures that were in part responsible for the government's gross errors in recognizing the lead-up to it." Several links were indicated here, supposedly to the writings of the now infamous DeeDee Morgan, but when Andie tried to call them up, they were inaccessible. *Oh, well,* she thought, *the ineptitude of the author applied to the person's technological abilities, or lack thereof, as well.* The bio ended strangely and abruptly, Andie thought. "DeeDee Morgan has the requisite skills and experience to be an exceptional asset to any agency interested in getting at the truth."

What? Where the hell did that come from? It wasn't a summary. It sounded more like a reference. What truth? Shaking her head, Andie just sat back and reflected, staring at what appeared to be a very recent photo of this DeeDee enigma. So . . . she was a whopping twenty-six years old and being sent to Iraq to represent the firm as *the* investigative journalist. This was crazy. Andie decided she couldn't wait any longer. She needed to talk with Simon. He answered her buzz and request to meet with a short "Come up at 11:00" response.

13

The VP was quite agitated. He knew he would have to comply with Jones's demands, but he could not stand the fact that Jones would get away with it. As he sat alone in his plush office, he stewed about the reversal of power and how he had let this happen. Damn! He hated Jones and all the baggage that came with him. As he stood up to pace, he felt a twinge in his knee and cursed again, hating himself for becoming so fat and out of shape. He knew he was unattractive, but the weight certainly didn't help. Then he admonished himself for getting off track. *Focus!* Jones could not get away with this. As he glanced out his window, he saw that the day had become increasingly dark and dreary. Good. He liked that. If he couldn't enjoy nice weather, he really didn't like the idea of anyone else getting out and flying a kite. It wouldn't be fair.

And he paced. Except for Jones, the plan was materializing as he had envisioned it.

Soon, the Terrorism Informational Prevention Systems presentations would be scheduled, and the potential informants would be receiving their inoculations. The tide of dissent would turn, slowly but surely. He knew it was actually the easiest way to go about changing the entire political landscape of not just the US, but . . . the world. He was going to accomplish what few had ever been able to do, and none would even consider in the Twenty-First Century. His name would be analogous with genius in the future. *In fact,* he mused, *he would be the most famous person ever to be known on earth. All six billion of them.* The lumbering pace continued, and so did the positive affirmations. He began muttering to himself. A habit he had had to work hard at stifling during his young years in politics, but which he often reverted to when alone. Words like *brilliant, talented, gifted, exceptional* were flowing from his mouth, almost an opposite of Tourette's syndrome. The secured phone abruptly interrupted his egomaniacal admiration. Startled, he grabbed for it quickly without thinking and twisted his knee again. "Goddamn it!" he snarled as he answered.

His Chief of Staff was on the other end thinking, *I haven't even spoken yet, and he's already started with the profanity.* Quietly sighing, he began, "Mr. Vice President . . ."

"What is it?"

"I'm calling to remind you, as you asked, to update you on the whereabouts of Jones and his activities."

"And?"

"He apparently has an office in Silver Spring. He . . ."

"Apparently, or confirmed?"

"Confirmed. He goes there quite frequently and is known to meet people there. A man and woman. Both have been seen coming and going with and without him, and alone, but never all together."

"What's in the office?"

"So far, our investigator has not been able to penetrate the security system. His observation indicates that Jones rented it under a pseudonym, just over two years ago, twenty-six months ago exactly." The Chief of Staff decided he better be as precise as possible so as not to elicit another criticism from the VP. "It's approximately, I mean it's fifteen hundred square feet and costs $2250 a month. The most interesting piece of information is that he leased it for three years, paying the entire amount up front. The lease will run out in ten months."

"First of all, it's not 'our' investigator. And second of all, get *your* investigator to get inside there and find out what the hell he's doing!" the VP shouted as he slammed the phone down. His Chief of Staff was such a non-starter. He'd thought of getting rid of him a number of times, but so much had transpired between the two of them that to do so could potentially jeopardize the secrecy of his actions over the course of the past fifteen years. It was easier to put up with the mediocrity than to forgo the loyalty.

As he began pacing again, his step was a bit lighter, even with the bum knees. *So . . . Jones was operating out of Silver Spring. Maybe he could still pull this off without giving in to his terms. Maybe.*

14

Jones and Maria were preparing the material that would be handed over to the VP once he came around and agreed to Jones's terms. In it they described what had taken place thus far and what would be the most expeditious way to "inoculate" people, so to speak. The beauty of it lay in its simplicity. Dr. Veritos, at the behest of Jones, had spent the last two years developing a superior form of subliminal messaging coupled with a chip that released serotonin, first on a programmed schedule, and over time by a person's own subconscious volition. The messages were what the VP would need to know, but the chip design and technique were, of course, always to remain a secret. Jones knew, even without the good doctor's constant reminding, that technique was everything. In this case, the technique allowed for the quickness with which people could believe in their convictions without waver. The chip, eventually triggered by a person upon hearing certain words and phrases, simply provided added endorphin support about their convictions. And those convictions just happened to be everything the administration touted, from the spread of democracy in foreign lands to religious righteousness in their own land.

"Where do you think they'll have these seminars?" Maria asked, shaking Jones from his thoughts.

"Maria, Maria," Jones said sarcastically. "They're not seminars; they are Terrorism Informational Prevention Systems, or TIPS, to be presented to the various audiences, TBA."

"Are you joking? No, I guess no one could make that stuff up," she sighed, shaking her head. "These poor saps. *Fear, fear, fear . . .*" Maria commented as she carefully labeled the DVDs. "You know, Jonesy, I think I'm finally beginning to understand the phrase *They drank the kool-aid,* so often used by the bloggers."

"Ah, Maria, if it were only that easy," Jones replied deviously. They both laughed.

No doubt about it, Maria thought a few minutes later. She was definitely looking forward to completing this project and leaving these mad people behind. She and Jones had never discussed where they planned to go, or how each of them would disappear. It was the polite way to handle it. Maria, for her part, was trying to systematically arrange things so when she dropped the bombshell on her husband, the "getaway" would be too enviable, or inevitable, to even question. He'd get over it. He loved her. He just didn't know she was working on a super secret project that would put her behind bars for the rest of her life if she were ever caught by legitimate police. "So . . . do you know where they'll be holding these TIPS?" Maria continued.

"Some of them," Jones said flatly. He was looking out of the two-story window, noting a black Lexus with tinted glass across the street. *Hmm,* he thought, smiling slightly, thinking that it stuck out like a sore thumb in this modest neighborhood. "They're in and around the federal buildings like State, the RRB, maybe Commerce." *The RRB was the most abominable building in the entire city,* Jones thought.

"I thought Commerce was in the RRB."

"Yeah, but Commerce doesn't mingle with the other two agencies there. They think they're at least a notch above them."

"How sad," Maria exclaimed. "Those poor people; they're so maligned as bureaucrats." She had just finished with the last DVD. "I think we're set to go, Jonesy," she said, stepping back and looking at her handiwork. Along the wall thirty DVDs were uniformly lined up, looking like a store going out of business.

"Just in the nick of time, too," Jones added, squeezing Maria around the shoulders.

"Why? I didn't know the VP had the seminars . . . I mean, TIPS, already scheduled."

"No, he hasn't, but we don't want to disappoint when he does demand them, do we?"

"I suppose not," she said, although she really could give a rat's ass what this VP wanted. "Do you think The Mascot knows about all of this?" Maria asked, walking across the room to put her coat on. Maria referred to the US President as The Mascot because of the seeming good fortune he had brought to his party, and . . . well, if truth be told, because of the way he would don outfits at the drop of a hat and play whatever role his team wanted.

"I don't know if *The Mascot* knows," Jones said, chuckling. "He may know but may not truly understand the implications of the activities. I don't think we should care one way or the other."

"Believe me, I don't. I'm calling it a night, Jonesy. Are you going to take care of these?" she asked, motioning to the software and supporting materials.

"Yes. No problem. Thanks, Maria. I'll be contacting you about the timing of our next steps."

"I'll be eagerly waiting to hear," she said, giving him a peck on the cheek. "Cheers." The door closed tightly behind her, locking automatically.

Concerned, Jones watched from the window to see Maria get safely into her car and drive off. He had slightly turned the blinds earlier so he would not be visible from the street.

Then faster than Jones could even blink another Lexus rounded the corner, almost rear-ending Maria. It then slowed enough to allow for a reasonable, non-alarming distance between them. Jones saw her head toward the exit to 275. He tried calling her, but remembered that the new law now prohibited cell phone use while driving and Maria was a stickler for following the law. At least most of them. "No!" he shouted. The other Lexus and the man Jones presumed to be sitting in it remained parked.

15

Just as Andie was approaching Simon's door, her phone rang. She thought she'd ignore it until she saw that it was Craig.

"Andie," he said without introduction, "are you alone?"

"Well, kind of, why?"

"Find a place to be alone." Andie looked around, deciding to try the women's restroom. It was empty. Most of the players on this floor were men.

"Okay, what's up? You're acting cryptic again."

"I just wanted to let you know about the Journalist List."

"What about it?"

"It originated at the DoD." There, he'd decided to just spit it out. She could handle it.

"Are you kidding me?" Andie asked, her mind racing. "Tell me you're kidding."

"Sorry, but no. It's printed and provided by the FCC, but sure enough, the DoD is the author. And, yes, your name is on it. It's thick, Andie. It's everybody, it's global, just as you suspected."

"Oh, no, Craig, do you know what this means?"

"It means a lot of things, Andie. Lots and lots, like you said."

"Please don't tell me my address is in it," Andie implored. "Please."

"Everybody's name, place of work, phone numbers of course, and . . . sorry to say, really sorry to have forgotten this part, but there are photos."

"Oh my God. How could you forget that?" she almost screamed.

"Andie, don't blame me. It was nothing to me until you mentioned it."

"I know. I know. But why did you receive a copy?"

"Yeah, that's another thing. It was sent to me by mistake," Craig said, waiting for the other shoe to drop.

"Oh, Craig. This is too weird. Way too weird. I need to see that List. When can we meet?"

"I can get it to you tomorrow. I have a big meeting this afternoon and then a reception tonight. "

"Okay. How about breakfast at that corner café in Georgetown? Say 7:00?"

"Yeah, okay. It's a bit early for my style, but yeah, this is important," Craig said, wanting to be supportive.

"Okay, thanks, Craig. I mean it. I'm sorry I yelled. It's just too weird," Andie said again.

"Agreed," Craig said. "Bye for now. Oh . . . Andie, are you still there?"

"Yes. Don't tell me you forgot something else that's even worse."

"No, I just wondered if you found out what the symbol on the three-by-five card meant."

"Depleted uranium. How's that for a kicker?" Someone entered the bathroom so she clicked off before getting his reaction.

16

Andie needed time to digest this latest bombshell, but at the same time she really needed to talk with Simon. The memorial was coming up, and she knew he'd be preoccupied. She decided to try to avoid thinking about the implications the List potentially signified for the next eighteen hours and concentrate instead on the new DeeDee and on Claire's tribute. She left the restroom and quickly reached Simon's office. She knocked on the door.

"Come in!"

Boy, he sounded mad. Mad or upset. "Hi, Simon," Andie said.

"I thought you were going to be here ten minutes ago. I've got about thirty seconds, and in that time I'm going to tell you that the layout for Claire looks good. Keep doing what you're doing. Now, what do you want?"

"Wow, Simon, what's wrong?" Andie asked with a concerned tone, noting his more than usual rumpled appearance and tangled long, thin hair. The room was awash again with the signature Chic-Fil-A cartons and diet soft drink cans.

"Nothing. And I mean that. What did you want to talk about?"

Given that the clock was ticking, Andie launched right in. "It's your new hire, DeeDee. Where did she come from?"

"Didn't you read her bio? That's why I sent it out."

"Of course I read it. That's why I'm asking you the question. Where did she come from, or rather where did *you* find her? She's a novice, and now you're sending her to replace Claire?"

"Oh, Andie, please let's not get into this," Simon said, slouching lower in his chair.

"Get into what? I'm just concerned that she's not up to the job. It's got to be a hell of a place to try to do investigative reporting. Do you honestly think she's got the guts to get out there?"

"No. No, I don't. This was not my hire. And if you say anything to anyone about what I'm about to tell you, I'll deny it. Do you understand? I will deny it."

"Shoot," Andie said, sitting down.

"She's been seconded from DoD. They insisted I hire her."

"What? Can they do that?"

"They've done it, Andie. I admit, it's probably not legal, but what are you going to do when you get a call in the dead of night and someone asks you to hold for the Secretary?"

"My God! You're kidding," Andie said as she sucked in her breath.

"Yeah, the Secretary of Defense called me. Can you believe that?"

"Why, what does he care about who WSSN sends to Iraq?"

"Apparently, a lot. He reminded me of Claire's death and said we needed to have someone who understands the context of the danger, so he didn't have to explain, over and over to the press corps and the public, why journalists were getting killed. He said it was the only way to do it safely and even more effectively, mentioning the embedded technique."

"But couldn't you have said no? You could have told him it's not how we do business."

"Andie, it wasn't a request."

The two of them sat without talking. Andie was appalled at what she had just learned, but realized that discussing it any longer was going to be counterproductive, given Simon's demeanor. He had become so distraught that he was holding his head in his two pudgy hands and just staring at his desk.

She decided she better change the subject. "Oh, well, don't worry. I imagine DeeDee will get up to speed rather quickly, once she's in country," Andie said, trying to sound convincing. "In the meantime, is there anything I can do to assist with Claire's memorial?"

At first Simon looked annoyed that Andie would acquiesce so easily. The mention of Claire's memorial, however, seemed to bring Simon out of the doldrums, if for no other reason than that he was accomplishing something for someone he truly admired.

"You know, Andie, I've been spending most of my time on this event. It's the least we can do for her. As I said, your outline looks very good. What are your plans for interviews?"

"Well, I've already interviewed a rather exhaustive group of colleagues, but haven't been able to identify a lot of friends from her past. I'm going to continue the process at the memorial and see if I can set up some times to talk with other folks, to get even more personal stories about her. And, of course, I've talked only briefly with her mother. I'm excited to meet her. The phone call I had was simply not sufficient. I need to have some one-on-one quality time. I was thinking . . ."

Simon cut in. "Unfortunately, her mother won't be attending."

"What? Why not?"

"She's simply too tired to make the trip. She's not in the best of health, Andie."

"Oh, dear. Well then, Simon, I'm going to need to make a trip to Ohio. She's in Columbus, right?"

"Westerville, to be exact. Okay. Arrange it. Make it sooner than later."

"I'll go right after the memorial. With Christmas coming, she may appreciate some company."

Now that she had him in a more casual mood and she realized the clock was not really ticking, Andie decided to try to get some information on one more loose end. "By the way, Simon, have you talked with Nathan lately?"

"As a matter of fact, I have."

"Really?" Andie was relieved to hear it, and surprised. "When? I mean, did you call him?"

"Actually, no. He called me. He was wondering about Claire's memorial and asked if he could make it back in time. I know he was upset. I told him it just wouldn't work. I mean, he's already there and now embedded, and to get back here would just not be logistically possible, unless the Concorde still existed *and* we could afford to send him on it."

"He must have been disappointed."

"Yes, he was. I told him that DeeDee would be out there in a few days. That cheered him up."

Andie thought this all sounded a bit off, but decided not to pursue it. She was just glad Nathan was okay. She'd find out later how his phone had ended up in Sadr City.

"Well, that's great, Simon," she said, smilingly broadly and standing up. "So, is there anything I can do for tomorrow?"

"Not really, Andie. Thanks for asking. Miss Ellie is up on *all* of the details, of course. I think this has gotten to her more than anyone. She really loved Claire."

"Everyone did," Andie responded somberly. "Everyone."

17

Dr. Veritos, Jones's other "deputy," didn't want to wait any longer. He knew it was a breech of protocol, but time was of the essence. *Jones knew that,* Veritos muttered to himself. Where the hell was that man? Veritos went down to the street to see if the pay phone was in operation. It seemed that it was pulled out of its base at least once a week. He knew it was just a matter of time before the phone company would just disconnect it. Fortunately for him, it was working this evening. Given this troubled neighborhood, he always looked around carefully before doing anything, whether it be to get out of his car or, in this case, to enter the phone booth. The streets were relatively deserted, save for the loud music coming from the tavern two blocks down. It was too early for the real violence to begin. Veritos stepped into the booth and then called Jones's cell. The big no no.

Jones answered immediately. "Doctor, I know I'm late." He didn't sound as angry as Dr. Veritos had thought he would be with the breech. "I'm in trouble. If I'm not there by eleven, leave and wait to be contacted." The phone went dead.

Dr. Veritos hung up quickly. He looked at his watch. It was 9:45. He glanced around again, cautiously. The parking lots and adjoining streets were also deserted. "Vhut kind of trouble?" he said out loud. Dr. Veritos was a native of Austria and had never been able to rid himself of the "V" for "W" speech pattern. He turned from the phone booth and made his way back to the "office." He and Jones had decided to give it the appearance of a toy repair shop. They figured that would be the least likely to be hit on by drug addicts or others looking for money.

Once inside, he went back to his video and began critiquing it for the hundredth time with his voice and time sensors. Some of the potential viewers of this video were going to be smart. Very smart. Nothing could be amiss. His strategy included not only the visuals, but the corresponding repetitive phrases. His experiment indicated that it was this repetition that was most critical. But the pictorial was essential for rapid absorption of the concepts and convictions. Of course, the "inoculation," as they referred to the chip, helped tremendously in this rapid absorption. *Ha, ha, ha,* Veritos chuckled quietly. *Just a bit of serotonin, and even the smart vhones vhill succumb to that endorphin high.* Jones was supposed to be here to view this final take and provide the DVDs for copy. He'd have to watch it later. And with that he clicked on the "show," as he liked to think of it.

The panoramic screen was huge compared to the rooms he had selected for presentation. It was his intention that plush seating be available so the audience could get comfortable, rather than be distracted by squeaky cafeteria chairs. The image he created evolved from a faint suggestion on one side of the screen, and quickly morphed into a crisp, clear, bigger-than-life Commander in Chief walking across what appeared to be the actual stage. As he did so, it appeared as if he was making actual eye contact with individual members of the audience, including his signature, thumbs-up gesture. The music, *Hail to the Chief,* played softly in the background, almost imperceptibly.

"How is everyone?" the President sincerely asks. "How are you?"

Dr. Veritos knew that at this point the audience would respond with actual nods and verbal okays, not realizing immediately that it was a delusion. Although it becomes obvious rather quickly, he was confident that the majority of viewers wouldn't continue to register this fact. The reality of the image was absolutely stunning. Reactions of adulation would be similar to those of movie star watchers.

The show proceeded to project six major points, in order, for developing a new belief system within the minds of the viewers. It unfolded seamlessly and faultlessly:

Fear is real—This Commander in Chief will protect you
War is justified
Dissent is unpatriotic

Our party is the party of the people
Judeo-Christian religion is your religion
Fear is real—This President will protect you

Images of the World Trade Center collapsing, news discussions of the anthrax attacks, bullhorn feel-good moments flowed across the screen, as the holographic President on the stage talked soothingly about his commitment to protect the people of the US. Facial images of members of his administration flashed in nanoseconds behind him, across the screen, as background. Near the end of the tape, after all presentations were over, the President reached out from the stage and shook hands arbitrarily with what appeared to be members of the audience. He then stood, looking humbled, and thanked all of those present for ". . . allowing him to serve them." Tears filled his eyes. He saluted while saying "God bless you all," and ended even more emphatically with "God bless America." *America the Beautiful* played in the background. Then, after turning on his heel, he left. The screen darkened, but not before there was one final montage lasting about three minutes. It showed Saddam's statue falling, Saddam's spider hole found, soldiers smiling, insurgents killed, Rockwellian American children smiling while they waved American flags at parades, Fourth of July fireworks, and finally a statue of the President on the Mall situated in front of the Washington Monument, overshadowing it, and now providing the reflection. Masses of people visiting the statue filled up the rest of the screen.

Ha! It was perfect! Even Dr. Veritos could not help but love his work. Of course, Jones had provided copy and review, but he, Veritos, was the one who had suggested the approach, and he was the maestro who had put it all together. And it was he who had ultimately provided the presentation to the VP. Ironically, the chip that he had designed was a far more significant development, but he had grown to appreciate manipulation through messaging more than any kind of implant. Bottom line, he was brilliant. He knew it. How his brilliance was put to use mattered not in the least to him. Somehow, sometime in the future, he planned on taking his due credit.

Veritos spent the next hour reviewing the other four "shows," then, glancing at his watch, he decided it was time to leave. Jones had said to get out by eleven.

Just as he had turned off the light, Jones burst through the door.

"Keep the lights off," he ordered, pulling Veritos to the floor with him as he simultaneously kicked the door shut. "Don't move, don't breathe."

18

The café was just opening when Andie saw Craig rounding the corner. *Good,* she thought. *It can get crowded here.* Craig waved as he approached, and kissed her lightly on the cheek when he reached her. "It's nice to see you in the morning," he joked.

"Same here," Andie said, smiling.

"Coffee, coffee, coffee," was the next expression coming from Craig's upbeat demeanor.

"Wow, you must have had a good banquet."

"Yeah. It was really good," he replied, grinning.

"Ohhhhh," Andie said suddenly. "You met someone?"

"Yeah. It shows?"

"No! Only from ear to ear. Who is she?"

"I'm not going there. It's bad luck. Let's just say it looks promising, which is a lot better than most of my attempts have been since, well, since Jane and I split."

Andie could tell that the breakup still hurt. "Okay, then," she agreed, "but if it progresses, you have to give."

"You'll be the first. Let's order."

Over coffee, fruit bowls, and freshly made egg sandwiches, they talked about the List, which Craig had brought to turn over to Andie. In the meantime, she noticed that the RW&B news program on the TV was discussing a bank robbery that had occurred on the West Coast the night before. *No war there,* Andie noted once again, wryly.

"I checked it again briefly," Craig was saying. "Yep, it's too bad, but your stats are front and center. It's listed alphabetically. You should have changed your surname. Personally, I don't know anyone else having a name starting with two As. What does Aaberg mean again? I know it's Norwegian, but what?"

"I told you, it's 'on the hill by the river.' My father would have disowned me if I changed his name. It's been around . . . well, forever."

"But you don't look Norwegian." Craig and Andie had had this conversation before.

"Come on, Craig. You know my mom was Greek. The recessive genes just didn't make it."

This was an understatement. Except for hazel eyes, Andie had jet black hair and an olive complexion. The Norwegian side showed up in her rather tall, angular physique. The combination was unique, to say the least, and quite striking.

"I'm just kidding."

"Yeah, yeah, yeah," Andie said, before finishing her coffee and the last bit of bread. "Okay. Gotta go. Thank you so much for meeting me here to 'hand it off,' " she whispered, looking around in an exaggerated manner. "But seriously," she asked, "how will you give it to me?"

Though the experience in Bethesda had been a benign one, the two of them had been surreptitiously, and constantly, surveying the crowded restaurant ever since they'd arrived.

"Just take it out of my backpack. It doesn't have to be a big deal."

Andie reached down and did just that. "Jeez, Craig, it's the size of a major city's phone book," Andie commented, quietly.

"It is a phone book," Craig responded sarcastically. "Only this one has lots of pictures."

"Yeah, don't remind me," she said, as she shoved it into her backpack.

"Okay, now I'm ready. How 'bout you?" Andie asked, a bit breathlessly.

Craig was already putting his arms into his bulky winter coat and nodding in agreement.

"When do you think you'll come to Claire's memorial?" Andie asked, as they headed toward the Metro.

"Oh. When is it?"

"Craig, it's tomorrow. Don't tell me you're not coming."

"Damn, I knew there was something," he said, snapping his fingers. "Sorry, but I can't. Big meeting. Well, it's not really a meeting, it's an all-day training, actually, I don't know what it is. It's about security."

"You're joking."

"No, I'm not. I have to go to something called TIPS. I'm truly sorry. I forgot."

"Well, skip it. It sounds stupid anyway. Security, security, security. It's all a ruse. If they really wanted to make us secure, they would deal with Al Qaeda."

"I can't. It's a mandatory seminar for everyone at Commerce; 'mandatory,' as in from the Secretary."

"Oh, Craig. That's so sad. I mean it."

"I know, I know. I'm truly sorry," he said again. "Please let Miss Ellie know how sorry I am."

"I will, but you need to let her know, too."

"I will, I promise," he shouted, as he ran toward the opened Metro train door.

Andie stood watching it leave the platform, which was aboveground at this station. The sign indicated that her train was delayed. The wind picked up, and the sky darkened with storm clouds. She felt very alone as the weight of the List on her back suddenly felt like an unbearable burden that she was forced to acknowledge without the means to escape it.

19

"Sir?"

The VP turned slowly to look at the man standing in front of him, George Bruce. *What a pathetic excuse for a human being,* he thought.

This guy was former air force pilot and CIA who had caved under duress when he and his team were ambushed during the first Gulf War. According to testimony, he had bawled like a baby when the Taliban even waved their weapons in his direction.

"Not true!" was the response from Bruce. He claimed the second-in-command, a Walter Trair, had actually been the coward, among others. Bruce contended that over the course of their captivity Trair had been able to convince the team that Bruce was responsible for their capture due to, in actuality, *his* cowardice. After their rescue, Bruce was relieved of his duties and put out to pasture, so to speak. Trair, on the other hand, had risen through the ranks, and the other members of the team were provided with raises and promotions as well, far faster than under normal circumstances. Bruce's reputation was so tarnished that no one would hire him. He had finally set up a small PI business, employing a couple of retired military he'd gotten to know during his time at the Agency. They kept him in the know as to what the Pentagon was doing, most of which he wished he did not know. But the business barely paid his bills . . . until recently. About six months ago he had received a call from the VP, who wanted Bruce to do some research and maybe follow a couple of people. At the time, Bruce could not understand why the VP would call on him for this rather superfluous task. He was about to find out.

"Have you identified her and her residence?"

"Yes, sir. I did it myself. Her name is Maria Stone. She lives at 23 . . ."

"I could care less where she lives. How many kids? What ages?"

"Two, sir. A seven-year-old daughter and three-year-old son."

"What's the husband do?"

"Works at the Department of Agriculture."

"What a loser."

Bruce said nothing.

The VP turned around in his chair, staring out his window. His back was to Bruce. His pancake hands were crossed behind his head.

When he turned back around, Bruce could have sworn it was another person. His eyes were angry, his color ashen, and the infamous pudgy face looked as if someone had pressed it in certain spots, creating permanent indentations that added up to a countenance of evil.

"Get the woman."

"Excuse me?"

"You heard me. Pick up the woman named Maria Stone."

Bruce crossed his beefy arms across his forty-eight-inch chest. "I don't think I understand."

"Of course you do. You just don't want to hear me, and you just don't want to understand me. I said pick up the woman."

"What am I supposed to do with her?"

"Put her in a secluded place. You have been given sufficient allowance to pay for such a place."

"I'm not sure I want to be involved in this. It's kidnapping, a felony."

"You work for me, you coward. If you can't figure that out, you really ought to have been killed by your captors, simply for being unacceptably afraid."

Inside, Bruce seethed, seeing for the first time how his reputation had been compromised once again, for working for the government. "How long am I supposed to keep her there?"

. "You asshole. I told you at the beginning of this contract. Don't ask obvious questions. I'll let you know what you need to know and when you need to know it. For now, just do as I say. Now get out of here."

"Yes, sir." George Bruce turned on his heel and left. *God . . . how he loathed that man.*

Walking to his car, George Bruce reflected on his life over the past thirty years, and had to admit that at times he felt regret. It was not regret about anything he had personally done, but regret about how he had not fought harder for a clean record when he knew he'd been set up as the scapegoat. And he knew why they had picked him to be the scapegoat, because he was loyal. He was not the kind of soldier or operative that would hire big lawyers or make a big deal about military "justice," regardless of how wrong it was. He had always known that he would have to fall on his own sword if the time ever came. And when it did, he would. But now, thinking about the VP and knowing how the man operated, he realized he'd always been a foe, always jealous of his, George Bruce's, integrity, fine military family upbringing, and most of all his undivided love for his country. George Bruce promised himself, even as he headed out to do his enemy's bidding, that he would never lose that love, that integrity, that loyalty. No matter what, he would always do the right thing.

20

Finally, after what seemed hours, Jones stealthily moved on his hands and knees as close as he could toward the door, ensuring that he did not pass in front of it. He waited. Nothing. He lowered his head so it lay flat on the floor and peered under the door. Nothing. No shadows. He then circled the room in the same manner, along its perimeter until he reached the windows. He raised himself up alongside one and peered out as best he could without becoming visible from the outside. The Lexus was there, as he had expected.

"I think I'm going to have to kill someone," he muttered.

Veritos heard him. "No. . . . Please don't kill," he whispered.

"No . . . no. I'm not. Do you have everything backed up on the memory stick?"

"Yes, of course. Two of them."

"Okay. This room is toast. Say good-bye to the equipment and, unfortunately, your paper files. Everything's backed up though, correct?"

"Yes. Everything."

Jones sat in the corner of the room, took off his heavy winter coat, and unzipped the lining. He turned it over to reveal a wide assortment of electrical wiring and other paraphernalia. Veritos watched as Jones then began threading the transparent wire along the door's frame, attaching it now and then with what appeared to be a tiny stapler. He continued rolling it along the baseboard to the file cabinet, where he tied it off using a kind of putty. He threaded the other side of the door's wire along the opposite baseboard and tied it off under the computer stand. He popped open the drives and took out the disks, leaving them open. He also removed the hard drive. Both of these items he put in Dr. Veritos's beaten-up leather briefcase. "Oh, yeah, you're going to have to lose this, too."

In fact, that briefcase did hold sentimental value for Dr. Veritos, but he didn't say anything.

"Okay, Doc," Jones began. "We're going to have to leave here now. We will be stopped. I was followed here, as you may have guessed. But I wanted to make sure no one would come up here after me, which thankfully did not happen. I think we've waited long enough to determine that the manpower against us is limited to one, maybe two at the most. These guys want what we have, obviously. They'll corner us as we approach my car. Act surprised. They'll be aggressive, so be prepared to be searched. That's when they'll take your briefcase. They'll be thrilled to see what's in it. Please protest as loudly and adamantly as you can when they take it from you. They'll let us go after a bit. We'll get the hell out of here before they approach this room. The explosion won't kill them, but it will hurt. Now, where are the memory sticks?" Dr. Veritos held them out to him. Jones removed their plastic labels. "Okay, come here for a minute, so I can look at your tie." Dr. Veritos was confused. Now he was standing only a foot from Jones. At this point, Jones took a piece of the transparent wire from his pocket and fashioned a tie clip with the memory stick across Veritos's shirt button and tie. It looked pretty legitimate. He then took his keys from his pocket and tied the other one to the existing key chain.

"This guy, or these guys, are ex-military. Let's hope they're not too familiar with the newer gadgets. Plus, it's dark, although I'm sure they've got state-of-the-art flashlights. If they do notice this and try to take it, then run to my car . . ." Jones gave him the keys, ". . . and get the hell out of here. Even if they manage to rip it from you, you'll still have this one. Go to a hotel. I'll delay him or them for as long as possible. Wait for me to call you."

Dr. Veritos couldn't believe Jones was saying and doing all of this, but they had discussed this possibility from the beginning. It had finally happened. "Jones? Can I ask vhun question?"

"Ask away."

"If vhe're going to confront them out there, vhy did you set up this booby trap. Vhy blow anything up? You'll be in big trouble if the police find out you did this."

It was a potentially fatal character flaw to be sure, and Jones knew it. "Because *he* pisses me off!"

21

Andie got to work a bit late due to the delay with the Metro. No matter. Most of the folks weren't there yet. She'd just settled into her desk when Simon called her. "Andie, I need to talk with you. Can you come up here?"

"Of course," she said, noting the urgency in his voice. She immediately headed to his office. She knocked lightly.

"Come on in. Have a seat."

Andie quickly removed the heavy backpack. Setting it by the chair, she sat down without taking her coat off, which was now quite wet from the sleet that had begun. It didn't matter though. The relief from the weight of her pack was well worth any other discomfort at this point. She observed Simon while she was tugging off her cold, wet mittens. The tips of her fingers were freezing.

Simon actually looked a bit better than the last time Andie had seen him. His hair was clean, and perhaps trimmed a bit? Unfortunately, however, he had a look of dismay on his face. Andie leaned forward. "What's up? You look like you just received word of the Titanic sinking."

"Worse than that. I just received a DoD directive indicating that twenty-five percent of our staff needs to attend an all-day seminar today, called TIPS. It's mandatory."

"TIPS?" *Where have I heard of that?* Andie thought. "What is it? Whatever it is, we shouldn't have to go to something with such a late notice. We have too many obligations, not to mention in this case a memorial, to just drop everything and attend. And besides, Simon, they can't order a private organization to attend a government-sponsored event. It's unheard of. Not possible."

"It means Terrorism Informational Prevention Systems, and the DoD is dead serious. Everybody from our company must attend over the course of the next six weeks."

"Well, bully for them. They can't make it a requirement. It's against the law."

"Hoffman agreed to it."

"What?"

"Yeah, he said yes, no problem." Doran Hoffman was WSSN's CEO. His grandfather had started the paper. The expansion to a televised news agency had come with the advent of cable TV.

"Simon, we can't. It's that simple. Call Hoffman. He should understand. He should be attending Claire's memorial, for Christ's sake."

"Yeah, but he's out of the country. Can't be reached."

"Then what?"

Andie was furious. So was Simon.

"I've already decided to make an executive decision based on extenuating circumstances. We'll have to ask for forgiveness later. I won't do this to Claire and all of the people who want to pay their respects."

"Oh, thank God, Simon. I'm sure we can all attend at another time. Thank you."

Simon looked extremely relieved himself. "I'd been debating this for the past several hours. Yeah. It's definitely the right thing to do. And to be honest, I agree totally that this is inappropriate. I'm sick of this administration trying to push us around. They're the jerks, you know?

They're the ones with the insecurities. If they're so afraid, and there's so much to fear, why don't they go over to Iraq and fix it themselves? Why don't we ask them that?"

Andie thought, *Maybe I will*. But instead she just shook her head. "Don't get cranked up, Simon."

"You're right. But . . ."

"Is there anything I can do to help with the memorial?" Andie asked once again.

"No. No. We're all ready."

"Okay, then. I'm going to get to work," she said as she rose from the chair, starting to heave her backpack onto her shoulder.

"Oh, Andie?"

"Yes?" Andie responded rather distractedly, noting again that the backpack was damn heavy.

"I've heard again from Nathan."

"*Really? So where is he?"

"He's on his way home. I told him to pack up and come home for the holidays. Kent and Sissy wanted to go, so they're replacing him. He won't be able to make the memorial, which really upset him, but he'll be here next week, back in the office. Then to West Virginia to spend some time with his folks."

"That's great, Simon. I've been worried about him. Can't wait to talk with him. I'll be back from Westerville on Wednesday. He'll still be here then?"

"As a matter of fact, he's leaving on Thursday, but I'll mention that you want to talk. I'm sure he wants to talk with you, too." Simon knew that Nathan looked up to Andie, just as he had to Claire.

"Thanks, Simon. See you at the memorial."

22

Jones and Veritos approached the street with trepidation. The main objective was to avoid losing the materials and plans that had taken over two years to design and develop to the thug, or thugs, depending on how many were waiting for them. Veritos still didn't know who they were, or why they were there, or even more mysteriously how they knew anything about the program.

The two peered out into the night after exiting the building. Jones recognized the Lexus. It was parked adjacent to the building. A man with crossed arms was casually leaning against the driver's side. Jones stopped in his tracks. Veritos made an audible gasp. The man grinned, only slightly.

"It's you?"

"Nah. It's not me," he said sarcastically.

"What are you doing here? How did you . . ." Jones's questions trailed off into nothingness.

"I talked those two guys into going to the tavern," the man said, motioning first toward the Lexus and then toward the bar down at the corner. "I told them there were some wild women in there, something they'd never seen before. We have a bet. We've only got a couple of minutes, they'll probably be back pretty soon."

Jones shook his head. "I'll ask again. What the hell are you doing here? Have you been following me?"

"Not a lot. But I know things are probably approaching show time, so I decided to take a proactive approach to finding out how far you've progressed. I guess I inadvertently saved you, huh?"

"Don't even go there. What are your plans? You trying to stop me? Us?" Jones glanced over at Veritos.

"I told you when I withdrew that I would not obstruct your progress, or even your completion. I just can't believe you're moving ahead. I had to see for myself. You've got a lot of enemies, or so it seems. Are you aware of that?"

"Including you?"

The man scoffed. "Not including me."

"Yeah, I've been tailed for some time now. I spend a lot of time losing them. This time, it was unavoidable."

"Is the place wired?" The man motioned toward the windows where Veritos and Jones had just been.

"Now."

"So . . . you're going to risk everything by blowing these two guys up?"

"Nah. It's mostly loud noises and smoke. They may suffer some tinnitus, nothing more. I just want to warn them. Push them back a bit."

"I doubt it will work. They're on a mission. This will just make them madder and more determined."

"Maybe. We'll see. It's true they want the goods. There's just not a whole lot they can do to me."

"Don't bet on it, Bro."

With that, the lone man took off toward the tavern. Jones and Veritos quickly turned in the opposite direction, using a side street to circle around to Veritos's car, leaving Jones's where he parked it, hopefully as a decoy, at least for a while.

"Vhell, that was a little different than you described in planning it out," Veritos commented to Jones, fingering his makeshift tie clip. "Vhere to now?"

Shortly after their departure, a muffled explosion could have been heard, or would have been heard if not for the loud music from the bar on the corner. The man standing in the shadows across the street watched as two men came stumbling out of the building, holding their ears. Slowly, they got in the Lexus.

23

George Bruce found a decent hotel room for his "guest." Getting her there was not such a problem. He was a gentleman, and therefore he simply went up to her when she was getting out of her car at the grocery store. The minute she saw him she knew something was up. Of course, she did not want to draw any attention, lest something evolve for which she was not prepared.

"Ms. Stone?" Bruce inquired.

"Yes?"

"I'd like you to come with me. You are not in danger, but believe me, you do not want to make a scene."

She'd already figured that one out.

He opened the back door to the black Lexus and held out his arm, as though he was escorting her to a ball. She looked back at her car, locked it with her remote, accepted his arm, and got in.

Bruce contacted the VP through the man's secure phone. All he said when the man he detested answered was, "I have the woman in a safe place." The VP grunted, hung up, and then turned to the window and stared out at the dark, stormy day. He was going to need some help.

"I need to see you. ASAP," the VP stated plainly to the recipient of his next phone call. "No. Now."

Twenty minutes later, the man entered the VP's office. "What for God's sake is so urgent?" The man was very red-faced and visibly angry. He was about six feet, five inches, which made him intimidating; his dark black mustache added to the overall look. Put him in a room with the former Russian oligarchy and he would have fit just fine.

"Calm down. You need to listen to me. Please. Just hear me out and then you can yell," the VP said, with obvious irritation. He then proceeded to catch the man up on his work and discussions with Jones to date, describing in broad strokes the purpose of the implant.

"You know how it goes. Any serious leader is going to use a few red herrings now and again to keep the critics and press from pawing at progress. Once we get this program underway, we can throw out red herrings by the handful, and they'll be eagerly embraced and repeated as new truth. Then we'll be free to get things done on our terms and our schedule. It's as simple as that."

The man was listening carefully, understanding, and agreeing with the sentiment.

Then the VP dropped the bombshell, complaining about Jones's demands and confessing to his involvement in the kidnapping of Maria Stone.

"You did what?"

"You heard me clearly. Now, here's what I suggest. You accompany me to the next meeting. If Jones has any doubt that we don't mean business, your presence will be critical for him to clearly understand his position. Believe me, he won't buck us if he realizes this is a government initiative and not a Jones initiative. He owes it to his country to turn over his designs, for the good of the country. He needs to be a patriot, not a greedy entrepreneur."

The man just shook his head. "I'll do it, of course, but this beats all. If you get away with this, I'll buy your next mansion."

"I'll take you up on it. I have a piece of land in Costa Rica."

"I'll see you there at the meeting," he said on his way out, shaking his head all the way.

The VP personally called Jones back, arranging for another meeting.

"Finally, this asshole gets it," Jones muttered to himself as he hung up. *Finally.* Smiling, he looked at himself in the mirror on the way out and admired his countenance. *Finally.* This was what he had worked for during the past ten years. *Finally. After all of the sacrifice, the loss of love, the loss of blood,* he thought.

24

Craig noticed that his office was unusually empty when he arrived in the morning; even Doris was gone. It seemed that folks decided to just head to the seminar, to begin at 8:30, rather than come to the office first. *Makes sense,* he thought, checking his emails. He wished he'd done the same thing. Now he had two emails that demanded responses. He left his office at 8:27, knowing he would be late.

While approaching the large conference room, Craig noticed that the line was snaking around the back of the exit. For what reason, he could not determine. Way up in front he saw Doris. Suddenly, he had to rub his eyes. It appeared that folks were getting some kind of shot. *Flu?* he thought. *Flu shots now? Too late. What else?* he wondered.

He came up to the end of the line, trying to see what was happening without really being noticed. He wasn't.

"What's up?" Craig asked casually, to the last guy in the line, a young, lanky, bespectacled person who fit the category of bureaucrat, Craig observed. "Are they giving us a shot?"

"They said it's to protect us against bird flu," the young man said. "The scab should fall off soon."

"Bird flu? Has the color alert been raised?" Craig was referring, of course, to the color coded alert scheme the Department of Homeland Security had invented.

"No."

"I don't remember any mention of a bird flu pandemic. What's the rationale?"

"Search me," the kid said. "They said something about us being out and about. It's not for general consumption yet, I guess. I think it's voluntary. You can ask when you get up there."

"But the bird flu hasn't even been identified in North America yet," Craig protested. He could have been talking to a wall. The kid had turned around and was already chatting with the young woman in front of him.

Craig stood there for a few minutes and then started thinking about Claire's memorial. Here he stood, waiting to be jabbed, and for what? "The hell with it," he muttered to himself, turning on his heel and walking out.

25

Andie had thought she would be arriving too early to Claire's memorial. Instead, when she entered the room it was already overflowing with people coming to pay their respects. Claire's favorite music was playing in the background, according to the memorial program's message provided to attendees. The message was also reflected, with the collage of photos depicting Claire in the field working for WSSN, on the large screen against the rear wall, which had been erected the previous day. The photos shifted periodically as the music changed. People were milling around drinking and eating, murmuring quietly, hugging each other, and wiping away tears. Andie was overwhelmed by the turnout. She was happy for Claire's mother, and extremely proud of WSSN. She caught Simon's eye across the room and nodded her head toward him, hopefully showing her appreciation. He smiled broadly. She began to mingle in order to locate some of the folks she'd spoken with on the phone, to thank them for their input about Claire and to give them her contacts in case they wanted to add to the upcoming tribute she was researching and writing. Soon, she guessed because she was being pointed out to others, people were coming up to her, introducing themselves, and offering to meet with her to provide stories about interactions with Claire and her good works. It was better than Andie could have hoped for. She was lining up a sizeable number of contacts who would really increase the robustness of her tribute to Claire.

One man with dark, thinning hair who approached her was turning out to be especially intriguing. He wanted to inform Andie about an incident he had with Claire while in Baghdad. "I was trying to reach you earlier, to warn you that she was delving into dangerous waters," he commented to her in hushed tones, looking around the room as he spoke.

"Really?" Andie said, surprised. "Did you call? I don't remember hearing from you."

"I tried subtly," was all he said, still looking around the room and still speaking in hushed tones. Andie definitely wanted to follow up with this man in more detail. She asked for his card. The man readily pulled one out of his suit pocket and handed it to her.

> **www.INFORMED CHOICE.com**
>
> *Tim Walsh*
>
> Remember, It's up to you

Andie learned that Tim Walsh blogged for his own site and had recently hired two other bloggers to work with him. "Can I call you next week to find a time to meet?" Tim inquired politely.

"Sure," Andie replied. "I'd be delighted." After thanking him again, she turned to get some punch and practically ran into Craig.

"Hello!" she said, happy to see him. "You decided to come."

"Hi. Yeah. I decided to ditch the seminar or whatever it was. From what I saw it looked kind of strange."

"What do you mean?" Andie was curious since she now knew that WSSN staff had also been told to attend.

"Oh, nothing, I'll tell you later. Boy, this is some gathering," Craig commented surveying the room, which was even more crowded now than when Andie arrived. "I'm so impressed and so glad I came. Have the comments begun?"

"No, not yet. I think they'll start in another few minutes. Want some punch?"

"Sure."

"Go ahead and mingle, I'll bring it to you."

"Okay, thanks," he said, as he headed into the crowd.

Once again, Andie headed for the punch. She was actually beginning to feel fatigued, with all the people milling around and all of the discussions she had been having. The punch turned out to be surprisingly helpful in reenergizing her. She filled up her cup again and got one for Craig. She was looking over the room, trying to locate him, when her eyes landed on a distantly familiar face. Elliot! He was talking with one of the reporters from WSSN. She came up and stood next to them, causing both men to stop their discussion. Her colleague, Joel, looked at her quizzically. Elliot just smiled.

"Hi."Andie stuttered a bit, noting how crowded it was, but not really knowing what to say now that she had deliberately interrupted them. "This is quite a nice event for Claire." Joel responded with a nod. So did Elliot. Silence. "Um, sorry to interrupt. Elliot, can I talk with you when you get a chance?"

"Sure."

"Okay." She walked off looking for Craig and feeling foolish.

Craig was talking with Simon, so it was easy to simply hand him the punch and let them keep talking, ". . . which is what I should have done with Joel and Elliot," Andie muttered to herself.

"They say as long as you don't answer yourself, it's okay," Elliot said, walking alongside her as she made her way to the rear of the room. It appeared as though Simon and Miss Ellie were preparing the group for testimonials about Claire. The lights were being dimmed and the music volume increased just a tad. People were beginning to take seats.

"I'm sorry to have interrupted you and Joel."

"You said that already. No problem."

"Well, it seemed awkward."

"It was a bit."

Andie now realized, even though she barely knew him, what she found annoying about Elliot. He just didn't say enough.

"You don't say enough," she blurted out.

"What did I miss?" he asked, raising his eyebrows, looking at her with a truly quizzical expression.

"Oh, never mind. What are you doing here, Elliot? Did you know Claire?"

"Yes."

"Yes? There you go again. Not enough words."

"Ask more questions."

"Okay. Can we go for coffee after the memorial?"

"Sure," he said. They sat down.

"Family, friends, and colleagues," Simon began. "We're here today to pay our respects to a fine woman and a fantastic reporter. She died doing what she loved best. Please let us share our time with Claire with each other now."

The attendees were not short on stories, nor were their stories short. Everyone, it seemed, had been touched by Claire in some way. She was funny, dedicated, serious, and thoughtful. She was compassionate, caring, and loving. She did anything and everything for everyone. She was truly a hero. The testimonies lasted over an hour. Everyone had a chance to laugh and cry as they reminisced. Finally, by the time it was over, Andie felt as though people had been able to grieve sufficiently and, hopefully, to begin to move on. Everyone except Claire's mother that was. But since she was unable to attend, the staff had arranged to tape the event for her. Andie was sure she would be pleased to receive it, and hoped it would help her with her grief as well.

For Andie, the event had provided a cleansing of sorts as well. She was pleased that so many of the attendees were so willing to talk more with her. She felt as though it was finally the beginning of her work about Claire, the beginning of filling in the blanks and hopefully discovering more about why she had died.

With a big sigh she looked up at the huge smiling photo of Claire and silently said good-bye. She left quietly, having planned on meeting Elliot in another hour or so at the coffee shop on 22nd, near State. Why there, Andie didn't know, but Elliot had suggested it so she quickly agreed. She decided to walk. She needed to walk.

26

The three men sat in the bunker, all stone-faced. "Who are you waiting for?" Jones asked, impatiently. The VP and his Chief of Staff said nothing. Jones began pacing.

"It's your time you're wasting," he said, as he sat down and pretended to write on a small pad of paper he'd brought. Again, the two other men in the room said nothing.

Twenty-five minutes later the door was opened by Agent Ingram, who escorted the man to the table.

"*You!*" Jones blurted, even before Agent Ingram had had time to depart. He could not believe his eyes. He now knew why the VP was eager to set up the meeting. His former friend, the Secretary of Defense, had now been brought into the mix. They were ganging up on him, and

Jones did not like it one bit. He realized that that was what the VP was counting on. *Tough,* Jones thought. *There's absolutely nothing they can do, even bringing up good old times or whatever their strategy was going to be, to coerce me into revealing the formula.*

27

The coffee shop was bright and busy. It made Andie feel better after such a stressful event. It had been a long day already. As she was ordering her coffee and a warm sticky bun, Elliot slid into the other side of the booth. "Same" he said, as the waitress looked over, pad and pen in hand.

"You knew you wanted a sticky bun, too?" Andie asked, smiling.

"Sure, it's why I come here. They're the best."

"Oh, I didn't know. They just smelled good, so I decided to try one."

"Bingo," he said.

Andie felt a bit shy suddenly. She didn't even know the man sitting across from her, but she felt as though she could get comfortable around him, if only he would open up more.

"So," he began, "how is your investigation going?"

She laughed out loud. "I was just thinking about what to say to you about my investigation," she said, still smiling.

Elliot thought she had the most beautiful smile he had ever seen. She just didn't use it enough.

"Well . . ." he said, waiting.

"Well . . ." she said, "I'm hesitant to tell you, but I will. Since Claire was killed, I have focused on writing a lengthy tribute to her, in order to get some recognition for her hard work. No one talks much about the journalists over there unless, well, unless they're dramatically kidnapped. Not when they're killed."

Elliot seemed to lose his coloring at the indirect mention of Claire's death. "So it seems," he said, nodding and looking grim.

"But," Andie continued, "I think the clues revolve around this whole issue of the role the media are playing in this administration. I mean, you already told me it's a leak. So that's another reason, a major reason, why I'm investigating Claire. Basically, I'm investigating the investigator, under the pretense of writing about her. It's for her and for me, I must admit."

Elliot simply nodded, and there was a moment of uneasiness.

"How did you know Claire?" Andie asked suddenly, breaking the silence. She had been angry earlier when she felt Elliot had lied to her, but now she was sure she would understand his explanation. Reflecting on the comments at the memorial had calmed her down a bit.

"I have read her articles for years and knew she was in Iraq and was used to seeing her reporting from there. I hadn't seen or heard anything for several days, and so I called the paper, your paper, and found out she had died while in Iraq. It was sad for me to hear. The person at the paper mentioned the memorial, and so I came."

Andie noticed while Elliot was speaking that he avoided looking at her, as though he was still hiding something. What it was, she couldn't guess. "So, do you take such an interest in all reporters?"

"Ah . . . that's another question. No. Claire was different. Definitely different."

"How so, I mean, what made her different?"

"I believe she was dedicated to finding and delivering information. She was able to keep her politics out of it. She was a true journalist, the kind they used to make. Not the ones that are on the evening news now. She's closer to what the bloggers are doing now, finally," he added.

"Boy, you must have watched her a lot," Andie commented. This made Elliot look more ill at ease, Andie thought, so she added, "She was one of a kind. I think the memorial was great."

"So do I," Elliot said.

Out of nowhere, piping hot, deliciously smelling cinnamon buns arrived with coffee.

Taking the hot steaming mug, Andie added warm, frothy milk and sugar. "So, have I worked through the clues sufficiently?" she asked, laughing, hedging her bets.

"You're getting close," Elliot said, enjoying the moment. "Believe me, you're getting close."

28

"Jones, calm down. You're not in charge of this anymore. We have some news that should help you to make some serious decisions and choices. Go ahead," the VP said to the newest member of the group. "Please explain to Jones what has happened."

As Jones listened, he tried to remain unemotional. It was not easy. He could not believe how low the VP had gone, although of course he knew that, in itself, it was nothing new. It was just new to him, because now he was the target. He had been on top for so long, he hadn't expected this. His mind was racing. He recalled the day he, Maria, and Veritos had toasted each other to their plan. The agreement had been that if any one of them was ever found out, and subsequently threatened, they would do everything in their power to keep from implicating the others. Of course, this agreement had been based on presuming that one or more of them should be arrested, not kidnapped, for God's sake.

While Maria had asked Jones if the VP was going to have him killed, neither of them had thought it might be the other way around, although Jones did not really think the VP would have her killed, but then . . . the VP was predictably unpredictable.

As the newcomer, the Secretary, finished describing the current state of affairs, Jones looked up to see all three men staring at him. Now he knew why they had placed him at the end of the table. It was to make him feel cornered. He didn't say anything. They waited, and they waited. Nothing. It was the VP who finally gave. He was the one who pulled papers from his coat pocket this time. With the tips of his fingers he shoved them at Jones. "You can just sign on the bottom line," he said with a smirk.

"I'm not doing this," Jones replied, standing up.

"*Sit!*"

"Like I said, I'm not doing this." Jones pocketed the papers and walked out.

29

After the coffee and cinnamon bun, Andie suddenly felt tired. She headed home. Elliot had been nice and walked her part way there and then had put her in a cab. The storm that had started earlier that morning had become increasingly menacing, but she didn't mind. She needed to pack for her trip to Westerville to talk with Claire's mother. Once she was settled at home, she prepared some tea and packed her suitcase for a two-day trip. Now, finally, she thought. She'd been waiting for this opportunity to look at the List. First, though, she went to the kitchen and poured herself a glass of white wine. Walking back to her office, she noticed from her sliding glass doors how dark it had suddenly become outside. The earlier storm had gotten a whole lot worse. As she settled into her office chair, she was glad she was here now, rather than later. Later, it would be a big mess. Metro delays, traffic delays, and a real nightmare for pedestrians. All hell broke out when it snowed in D.C.

Finally, she pulled the List out of her backpack and placed it on her desk in front of her. The envelope it was wrapped in had her name on it. That was nice of Craig, she thought as she carefully removed it, wadding it up. "Okay," she muttered to herself, bracing for what she was likely to see. She opened the hard cardboard cover.

SOLE PROPERTY OF
THE DEPARTMENT OF DEFENSE
U.S.A.
CLASSIFIED
(UNAUTHORIZED REVIEW OR DISTRIBUTION IS STRICTLY PROHIBITED)
Updated November 9

Classified! Craig hadn't mentioned that little tidbit. *Uh, oh.* Andie was just a wee bit nervous now. *Oh, screw it.* This administration classified everything. "Hell, they classified information that was already printed in the mainstream. This was no exception," she rationalized.

Turning the page, she realized what Craig had meant. There she was— first name on the List. The photo was recent, but not the most recent. She tried to place it. When had she had that taken? It wouldn't come to her. Not so long ago, she decided. It was fairly accurate: same hair and a current blouse. But . . . oh well. It didn't matter. What did matter, however, was the detailed information, beginning with her full name:

Aaberg, Anderson "Andie"

This was followed by her birth date and place, her address, her work address, her latest graduation date, her title, cell number, social security number, passport number, and then there was the photo.

Andie sat stupefied. Who the hell had compiled this? Who the hell had the right to put this information all in one place without her knowing it? It made her feel sick.

She began flipping through it, noticing familiar faces, stopping here and there to note information she obviously hadn't been privy to before. "Jeez, she's that old?" "He never even graduated from college?" Then she stopped cold. There was Michael's photo. Cruelly, a big red circle with a line across it and the word *Deceased* plastered on what had once been his pleasant face marred the photo. Place of death: Baghdad. Additional information included the remaining family members' names.

Andie reflected back at seeing these red swaths now and then as she had been flipping through it. She felt sicker. This was a sick publication. What was its purpose? Flipping back to the front, a page stuck to the next one, creating a ripping sound. Andie stopped and slowly pulled the two pages apart. The page she had accidentally opened to held Claire Thompson's photo. She noticed it immediately. There was a red swath across it. She stopped.

Claire had been killed in December, almost a month after this update.

30

Jones read the proposed contract from the VP. He still couldn't believe that the jerk had brought in a heavyweight and former friend to continue the intimidation routine, especially on top of nabbing Maria for extra emphasis. Poor Maria. What must she be thinking? What must her husband be thinking? How long had it been so far? At least eighteen hours. "Absolutely not!" Jones exclaimed. Then he ripped the contract in half.

31

Mark Stone was an easygoing, nice-looking, forty-year-old Ag Department Undersecretary. He came from the Midwest, still had some land there passed down through four generations of the Stone family, and really appreciated the small farmer because of this background. He had met his beautiful wife, Maria, through a mutual friend, and it had been love at first sight. At least for him. Actually, she didn't need much coaxing. Maria had quickly grown to love him because he was passionate, considerate, and loving. Today, however, he was anything but. He had talked to the Maryland, D.C., and Virginia police. His wife had not returned home. They could care less. "No, sir, not for at least seventy-two hours" could they do a damn thing. "What if I was important," he had finally screamed at the phone to the Maryland cop? "Well, sir, it sometimes appears to make a difference, but no, sir, seventy-two hours is the rule." Mark Stone slammed down the phone for the fourth time in as many hours.

Okay then, he thought. He dialed the international number connecting him with his wife's family in Venezuela. Within ten minutes he had accomplished more than he had been able to do for over the last twenty-four hours. He was totally satisfied now that every inch of the Beltway would be combed, and pronto. Maria would be home soon, he thought; he was absolutely sure of it.

32

Andie had gone to bed but was unable to sleep. She was so troubled. The List suggested that Claire's death was pre-known. Of course, it could have been a typo, the date on the DoD document could have been December. Or it could have been a mistake to have ID'd her as deceased. There were explanations, but no one to check with. No way to investigate it. She couldn't just call DoD and ask who had compiled the document. She wasn't even supposed to have it. Craig wouldn't know. She didn't know if she would even tell him. Why distress him when he couldn't do anything either. She finally fell into a fitful sleep, dreaming that when she opened the List and saw her photo for the first time a red swath was already across her face.

The alarm was just too much. She slammed it off and turned over, only to jump up when she realized she had to get to Dulles through morning rush traffic. She prepared some coffee and quickly showered, trying to leave enough time to have a bite to eat before the taxi arrived. Out of habit, she turned on the TV in the kitchen while she toasted some bread and gulped some coffee.

Low and behold, DeeDee suddenly appeared on the news, reporting from the Green Zone. My God, Andie thought, how could she be up and ready so soon? She'd barely left. Here she was reporting on what? "Good, soldierly deeds, thankful Iraqis," and what? "clean streets?" Where? Andie wanted to see them, not just hear about them. Where was the proof? Where did DeeDee get this?

The buzzer by her door rang, indicating that the cabbie was there. She quickly turned off the TV, unplugged the coffee pot, grabbed her suitcase and laptop, and ran to the elevator. Just as it arrived, Andie thought back to the List. Wait, she should have looked up DeeDee, too. She needed to know more about the mysterious woman who just showed up and was now a wartime correspondent. Andie quickly turned, ran back to her apartment, struggled with the items she was carrying to find her keys so she could re-enter it. Finally, she got inside, dropped the suitcase, and with the computer still over her shoulder, she ran back to her bedroom and picked up the heavy document. She rapidly flipped through it. Upon hitting the M's section, as in Morgan, she grabbed hold of a section that she felt would include DeeDee and ripped it out. She hated to do it, but she didn't have any more time or she'd miss her plane. Then, holding the List in front of her with both hands as though it was contaminated, she looked around frantically for a hiding spot. Suddenly, she did what millions of people around the world had done at some time or other. She hid it under her mattress.

The buzzer began to ring again just as she was running out the door, all the while cramming the dozen or so sheets into her computer case. *What a way to start a trip,* she thought. *What had happened? I used to be so organized,* she muttered to herself. Too much out of her control was the only plausible response, she decided, as she slung her suitcase into the back of the taxi and hopped in.

"Where to?"

"Dulles, Northwest Airlines."

The cabbie, who sounded Ethiopian, did a U turn in the middle of the busy, four-lane road, eliciting deserved honks, only to get trapped behind a bus. *Never fails,* Andie thought.

33

The VP answered his secure phone with a gruff "What?"

The Secretary of Defense on the other end simply said, "I'm coming over. I'll be there in ten."

The VP wondered what the hell was up. He didn't sound good. *God . . . what now?* He had too much on his plate already. He had actually hoped that it was Jones on the line. He kept expecting him to call and say he was ready to deal.

The knock was brusque. His entrance followed immediately.

"Check this out," he said, as he tossed a piece of paper to the VP. It was a letter from the President of Venezuela. It was brief.

> Dear Sir,
>
> It has been brought to my attention that my niece, Maria Stone, has been missing for over thirty-six hours. Police in Maryland, D.C., and Virginia have not responded to requests for assistance in locating her. I am putting together two teams of investigators from within the US to begin searching immediately. This is simply a notification of my action, as a courtesy from one country to another. Thank you for your understanding.

"It's a legitimate signature," the man said. "I had it checked out."

"Jesus Christ," the VP said, throwing back his head, sighing loudly. "How the hell did this happen?"

"You did it."

"I know, I know. Who would have thought that this woman was his niece, for God's sake? I had her checked out. Her husband's a bureaucrat. Why would his niece marry a bureaucrat?"

"I guess it was love," the Secretary said, nonchalantly. "I'm more concerned about getting out of this mess than I am as to how it happened. Where is she?"

"I don't know."

"What?"

"I had her taken care of by someone, I didn't ask questions. I thought the less I knew the better."

"Well, now it appears that you had better know as much as you can. The President is calling a cabinet meeting in two hours. He greatly resents the Venezuelan President interfering in US law enforcement. He wants to find out how something like this has happened and expects the team to problem-solve, so no other country will ever, ever interfere like this guy is doing."

"*Oh my God.* What an idiot. I've got to get to that meeting. Why wasn't I formally invited?"

"Regardless, you better let him know you have been contacted by someone, not me, of course, but someone, and then . . . I don't know, you decide."

"Yeah, I'm going. I'll see you there."

34

Except for the rude treatment by TSA at Dulles, the flight to Columbus was uneventful for Andie. She got a rental and drove to Westerville, which took about an hour due to traffic, even though it was only fifteen miles north of Columbus. She arrived early, checked into a hotel, and then stopped at a local coffee and doughnut shop to get organized and to gather her thoughts before meeting Sadie Thompson, Claire's mom. Andie got a self-service cup of coffee and grabbed the last booth in the front of the shop. It was a *hoppin' place,* she observed. The line at the register was nonstop, and the takeout window had cars backed up to the street. The TV in the corner had the RW&B news channel blaring. The newscaster was seen describing a snow blizzard in the west. *Breaking News* was flashing frantically, while the woman at the scene, dressed like an Eskimo, screamed into the mike so she could be heard above the howling wind. Meanwhile, Andie noticed with outrage, the ticker tape indicated that four more American soldiers had just died in Iraq. *Isn't that breaking news?* she thought wryly. *How many souls have died?* she wondered. It was too unfathomable to imagine.

She looked out the window, depressed, and then reminded herself that right now she needed to focus on Mrs. Thompson and Claire. Andie had to admit that she was very nervous, even given all of her experience as an investigative journalist. This was so personal and close to her that she really had to concentrate on not letting her emotions get to her in front of Claire's mom. Mrs. Thompson had sounded fine on the phone, Andie remembered, but she really wanted to pry into things that Mrs. Thompson may not be willing to talk about. She decided that she would need to play it by ear. There was no way to predict the mood Mrs. Thompson would be in and how receptive she was going to be to Andie's inquiries at this point. Andie was glad she had the recording of the memorial at least. She knew that by handing that over it would help to break the ice, if it needed breaking. With that thought, she took a deep breath, gathered her belongings, and got back in her rental. Sadie's home was not far.

The single-story house was quite modest, and quite old. Andie figured it must have been built in the mid-forties, early fifties at best. She collected her laptop, got out of the car, and walked toward the front door along the sidewalk, which was cracked and raised here and there due to the roots of the huge elms that surrounded the driveway . The yard was obviously well cared for and maintained. She reached the single storm door and rang the bell. About thirty seconds later the oldest, shortest, and most wrinkled black woman Andie had ever seen opened the door.

"Good afternoon, Andie. It's good to finally meet you after our brief talk. Thank you for coming. Please, come in."

Andie smiled and entered the foyer, immediately noticing that the house held that homey odor of past meals and candles and wood fires, desserts, coffees, teas, and whatever else had been enjoyed with friends and families. She felt warm all over.

35

The cabinet meeting was called to order. The President began: "Thank ya'll for coming together on such short notice. I feel I have pressing business to bring to the table. You all have been informed of the letter I received, or actually the Secretary of Defense received. I want to suggest that we do not take this lying down. I mean, this is an infringement on our sovereignty. We cannot let another president interfere in our law enforcement. There's no other way to view it. Comments?"

The people sitting around the oval table looked blandly at the President. No one said a word.

"I mean, something needs to be done to this man. He can't just send a letter that basically says he is taking over."

No one said a word.

Just at that moment the VP entered. A slight, discernable scowl crossed the President's face. Relief could be seen in many of the participants' faces.

Even before the VP had walked a couple of steps, the cabinet member closest to the President jumped up and gave his chair to the VP, moving to a back chair next to the President's Chief of Staff. The VP sat down.

"As I was saying," the President started, ignoring what he visibly perceived as an interruption, "we must take some action against Venezuela and this president."

"We need to ignore the whole incident," the VP stated simply.

The President frowned. There were some audible sighs and a couple of nods in the affirmative. Glancing eyes could be seen furtively looking back and forth to both men.

"That's not gonna be acceptable in my book. I'm the Commander in Chief."

"If we make a big deal, it will hit the media. You'll be expected to give a press conference to explain what has happened, why there are Venezuelan agents readily available in the US, what you're going to do, and what stopped the law enforcement agencies from looking for this woman."

The President looked uncomfortable at this description of a media inquiry. "We need to prevent this from happening again, another country threatening us, for God's sake," the President said resolutely.

"No one will know about this if we keep this amongst ourselves. No other country will try it. Let's ignore this affront. I recommend that the Secretary of State call the president there and let him know we'll work together to search for his niece. Hopefully, we'll find her at a friend's house with a big hangover and full of apologies for creating any problems." He paused. "Whatever the result of the search, however," he warned the cabinet, looking around slowly, making eye contact with each and every one of them, "no mention of her, this letter, or these Venezuelan law enforcement teams must ever be made. We each know who is present here," he said, threateningly. The cabinet had heard this part all before. The day they were initially convened, they were informed that their first loyalty was to the President and Vice President. No ifs, ands, or buts. So far, few had strayed from this policy, and when they did, they were finished.

36

Jones was in the repair shop waiting to pick up his car. *What a mess,* he thought, worrying about Maria but unwilling to be blackmailed, even for one of his team. Veritos had agreed with him, but, of course, he would. Veritos only considered himself, Jones thought wryly, unable to reflect that he was behaving similarly. He felt it was unfortunate that he had already provided that one-day demo with some of the government departments' staff. Oh, well, he couldn't take it back. Veritos said it had gone "vhery vhell." Only a few from the Commerce division had refused the "vaccine," and many from the private media actually showed up, ready and willing, even though, technically, they were not obliged to do so. Apparently, most of them were still too naïve to realize that their media CEOs were already working in concert with the administration. Those guys would willingly do whatever was requested of them in order to keep their multiple business contracts related to the war and other adventures, including whatever news was necessary to keep things on track.

"Mr. Jones? Your car is ready," the young woman said, pushing the bill under the window.

It was $4,800.00. Jones whistled. "Maybe I should have bought a new car," he said.

The girl just shrugged.

After he and Veritos had left the "office" the other night, they had camped out in a shoddy motel on the other side of town. Early the next morning, Veritos had driven him back to pick up his car. As they approached the "office," they noticed the windows had been blown out, but it wasn't obvious why. Given the neighborhood, someone could have shot them out, although conceivably all of the glass would not have been on the ground if that had been the case.

"I don't think the police will care how it happened," Jones replied, when Veritos asked if he was ready to be questioned.

"They vhill look for the tenant, don't you think?"

"I'm not the tenant," Jones had replied.

He doesn't miss a trick, Veritos thought.

Apparently, Jones's car had not escaped being ID'd by the two men following them that night, however. It was keyed, the windows were smashed, the sound system was ripped out, the leather seats had been knifed, and the tires ruined. "Well," Jones said, "I wished they'd totaled it. Insurance will want it repaired."

Sure enough, that was the bill he was now staring at. Too bad he had selected a $2,500 deductible.

He paid, got in, and drove home, wondering all the way what he was going to do about the VP's proposition. Stalling would work for only so long. And even though she knew and had agreed to the stakes, Maria must be getting very worried.

37

"Please, have a seat," Mrs. Thompson said, waving her ancient hand toward an overstuffed salmon-colored chair near the fireplace. Bookshelves lined two walls, filled with paperback books and bound hardbacks. A similarly colored love seat, across from the chair, provided a place for newspapers and magazines, which were draped over the arms and against the pillows. "You must be tired, would you like some coffee or tea?"

Andie felt as though she shouldn't ask anything of the frail woman, but it looked as though she wanted to do something for Andie.

She must have been reading Andie's mind. "Don't worry, it's not putting me out, I've already prepared both."

"Coffee would be great," Andie said, somewhat embarrassed that she'd been caught. "Can I help you?"

"Sure."

Andie followed her slowly into the kitchen, noting the pink fluffy slippers, the turquoise sweat suit, and the brown crocheted shawl that swung to and fro as Sadie Thompson moved.

The kitchen was located behind a partial wall that separated it from the living room. It wasn't far.

Andie was in for a treat.

The kitchen looked to be as old as Sadie. Well, not quite. The counter was comprised of a celery-green-and-white mix of tiny little tiles. The cupboards looked to be the original that came with the house. They were painted, or had been painted, a dark green at one time. The floor was a distractingly patterned terrazzo. The faucet sink and even the sink itself had never been replaced. Though Andie was no expert, she was sure a Sunbeam MixMaster sat in one corner and a toaster that toasted only one side at a time in the other corner. The fridge and oven looked like the kind she'd seen in photos from her mother's childhood. A back door provided an entrance from a small enclosed porch. Andie could see the backyard as well, which appeared to be filled with trees and the ground covered with leaves. As she stood there smiling, taking it all in, she saw Sadie pouring a cup of coffee from, again, a very old percolator.

"Claire wanted to refurbish this kitchen for me," Sadie said, again seemingly knowing Andie's thoughts. "I resisted, and now I understand I'm right in vogue," she said, laughing. "Milk? Sugar?"

"Yes," Andie said. "Thank you. Who told you you were right in vogue?" Andie was curious how she knew.

"Oh, the girl next door helps me out from time to time, and she said that folks are paying a lot for, let's see, what was the phrase, 'retro' kitchen appliances. She wanted me to sell these to make money. I told her I appreciated it, but I wasn't interested. She was so disappointed that I told her I would keep it in mind. That seemed to satisfy her. Ever since then, she has spent more time wiping and shining all of these kitchen things than she has dusting and vacuuming. I'm not complaining though, no, ma'am," Sadie added, stirring the coffee. "Let's go sit by the fireplace," she said, moving ever so slowly, "I'm chilled to the bone."

Coming back to the small but comfortable living room, Andie tried to imagine Claire in here, growing up here. It was so homey. She must have loved coming home, whether from school or, later, from work. Photos on the mantle showed that Sadie and her husband had obviously been very proud of their daughter. Claire's beauty was evident from a young age. Her large eyes, coupled with the dark, creamy skin and high cheekbones, were absolutely stunning.

There was some silence as they both sipped their coffee.

"So, Andie, my dear, tell me what happened to Claire," Sadie said, suddenly looking wistful.

For the first time, Andie noticed the pale brown eyes behind the large rimmed glasses. The woman's white, white hair framed her face, which appeared to be saying, *She has seen it all.*

"Well, Mrs. Thompson . . ."

"Call me Sadie."

"Well, Sadie, she was caught in some crossfire, apparently," Andie replied, reluctantly, envisioning the red swath across Claire's photo. "No one's really sure."

"Come, Andie," Sadie said, as she reached over with a slightly shaking hand to put her cup and saucer on the end table. "Wasn't she murdered?"

38

Jones entered his house, disturbed and pissed off. No call from the VP. Fine, the demo was it. They weren't going to get any more.

"Hi, Jonesy."

"Yaaaaa," Jones screeched, whipping around.

Maria was sitting in the shadows, lighting a cigarette, which Jones knew she'd given up over seven years ago when she had first become pregnant.

"My God, Maria. You scared the hell out of me." He raced toward her, ready to hug her.

Maria didn't, apparently, hold the same sentiment. She began to smoke, looking up at him slightly.

He sat down in the chair opposite her.

"How? When?" he asked, then stopped. Maria was obviously not a happy camper.

"Jonesy, you didn't even try."

"Maria, you know they'd have been all over me. Come on, what did you expect? We talked about this."

"We talked about the police nabbing us, not the government."

"I'm as surprised as you are."

"Really?"

Jones was still trying to figure out how she was here. He didn't know what she knew. He decided not to lie. "I wasn't about to give in. They wanted me to cave. They wanted me to give them the whole program, the formula, the 'show,' the whole shebang. They were blackmailing me. We would all have ended up with absolutely nothing. Is that what you wanted?"

"Jonesy, I wasn't going to get anything dead. What about that? Did you think about that?"

"Maria, I did not seriously think that the government, our government, would do harm to you. I imagined they would eventually have to let you go. You would not be allowed to just disappear."

"How do you know?" she screamed. "I have children, a loving husband. How do you know?" Tears were streaming from her eyes; she took out another cigarette. Jones reached over to light it.

"Maria," he said lovingly, sincerely. "Maria, please, I never imagined they'd do away with you. Never, never."

She sat there with her arms crossed, moving forward and backward, biting her lip, cigarette between her fingers, the tip burning. Her beautiful thick black hair cascaded across her shoulders. Her eyes continued to fill with tears. She looked sad and hurt.

Jones waited.

Finally, she stubbed out the butt, never having taken a puff, and shook her head like she had just taken out a ponytail. After taking a deep breath, she said, "I'm out of here, Jones. I want my share. My work is done."

"But, Maria, I don't have it yet."

"Get it," she said, standing up. "Get it fast. I want it by tonight." She grabbed her purse and coat and walked toward the door.

"Maria?"

She turned to look at him.

"How is it that you are here?"

"Jones. You must have forgotten who my uncle is. Fortunately, my husband did not."

Jones waited for the glass in the front door to shatter. It took about ten seconds after the slam.

39

"Sadie, what makes you think that Claire was murdered? I mean, did she say anything to you? Was she afraid?"

"She mentioned that she was getting some strange calls and some threats, both written and verbal."

"Did she show you any of these?"

"No . . . no. . . . She didn't want to scare me. Frank had just passed away, and she didn't want to alarm me, I'm sure. But I was sure there was something wrong."

"Frank was her father, your husband?"

"My, my, my, Andie, are you sure you're an investigative journalist?" Sadie chided.

Andie could feel her cheeks turn hot. "I'm not sure what you're getting at," she said calmly, although she was really quite hurt.

"Oh, my dear, I didn't mean to embarrass you," Sadie said, realizing she had put Andie on the spot. "It's just that, well, tell me, how old was Claire, do you think?"

"She was thirty-five, I know for sure." Realization struck Andie like a clap of thunder. "Oh. You're not her mother," Andie said, meekly.

Sadie laughed lightly. "Now you're thinking, girl. No, Claire was Frank's and my granddaughter. We raised her."

"Oh. What happened to her mother, if I may ask?"

A dark shadow crossed Sadie's face. "She disappeared. She was a student at OSU, living at home. We cared for Claire while she was at school. One night she didn't come home. The police said she must have run off, but there couldn't be anything further from the truth. Christine would never have abandoned Claire. Never. I don't know what happened to her. She was a cold case before the ink had dried on her missing person's report. Maybe she's still alive somewhere, but I'm afraid that's probably not true. It's been a long time now, but you know, no one can convince me that she left her baby. Fortunately for us, Christine did not want the father to know about her, so it was easy for us to continue to raise Claire. He was a good man, but, well, Christine just didn't want him around."

Andie was speechless. Finally, she said, "Sadie, I'm so sorry."

Sadie smiled wanly. "Don't fret, dear. Like I said, it was a long time ago. I'll tell you one thing, though, I'm not as complacent about Claire's death. I have become increasingly informed over the years," she said, her eyes roving across the books, newspapers, and magazines, "although now there's no real news available through television or radio, except WSSN, of course. I never became computer literate, unfortunately, and

I understand that's where the real facts can be researched, but that's okay. I have you."

Andie was a little surprised by this comment, but found it to be endearing all the same. "Well, thank you. I do have to say again that something must have happened for you to have made such a bold statement about Claire's death."

"Oh, yes, something happened all right. Two men in gray suits showed up here about three days ago. They wanted to search the house, especially Claire's room."

Andie felt alarm prickle all over her body. "Oh, Sadie, what happened?"

"I told 'em flat out, no. They said they had the right to, and flashed some kind of badge at me. I told 'em I didn't care if they lived at the White House, they weren't comin' in. They just stood there. They said they would wait out there until I agreed to let them in. I said fine. Then I called Harry at the Westerville Police Department. Harry is Chief of Police. Westerville is still a small town. I told him I was being harassed. He sent two screeching cars over here right away. The men were told to leave and not come back." Sadie was laughing hard now. "I keep wondering what they must have thought, having those police show up so fast. It must have startled 'em to say the least."

"Well, good for you."

"That's what I said. Good for me. Claire would have been proud."

"You don't think they would have found anything, do you?" Andie asked, curious.

"Yes, ma'am, I sure do. Let me show you. Just wait here."

She slowly got up and walked over to a small box about six by six inches under a framed photo on the mantle. She brought it back and sat next to Andie on the love seat, by pushing some pillows and magazines out of the way. She opened it and brought out two CDs. "I know they're not records, 'cause they're too small, but Claire sent me these express mail."

Ooooh, Andie thought.

40

Even as Andie was about to become privy to new information, the VP was still trying to fight a twenty-year-old foe. Gritting his teeth, he called Jones. "Let's meet and get this over with. I'll see you there this afternoon."

"Fine with me."

"Jones?"

"Yeah?"

"Why didn't you tell me that the woman was related to the Venezuelan President?"

"It was none of your business."

"You're crazy."

"I don't think so," Jones said, smugly.

41

While the two men were taking pot shots at each other, Andie was learning more and more about Claire. The two women talked all afternoon. By now, the light was waning. Throughout the entire time, the discussion had varied only a little. It was obvious to Andie that she had come at a good time. Sadie was lonely and wanted to talk about what a great granddaughter Claire was and how much she was missed. Andie was the perfect guest. She spoke when it was important to do so, but mainly she listened and nodded when it was appropriate.

"You know, she graduated valedictorian from high school and summa cum laude in college."

"Really?" was all Andie said.

"Yes, ma'am," Sadie said proudly. "And she almost had two majors."

"Really?" again from Andie.

"Yes. She began with her heart set on becoming a chemist."

"A chemist? Well, that's a far cry from becoming an investigative journalist."

"I know. But Claire loved chemistry. It was her passion. She felt that she could solve the world's woes through knowing and using chemistry to understand problems affecting us in the Twenty-First Century, global warming for an example, or farm production shortages. She was extremely altruistic."

"Well, what made her change her mind?"

"A good friend invited her to attend a class in mass media. It was there that she learned how critical it is for, let's see, Claire used to always tell it to me this way: 'It is important for people all over the world to have the right to make informed choices.' She felt that if she could get the information out there, then people would do the right thing. She felt she would have a greater impact that way, so she quickly switched over, in her third year, doubled up on her course work, and the rest is history."

"Well, good for Claire," Andie said sincerely. "It's important to figure out what you want to do sooner, rather than later, and then to excel at it so well. You're right, Claire was very special."

Sadie just nodded. Finally, she was growing weary. Andie could see it in her posture and hear it in her voice. "Andie, it's getting quite late. Why don't we have some supper?" Sadie asked. "You can stay here for the night."

"Thank you, Sadie, I would like that." Andie had hoped she would ask.

After the meal, which consisted of store-bought country smoked ham and boiled potatoes, Sadie commented that she felt like retiring early, although, actually, it had become quite late.

"That's fine," Andie replied. Sadie showed her to what had once been Claire's room and said her goodnight. The room was starkly furnished with only a desk and hutch, a dresser, and a twin bed. The dark blue curtains looked rather faded, but well-pressed. Andie immediately set up her computer on the desk and punched in the CD simply labeled #1. It was arranged according to a table of contents. *Claire was so organized,* Andie thought with admiration. The screen showed six chapters, or sections:

1. DU Formula
2. History of use
     U.S.
     Britain
     Others
3. Photos from Fallujah
4. Health hazards
5. Political arguments
6. Cleanup approaches

DU? Where had Andie seen that before, she wondered? *Oh, depleted uranium. Oh . . . the card in the envelope.* After selecting the first choice, the screen opened to the same formula Andie had identified. She just hadn't had time to pursue researching it as of yet. Now it looked as if she was going to find out just exactly what it was.

^{238}U, Claire's written research findings began. Andie noted that she was quoting from the IAEA web page.

> In order to produce fuel for certain types of nuclear reactors and nuclear weapons, uranium has to be "enriched" in the U-235 isotope, which is responsible for nuclear fission. During the enrichment process the fraction of U-235 is increased from its natural level (0.72% by mass) to between 2% and 94% by mass. The by-product uranium mixture (after the enriched uranium is removed) has reduced concentrations of U-235 and U-234. This by-product of the enrichment process is known as depleted uranium (DU). The official definition of depleted uranium given by the US Nuclear Regulatory Commission (NRC) is uranium in which the percentage fraction by weight of U-235 is less than 0.711%. Typically, the percentage concentration by weight of the uranium isotopes in DU used for military purposes is: U-238: 99.8%; U-235: 0.2%; and U-234: 0.001%.

However, and now Andie noticed that Claire's research source had changed to another web site www.wise-uranium.org, the military found an effective use for DU in its weaponry. DU is used in armor-penetrating munitions because of its high density. However, DU is both radioactive and toxic to the human body. Exposure to DU can cause a myriad of ailments related to the kidneys, lungs and immune system.

As the information and photos, staring at her from a dead woman's work, began to sink in, Andie became increasingly incensed. She began paging down, scanning the history of its use. Claire began by quoting from a source labeled www.eoslifework.co.uk.

> The facts about DU weapons are well known to military experts and arms manufacturers in the US, the UK and at least 30 other countries. The conclusions have **immediate implications** for the health, safety and welfare of civilians, troops and aid workers in Afghanistan [and now Iraq]. They question **the role of Governments, UN agencies** and the **validity of official research studies** concerning Depleted Uranium (DU) to date. They raise serious questions about the **global proliferation of DU** in military and

civilian applications and its suspected widespread use in Afghanistan [and now Iraq]. They have fundamental implications for the
classification of **DU munitions** as **weapons of indiscriminate
effect** as defined in the **1st Protocol additional to the Geneva
Conventions**. Their use is a **war crime**.

Quickly scanning down, she started reading about the health hazards
due to exposure. The medical findings related to DU's use made Andie
even madder. "Incredible," she whispered. *Why had anyone created this
weapon, knowing about its uncontrolled side effects?* She was now reading from a web source titled www.citizen-soldier.org/CSO9-uranium.

> The American and British militaries first used DU weapons during
> Operation Desert Storm in the Persian Gulf in 1991. When a DU
> shell strikes its target, up to 70% of the depleted uranium vapor-
> izes into fine dust, which then settles out in the surrounding soil
> and water. Over half of the aerosolized particles are smaller than
> 5 microns and anything smaller than 10 microns can be inhaled.
> Once lodged in the lungs, these particles can emit a steady dose
> of alpha radiation. An additional hazard is DU's chemical toxic-
> ity. An Armed Forces Radiobiology Research Institute study of
> rats after the Gulf War found that DU exposure damaged their
> immune and central nervous systems and may have contributed to
> some of the cancers they developed. While the Army intensively
> studied DU's value as a weapon, less effort was made to learn
> about its possible hazard to health. In fact, the Army's Environ-
> mental Policy Institute criticized the command in a 1995 report
> for its failure to "closely coordinate the planning and performance
> of experiments for DU health and environmental assessments.
> All told, the Pentagon has estimated that 320 tons of depleted
> uranium was [were] fired by US and UK units. As of today, not
> an ounce of this toxic residue has been removed by either the US
> or any other agency.

And then there was this startling bit of information from an article
titled "Spreading Cancer" by Robert C. Koehler.

> **"We used to think (DU) traveled up to a hundred miles. . . ."
> Busby [indicated], a chemical physicist and member of the
> British government's radiation risk committee, as well as the
> founder of the European Committee of Radiation Risk, has
> monitored air quality in Great Britain. Based on these find-
> ings, "It looks like it goes quite around the planet."**

To be fair, Claire had included facts repudiating the danger of DU quoted from a Defense Department's article.

> A VA program in Baltimore is assessing the health effects on 33 of these service members. About half still carry DU fragments in their bodies. They've shown higher than normal levels of uranium in their urine since monitoring began in 1993, while veterans with no retained fragments show normal levels, VA officials said. Overall, Morris said, the study has found no adverse health effects that can be attributed to DU. Tests of kidney functions in the 33 subject veterans have all been normal. Their reproductive health also appears to be normal—there have been no birth defects in any of the babies they've fathered since 1991.

Andie looked at her watch and was startled to see that it was almost 4:00 a.m. There were screens and screens of information that Andie had to skip. No time. As she was trying to find the political discussion about DU, she suddenly became very frightened. My God! How could she be so stupid! Somebody besides the bald guy who had slipped her the envelope also knew what Claire was working on. On a hunch, she got up, turned out the lights, and went to look out the window. She jumped back, stifling a scream. Not more than thirty feet from her window a dark large car was parked. She could see that two men were sitting in it, apparently because of a lit cigarette one of them had. A cracked window allowed for the smoke to escape, creating a contorted cloud. They appeared to be chatting away and, fortunately, not looking in her direction. She closed the curtain quickly, turning the light back on so they would not notice any difference.

This was not good. She went to the bedroom door and looked out. It appeared that Sadie was asleep, as no light emanated from under the door. Andie stood there, trying to decide what to do. Were they here because she was, or because Sadie had refused them entrance? It must be both, Andie reasoned. Sadie may have gotten the police on their tail during the day, but she would not know that they were around after dark. They were just waiting to get lucky. So . . . here sits her rental. Now their patience had paid off. If she waited until morning, what would they do? Sadie would have to call the police again, but the two men would know that whoever's car it was, that person would have to leave . . . sometime. They could just wait up the block.

This was scary. They must know or think, well, maybe not them, but someone, that Sadie and now Andie had something they needed to find.

Andie formulated a plan and decided to go for it. She wrote a note to
Sadie, asking her to destroy it, and left it on her bed along with a gener-
ous amount of cash for Sadie to arrange for her rental to be towed back
to Columbus. She then called Sadie on the phone, knowing it was next to
the TV, which would require her to turn on the lights. Once she headed
in that direction, Andie slipped out the back door with her computer
and bag and, most importantly, the two CDs, one of which she still had
not had a chance to examine. She securely locked the door behind her.
Sadie was answering.

"Sadie, the men in suits are back. I left a note on the bed. I'll be in
touch." As she weaved through the backyard to another yard, she saw
the red taillights of the car turning the corner. *Boy, Sadie really had had
the cops put the fear of God in those guys. Good,* she thought.

Andie made her way back to the hotel by following the blinking stop
lights. She roused a few dogs here and there and had slipped a few times
where patches of ice could not be seen. She felt like a little girl running
through the neighbors' backyards, only this wasn't for fun and she wasn't
little anymore. Once, maybe twice, she thought she saw a light turn on
inside a house as she passed through the yard, but she kept moving. It
wasn't a long distance, but because of the circumstances, she was quite
out of breath when she reached her hotel room. She quickly entered,
gathered her other bag, and went to the desk. The night attendant looked
irked that she had awakened him, but by now it was close to 6:00 a.m.

"I need a cab."

"Call one."

"Could you call one for me? I don't know which companies go from
Westerville to the airport"

"Lady, there's only one." He picked up the phone and begrudgingly
called. Andie had been in D.C. too long.

Though she had several hours to wait at the airport, Andie had a corporate card to get into one of the airline lounges. She felt inconspicuous
there. She found a relatively secluded alcove and settled in, quickly setting
up the computer, not wanting to waste any time in finding out what else
Claire had discovered. She was not disappointed. She was mortified.

42

After her coffee and toast, Sadie went to her back porch. It was coldish, but not freezing. She sat down on her lounge chair, a metal porch glider with Harley fenders. It was a faded green, which had matched the kitchen décor at one point. She held Andie's note in one of her hands. Quietly, she lit it with a lighter and let it burn, finally dropping it on the cement floor. With the lighter still going, she lit a cigarette and began to rock. She allowed herself three a day. *Something was going to happen now,* she thought as she exhaled, smiling grimly.

43

Jones headed toward the bunker, for the last time he thought. While the meeting place was the same, this time Jones believed he had the upper hand, or at least it would seem so. He was counting his money and the money for Maria. He hoped she would find it in her heart to forgive him, someday.

The VP sat quietly. His Chief of Staff was here as usual, eyes downcast. His partner in crime, the new addition to the pair, the Secretary of Defense, was again in attendance. His purpose, Jones knew not what. Also, as the last time, the three sat on one side. Jones was obviously forced to sit juxtaposed to create a sense of vulnerability. He could tell by this arrangement that they were well ahead of him. *So what?* he thought. *They have no means to threaten me anymore.*

"Jones," the VP began, "we've discussed your request and believe you should reconsider. Your demands are unpatriotic and represent a threat to the security of the US. You are a mere citizen asking, let me rephrase that, demanding special consideration and remuneration. If nothing else, it's unseemly." The Secretary nodded in agreement. Nothing was said by the Chief of Staff.

Jones was stupefied. "Are you nuts? What the hell do you think you're doing? You think this was a war of necessity? You're the criminal."

"Whoa," the Secretary of Defense said, starting to rise. The VP held up a hand, halting him.

"Let me explain the situation, Jones," he said through gritted teeth. "You were still mowing lawns to supplement your allowance when I conceived of this effort. We've worked," he threw his head in the direction of the Secretary, "for thirty years waiting for this opportunity. It's been painstaking and has required a lot of sacrifice."

Jones winced when he heard the word *sacrifice* uttered.

"Then you, you waltz in here and expect, well, a percentage that you haven't earned."

"I thought you said the problem was patriotism," Jones said evenly.

"Patriotism is part of sacrifice. You haven't participated."

Jones stood up. "I told you I would walk, and I will. Good day."

The three men stared. "Jones, here's your contract." The VP said, snapping his fingers so the Chief of Staff would know it was time to hand it over. As the assistant tried to pass it behind the Secretary of Defense, the contents dropped out of the envelope, scattering to the floor. The VP just sighed. Once the Chief of Staff had gathered it up again and shoved it back into the envelope, he walked it over and set it next to the VP. "Okay, you can leave us now," the VP said. "Wait outside." The man briskly walked out. He would gladly spend a little time with Agent Ingram. It was a relief.

Jones pulled the contract out, read it carefully, very carefully. Never could he underestimate the level to which this man would stoop to cheat him.

Over an hour later, he looked up. "I need a down payment. Today."

The VP shrugged. "As you wish. It will be transferred to your bank. Give me the account number."

Jones had been prepared for this. He had established an account this morning. He pulled the card from his front pocket and slid it over. "The rest is to go to the overseas account."

"Fine."

Jones stood up. "That's it," he said with finality.

The VP simply nodded. Jones walked out, past Agent Ingram and the Chief of Staff, sighing with relief. Now he just had to deliver . . . to everyone and for everyone.

44

Not far from the old bunker where history was being made, Craig was getting the cold shoulder at his office at the RRB. He was sure of it. His jokes at the staff meetings weren't receiving the belly laughs they used to generate. His requests for information created a frenzied response that included a much too serious look when delivered, as far as he was concerned. He often prided himself that he ran a tight but relaxed ship. He felt that his team was no longer the one he had worked so hard with for the past five-plus years. What the hell had happened?

Now he was looking at them all staring back. The issue of establishing a daily prayer meeting had just been raised. Inside and out, he was speechless. He hoped it didn't show. He could tell the group was dead serious. Doris, of all people, was staring at him intently. He'd never known Doris to practice any religion. She used to talk about how she enjoyed her Sunday mornings so much when she could enjoy a leisurely walk with her beloved mutt named Sputnik. *Seriously, what the hell was going on here?* Craig wondered.

45

Jones checked to see if his newly established account held newly transferred funds. It did. He then called Maria. "Let's meet at the office in Silver Spring."

"Let's not. Transfer the funds to the account number I gave you, Jones."

"Maria," he pleaded.

The phone went dead.

Maria was furious. She didn't have any interest in meeting with Jones, nor the time. She needed to get her family out, and fast. Her husband had not been pleased to find out about Maria's clandestine life, to say the least, but he had been so happy to have her back safely that he had told her he was forgiving her, momentarily. She gathered by that statement that they would be talking about this, probably for the rest of their lives. So . . . as it turned out, she was now on her way to meet him and their kids at the airport, as planned; leaving for good, also as planned.

It never happened. Whoever ran her car off the ramp on the Beltway and into a tree was never identified.

Jones wept.

46

The return flight was on time. Andie had a good seat to D.C., against the window, and fortunately, no one sat next to her. She was so troubled by what she had read. She kept mulling it over, and over, and over again. The information collected by Claire was enough to fill two lengthy volumes. She obviously had been researching DU since her days as a novice investigative journalist. Now, Andie had to decide what to do with this information. And to be quite honest, she did not know, at least not yet, what action to take. She still had not seen the second CD. Of course it would be necessary to view it. Perhaps it would lead to some kind of decision. She sure hoped so. For now she was stumped. It was just at this moment that Andie remembered the ripped pages from the List that she had taken so hastily on her way out of her apartment. She had just been so busy and so much had transpired that she had totally forgotten about them.

She got up to pull her computer and case down from the overhead and sat back down. She reached into the side pocket and extracted the bunched pages. They were quite crinkled because she had been in such a hurry. She thumbed through them, looking for DeeDee Morgan. Boy, there were a fair number of reporters with last names starting with M and a lot of Morgans, Andie noticed. For a second, she thought she had actually missed grabbing enough pages to include her, but then, there she was. Kind of.

Every muscle in Andie's body suddenly felt limp as she looked at DeeDee Morgan. DeeDee was a nickname, Andie read. Deidre was her proper first name. As Andie peered closer to the photo, which was now creased, she recognized DeeDee. Nonetheless, there was something peculiar about the way she looked in the picture and the way she appeared both at the office and on TV. Now, her hair was more severe and her attire was conservative, with turtlenecks and buttoned collars. This photo showed a grinning woman, with a semi-low cut blouse and loose hair. The bio was short, and pretty much reflected the same story that Simon had sent out, except for one piece of information. Her parents had been killed in a freak plane crash in Tanzania, not in the bombing. Andie wondered why it had been changed and which version was correct.

But even with all of that, there was something more ominous and eerie about this whole discovery. It was what had originally made Andie feel weak. The name Deidre was so unusual, this had to be the woman who had been calling her. Once she had digested this epiphany, Andie began reflecting upon the bizarre occurrences recently, many of which had affected her directly. Deidre had quit calling shortly before DeeDee had arrived on the scene at WSSN, supporting her proposition that these two were the same woman. The bios did not match with respect to DeeDee's parents, and a classified document titled the Journalist List had made it into her hands, which had provided her with this newest information. Plus, she had a new acquaintance named Elliot, who apparently was trying to help her, but in such a vague, euphemistic way that she could not get a handle on it. Somehow, however, she now believed he might be key in deciphering the mystery surrounding DeeDee Morgan. As the plane's wheels touched down, for the first time in a long time Andie felt as though she was starting to chisel away at the blank wall that had been erected since the first call from Deidre. She sighed audibly.

The minute she entered her apartment, she knew something was wrong. She had turned off the light in her bedroom when she left yesterday. It was now on. What to do? Who and why? Was someone still here? She was afraid, and mad. Mad because she was afraid. She slammed the door shut and reopened it quickly, thinking if she startled someone and he came running out of the room, she would have a chance to run. Nothing happened. She set her bags and computer down and approached the bedroom.

She gasped. The bedroom was a mess. The closet and drawers had been emptied onto the floor, and . . . sure enough, her mattress had been tossed. Oh . . . now she knew. Someone was looking for the List. *No!* Andie suddenly ran to the other end of her apartment, to her office. *Oh, no!* They must have started here. It was demolished. *Oh, God.* The implications were tremendous. *Craig. She needed to call Craig.*

"Craig, I'm at my apartment. Please come. Please come now."

"Andie, it's 1:00 in the afternoon. What's happened?"

"Please come as soon as you can."

Andie sat at the kitchen table, staring out the window. She could not for the life of her figure out who had done this. Within the hour a knock at the door made her jump.

"Andie, it's me," Craig shouted from the other side of the door.

Thank God, Andie thought, as she ran to open it.

Craig entered quickly, looking at Andie carefully. "What's wrong? What happened?"

She pointed.

Craig stopped at the entrance. "What the? . . ."

"Someone took the List."

"Uh, oh."

"Yeah."

"Where was it?" Craig couldn't tell. The room looked like a tornado had hit it.

"Under my mattress."

Craig turned and stared. It would have been funny if it were not so serious. Andie looked devastated.

"Craig, it's not just that it's gone. It was *classified*. Someone knows I had it. Probably lots of people know it by now. I doubt the person who broke in just happens to have a hankering for possessing the List."

"You're right there, I'm sure," Craig said, shaking his head. "What are you going to do?"

"I didn't call you just to see this, but to help me brainstorm, too. Who would know I have it?"

"Oh, Andie," Craig said, experiencing a very sinking feeling.

"What?"

"I think I know who . . ." he faltered for a moment, "who may be responsible. At least in part."

"Who?"

"Doris."

"Who's Doris?"

"Doris is my secretary, my admin assistant. She's very dedicated. She's very decent. But . . . " Craig's voice trailed off.

"But what?"

"Well, lately she's been acting strangely. She's become, how do I describe it?" Craig thought for a moment. "Rather pious and patriotic," he declared.

"So, why?"

Craig explained as carefully as he could what had transpired between the two of them and then added the bit about the "transformation," as he chose to describe it. "It's been really bizarre, to say the least. I have half my staff attending a Christian prayer meeting every morning now, including Doris. The jokes I used to make, especially the irreverent political ones, are treated with an uncomfortable avoidance of recognition, as though I hadn't spoken them. I've quit trying. It's no fun anymore."

"So. Doris called the DoD and confessed that the List went to the wrong person?"

"That's the only thing I can think happened. She's the only other person who knew that I had it."

"But why not rob your place?"

"I know, that's the catch. Unless . . ." Craig paused to think.

"Unless what?" Andie could not disguise her impatience enough.

"Well . . . I was in a hurry that day, so after she brought it to me, I asked her to prepare an envelope for you."

Andie could feel herself becoming unglued. "Craig, this is really serious now."

"I know, I know. I'm sorry. Something has happened. My team is no longer my team. Doris is no longer Doris. I would not have intentionally put you in danger."

"I know, Craig," Andie said, crossing her arms across her chest in a protective manner, and shaking her head.

Andie's visible distress was too much for Craig. "Come and stay with me. I've got two bedrooms. It's not as neat as your place, but it will work for the time being."

"No . . . no," Andie said, taking a deep breath. "They got what they came for. They would have arrested me if everything was on the up and up, but they're the ones who broke in. I mean the DoD. I don't think they want the general public to know about the List. I'm not afraid, at least not yet. I'm just really, really angry. They took my evidence."

"What evidence?"

Andie described the photo of Claire with the red swath.

"Unbelievable."

"I know. Now, it's gone. No supporting evidence that anything was fishy about Claire's death. Nothing. Poof."

"What are you going to do?" Craig asked again.

Andie decided not to mention Claire's CDs and the incident with the men in the car. Nor did she want to bring up DeeDee. She didn't know why. She just thought that, for now, she needed to see the CDs and digest them. It was just too much and too hard to describe. Even to her best friend. She did, however, now believe the two incidents were related.

"I'm going to clean up this apartment and get some rest."

"Okay then, I'm at work if you need anything. I'll call later," Craig said hesitantly. "Are you sure you're okay?"

"Yeah. Thanks for coming by. I was freaked out, but now that the mystery is solved, it's not as bad. Still bad, but not as bad."

It took Andie four long hours to clean up the mess. Damn, she should have just left the List on the table where it was. Why did she hide it? It was the *classified* part that had spooked her. That's why.

She had clicked the TVs on in both the bedroom and office to keep her company. As always, with little hope, she channel surfed the news, often stopping on WSSN to get the most reliable stories. In her mind, the others had turned into the classic soap opera. The "newscasters," as they liked to refer to themselves and each other, were really just two people sitting at a desk talking. Periodically they would become struck by dissonance, indicated by the *Breaking News* scrolling across the screen, whereupon they would grasp for clues aloud, often joking with one another. Then, after some inane discussion, they would hone in on the terrible realization, verbalized though with intense looks that *something* was indeed happening, but they were no more than bit players trying to discover what that something was, along with their audience. Andie blamed the OJ Simpson fiasco as the beginning of the end of sound journalism. The ticker tape did not make up for the vacuum.

Suddenly, there she was, front and center on the screen again. Speaking from Baghdad, DeeDee Morgan was looking right into the camera. Her big brown eyes took up most of the screen. Or was that just Andie's jealous interpretation? The discussion focused on the commitment of the troops to continue to do their duty. A young military man was standing next to DeeDee, responding to her questions. What news? This was chitchat. It didn't matter that Andie was still investigating why Deidre had changed to DeeDee. The woman was a disgrace to WSSN's standards. Andie called Simon. No answer. She tried his cell. No answer. She couldn't take it. She switched out the TV for music. Much, much better.

47

While Andie was cleaning, the two men sitting in Jones's apartment were arguing. "The rollout must begin, vithout Maria," Dr. Veritos entreated Jones. Jones had become despondent over the death of Maria. Dr. Veritos needed him to help comprehensively arrange for the shows. There was no time to grieve.

"Vhe must finish our contract. Maria vhould not vhant you to act this vhay."

Jones thought this statement was probably the farthest thing from the truth. God, he wished he could just disappear. He sighed. Soon.

"Okay, let's go," he said, reluctantly rising from his chair. The final sessions of the mass indoctrination were to begin that morning. State, Commerce, the rest of Defense, and most media organizations had been targeted to attend, and many had already done so. The invitations, or rather the directives, had been sent out a couple of weeks ago. The pre-tests had not indicated any severe problems. Based on the videos that were shot during the tests, there were a few in the audience who did not appear to be star-struck, but that was within the normal standard deviation. The only other possible glitch was the lack of compliance from many, although not the majority, of the viewers to be "inoculated" with the vaccine. Dr. Veritos was not concerned about this setback, relying on his strong belief that the media blitz and subliminal format were sufficiently influential even without the implant. Jones decided he didn't care what happened after the events. This was a hundred-eighty-degree turnaround from his original, self-aggrandizing image of being the designer of the first successful mass mind altering program. His dreams were shattered. Now, he just wanted to get his money and . . . all be told, get even.

At the same time Jones was thinking of revenge, Simon had felt so content with Claire's memorial that he decided he did not mind his staff attending the TIPS. He still didn't agree with the notion that they were obliged to attend, so he made it voluntary, but stressed that it would be greatly appreciated. More than half had shown up. As Simon sat in the audience with many of them, he was struck by the expense that must have gone into these presentations. He didn't even know that this audito-rium existed: the plush seats, the huge screen, the relaxing lighting, *who would have guessed?* he mused. He felt a bit humbled because of it. And to get a preventive for the bird flu was a real added benefit, he thought, rubbing the spot on his arm where the injection had been given. Now he wished he had told everyone that they must attend. Instead, he had left it up to each individual. Well, he reasoned, he could let them know once he returned. But then he could not. They had been informed that the injection availability should not be relayed, even to family members, or it would create a panic, especially since there was a limited supply. He judged that to be a reasonable request. Lips would be sealed.

Suddenly, the lights dimmed and the show began. *Oh my God,* Simon thought. *The Commander in Chief was actually involved.* Well . . . not really, but he had participated in the making? Simon was confused, but impressed. By the end of the presentation, he was more than moved. He was committed.

On his way back to the office, Simon decided to initiate a new division. It would be called *The War Column* and would be utilized for both written and visual news clips. He wanted this initiative to ensure that their audiences were fully informed, informed to make choices about their support for this war, the folks fighting it, and most important, the leaders who had to make the tough decisions. His mind was racing with all kinds of interactive scenarios. He had seen DeeDee's recent reporting, and now it seemed even more apt. She was spot on. He was happy to have her on board now. At first, he had to admit, he was as hesitant as Andie had been. Too bad Andie hadn't been able to attend today. Simon was sure the TIPS would have put her angst about DeeDee to rest. He scratched his arm where the shot had been given. It sure did itch.

48

Statistics regarding the effects of the TIPS were being monitored on a daily basis by the VP's office. He had just collected today's tally when the Defense Secretary entered. The VP was feeling fat and sassy. He picked up his drink and leaned back in his chair. The Secretary sat down across from him. "So, you're pretty pleased with yourself, I see."

"You bettcha," the VP replied, smacking his lips. "Do you realize that over a dozen prayer groups have sprouted up since we started the TIPS?" he asked, taking another drink from his tumbler.

"So, what does that do? I've always wondered what the emphasis was on starting and maintaining these groups."

"Oh, come, man, you don't get it? The religious right has tons of money. They help get us elected. Without them, we'd lose our base. Call it proselytizing for the sake of the country. The sake of the country as we know it, rather. They love to see these groups forming up and praying in the workplace, on the taxpayer's dime. You want a drink, friend?"

"No. Not now. I'm concerned. New Christian recruits may be joining your teams on your timetable, but for me, I'm losing the military recruits. I can't keep the ones we have and am missing my quotas for new ones."

"I told you not to worry about it."

"What do you mean, don't worry about it? I can only fudge the numbers and their implications for so long at these ridiculous press conferences. What's your solution?"

The VP sighed, looked around his huge, plush office with the dry bar, the relics from Afghanistan and Iraq, the photos of himself with presidents over the past decades. It was a war room treasure chest. "It's really quite simple," he said patiently. "We lower the recruiting criteria." By this time the VP had stood up and was pacing, all the while shaking his glass so the ice continued to circle it, making a clicking noise that irritated the Secretary to no end.

"We've already done that," he responded, sighing.

"No. I mean we really lower it. We let convicts in."

"What?"

"Well, there is a caveat. It's actually quite brilliant. We only let those prisoners who have been involved in armed assaults apply. The carrot, of course, is that they get to count their time in Iraq as time off their time in prison, plus we feed them and pay them, although at a somewhat reduced salary, given of course that they're criminals."

"I'm not getting it," the Secretary said, shaking his head.

"Subtlety is part of the brilliance. The convicts I'm speaking of have armed experience, right?"

"Yes."

"So, now we can cut down on the time needed to train them. They can handle a weapon already. That's the main skill that's needed. *Can you shoot?*" he said, mimicking a person shooting a gun. "We'll get your recruits and save a ton of money by cutting the training time, perhaps in half, and cutting money from the federal prisons budget."

"You've . . ." the Secretary started.

"Not done," the VP interrupted. "There's more good news to be had with this plan. Guess who's going to love us for doing this?"

"The prisoners?" his partner asked, innocently enough.

"Yes, of course. But they're not the ones with the money, are they?" the VP asked, rhetorically. "I'm speaking of the NRA. Can't you just see it? *Uncle Sam wants you! If you've proved you can shoot!*"

The Secretary nodded affirmatively. "I'm beginning to get it," he said, walking to the bar and pouring himself a stiff one. "So, what's the plan? Who lays this out? Who's going to sell this to the public? I can see a lot of folks who will freak out. They'll cry foul and ask where's the justice? The other side will point out that the majority of these folks are minorities."

"Yeah, yeah, yeah, they will say all of that, and more," the VP said, shaking his hand dismissively. "We'll get You Know Who to sell it. *He* commented recently that he wished it was an election year. He's bored and wants to do some campaigning."

The Secretary smiled and walked over to the VP. "Cheers."

49

Andie was truly exhausted. She had finally finished cleaning her apartment. The perpetrator had done a real number on her stuff. It had been strewn everywhere. She sat down in her living room, scooting her chair up to the balcony window that overlooked Rock Creek Park. When Andie's parents had died unexpectedly in a trekking accident in Nepal, she'd been surprised to find out that they had set aside enough money for her to be quite comfortable for, well, for the rest of her life. While she managed her money well, she did take advantage of her financial well being by moving to this rather posh apartment overlooking Rock Creek. She sighed as she looked at the gloomy weather and thought about Christmas without her parents, now for the second year. Sure, she'd plan on going to some parties and such, but she would be alone nonetheless. That was fine. She needed to go over Claire's CDs with a fine-tooth comb and come to a decision about her findings, or rather, Claire's findings. She decided to check the second CD now, before she called out for some dinner.

This one, # 2, was already different. Claire was there. Looking straight at the camera and talking.

"If you're looking at this, I imagine it means I'm gone, either dead or imprisoned," Claire stated calmly. Andie observed that when people say these things they must not *really* believe them, or they'd be much more emotional. "My Sadie would not give it to just anyone," she continued. "I can only guess who she decided to trust, but I'm betting it's you, Andie." Andie gave a start. She felt the hairs go up all over her body. "Sadie would not have released my reports to anyone who did not demonstrate to her a commitment to the truth. (Actually, I gave her a hint)," Claire said laughing slightly, but then frowning.

"Andie, I wanted to document what the US is doing. The use of DU is deplorable. By now, you've probably seen the first CD. I imagine you are as outraged as I was. Well, hold on to your seat, lady, because the second CD is worse. This one is actually Michael's story, his story of those affected by DU. We started to collaborate once we realized we were both working on the same topic. It took a while, however. We didn't trust each other. Andie, I know someone you can trust one hundred percent. I want you to try to locate him. I believe you may have met by now. His name is Elliot. By this point in time, he is the only one you can trust. There are some in the government involved in a deceitful, despicable, and clandestine operation to brainwash people most likely to contest their actions. Staff from all over the government will soon be, or perhaps they are already, victims of a plant. These efforts are targeting the press, too, in case you haven't noticed. That's why you are not going to be able to trust anyone. You are now in danger, and for that I am sorry."

Andie stopped the disc and got up to pace. She was unnerved now for sure, "as though I wasn't before," she muttered to herself. She poured herself a glass of wine and went back to watch and listen.

"The DU program is insidious. It's an evil strategy. It's not simply a means for addressing a current military need, as the Pentagon wants its users to believe. And for this reason they will do anything to keep its use and the ulterior motives a secret."

At this point, Claire looked over her shoulder, as though she had heard something.

She returned to gaze into the camera. She continued. "Note carefully who has been damaged by the effects of this weapon, and I don't mean just that women and children are included. This is a weapon of mass destruction, and it's the fact that. . . ." At this point Claire jumped up. She turned to look behind her and then raced toward the camera. The screen went dark, faster than Andie could blink.

Andie's heart sunk. She fast forwarded the CD but to no avail. Claire never appeared again. *Oh,* Andie sighed. *Oh, no. No, no, no.*

50

The Secretary had left upon receiving an urgent call from his office. "Probably nothing. These yoyos jump at anything. They think I should drop everything every time there's a call from a general in Iraq. Hell, my biggest focus these days is keeping the contractors in line and alive so we can keep the money flowing. I'll see you later," he had said over his shoulder while closing the door.

The VP continued to sit at his desk for quite some time, savoring the coup he had just accomplished, for the Secretary of Defense was not an easy man to persuade. The VP glanced out his window, noting the gloomy weather made even worse by the developing nightfall. Winter stormy days in D.C. barely allowed for any daytime.

He didn't care. He then turned in his chair and speed-dialed a number. A man with a distinctive New Orleans accent answered quickly.

"Hello?"

"Bobby?"

"Yo! What's up, big man?"

The VP was short on words. "I need you to do something quick."

"You got it."

"Okay, listen. I have a new recruitment strategy that I want disseminated yesterday. I already have the final copy. The focus groups loved it. It's on its way over by courier."

"At your service, consider it done."

"There's one more thing."

"Yessir!"

"The commercials need to be aired three times more frequently than is legally allowed."

"Oh, don't worry. I'm the FCC Chairman. What are they going to do? Arrest me?"

"Not today," the VP agreed, laughing, "Ha, ha."

"Damn right. Look for it tomorrow, anytime, any channel, TV or radio. We've got it cataloged. That's propaganda speak."

The VP grunted his approval and hung up.

The FCC Chairman chuckled to himself all the way to his private club.

The VP had one more thing he wanted to do before traveling to his undisclosed bunker, his home. He was tired, but this was going to be cathartic.

He rose slowly from his huge, plush, leather chair and went to his concealed safe, behind books featuring his notorious notables: Machiavelli, Rasputin, Lenin, and of course Pol Pot. He had learned one of his first political lessons from Lenin: *If you say something often enough, with enough conviction, everybody will believe it.* He thought anyone seeing the volumes there would think of them as readings for lessons learned, pitfalls to avoid, dangers requiring detours. He laughed to himself, knowing in reality how much he depended on their contents for guidance. He dialed the combination, which he changed every week, and pulled out the only item in it: a document containing some eight hundred pages. He held it lovingly, while moving over to the large conference table. Then he pulled out a section of it, which he unfolded.

This was the blueprint. He leaned over it with his palms resting on the table on each side of it and peered into the image. It was a map of the world. A careful observer would notice slight variations, however, from the current situation in the Middle East, South America, and even . . . yes, even Eurasia. The changes were not different borders as might be expected, they were infrastructure. Roads, bridges, and walls had been erected here and there joining certain borders, others had been taken out. These were marked in a bold purple. He smoothed the paper and using his index finger traced these lines, here and there. That was all. He folded it back up and replaced it within the report. He then sat down and pulled out a calculator, which he began rapidly punching. He wrote a number in the margin of the report's chapter titled *Manpower*. Next to the number he added a + sign. This was a reflection of his just-completed meeting with the Defense Secretary. He calculated that, with the new recruiting plans, he would increase his military by one hundred thousand. He did not, however, move to the next chapter, titled *Benefits,* to adjust those numbers accordingly. That could wait until his operations had been executed. Suffice it to say, the US might be a lot better off without the burden of paying for, and rehabilitating, the criminals (something he had never believed produced a viable outcome anyway). It would be much better to have them serve and perhaps sacrifice for their country. He estimated that, at most, twenty percent would be returning, given the nature of the operations and the length of their service. Their "benefits" could be calculated later, once the real numbers were in. He returned the document to the safe. His plan was on schedule. Time to go home for the day.

The VP had barely left his office when he got a call from the Secretary of Defense. "We've got trouble."

"What?"

"It seems some information has gotten out."

"What information?"

"The List."

"Oh my God. Who and how?"

"Doesn't matter. It wasn't intentional. Just a bureaucratic fluke."

"Good. What are you going to do?"

"We've already found it, so I'll start with that. I'm going to track down the loose ends. I'll keep you posted," the Defense Secretary said.

"Whoa, don't be so hasty. Who had it?"

"A woman named Andie Aaberg," the Secretary said before hanging up.

The VP just shook his head. No one seemed capable of doing anything right, except him of course.

While the Vice President and Secretary of Defense were making plans that seemingly involved Andie, she was fortunately not aware of them or, perhaps for her, unfortunately.

Instead, she was driving as fast as possible to an address in Frederick, Maryland. She'd decided to contact Elliot as Claire had requested. Once he learned of her experience in Westerville and then the apartment break-in, he had asked her to come to his house right away. "Time is of the essence," or some such phrase had been used by him as he urged her again. She was a little nervous, but, hey, it was better than staying in her apartment right now. It still had an uneasy air about it, given that someone else had been in it, uninvited. She sensed that she could smell the person, a musky odor suggesting too much cologne, perhaps. Maybe it was just her imagination. It didn't matter. She was leaving. She called

Craig on her way out and told him she was going to visit a friend and not to worry about stopping by tonight. He offered again that she could stay at his place, but she declined, again reassuring him that all was well.

Elliot had said it was going to be a bit difficult to find his house, but not to call him again from there. If she didn't arrive by 8:00, he'd meet her on the steps of Town Hall, which couldn't be missed.

He was right. She kept driving up and down the street he said he lived on. He had said it would be impossible to see the address in the dark, as he used a P.O. box only, so there was no street mailbox. The only address was on the house. He said he lived on a hill. She drove back to the corner, to confirm again that she was on the right road. She was. She decided to try one more time. It was getting late, and she'd have to get to Town Hall. She reached the end, again with no luck. As she turned the car back around, her lights caught the silhouette of a house that looked as if it was sandwiched between two other ones. She drove to where she could see it from the road, and sure enough, there was a narrow, paved driveway leading up to it. The fact that it had appeared squished between other homes was actually an optical illusion. It was quite isolated in reality. It was downright spooky.

She pulled her car up to the single detached garage with a barn-like door and cut off the engine. She saw a light come on in the back of the otherwise totally dark house. A man walked out of a side door. She could tell it was Elliot by his lanky shape. A big sigh of relief escaped her lips.

"Come on in," he said quietly. "It's really cold out there."

Andie couldn't agree more. She gathered her suitcase and computer and joined him at the door.

He took the suitcase from her and held open the door for her to enter.

Andie heard the door lock automatically when it closed, as if by an electronic device.

The room she entered was quite cozy. A huge brick fireplace with a large fire provided both heat and flickering shadows against its surrounding walls. It was built into the corner. Filled bookshelves covered the opposite wall. Subtle lights on the walls and from large candles around the room provided a warm glow, not visible from the road. A thick, dark red carpet covered most of the room, and the leather furniture finished off the lodge-like quality.

"Have a seat," Elliot offered, setting the suitcase against the wall. "Did you have trouble finding the place?"

"As a matter of fact," Andie said sitting down, feeling as though the overly large chair would envelope her, "yes."

"Sorry. I like it, but it is hard for anyone who doesn't know it's here to see it. Especially at night," he added, sitting down across from her.

There was a moment of uncomfortable silence. Andie started. "So . . . you said you had been expecting a call from me?"

"Yes. I knew you would be calling soon. You were getting close, which is why people, or rather goons, are noticing you. You have to be very careful, Andie, especially now."

"There you go again," Andie complained. "Cryptic, cryptic, cryptic."

"I don't mean to be. It's because of my past."

"Meaning?" Andie asked, and they both started laughing.

"Can I get you a drink?" Elliot asked, picking up an empty glass on the table.

"White wine if you have it."

"Of course," Elliot said as he left.

It was a bad habit, but Andie couldn't stop herself: whenever she was in a person's home for the first time, she liked to see what they read. This time was no exception. She automatically walked over to the bookshelves. The selection was quite eclectic; from Plato's *The Republic* to Sun Tzu's *The Art of War*, and Voltaire's *Philosophical Dictionary* to biographies on Benjamin Franklin, Thomas Jefferson, Hitler, Stalin, Dickens, and Twain. An entire three shelves contained books on science and scientists. *Wow,* thought Andie, *I'm stupid.* She picked up the book by Voltaire to see if it was in French.

"Those who can make you believe absurdities can make you commit atrocities."

Andie started. "Excuse me?"

"Oh. Just a quote from Voltaire," Elliot said, handing her a glass of wine. "Pinot Grigio, I hope you like it." He reached over and pressed a switch inside the bookshelf, providing immediate light from within. "You can borrow anything you see," he said casually. "If you like Voltaire, I recommend *Candide*. It's helpful in reminding me of priorities from time to time."

"I've never read it," Andie said, rather softly.

"Then by all means," Elliot said, reaching up and pulling down a very thin, older looking hardback. "Please." He handed it to her.

"Thank you," Andie said.

"Cheers," Elliot said.

They both took a sip. "Let's sit down and catch up," Elliot suggested.

"Good idea." They returned to their former seats.

"I knew you'd be contacting me soon," Elliot said again. "I knew because you were writing a tribute about Claire that you would eventually be calling me. It was Claire's desire that you would be the one at the office to want to dig where she had been digging."

"So you actually talked with Claire?"

"Yes. I lied earlier, but only to help you. Actually, I knew Claire well," he said. "I loved her."

Andie was blown away by this admission. She didn't know where to begin. "I didn't know Claire was seeing anyone."

"Oh, I didn't mean that. We had a platonic relationship. I said I loved Claire. She knew, but she didn't have time for me, really. She was married to her work, if I can be so trite," Elliot said, shaking his head. "She always worked with such fervor. Her commitment was truly admirable, but . . ." he paused, looking thoughtful, "it didn't allow for anything else, or anyone else."

"But . . ." Andie was still trying to digest the fact that the two people knew one another. "But . . . I mean, how, why . . . I guess I mean, when did you meet her? What started the relationship?"

"Oh . . . that," Elliot said, almost forgetfully. "It was a long time ago. It's a long story."

"I've got time," Andie said. "That's why I'm here, right? I need to know enough to take over where Claire left off, and so some background would be a bit helpful. At least for me. I mean, some context at least."

Elliot's countenance took on that distant look that Andie had noticed in the bar the first time she met him, when he was looking out of the window.

"She was a college student of mine."

"Sorry, Elliot, but you don't look that old."

"I was a graduate student, teaching Intro to Chemistry. So . . . you're right, I wasn't much older than she was at the time."

"Oh." Andie tried to imagine a professorial Elliot.

Elliot continued. "She stuck out immediately because she sat right up front and took extensive notes. Of course all students hoped they could pass with a decent grade, but Chemistry is not everyone's favorite subject, you know. But Claire relished the course, you could see it in her eyes."

Andie nodded.

"Anyway," Elliot carried on, "she earnestly wrote everything I said down, aced her first test, and then lobbed a loaded question at me for which I still do not have an answer." He paused, thinking back to that day.

51

"Professor, do you believe that the use of chemistry can ever be construed to be a benign science? Or are you of the opinion that it is used for either good or evil?" Claire asked simply. It was not meant to be a challenge.

"I don't know. I haven't really considered it in that light. What do you think?" Professor Elliot asked back, noting that the rest of the class was actually interested in this discourse.

"I don't think, by its very nature, that it can be used benignly. I just wanted to know what you think."

"Well, as I said, I haven't given it any thought. Let me consider your question, and I'll get back to you."

"Okay."

Now Elliot was totally intrigued, with both the question and the woman. He actually went to the registrar's office and called up her file. She was a straight A student, he discovered. A high school valedictorian. He could believe it.

The rest of the quarter went quickly. Elliot wanted to ask her out but, of course, knew that would be suicide for both his graduateship as well as his dissertation. He had a lot of work to do and needed to stay focused.

He ran into her quite often in the library, however. One time, when they saw each other there, she asked for his advice and help on a paper she was writing.

"Let's discuss it over coffee," Elliot suggested.

"Good idea, I'd like that," Claire responded, with a big smile.

They had a good time together, lots of laughs, and a decision by Claire to write a "simple" paper so her professor would not feel too confounded.

It had become late, so Elliot offered to walk her to her dorm. Claire readily agreed.

"Can I call you?" Elliot asked timidly.

"What for?"

"I'd like to spend some time with you," Elliot said, smiling at her naivety.

"Oh, Elliot, thank you, but I don't know. I'm so busy. I've actually decided to combine my major. I'm interested in journalism."

"Journalism." Elliot was crestfallen. "Why?"

"I like it. I think I can do something with this. My chemistry background can be my focus for helping connect laypersons with issues going on around us. I can write about it so everyone can understand it, even a kid. It's a challenge that I feel good about."

"Well, good for you." But Elliot didn't mean it. He thought Claire should be a chemist and just a chemist. "I imagine you'll still have to eat, though."

"Indeed I will," Claire said, again smiling. "So by all means, call whenever and let's see."

Elliot did just that. He finished his dissertation around the same time Claire graduated from college. It had been a good two years of studying and having fun.

52

"So, you did get to know her well?" Andie interjected.

"Yes, but we were more like brother and sister. It was a tight friendship."

"Then what happened? I mean, we're talking ten, fifteen years ago?" Andie asked.

"Yes. We first met in 1990. So . . . that does take us back a bit."

"So . . . what happened?"

"Oh, we stayed in touch," Elliot said. "I became a contractor here in D.C., Bethesda to be more accurate, and Claire started working for a newspaper in Columbus as a reporter covering health issues, given her science background, we surmised. We kind of laughed about that one, but who cared? It was a prestigious newspaper, so she felt lucky. It seemed like such a waste to me, but I guess now it could be viewed as a springboard for her. She received an award for her piece about Vietnam Veterans' mental health problems and the relationship to homelessness, and that helped her catapult to the next stage."

"Which was?" Andie asked, very much interested.

"Actually, moving to D.C.," Elliot answered. "She called me out of the blue. I don't think I had heard from her in over six months at the time. It was springtime, as I recall," he said gazing upward a bit, remembering the day exactly and the phone call. He'd received it at his office.

53

"Hi, Elliot."

"Claire?"

"Yours truly."

"Hi. How are you? Where are you?"

"I'm here in D.C. How are you?"

"Fine. What are you doing here?"

"I'm here for an interview. I think I've hit the big time, Elliot."

"That's great, Claire. Who is it with, I mean, which newspaper?"

"It's the *Gazette*."

"Wow. Congratulations. When's the interview?"

"This afternoon. Can I come by your office afterwards, or do you want to meet me somewhere?"

"Sure, Claire. Why don't we meet at the Golden Mushroom around 7:00? It's on Connecticut, north of Dupont Circle."

"Great! See you then. Wish me luck."

"You don't need it. Your merit will carry you."

"Thanks, Elliot."

When she entered the restaurant and waved to him, he could see from the smile on her face that she felt good about the interview.

"Things went well?"

"Yes, indeed. They offered me a position."

"You're kidding," Elliot responded with astonishment.

"No, I'm not!" she said indignantly.

"No, I don't mean that," Elliot said. "It's just that I assumed they would be getting back to you. I didn't know it would be so immediate."

"Me, either," Claire said laughing, brushing off the momentary hurt she felt. "I'm really, really happy. This is the greatest day of my life. I wish my mother were here to share it with me," she added, looking a bit down, but then she perked up. "I called Sadie and Frank. They are thrilled for me. They told me how proud they are of me. It was really touching."

"So, what will you be covering?"

"That's the best part, Elliot. I'm to cover wars."

"Wars?" Elliot's heart sunk. "Why wars?"

"Well, first there's my award winning article," she said modestly, but defensively. "Then, there's the fact that there are a lot of wars these days. The *Gazette* wants investigative coverage so they can stay on top, especially with any new uprisings. They believe there will be increased problems since 9/11. They just want to be on top."

"Well, what are you supposed to do exactly? Not go to where they are occurring?" he questioned incredulously.

"I sure hope so. That's the only way I can do my job," Claire said, shaking her head up and down and looking eager to begin.

"And Sadie and Frank . . ." whom Elliot had met on several occasions, "Sadie and Frank are all for this?" he asked, concerned.

"Well, I didn't tell them this part yet," Claire said flatly, as though she might never tell them.

The waiter arrived with a bottle of champagne. Elliot had ordered it in advance, not knowing how very appropriate it was going to be.

"Oh, Elliot, thank you so much." Claire was absolutely ecstatic.

For this reason, Elliot decided not to harp on the dangers of the job she had just accepted. He really didn't want to spoil this evening for her. "You're welcome. Congratulations again. When will you be moving here?"

"This week. They want me to start by the first of the month, so I need to locate an apartment and get my stuff here, for what it's worth. Can you help me find an apartment?"

"Absolutely."

Elliot helped her find a modest apartment located near the newspaper's headquarters. It still cost a fortune for a fledgling investigative reporter, but it was the best he could do, given the timing. Claire didn't seem too badly affected by sticker shock. "I'll be upgrading directly," she said laughing, knowing it would take some time to do much better.

"Elliot, I really do appreciate all of your support," Claire began, after moving in and starting work. "I just want you to know that I'm going to be very busy, especially at the beginning of my new job, so please, please don't get upset with me if you don't hear from me for a while."

"It's fine, Claire. I've known you too long to think you'd spend much more time just hanging out. Go get 'em. Show them what you've got. Call when you feel like it to chat or whatever," Elliot said nobly, but feeling forlorn at the same time.

"You're a doll," Claire said, kissing him on the cheek. "I'll have an open house in a few weeks." They both laughed.

54

"I never knew she worked for the *Gazette,*" Andie said, abruptly breaking Elliot's concentration.

"Well, wait, I'm about to get to that," Elliot replied quickly, not wanting to lose his train of thought.

"I wasn't too surprised that it took so long to hear from her. It was about two months later that I received her call."

55

"Hi, Elliot, it's Claire. How are you doing?"

"Fine, Claire. Is everything okay, you sound a bit down."

Claire sniffled a bit. "No, it's not," she said.

Now Elliot could tell she was crying. "What's happened? Is it Sadie or Frank?"

"No . . . they're fine. Thanks. It's, oh Elliot, I've made a big mistake taking this job and working for this, this . . . this corrupt company."

"The *Washington Gazette News* is a corrupt company?"

"Don't call them a news company. They're not. They're just . . . terrible. I need to quit."

"Claire, where are you?"

"Home. At my apartment. I just couldn't go in today."

"I'm coming right over."

"No. You don't have to do that."

"I want to. I want to find out what's up. It's hard on the phone."

"Okay, Elliot. Thanks. I'll try to explain it. It's not easy."

"I'll be there within the hour. Make yourself a cup of tea."

Elliot had forgotten how small Claire's apartment was. The furniture definitely made a difference, but he had to admit, it was quite cluttered with magazines, books, and newspapers lying around. *Oh, yeah, that's how her grandparents lived, too,* he thought. Claire motioned for Elliot to sit down. She had a hanky in her hand and her eyes were red. She sat down with a huff next to him.

"Claire, what's happened?" Elliot asked, concerned.

"The *Gazette* is a journalistic fraud. It's not interested in investigative journalism. It's interested in circulation."

"Well, all newspapers are interested in circulation," Elliot reminded her soothingly. "It's how they make a living, or should I say a profit."

"Yes, but this one is interested *only* in circulation. They're tooting the administration's horn every chance they get. It's pathetic. I've been working on a piece for six weeks. It's valid, and my sources are reliable. Yet . . . it's a bit 'anti-administration' I've been told."

"Well, I'm sure if you explain your perspective, they'll reconsider," Elliot said, continuing to try to console her. As he sat there rubbing her shoulders, he looked around the room, seeing it more clearly now. There were several plants, some doing better than others, vertical blinds had been added, and a TV and compact stereo were side by side on the far wall. Only a few pictures had been hung. One, a framed quote, was on the wall in front of them.

> As democracy is perfected, the office of president represents, more and more closely, the inner soul of the people. On some great and glorious day the plain folks of the land will reach their heart's desire at last and the White House will be adorned by a downright moron.—H.L. Mencken (1880-1956)

Elliot winced seeing this, thinking that her attitude just might play a tiny role in their perception of her.

"Elliot, they won't," Claire said definitively. "I have seen pro-administration changes to my pieces even in the short time I've been there."

"Well, why, do you think?"

"The administration is buying these folks with money and favors. I'm not kidding. The executives and reporters who kowtow are invited to the fancy gatherings, to their homes, to the White House Press Corps dinner, you name it. It's just disgusting."

"Are you sure this is the case for everyone there? Maybe it's just the impression you're getting from a few of them?"

"These are not impressions, Elliot, I assure you," Claire said with conviction, losing some of the tears. "To put it bluntly and succinctly, the *Gazette*'s ownership has told us not to challenge the administration about anything. Before a press conference with any member of the administration, my colleagues are receiving questions that come directly from the White House."

"Aren't they upset?" Elliot asked, becoming a bit alarmed at what he was hearing.

"Not at all. They are convinced that they are receiving preferential treatment and do not want to jeopardize their status. In fact, Elliot," Claire had gotten up and was pacing back and forth, "they, the newspaper's owners, tell us they support whatever *he* does. This from the paper that used to be the most objective in the country."

"Oh, Claire, I'm sorry. You could be right. I know you won't cave like the rest, so I'm proud of you and agreeing with you that you should look elsewhere. It doesn't sound like the perfect match we thought it was going to be at the beginning," Elliot said, and meant it.

"I know, I know. It's just so depressing. I had such high hopes, and they are the best, or should I say, *were*."

"It's their loss," Elliot said supportively.

"Well, it doesn't matter anymore," she said stoically. "I'll just have to find another job. It's as simple as that. I can do it, and would rather do it, than continue with this farce."

"When are you going to quit?" Elliot asked, trying to help her move on.

"Today!" Claire said, triumphantly. "And I don't mind telling them why."

"Won't you need references? I mean, it may be risky to be critical on your way out."

"No one there will give me a good reference anyway. I've made my professional ethics known. They're not happy with me, believe me."

"Good, I was hoping you'd say that. Can I see the letter when you're done?" They both laughed, knowing it would be a good one.

"Sure, I'll even frame it for you," Claire said, nodding toward the quote from Mencken, smiling hugely.

56

The Defense Secretary was worried, and mad. His second in command, Fritz Jackson, had not wanted to bother him about the List, so he'd taken care of it himself. The Defense Secretary was reading over the report produced by Fritz at this time. What he saw alarmed him. A woman working at WSSN had apparently gotten hold of the List, and had hidden it under her mattress. What she had inferred from this document, whether she had photocopied it, and where she had gotten it were all unknowns, at least to date. And some pages had been ripped out. Whether she had ripped them out or they were gone when she obtained it, no one could know. Then he read about a possible coincidence. A team from Defense had staked out a residence in Westerville, Ohio, to watch comings and goings. It was suspected that certain tapes might be at this residence. Tapes of what, they could not say, but he was pretty sure they would implicate the Pentagon in some way or other. While they were watching the house, a young woman, fitting the description of Andie Aaberg, arrived at this residence and spent the night. Somehow, she had departed without them knowing.

What? the Secretary wanted to yell when he saw this part of the report. He was sitting there mulling this over when he received notification of yet another kidnapping in Iraq. At first, he just glanced at the message. Kidnappings occurred by the dozens on a daily basis there. It was only when it was someone prominent that the US mainstream news spent time on it. Then he saw it: *UK Ambassador*. Uh, oh. Oh, no. "Big time trouble now," he muttered to himself. He tossed the report from Fritz over to his leather sofa and got on the secure phone to the VP's office.

"Still there?"

"Yeah, I was just leaving. What is it?"

"We've got big-time trouble. The UK Ambassador to Iraq has been kidnapped. I'm sure it's all over the news in Europe by now. It won't be long before it hits the airwaves here."

"I'll call you right back." The phone clicked dead.

The call was not forthcoming. The Defense Secretary paced and paced. The story was already on RW&B, the only station allowed to broadcast in all federal offices. So far, the story was vague. The newscaster suggested that it might simply be a rumor. God, the Secretary sure did hope so. The percentage of released-alive hostages was not good. And given that this guy was a leading ambassador, the ransom, which had not yet been posted, and the final outcome were big-time worries. Why hadn't the VP called?

Finally, it came. "All is taken care of," he grunted. "Change the channel to WSSN."

"WSSN? That's a new one," the Secretary said, as he picked up the remote and switched it. There stood a waif-like woman reporting on the kidnapping that had just been discovered.

"We have reports from anonymous staff and bystanders, who were afraid to be identified, that Ambassador Parker was last seen leaving the safety of his office compound heading for a meeting at the newly built Parliament building. His motorcade was rerouted, supposedly due to debris in its path. Apparently, this was planned by the hijackers. After turning along another route, the bulletproof car headed into a cul-de-sac, whereupon two men started to blowtorch the limo's back door, again from other anonymous bystanders."

At this point the young woman frowned slightly, took a quick breath, and continued.

"Apparently due to the heat from the blowtorch, or the fear of unknown damage, the ambassador, who is not a young man nor a slight one, jumped from the SUV on the other side, where three men grabbed him, hooded him, and dragged him to a nearby truck, which then sped off. The men with the blowtorch ran away, as US helicopters began circling over the incident," the woman stated matter-of-factly. "One helicopter followed the men fleeing by foot. A military sharpshooter shot them both down. Other helicopters followed the vehicle now holding the ambassador as it weaved in and out of traffic, trying to escape.

"We will continue tracking this story and make sure you receive the most accurate and up-to-date events as they unfold," the reporter said. "Just let it be known that at this stage the US military is doing a fantastic job at cutting this incident off at the pass. This is DeeDee Morgan, reporting for WSSN from Baghdad," the woman said, ending with a big smile as though she had just won an award, rather than reported a tragic kidnapping and subsequent deaths.

The Defense Secretary had sat glued to this report. He was dumbfounded. *Why would WSSN be so effusive about the military and its operations?* he wondered. But he just could not believe the part about the helicopters and the sharpshooter. He should be well informed about this by now, and yet he had not heard a peep. He called the VP back.

"What's going on?"

"Pretty fantastic, wouldn't you say?"

"Yeah, too fantastic. Who do you think is going to believe that BS?"

"Everyone. They'll love the chase and the heroism. It's a win-win, especially with WSSN reporting," the VP responded, chuckling.

"Where's the ambassador?"

"I'm checking on that right now."

"Your 'contacts,' as you refer to them?" The Secretary of Defense was talking about the VP's network of Middle Eastern men, from Iraq, neighboring countries, and even elsewhere, that he kept on a revolving payroll, so as to be able to bribe them whenever he needed information. It was an expensive endeavor, over a billion a year, but well worth it. It was the only way to achieve his end goal.

"Yes, they'll let me know where he is and what the demands are. I doubt we'll be able to save him, but we'll make sure we can take advantage of whatever happens. It will look good, don't worry," the VP responded, not being totally honest.

"Okay. Can you get *him* ready for a press conference? And can you make sure the names are spelled phonetically on the teleprompters? I thought that was a given, but last time it was a fiasco. He mispronounced Fallujah each and every time, and each time it was vaguely Spanish, and every time it was a different pronunciation."

"Yeah, yeah, yeah, I've already talked directly to *his* Chief of Staff about it. It won't happen again."

The Secretary sighed as the VP clicked off. He turned off the TV and called his assistant to arrange for a staff meeting for first thing in the morning.

At the same time the Secretary was turning off the TV, Craig turned his on. He couldn't believe what he was seeing and hearing. This was the first time he'd seen the woman named DeeDee described by Andie. He was confused by her wrap-up, to say the least. But it was her overall behavior that most confused him. She seemed almost mechanical. Almost as though she didn't believe what was coming out of her mouth. He called Andie.

The phone disrupted Elliot just as he was recalling Claire's excitement about meeting Michael at WSSN and her entrée into that newspaper.

"So sorry," Andie said, grabbing the phone. "Excuse me, Elliot."

"Andie, turn on the TV," Craig said excitedly. "Turn it to WSSN, I think they'll play it again soon. Gotta go."

Andie looked around, not seeing a TV anywhere. "Elliot, excuse me, but do you have a TV somewhere near? A friend's suggesting I watch WSSN for a few minutes."

Elliot reached for a remote on the table, and with the push of a button, the bookshelves opened outward revealing a huge TV screen that he'd already turned on. WSSN was reporting. "Jeez, Elliot, where's the tunnel?" Andie asked jokingly, looking over at Elliot. Elliot did not respond.

The two of them learned quickly that the UK ambassador had been kidnapped. Within minutes, the clip showing DeeDee was replayed.

Andie put her clinched hand to her mouth. Elliot shook his head in the negative. They both saw a report that was empty and misleading. "Elliot, there's something very strange about this reporter. I still need to find out more, but she's not exactly who she appears to be."

"What do you mean?"

Andie proceeded to tell him about the phone calls she'd received from Deidre, emphasizing how scared and confused the woman had sounded. She added that recently she'd been able to identify a discrepancy about her in the List.

"Now that I am actually hearing her, I recognize the voice. But I'm not sure why she's chosen to go by DeeDee and why she's behaving this way. I mean, I've never seen her reporting before she joined WSSN, but her actions . . ." Andie stopped talking to observe the last comment and then continued "and that silly, inappropriate smile there," she commented.

Elliot crossed his arms on his chest and continued to shake his head. "She's simply a victim," he said.

"A victim of what?" Andie asked, concerned and a bit scared.

"More like who," Elliot said disgustedly. "More like who."

"Well, whatever or whoever, she appears to be half brainwashed."

"Bingo."

With this utterance, Andie's mind began to race. Her wording had been somewhat of a slip, but now she realized how apropos it had been. Oh my God, this is exactly what Claire had mentioned. And then Andie remembered Deidre's first call. What was it that Deidre had said to her? *I don't know how I got here, I'm afraid,* and so forth, and then days later, *I'm feeling better. I'm not scared anymore.*

And Andie could not forget that Deidre was the person who had mentioned the List. Deidre was the clue that she had stupidly overlooked. Now, Deidre was a different person, or so it seemed. Certainly, the name had changed. Certainly, her arrival at WSSN was unusual, and certainly the type of coverage was much closer to the tabloid reporting that RW&B and other stations practiced. Brainwashing was not as inconceivable as one might think.

"You know for sure that's what's happened?" Andie asked.

"For sure."

"Why didn't you tell me at the bar . . . at Claire's memorial . . . when we had coffee?" Andie sputtered furiously.

"Well, to be quite honest, if you had told me that you were receiving calls from Deidre, I would have known more and might have been able to talk with you about it. But the bottom line is that you still wouldn't have believed me. I imagine that you probably thought of me as a kook as it was. Add to that incredulous facts, such as a scheme involving brainwashing, well, it just wouldn't have computed. You had to figure this out for yourself, Andie. I've been telling you that since the first time we met. Now you can believe that the incidents you have been experiencing are not by chance. Now you are not only informed, you've become part of the saga."

"Why should I believe you now?" Andie asked defensively.

"You don't have to. But please don't ignore your own eyes and ears."

"That was uncalled for, I apologize," Andie said. "Of course I won't ignore what I'm seeing and hearing. But how is this scheme working? Do you know?"

"I know the scientific part of it only. I would consider it a form of brainwashing. It is being done by an office in the government, maybe more. That's why I'm living under these circumstances, Andie. There is someone who knows that I know what's going on, and I'm just not sure I can trust him."

Andie thought quietly for a while. "So . . . who's being brainwashed? Everyone?"

"I don't know the targets. I just know that the means to do so exist. And now you've confirmed that at least one person seems to have been exposed to it somehow."

"So, this is part of Claire's warning," Andie commented, hoping to put more of the puzzle pieces together.

"Yes. She believed that some in the government would go to great lengths to keep people from asking obvious questions," Elliot said, shaking his head.

A long silence ensued.

"It's late," Elliot said suddenly. "We've got a lot of work tomorrow to peruse those CDs that Claire put together. Hopefully, we'll have a plan by the end of the day on how to continue her work. Let me show you where we're going to work tomorrow." And with that, Elliot used his remote again, and the TV screen slipped behind one of the opened bookshelves. A metal door was revealed. Elliot walked toward it and applied his hand to a glass cover. The door opened. "You were asking earlier about a tunnel?"

"You're kidding!" Andie exclaimed. But after stepping through the metal door, she could see that indeed he was not.

57

George Bruce was sitting in his truck, down the street from where Elliot lived, watching the driveway where Andie had disappeared over three hours ago. He was going to have to go in there at some point if she didn't come out. He figured once he nabbed her, she'd be more than willing to describe what she had learned from the List and how she had come to possess it. He did not stop her en route to her destination because he thought she might be missed by somebody who was expecting her. He figured he was right. She'd entered a residence. He hoped to get her returning to her apartment from where he'd followed her, and perhaps to observe her here at this residence to see who she was talking to, what she was doing here.

As he sat there, he reflected on this latest development. He despised the situation he found himself in. It was simply untenable, but he really did not know what to do at this point. He laughed out loud at that thought. Here he was, a former Air Force pilot and CIA operative and he couldn't figure out how to get out of a tight spot. Boy, had he ever allowed himself to be manipulated. After the last incident, the one with Ms. Stone, he swore he'd never lift another finger for the VP. He still didn't know who had been responsible for mowing her down on the Beltway, so to speak, but he was sure it had been no accident. And now this. The call had come only hours ago.

"Go find out what she knows. She was involved in the unlawful possession of a classified document. She may hold other illegal materials," the VP had growled.

"Nothin' doin'. I told you after that sorry accident on the Beltway, no more. I'm a free agent. I don't work for you," Bruce had retorted.

The sigh was slow and menacing, if a sigh could be interpreted as such. "I hope DoD doesn't have to reopen your Afghanistan case. I've heard rumors. It seems some would like to eliminate your retirement benefits, believing that it would set an example for others who might find themselves in your situation."

"What's that supposed to mean?" Bruce asked tersely, thinking of his family and friends. He'd been divorced for quite a while now, but still, he didn't want to drag them through another fish-bowl exercise. Plus, he didn't think he'd survive another investigation. His temper would do him in.

"Don't know. Take it for what it's worth. I, on the other hand, know you to be a patriot. I imagine you would not want classified material in the wrong hands."

"Don't patronize me."

During the long silence, prior to agreeing, Bruce wondered if he dared turn down the most powerful person in the world. Obviously he had not, or he would not be sitting here now.

But as he returned to the present, he recalled that when he had observed the young woman leaving her apartment, she did look around at her surroundings. She glanced in the rearview mirror as she headed out of D.C., and she did not use a cell, even when she appeared lost on the street. In summary, she acted as though she had something to hide, as though she did not want to be followed or observed. Now Bruce was curious. He decided to at least do a decent job investigating this woman. He would wait another half hour and then go check it out.

At the same time that Bruce was mulling over his unfortunate circumstances, Elliot introduced Andie to the bunker. "It's about ten feet below ground," he said, as they made their way down very steep and narrow stairs. He flipped a switch, illuminating a huge office and an even larger laboratory. A surveillance camera showed the snow-covered yard surrounding the house above. There was also a small kitchen and bath, plus lots of storage. All in all, it was quite comfortable in appearance.

"What's it for? I mean, did someone build this during the Cuban missile crisis or something?" Andie asked innocently.

"No . . . it's much older than that. At least the original one. It's a former underground hideaway used by slaves headed to Canada."

Andie felt chills down her spine. "Oh my God. What a history."

"Yeah. People forget that Maryland is south of the Mason-Dixon Line. Sometimes I stand here thinking about what it must have been like to have been down here, congregating with a group of people, some of them strangers, no electricity, just a lantern or candles and the smell of the earth, knowing there was limited oxygen, wondering if you would ever see daylight again. . . ."

"Okay, Elliot. Enough. You're creeping me out. It must have been hell."

"Sorry. But it must have been mixed: excitement and fear, with the possibilities of freedom or capture."

"Where did the people go from here?"

"To Pennsylvania, I imagine. They still needed to make Canada in order to really be safe, though. But I'm not sure where the next stopping place was before they crossed the border from here, if there was one. I found an escape hatch of sorts, where that storage area is located now," he said, pointing. "I didn't really check it out, though."

"How'd you know about this?"

"I was looking for a house with one, or at least hoping to find one. I figured there had to be some still in existence."

"Why did you need to find a location with one?"

"For this exact reason. As I said, I have a peppered, somewhat regrettable past. I have enemies, at least one, I'd like to protect myself from the best I can, for as long as I can."

"The regrettable past?"

"Yes, it was due to the regrettable past that I built out this underground and built this house. The lot was empty, but I knew from the maps I'd seen that there used to be a rather large estate here. Rumor had it that it used to be a safe house. Once I got onto the land, I found it. I needed to conduct my scientific work in total secrecy. Claire knew of it, but she never got a chance to see it. It's because of Claire, Claire's death rather, that I have to get involved again, so I think we should work in here," he said, setting Andie's laptop on the desk.

"Involved in the DU investigation?"

"Yes, that and more. There's always more when it comes to war and politics, isn't there?"

"Yes. It seems so, Elliot," Andie said. "I have always limited myself to smarmy politics in the past, though."

"Well, this time the smarmy politics and a very smarmy war are inseparable," Elliot said with finality.

The two glanced around again before leaving.

"Your bedroom is near the kitchen if you want anything during the night," Elliot said, as he led Andie to it. "Coffee maker's set for 6:30."

"Thanks, Elliot. And thanks for letting me stay here. I'm ready to tackle Claire's work."

Elliot smiled wearily. "No more reporting from the front lines, though. I don't think I can take knowing another person wiped out in this war."

"Don't worry," she agreed. "Simon wants DeeDee there, and to be quite frank, I'm too scared to go."

"Good."

58

George Bruce stealthily ascended the driveway, in the shadow of the trees and the moonless night. It was about 2:00 a.m. The ground was damp from light snow and slippery. As he approached the woman's car from behind, he made a wide swath in case she had an alarm. It was this move, although he would like to think it was his training, that was his lucky break. He saw the camera right before he stepped into its viewing range. "Jesus," he whispered under his breath. He squatted to the ground and looked around. The place was covered with motion detectors and cameras. One, the one he had been able to avoid, was almost right on top of him. *Who lives here?* he thought. He turned around and retraced his steps to the bottom of the driveway. He'd have to wait for her. It was going to be a long night.

59

The next morning, Andie sat in the leather, overstuffed chair in Elliot's "lodge" and argued with Simon. "I can't come in right now. It's just not possible. And by the way, Simon, why is DeeDee providing such an unsupported report. It's so biased."

"It's not unsupported, Andie. That's one of the reasons I wanted you to come into the office this morning. I've had an epiphany: *The War Column*. You won't believe what kind of reception I've already had to this idea."

"*The War Column*? What's it about?"

"About our troops and what a grand job they're doing and how their hard work needs to be highlighted on a regular basis."

"Well, I don't know, Simon. Anyway, nonetheless, I'd really like to ask your permission to not come in today. I'm pursuing Claire's tribute. I've almost finished," she lied.

"Okay. We'll let you pass today. We're having a big meeting about this new column's potential today, but I'll have someone fill you in. Oh, and Andie, Nathan is here. He said he wanted to get together with you."

"Oh," Andie said sheepishly. She had totally forgotten about Nathan's return to D.C. "Okay. Well, let me get busy, and I'll try to get there first thing in the morning."

"Good! I'll let him know. See you then. You're going to love this new initiative."

Wow, Andie thought. Simon was downright giddy. How strange. It was uncharacteristic of him to be so euphoric. And what about *The War Column*? She'd have to be honest with him, but he sounded too elated to say anything more negative just now about DeeDee's reporting.

As she finished her coffee, she heard Elliot in the kitchen. Good. She wanted to go to her car to get materials she had left in the trunk but was a little nervous about leaving the place, given the alarm system.

"No problem. Let me show you." He opened a small window-sized door against the wall and simply pressed *Deactivate.*

"Simple," Andie said. "Thanks." She took her keys and walked down the driveway and around to her trunk. That's when she saw the footprints. She quickly looked around. It was a cloudy day, and the street seemed quiet, but she was spooked. She picked her satchel out of the trunk and quickly returned to the house.

"Elliot! I'm sorry, but we've got trouble. I must have been followed last night."

Elliot looked alarmed, but remained calm. He went to his security system and backed up the cameras near the driveway. The only thing he could discern was a shadow. It was a hefty one.

"He must have seen the cameras or detectors," Elliot commented. "Smart fellow. No harm done, at least not yet. He'll eventually try to find out who lives here, but that's virtually impossible. Aside from entering with a warrant, which I doubt he'd like to do, he can't do anything."

"Except wait for me."

"Except wait for you. We'll have to develop a decoy, but let's not get carried away. We have too much work today."

Andie didn't look convinced.

"Lighten up," Elliot said, smiling. "He didn't find anything. He knows about you, but obviously doesn't know much or he'd have accomplished more. He ran away."

"Okay," Andie said, shaking her head. "Let's look at the CDs."

While they moved into the tunneled extension with their coffee and bagels, sticky buns were being laid out at the DoD in advance of the staff meeting called by the Secretary. He expressed impatience with these niceties, but they were provided nonetheless.

The Secretary had had a sleepless night. He was tired. His friend, the VP, was confident. He, the Secretary, was constantly being put in the spotlight and trying to explain away ridiculous events. He needed to change his position in this relationship. He was tired of being the lackey. This time he was not going to wait for direction. He was going to use his own intelligence to find the ambassador, and finding him was going to be his utmost priority from this point on. He didn't want to go down in the history books as a lightweight. He had been told that history would be rewritten to ensure they would all be heroes. *But what if it wasn't?* he thought as he'd shaved, noticing the creeping signs of age on his cheeks. *What if things changed and his true actions were exposed? No. He needed to be a hero.* It was not in his nature to be such a wimp. What had happened to him? Before going to the staff meeting, he checked with the folks in his intelligence gathering room to see if they'd heard from the OVP regarding news about the whereabouts of the ambassador. He didn't need to ask. Three men were standing in front of the GPS tracking board, similar to the one in Craig's office, pointing to a green blinking light.

He called his meeting to order and looked around the room. The persons seated were a combination of a small number that had been culled from the original team he'd inherited, and the rest had been handpicked by him and the VP. These were all loyalists. And now, he had to admit, their attendance at the TIPS had made them all overly devoted and somber. They were more than eager to be engaged. It was downright eerie how serious and religious they were becoming. All of them had worn the flag on their lapels or collars since 9/11, but now he noticed many were wearing gold necklace crosses, even the men. Coincidently, one of them, a big, hefty guy he'd know for years, looked as if he was going to scratch his arm off. The Secretary stared at him for a while, and the man finally stopped.

Over the course of the next five hours, strategies were laid out, based on information analyzed throughout the night, to save the ambassador. The die was cast by 1:00 p.m. Orders were dispatched. The Secretary had made a break, for good or bad. The OVP was going to have to sit this one out.

60

On the other side of town, Craig called Andie on his way into the TIPS. "Did you catch her?"

"Yeah, pretty amazing transformation for WSSN."

"No kidding. It was strange, to say the least. Listen, I've finally been *ordered* to go to this stupid seminar, so I just wanted to touch base and see how you're doing. I'm going to be out of commission for most of the day."

"Okay, no problem. Wait a second, Craig."

"What?"

"How can they *order* you?" Andie's head was spinning. She looked over at Elliot. He was staring at her quizzically.

"I mean, how can Commerce force their employees to attend a seminar, it doesn't make sense," she continued, making it a comprehensive statement so Elliot could hear it fully.

Now he looked alarmed. He took his forefinger and crossed it across his neck, shaking his head vigorously.

"Craig, don't go," Andie warned. "Don't go. I'm warning you. Please don't attend this meeting. Think back, isn't that when your staff started to act strange, after they returned from there? Didn't you tell me it looked strange to you when you skipped out to come to Claire's memorial?"

Craig stopped in his tracks on Pennsylvania Avenue and looked around.

"You're right. What's going on, Andie?"

"Something very bad. Call in sick. Admit yourself to GW if you need to, but don't go today."

"What, though, can't you tell me?"

"Not now. Just trust me. It can't hurt to avoid it. It might hurt to go. I can explain later."

"Okay," Craig said, resignedly. "I'll talk to you later today?" he asked hopefully.

"We'll see. It may not be safe. I'll get in touch with you."

"Okay, Andie. By the way, where are you?"

"With a friend. Everything's fine."

"Okay."

Andie turned to look at Elliot. "Elliot, let's go over the CDs and then, please, please, please tell me what's up. I don't like what I'm thinking. I hope you'll change my mind."

"You'll know by the time we're finished," Elliot said somberly. "It will be quite clear what we're up against. What Claire and Michael had been up against. Believe me."

61

Veritos was bugging Jones no end. "Vhen do vhe get the rest of our money? Vhen? It's been almost a vheek!" he said with exasperation.

"Okay, okay. I'll contact him again today."

"Who is *he*, anyvhay?"

"You don't need to know, I've told you that a number of times. You should count your blessings you don't know."

"I don't know anything about blessings."

Jones just shook his head. He had never confided in Veritos the way he had in Maria. It had never occurred to him to do so. Now, he realized, he had no one. Absolutely no one. He was all alone in the world. He shook his head again. Things were not as he had imagined they would be by this time.

Jones had not told Veritos, but he, the VP, had been avoiding his efforts to contact him for the past week. Every contact and contact conduit he knew of he had tried, but no cigar. It was as though the man had disappeared. He had finally decided to call him on his secure phone. He knew he had sworn that he would never, ever, do so, but he had no choice. He placed the call once he left Veritos sulking at their "office."

He called from a hotel lobby. "How did you get this number?" the VP asked gruffly.

"The TIPS are almost finished. I'm sure your stats indicate it to be a success. I need the last installment to be made, as agreed. There's been no indication of a transfer."

"Who is this?"

"Look, don't play games with me. I want the final installment," Jones said impatiently.

"I don't know who you are," the VP replied, leading Jones to slam his fist against the wall.

Jones could hear the VP laughing hysterically as the man hung up.

While Jones was getting what the VP considered his comeuppance, Craig was walking up and down Pennsylvania Avenue still trying to decide what to do. He looked at his watch. He had nearly half an hour yet to make up his mind. He was curious. Why shouldn't he attend the TIPS? Why hide? I mean, he knew Andie wouldn't mislead him, intentionally. But perhaps she was just overly concerned. He considered her to be a bit too cautious, and a bit paranoid, if the truth be told. She had too many conspiracy theories going on. And with that, he turned on his heel for the umpteenth time and headed for the TIPS. He was actually excited about the prospect of seeing what his staff had seen and why people were "changed," so to speak, convinced that whatever it was, he could observe it without succumbing to it.

The line was much shorter this time. Craig guessed because so many had already attended, this was the tail end of it. He could hear the nurse and the man in the suit standing next to her discussing the shot they were offering to administer to the person in front of them.

"It's to protect you against the bird flu. I'm sorry, but no, you cannot tell anyone about it, especially not your family members. We don't have enough in stock just yet, but because of your important role in the national government and therefore national security, we believe you to be deserving of the limited supply. If you can agree to these terms, please sign here, and we will proceed."

Craig suddenly recognized that the young man they were speaking to was Nathan McCabe, the photographer from WSSN. He could see by Nathan's body language that he was not happy with the offer. The man was holding the pen out to him along with a sheet of paper on a clipboard. Nathan studied it for another thirty seconds and then shook his head no. The two people looked exasperated, but tried not to show it. The Suit then smiled and opened his arm as an entrée to the auditorium. Instead, Nathan turned around and walked in the opposite direction, down the line, toward the exit. In doing so, he passed Craig. They had met a couple of times after work when Craig was meeting Andie, before Nathan had gone to Iraq.

As he passed, Craig stepped out of the line. "Hey, buddy," he said, reaching out his hand.

"Craig," Nathan said, surprised.

"Long time. How are you?" Craig asked.

"Could be better. You?"

"Okay. I was sorry to hear about Claire."

"Thank you. I miss her very much," Nathan said, with downcast eyes. Craig noticed that he had matured significantly since he'd last seen him, and no wonder.

"You decided to skip this event?" Craig asked, changing the subject.

"Yeah. I don't have time to waste. I've got some friends I want to see before I head to West Virginia to see my family. Then I'm going back."

"To Iraq?"

"Yeah."

"Well, that's great," Craig said, a little surprised. He was sure that Andie had told him Nathan was coming back for good. "Have you seen Andie yet? I know she wanted to talk with you."

"Not yet. Probably tomorrow."

"Well, that's good. And have a good time today," Craig said.

"I will," Nathan said, as he started to turn.

"Oh, Nathan?"

"Yeah?"

"I'm curious, what are they offering up there?" Craig asked, nodding toward the nurse.

"Bird flu preventive," Nathan said flatly. "I don't need it. Last I knew there was no bird flu. And hell, after being shot at, the bird flu doesn't seem so scary. I don't have time for this nonsense. I just came here because I was trying to please Simon."

Craig looked back at the nurse and Suit. The Suit was watching them talking. Craig felt uncomfortable. "Okay, buddy. Well, have a good time and be careful."

"I will," Nathan said, ambling off. Craig noted again that even though he still looked like the handsome kid he did before Iraq, his demeanor offered not only a much older person, but a much sadder one. He figured Andie would find out what happened to him after Claire was killed, and maybe why he never answered his phone.

Craig was now about fifth in the line before the injection station. He still had time to leave, but he'd made up his mind. He decided to go all the way and do the shot, do the presentation, and then tell Andie there was nothing to it.

In the meantime, Andie was quizzing Elliot on his knowledge of the seminar. "Elliot, what can you tell me about the seminar that Craig was going to attend?"

"Nothing specific. But I do know that something's going down with the government and their commitment to secrecy. They are unwavering in their desire to keep people from getting substantive information and making informed decisions. They hate any press they cannot control. That's why I'm just as curious as you are to see the CD. Claire was on to something."

Andie started with the second video, the one with Claire, since Elliot already knew she was investigating DU. Elliot was obviously moved when he saw that Claire appeared to have been forced to stop the taping. Andie asked, "Do you know why she quit there? Who was she running from?"

Elliot just shook his head. He really didn't know. "Something obviously spooked her. It could have been a benign incident, maybe a friend coming in and she just didn't want him or her to see what she was doing."

"But then she would have come back at some point to finish it, don't you think?"

"Yes. That would be the obvious thing to do. You're sure she doesn't continue it somewhere else on the video?"

"I checked over and over. Believe me."

"Okay, let's proceed," Elliot said, with sad resignation. The personal stories Michael had uncovered were enough to create a heartache for a lifetime. The DU was lethal. As Dr. Jawad Al-Ali, Director of the Oncology Center at the largest hospital in Basra, said, speaking in 2003 at a peace conference in Japan:

> Two strange phenomena have come about in Basra, which I have never seen before. The first is double and triple cancers in one patient. For example, leukemia and cancer of the stomach. We had one patient with two cancers—one in his stomach and kidney. Months later, primary cancer was

developing in his other kidney—he had three different cancer types. The second is the clustering of cancer in families. We have fifty-eight families here with more than one person affected by cancer. . . . My wife has nine members of her family with cancer.

Children in particular are susceptible to DU poisoning. They have a much higher absorption rate, as their blood is being used to build and nourish their bones and they have a lot of soft tissues. Bone cancer and leukemia used to be diseases affecting them the most. However, cancer of the lymph system, which can develop anywhere on the body and has rarely been seen before the age of twelve, is now also common.

Michael continued to quote the article's author, Robert C. Khoeler:

We dropped at least three hundred tons of it on Iraq during Gulf War I (the first time it was used in combat) and created Gulf War Syndrome. This time around, the estimated DU use on defenseless Iraqis is seventeen hundred tons, far more of it in major population centers. Remember shock and awe? We were pounding Baghdad, in those triumphant early days, with low-grade nuclear weapons, raining down cancer, neurological disorders, birth defects, and much, much more on the people we claimed to be liberating. We weren't spreading democracy, we were altering the human genome.

As we "protected ourselves," in the words of the President, from Iraq's non-existent weapons of mass destruction, we opened our own arsenal of WMD on them, contaminating the country's soil and polluting its air—indeed, unleashing a nuclear dust into the troposphere and contaminating the whole world.

"I'd seen reference to the three hundred tons in the other CD," Andie said to Elliot, "but not to seventeen hundred tons."

"Let's look at the interviews," Elliot suggested, obviously disturbed by this author's report.

The first interview by Michael was with an Iraqi family caught up in the fighting from the first Gulf War. The father described the incessant shelling and his efforts to get his family out of its range, to no avail.

"The terrain was demolished before we had a chance to run . . ." the emaciated man explained in a raspy voice. Michael had introduced him as a thirty-seven-year-old father of seven. He was, or had been, a shepherd. ". . . and the air was filled with gray dust that took quite some time to settle. Once it did, it covered the debris following the shelling." He had told his kids and wife to stay away from it, but the only available water was filled with it. The majority of his herd had been wiped out by the one-day incident. He had had great difficulty in repopulating it since that time. Michael's camera panned the remaining animals at that point. There were a half dozen skinny goats staring vacantly at the camera. Michael held their gaze for at least a minute. The children were roaming around while their father spoke. They were dirty and emaciated as well. The youngest two had limb deformities. Their dark eyes appeared to take up half their faces, due to their sunken cheeks. He went on to say that his wife had died recently due to a really bad cough. He figured it had been lung cancer, although she had never smoked and was only thirty-two years old. He could do nothing for her.

At this point, Michael had shown a slide of an excerpt from the White House Web page.

DEPLETED URANIUM SCARE

During the Gulf War, coalition forces used armor-piercing ammunition made from depleted uranium, which is ideal for the purpose because of its great density. In recent years, the Iraqi regime has made substantial efforts to promote the false claim that the depleted uranium rounds fired by coalition forces have caused cancers and birth defects in Iraq. Iraq has distributed horrifying pictures of children with birth defects and linked them to depleted uranium. The campaign has two major propaganda assets:

Uranium is a name that has frightening associations in the mind of the average person, which makes the lie relatively easy to sell; and Iraq could take advantage of an established international network of anti-nuclear activists who had already launched their own campaign against depleted uranium.

But scientists working for the World Health Organization, the UN Environmental Programme, and the European Union could find no health effects linked to exposure to depleted uranium.

The next story was from Iraq, but almost mirrored the first one. After a number of, again, similar stories from Iraqis, Michael moved to American soldiers, noting that the research was quoting from a *USA Today* article.

> Gerard Matthew Reed, Raymond Ramos, Hector Vega, Augustin Matos, Anthony Yonnone, Jerry Ojeda, and Anthony Phillip all have depleted uranium in their urine, according to tests done in December 2003, while they bounced for months between Walter Reed and New Jersey's Fort Dix Medical Center, seeking relief that never came.
>
> The analyses were done in Germany, by a Frankfurt professor who developed a depleted uranium test with Randall Parrish, a professor of isotope geology at the University of Leicester in Britain. The veterans, using their positive results as evidence, have sued the US Army, claiming officials knew the hazards of depleted uranium, but concealed the risks.
>
> The Department of Defense says depleted uranium is powerful and safe, and not that worrisome.
>
> Four of the highest-registering samples from Frankfurt were sent to the VA. Those results were negative, Reed said. "Their test just isn't as sophisticated," he said. "And when we first asked to be tested, they told us there wasn't one. They've lied to us all along."

By the end of the day, Andie and Elliot were numbed by the experiences Michael had been able to capture in both his investigations and his photos representing the abject misery to humanity the DU had caused. "What else can Claire have wanted us to see or learn?" Andie asked for the umpteenth time with exasperation. "This is damning enough. Why didn't she go with it? She has more than she would have needed to make a profound statement."

"Maybe she wanted more absolute proof. It's the only thing I can think of, but I'm sure you'll figure it out," Elliot said.

"Me?"

"You're the investigative journalist," Elliot said smiling, trying to help them both shake the depression that had set in. "Tell you what," he continued, "let me make some dinner for us, and while I do, I'll lay out your escape tonight, as well as your re-entry tomorrow. You'll see, it's easy and danger-free."

Andie smiled and agreed readily. She was hungry, as the food in the bunker was primarily cans of soup and other non-perishables, and she also couldn't wait to extricate herself from the morbid visions that kept flicking across her mind. *How did Claire and Michael do it?* she wondered. They carefully stored the CDs in Elliot's safe and made their way upstairs. Three hours later, they initiated Elliot's brilliant plan.

Suddenly, out of nowhere, four Frederick police cars were screeching past Bruce on this quiet street, slamming on their breaks at the house adjacent to the house he had been monitoring.

Uh, oh, he thought.

Sure enough, the first cop to get out of his car came charging at him with a lit flashlight. It must have been around 9:00 p.m. "Get out of here," he shouted. "Get out! Police business. Turn your car and leave this area." He stood in front of the parked car, hands on hips, waiting for Bruce to do what he demanded. Bruce had no choice. The other cops were spreading yellow tape, preventing entrance around the perimeter of the house they had targeted. Bruce sighed, turned on the ignition, made a three point turn, and left. He thought he'd wait around the corner, but nixed that idea when he saw the cop at the end of the street and then another in each direction. He simply had no place to hide out. Resigned to failure due to this wrinkle in the plan, he started back to D.C. Shortly afterwards, Andie drove out of Elliot's garage in his VW, circled around her parked car, and after waiting for the cops to motion her onward, drove off and out, similarly to Bruce. "Piece of cake," she said, smiling to herself. Elliot was indeed a good guy. Although she was tired of the research due to its grimness, she had to admit that she thoroughly enjoyed Elliot's company. She was so glad that Claire had told her to trust him. It was the best thing that had happened amidst all of the sadness and mystery.

Her win obviously resulted in another person's loss. While the VP was railing at him for failure, Bruce couldn't help but notice how much the man had begun to resemble caricatured depictions of Lucifer. It seemed that his shoulders had become narrower while his hands had grown larger and whiter. The nails were kept up impeccably by a manicurist, but Bruce could swear that they had taken on a rather gray-yellow appearance. He half expected a raven to materialize and settle on the back of the man's chair. The observation so obsessed him that he was unable to concentrate on his agitated indictment of Bruce's incompetence. It just sounded like background gibberish, notwithstanding the bits of spittle that also spewed from the VP's dark, cavernous mouth. It was the word *fired* that finally got Bruce's undivided attention however.

"Get out of my sight. You're fired, you worthless imposter. You coward. You're no better than a little girl."

Bruce looked at the man intently, thinking what he would like to say or do when he decided he'd have another chance, some day. Actions would speak louder than words, as the old cliché read. Bruce turned and left, knowing he'd never receive a dime for his services. It didn't matter. He was finally freed from an unconditional, undeclared, slavery.

The whole while the VP was chewing Bruce out, Lowell, his Chief of Staff, sat watching silently, as usual. He had begun thinking lately that it was time to get out. He needed to get on with his life. He'd given too much of it to this man already. How many years had it been? Going on twenty? It seemed impossible. And to have him say he didn't trust him. That had really been gut-wrenching. It was then that his sentiments had shifted, he recalled. Plus, the man had become increasingly obnoxious, both paranoid and aggressive. But . . . how could he quit? They had too much between them. The VP would not allow it. He was sure. He feared he was tied to him for the rest of his life, or the life of the VP, whichever came first. It was a sad realization.

The VP turned abruptly to him after Bruce's exit. "Get me DARK-SAND."

"DarkSand! Isn't that a bit extreme?" Lowell asked, shocked that the VP was taking a vague incident about a young woman and the List so seriously. DarkSand provided contractors to Iraq. Contractors or mercenaries, it was hard to know the difference.

"You're not really paid to ask questions, are you?" the VP retorted.

"No, sir. I'll get right on it," Lowell said, getting up quickly to leave.

"Get me the CEO, not some mid-level airhead."

"Yes, sir."

The VP sighed as the man left. He was not going to let a nobody mess up his plans. He had to find out who had obtained the List, if only temporarily. He had to know everything she knew about it and who else might know of its existence outside of Defense. He had to.

He got up, locked his door, and looked around before going to his safe again. He really, really, did like this room. He loved the memorabilia, especially the genuine weapons that had been presented to him by various politicians and military commanders, from a myriad of countries spanning the Gulf I war, attacks on Afghanistan, and even some from the current Iraq war. These items, gas masks, swords, knives, guns, batons, and so forth, gave him a sense of manly strength. He, himself, could not, or would not, go to battle, but he could hold these items in his hands and imagine himself leading his troops to victory. The image of a Teddy Roosevelt moment would often come to mind. Unbeknownst to the egomaniac, the war memorabilia also provided the spirits surrounding them a convenient place to congregate, languishing near death's causes. Pulling out the map, as he had done so many times before, he traced the new infrastructures with his index finger, as usual. He then did something unlike anytime before. He walked to his drawer and removed a double-edged razor. Walking back to the table, he reached down and carefully scratched the name of one of the countries off the map. It took less than a minute. And while he was careful in his effort to hold the paper taut with his left hand and get all of the country's name's letters without tearing the paper, he nicked his opposing thumb, just slightly. At that, he jumped in pain, but not soon enough. A slight drop of blood trickled in spots across the now unnamed country.

The observing spirits moaned and retreated further into their crevices, their eyes filling with dread.

62

Andie entered her apartment with trepidation, but all was untouched. Even the musky, rather unpleasant odor she had observed before was gone. She decided she'd try to put the incident behind her. She even began to convince herself that it was a closed case. DoD had its directory back. End of story, she thought, over and over again.

In an effort to relax, she took a hot shower and slipped into some fuzzy cotton sweat pants and a long sleeve tee. Then she plopped herself down in front of the TV. Before turning it on, however, she called Nathan. He answered on the first ring.

"Oh. Hi, Andie. How are you?"

"Fine, Nathan. And you."

"Could be better, always. Are we going to meet tomorrow?" he asked, rather anxiously.

"Yes, of course. I hope Simon told you I'd be coming to the office."

"Yeah, he did. He just didn't say when, and I was beginning to wonder . . ." his voice trailed off.

"I'm sorry I didn't call sooner. I've just been so immersed in researching and writing this tribute to Claire that time got away from me."

"It's okay, Andie," Nathan said sincerely.

Andie had always felt that Nathan had a small crush on her. She could sense it now. She felt more like an older sister, however, than any kind of girlfriend.

"Thanks for understanding, Nathan. I appreciate it. What's a good time for you tomorrow?" Andie continued.

"Anytime. How about 10:00?"

"Great. I'll be there," Andie said.

"Andie?"

"Yes?"

"Let's not meet at the office. It's too . . . it's just not conducive to having a conversation," he concluded.

Andie thought about this for a second. It was noisy, true, but that had never stopped Nathan from just sitting himself down next to her and having a chat. She figured he wanted privacy.

"Sure, okay. Where then, just name it," Andie replied agreeably.

"Um, how about the Natural History Museum's café?" he suggested.

Andie was quite surprised. "Okay, sure. I'll see you there at 10:00, Nathan. Have a good evening, at least what's left of it."

"You, too, Andie," he said before hanging up.

"Hmm," Andie muttered to herself. Now she was even more intrigued to talk to him. As she had suggested to Elliot, Nathan could very well be the key to unraveling what Claire's true goal had been.

She resumed her supine position and clicked on the TV, feeling warm and cozy for the first time since she had received the spooky call from Deidre. Flipping through the news channels, all she was seeing was an earlier press conference of sorts with the President. No . . . in fact, he was in front of one of his canned audiences, a practice that this President had turned into a regular and accepted event. No real questions were ever allowed. The audience was screened ahead of time to ensure that they were true, adoring loyalists, and the President never knew that anyone in the whole wide world disagreed with him, Andie thought incredulously. She started to flip to a movie channel when the background banner caught her eye.

OPERATION REHAB SOLDIERS for IRAQ

What in the? Andie clicked off the mute.

"We're fortunate to have so many skilled men and women to assist," he was saying, smiling largely.

"It's a win-win. When you have skilled men and women just sitting behind bars, being supported by the citizens' taxes, and we got insurgents goin' after innocents, it's time to rethink and retool. And that's exactly what we've done. See . . . we're putting them to work, folks. They will fight the fight because they're good at it. They got experience. They're whatcha call veterans, even though they haven't been in the military yet," he said, chuckling. Members of the audience, which Andie noticed reflected an unusually large number of minorities, could be seen to be laughing with him although a few had that deer-in-the-headlights look. Soon people were actually applauding. The President nodded enthusiastically and then pointed to someone in the audience.

"You have a question?"

"Yes, Mr. President. How are you selecting them. I have a cousin, I mean I have a friend who has a cousin, who's in the pen, and I'm sure he'd like to benefit from this opportunity."

"That's a good question. We decided to prioritize the selection based on experience, just like any employer would do. Did your friend's cousin use an AK-47?"

"I . . . don't remember," the man said.

"Well, let's hope he did, because it's people like him who will be contacted first. Next question," he said, pointing to a young black woman.

"How much will they be paid?"

"Another good question. Does everyone here have a Ph.D. or what?" the President extolled.

The audience roared.

"There are a lot of factors that go into deciding how much each person will get. It'll depend a lot on how much time the person is in for and the nature of the crime. But it's more than they're making now, right?" he cheered.

Everyone could be seen to be nodding and clapping in agreement.

"So there you have it, folks. The new *Operation Rehab Soldiers for Iraq* is a vision to the future. Let's give a hand to our new, brave men and women who will be fighting to protect you rather than sucking up your tax dollars." The crowd could be seen giving a standing ovation.

As the clip ended, the camera turned to the pretty news anchor, who smiled broadly. She turned to her co-host saying, "Apparently, Jim, there's so much enthusiasm for this initiative that we're told the President's approval rating has taken a big jump."

"Yes, that's what I'm hearing again, too. We haven't seen the actual numbers yet, but some are saying it's past seventy percent now. We'll just have to wait for the final tally." The program went to commercial.

Andie had been sitting on the edge of her couch for some time now, eyes mesmerized on the TV. Gone was the warm, cozy feeling, gone was the contentment to just relax, gone was any semblance of sanity. Andie was simply stunned. This was a big step back from civilization. A very big step.

She called Craig. "Hi. Is it too late?"

"Not yet, I hope."

"Very funny. Have you seen the new scheme by the administration to send criminals to Iraq?"

"Yeah. Pretty clever, huh?"

"What?"

"Yeah, everyone's talking about what a good idea it is."

"And what do you think?"

"It's good. I mean, what else? They're just sitting there."

"I can't believe I'm hearing this," Andie muttered.

"Oh, Andie, don't get yourself all in a tizzy. It's just another chapter of life for those folks. They're glad to get out."

"How do you know?"

"Wouldn't you be?"

"No."

"Don't be so sure."

"Craig, you can't be serious. This is analogous to what the Romans did when they captured slaves."

"What are you talking about?"

"They used them in their military," Andie said, tersely.

"And look how long that empire survived. Besides, these criminals are going to be paid. They're not slaves."

"*That* empire!" Andie was feeling the anger rise. "Craig, please tell me you're joking. Are you really supporting this President?"

"Relax, Andie. He's not so bad. Listen, I've got to go. I've got a busy day tomorrow."

"Fine. Have a good night, if you can sleep." Andie switched off her mobile as hard as possible. "Ughhhhhhhh!" she yelled.

While Andie had a restless, nightmarish sleep, with images of Nineteenth Century prisoners, including her, being rounded up and sent to a bloody ugly war, which did not have a name, the VP slept like a baby, awaking with a sense of accomplishment and exciting objectives to be tackled.

His wife always put a copy of RW&B's newspaper and a cup of hot, steaming coffee containing four teaspoons of sugar and real cream on the table next to the bed. This morning the sense of contentment quickly evaporated, however, when the VP opened the paper to a startling headline.

US RESCUES UK AMBASSADOR

He could feel his heart literally skip a beat. The breath he sucked in caught in his throat. He felt that he couldn't breathe. He then tried to raise his hefty torso, but laid back down. The energy required to sit up and throw his legs over the side of his mattress was sapped.

He lay there panting like an overweight kudu narrowly escaping death from a lion. Ten minutes later, he sat up and screamed for his wife. She appeared within seconds. He ordered her to bring his secure phone from his office. She looked scared as she ran off to get it, knowing only too well not to ask questions.

The VP was now able to get out of bed and stumble to the bathroom. He splashed cold water on his face and neck, leaning his head into the sink finally and letting the water pour over him. Eventually, he felt better and was able to stand up straight. As he dried his face after shaving, he moved closer to the mirror. He noticed the bags appeared heavier and the slack jowls longer. *I've got to use my gym,* he thought. *I'll start Monday.* But the pasty face with sunken eyes that looked back at him appeared stonily unconvinced and uncooperative.

When he came out, the phone was sitting on his night stand. No wife was present. "Good," he muttered, as he hit the speed-dial number.

"What the hell are you doing, man?"

"Pretty impressive, huh?"

"You're pathetic. Who do you think you are, anyway?"

"The Secretary of Defense, that's the reason I moved in to rescue a high profile prisoner. It's my job."

"Wrong. You're job is to coordinate with me. I call the shots, and if you can't abide by that, let me know now."

The Secretary felt first anger and then sadness. *So, it had come to this,* he thought.

Instead of acquiescing, he moved on boldly. "What part exactly of rescuing the UK ambassador do you find so distasteful?" he asked smugly.

"The part about his kidnapping being orchestrated by me so he would have a sensational rescue that could be used in thirty-second commercials during the upcoming election."

This bombshell hit the Secretary of Defense with such a thud that he could not think coherently for several seconds. The hubris was overwhelming.

"Sorry to have rained on your parade." He hung up, his mind reeling.

"Too bad for you," the VP commented to no one in particular, assured that the Secretary was sufficiently cowed so as not to muck up any more of his plans. He sighed heavily. Now he'd have to come up with a new surprise for commercial viewing.

When Andie awoke the next morning, she realized with relief that her hands were not shackled and the dark woman next to her was not dying of consumption. The nightmare had been so real. She needed to shake it from her memory, so she decided to go for a jog in Rock Creek Park. The subsequent endorphins helped her, somewhat, to shake her malaise from the newest encroachment on decency and to focus on her upcoming meeting with Nathan. She hated to admit it, but she wanted to get a lot of information from him. At the same time, she didn't want to come across like she didn't care about what he had experienced during and following Claire's death. Suddenly, without warning, as she rounded a bend, she practically ran head on into another jogger. He looked very familiar, but he passed so quickly, she didn't really have a chance to look closely. As she prepared to head to meet Nathan, three hours later, she still couldn't get his appearance out of her mind, vague as it was.

Nathan was sitting in the corner, near a window, with his back to the wall. It looked like he was drinking a beer. Yep. A big twenty-ouncer. Because it was still early, the restaurant was virtually empty. Laughter and chatter from the servers could barely be heard above the soft classical music.

"Andie!" the strapping man said, standing up to hug her and peck her on the cheek. "So glad to see you."

"You, too, Nathan," she said, hugging him back tightly.

"You look as beautiful as always."

"Thank you, Nathan," Andie said modestly.

She sat down across from him so they could both look out the window from time to time.

After ordering a turkey sandwich and hot cup of tea, Andie asked when Nathan was leaving D.C. to visit his family.

"This afternoon. I'm looking forward to seeing them," he said. "It's been a while."

Andie noticed that he appeared preoccupied.

"Nathan, I'm so sorry, again, about Claire's death. I'm sorry I couldn't help any more. I know it must have been a terrible event for you."

"Actually, Andie, it was not unexpected, it was just so shocking when it happened, to actually see it. It's one thing to think about it or talk about it, it's another to experience it."

Andie bit her lip upon hearing this confession. "You mean Claire and you talked about the dangers and possibility of being injured?" Andie asked, not wanting to suggest what she feared most, that the death was intentional.

"Yes, of course, it's a war zone," Nathan replied.

"I know, Nathan. I know. I guess I don't know why you would think and talk about imminent and violent death, when you are supposed to be embedded and protected, that's all," she said softly.

Nathan scoffed at this comment, then he looked down at his beer rather sheepishly. "Sorry, Andie, but you don't know what it's like there."

"You're absolutely right. I don't," she agreed again.

There was a long pause. The server came with the sandwich and tea. Nathan ordered another beer. Andie put some sugar in her tea and stirred it far longer than necessary.

Once Nathan's beer had come, and he'd taken a big gulp, he started talking, leaning in toward Andie, speaking ever so softly.

"Claire was murdered, Andie. And yes, by us. By the US. By our side. I hate to have to tell you this, but it is indisputable. We were set up, and then they took her out."

Andie lost her appetite immediately. She felt shaky. She couldn't swallow. She sat up straight and tried to breathe through her nose so as to stop the light-headedness.

"Are you okay?" Nathan asked, looking concerned.

Andie shook her head yes, but the tears filled her eyes and rolled down her cheeks. *How could this be? Her country. She knew what Nathan had said was probably true. But hearing it . . . the reality was so stark.*

Nathan pulled out a handkerchief and handed it to her, while he put his other hand on top of hers. He squeezed it tightly and looked intently into her face. His eyes expressed so much concern and, Andie realized, so much of life's hurt as well. She forced herself again to breathe deeply, feeling foolishly weak and cowardly. Here was the man who had been right next to Claire when she had been killed.

As if reading her mind, Nathan said, "Don't be too hard on yourself, Andie. I've had a bit of time to internalize that terrible day. You haven't. Yes, Claire and I talked about it. I don't think either of us actually visualized such an event, however. For Claire, the end was immediate. She did not suffer. But . . . she was not able to finish what she started, which is a great tragedy."

Listening to Nathan, Andie began to regain her balance and composure. He was so young to be so mature.

". . . she was doing her job when she was murdered. She was simply trying to inform Americans as to the truth that was occurring then and there. That's what journalists are supposed to do. Most of the ones from the States, however, were too afraid and too glib to go for the actual, factual, on-the-ground activity. She was shunned by her fellow colleagues, you know." Andie shook her head no this time.

"At first we thought it was because she wore the burka, but then we realized that most of them were defensive because they were afraid to do what she was doing and consequently jealous. They were really nasty."

"How so?" Andie asked, becoming increasingly more engaged in Nathan's story and less focused on the event of Claire's murder.

"They didn't want her to sit next to them, but sometimes there were no empty seats in the cafeteria, so she'd sit down next to someone and that person would actually get up and leave, even if it was obvious that he or she was not finished eating. Really childish," he concluded.

"So what happened, Nathan?" Andie was not so much impatient as concerned. She wanted to know what he knew and try to help finish Claire's work. Andie figured she should not have died, and certainly should not have died without closure.

Nathan sighed. "Okay. Let me start from the beginning, or at least my beginning. I had been with her since we arrived together in the early part of January. It was chaotic back then, although it's become much worse. There were few rules within the Green Zone and tons of rules about leaving it. So everyone hunkered down, except Claire. She'd cajole and sweet talk anyone into going into the field for a few hours or a day. That's how she was able to report like she did. She was front and center, and the reports were not rosy, as you may well remember. She was dogged about her research, but in the meantime, she'd be conducting interviews with people to discuss their experiences and health, and any aspect about DU, of course. She was following up on Michael's work. I guess you know that they realized they were working on the same impacts and outcomes of the use of DU in war, on the people caught in the middle, both Iraqis and soldiers, ours and theirs."

Andie nodded yes.

"Well, the day of her murder she had invited me to her room. She was all secretive, whispering as though someone might hear us, looking out her window, but not getting too close, and carefully organizing her materials on her makeshift desk, in the corner," Nathan recalled, reliving the time.

63

Claire had closed the door quickly behind him. "Thanks for coming, Nathan. I just received a call to go to Fallujah. There's something up. But you don't have to go . . ."

"Of course, I'll go," Nathan responded, hurt that she had even suggested he might not want to accompany her.

"By the way," Claire continued, "I want you to know that I sent Sadie my research in two CDs."

"Okay. Good," Nathan replied, not really listening very intently. He was preoccupied, thinking about how they were going to get in and out of Fallujah.

"I have one other one, I want you to get it to her. I have the copy here, but you keep the original."

"Why? Why not mail it?" Nathan asked, becoming alarmed and not liking what he was hearing at all.

"I don't have time now, we've got to go, pronto."

"I mean later, when we get back."

"It's better if you take it now. I know you'll get it to her, but I get absentminded," Claire responded, unconvincingly. "This one is especially important, so please be a dear and make sure you keep it safe," she said, as she slipped it in his jacket's inside pocket while she gave him a quick kiss on the cheek.

Nathan could do nothing but accept the task. It wasn't fair when she manipulated him like that, but he put up with her flirting just to be around her.

"So, go get your gear, and I'll meet you down in the lobby in twenty minutes," she said, again looking nervously out the window. "And, Nathan, sit in the corner or something, I don't really want anyone to see us leave."

"Whatever," Nathan responded, a bit irked.

64

Andie interrupted his story. "So, weren't you curious about who called her?"

"Yeah, but the CD thing came up, and I forgot to even ask. I ran up the stairs to my room, organized my support equipment, took care of the CD, and barely made it down to the lobby in time. Then we jumped in a car with an Iraqi driver that she had pre-arranged and off we went. She continued to talk about the need to catch everything that was going on when we got there on film, because from what she could tell, the true story was not being reported in the States. She said she had already prepared the beginning statement based on her current knowledge and wanted me to get her in front of any action or activity or commotion that would give the viewers a sense of what it was like to be on the ground there. She said to also look for DU and get photos.

"I kept saying, 'yeah, yeah, yeah. Claire, it's what we always do,' I had said.

"I remember still feeling down, used, I guess," he paused here and took a big gulp from his mug.

"So then what?" Andie asked impatiently.

"Well, Claire was sitting in the front seat talking into her mike. I guess she was preparing her evening report or the one from Fallujah. I stared out the window for a while. It's a scary trip. Fallujah is about forty miles west of Baghdad. The road is loaded with mines and debris, not to mention opportunistic killers and hijackers. That's one of the reasons for Claire's burka and, of course, the Iraqi driver. For my part, I kept my head down and slouched for most of the trip, which took almost three hours.

"Once we arrived, there was already fighting occurring in different parts of the city. You could see smoke plumes and hear the gunshots. Claire asked the driver to take us to the one remaining, standing hotel. She told me that's where the caller said to hang out. An incident was going to occur nearby. So . . . we hung out. The city was pretty much gone by that time. I mean, I couldn't understand why we were even sent there. There was nothing left. No civilians, at least none that were still alive. It was just a squalid piece of territory filled with debris, dead foliage, bombed-out buildings, an acrid decaying smell, and lots of DU. Yeah, the DU was everywhere, glistening in the sunlight. It gives me the creeps to even see it, knowing that we're dropping it on these cities where innocent people live and work."

"Aren't you afraid to be around it?" Andie asked, alarmed.

"You just watch your step," Nathan replied. "It's possible to avoid it if you know what to look for and you don't have to go too far. Trouble is, most civilians, especially the children, haven't got a clue. And of course, our soldiers can't always avoid it. They're fighting in and around it once it's dropped. Ugly, ugly business," he concluded, taking a gulp from his beer and looking around. Resuming, he said, "It was maybe thirty minutes or so before we started sensing that something was up. And that's when it happened, everything I described to you on the phone. It happened really, really fast."

Nathan finished his beer and motioned for the waitress to bring him another. Andie wondered if he was driving to West Virginia, but decided to ask before they left each other. She decided she would take him if need be.

"Can I talk with you about it now?" Andie asked. "I mean, can I ask questions about what happened afterwards?"

"Yes, of course," Nathan said, again turning his head to look out the window. "My biggest goal now is to get back there and help to continue Claire's work in any way I can, even if it's just the best camera work around. It's such a cloistered environment. I might try some freelancing, with some bloggers."

"You'd leave WSSN?" Andie asked, surprised.

"Yeah, not a problem," was his only response, which surprised Andie even more. She had always thought Nathan cared deeply for the company. "So, go ahead, ask away."

"Well," Andie hesitated, looking down at her uneaten sandwich. "What happened to Claire? I mean her body?"

"Military took her. I don't know what happened, did Sadie say anything?"

"No." Andie felt a blush of guilt wash over her. She had never discussed it with Sadie. She felt badly that it had never occurred to her. Nonetheless, she continued. "What happened to you? I mean you said they smashed your camera, what then?"

"I tried to run, but two contractors stopped me and patted me down. I was worried that they were going to take my passport, but they just took my water, money, and candy bars, and a couple of pens, I think.

"Then, I walked more slowly, trying to hug any shadows that could be found in the rubble, which is not easy, and slowly made my way to the hotel, wondering if I'd ever get out of Fallujah alive. I hung out there for . . . I don't know . . . at least two hours. I was in shock, I realize now. I was staring stupidly out the window, from the far corner of the room, when I saw the taxi driver who had brought us, trolling by, looking around. I remember checking to see if anyone was watching me, and then I bolted, running as fast as I could to get in front of his car. He pulled over, motioned wildly for me to jump in, and we sped off. I didn't know it, but he could speak English. He said he'd heard that Claire was shot. He said he'd get me back.

"I was really terrified by this point, hoping beyond hope that we could avoid gunfire. We did, obviously. He dropped me off near the Green Zone a few hours later. It was dark by then. I felt badly, I couldn't even pay him. He said, no need. It was a favor to Claire. And you know what, Andie . . . " Nathan asked rhetorically, "by the time I got inside the lobby of our hotel, a notice about Claire's death was already there. It just seemed impossible to me that with all that chaos, a notice would be posted. I'm just telling you this because it added to my conviction as to what had happened."

"I can imagine," was all Andie could say. Mentally, however, she made a note to follow up on the sequencing of notices such as this. Shouldn't the families and relatives be contacted first? Was that done? She needed to know. Given the time difference, she doubted it.

"So, when I called you . . . " Andie continued, wanting to keep Nathan engaged, "you were with a couple of guys, some colleagues, I guessed?"

"Noooo," Nathan said, emphatically, "I was going to get to that. *That* was a big mistake. I should have just gone to bed, but instead I went up to my room and washed up then headed to the bar. Those guys were waiting for me, which is another peculiar incident, adding just another layer to the whole morbid event. I was a sitting duck," Nathan shook his head remorsefully. "Anyway, I did manage not to talk about Claire's murder, even after several drinks. I just complained about the Green Zone and the rules and the concept of 'embedded' and whatever I was furious about in order to release my hurt, anger, and frustration. Nonetheless, they were after something. Later, I realized that they were there with me precisely because of her murder. Maybe if I had told them what I thought about it I wouldn't be here today. But anyway, after quite a while they wanted to help me to my room, I said no, but they each took an arm and took me there. By the time we got to my door, my head was swimming. They must have dropped something in my drink, because I can handle it," he said, rather boastfully. "Next thing I knew, it was morning, and I had a hell of a hangover. I could barely get out of bed, but when I did, I saw that they had ransacked everything and had taken my backpack. My empty wallet and passport were the only items on my bed stand. A note of sorts was on top."

Andie was beginning to wish she didn't have to hear all of this. It was rather embarrassing.

"What was written on it?" she asked, innocently enough.

"Go home, WV DB."

"I don't get it," Andie said.

"Everyone in the Green Zone has a nickname. Mine is West Virginia Dumb Boy."

"Oh, that's not nice. Why?"

"I don't know who started it, but I decided to play up to it, so in part it's my fault," Nathan said, grinning for the first time. "I guess I fit the description that night, though," he said, looking down at his beer. "For the first time it hit me, I should have checked Claire's room when I got in. I ran down to it, but it was too late. The door was ajar, and the room was ransacked. Everything was turned upside down."

"Oh," Andie said with concern, her eyebrows pinching together, "the CDs were gone?"

"Yeah, mine, too." Nathan said, looking into her eyes. "Those guys even took my coat."

"Oh, no," Andie said, putting her fist to her lips, remembering that the GPS indicated his phone was in Sadr City. It must have been tossed there. *Thank God they did not kill him,* she thought.

"Yeah. Fortunately, I made a copy before leaving for Fallujah," he said grinning, reaching into his pocket and pulling out a memory stick.

Andie's frown turned into a huge smile. "Thank you," she said, reaching for it. Nathan released it easily. "Have you had a chance to look at it?" Andie asked, curious for a couple of reasons.

"No. I couldn't bring myself to view it. I thought about it, but just couldn't." And with that he put his other large hand on the table, palm down with his fingers wrapped around something.

"What is it?" Andie asked a bit apprehensively.

He turned his hand over and opened it. A small cell phone lay cushioned within his palm. "It's Claire's," he said, smiling again.

"Ooohhh," Andie said. "May I?"

"Of course."

"Thank you, again." She examined it closely, realizing it was a state-of-the-art phone. *There must be photos, messages, and text messages as well as numbers,* she thought. Then she quickly dropped it in her purse. "So, who were those goons? The two guys."

"Contractors too. They're everywhere. There are more contractors in the Green Zone," Nathan said, "than military."

"Really?"

"I'd bet on it," Nathan said, looking out the window rather wistfully. Then he yawned and looked at his watch. "By the way," he said suddenly, "I have a new number. Let's stay in touch once I'm back in Iraq."

"Definitely," Andie agreed, as she punched his number into her phone. "I have to admit, I'd love it if you can get more of the DU photos that were destroyed when the soldier crushed your camera," Andie said, sensing that their meeting was over.

"Believe me, that's my goal, too," Nathan replied.

Andie hesitated a minute and then added, "Do you think it would be possible to do more?"

For the first time all morning, Nathan looked energized. "What do you mean?" he asked eagerly.

Andie leaned toward him and practically whispered her plan.

Nathan immediately began nodding in agreement. He added to the plan as she laid it out. Five minutes later they were grinning at each other, eyes locked in mutual understanding. "Okay, then, I guess I'd better get going," Nathan said enthusiastically, but suddenly yawning again.

"Are you driving home to West Virginia?" Andie asked, concerned.

"No," he said, laughing big, "not in this condition. I'm going to mosey over to Union Station and catch the train. My brother's picking me up in Martinsburg."

"Well, good for you. Listen, Nathan, I really want to thank you for this opportunity. I admire you for your courage," Andie said as they stood up, converting back to regular, professional banter.

"Oh, you don't have to say that, Andie. It's been my pleasure. I needed to get some of this off my chest and, of course, get these items to you," he said modestly, pushing his sandy hair back again.

"Okay, then," Andie said, "I've got to go, too. I need to get to the office and check on things. It's been a few days since I've been there."

"Oh. You're going to be seeing Simon?" Nathan asked.

"Yes, of course, well, most likely," Andie replied. "Why?"

"Good luck. He's been tied up in meetings lately."

"What about?" Andie asked.

"You'll see," Nathan said, sardonically.

"You won't tell me?" Andie asked, a bit hurt.

"It's too hard to describe."

"Oh, try." Andie attempted to egg him on.

"No. It's too weird. You'll see. Call me and tell me what you think. Maybe it's my imagination. I don't want to prejudice you."

Andie was somewhat satisfied with this explanation. "Okay. Let's go. I'll walk with you. I'm going that way."

"Thanks, Andie. That's nice."

As the cold air hit them upon leaving the museum, they interlocked their arms and walked off toward the station.

"Who's the dude with her?" the man asked into his shoulder mike.

"A kid from West Virginia and apparently a pretty gullible one. He's not a target. It's the woman we need to watch," the man opposite the mall in the middle of the Smithsonian said into his mike.

"I got the same marching orders. I know it's the woman, just wondering what he's doing with her. Can't be too safe."

"I told you, a nobody," came the response. "Let's just keep tracking her until we get more orders."

"Got it."

Obviously, Andie could never have imagined that she was being observed by hooligans. Why should she? Who would have thought that this kind of behavior by officials in her own government was possible?

65

The phone rang while the VP sat at his huge pine desk, contemplating a new PR propaganda strategy in Iraq. It was the Defense Secretary. The VP had not expected to hear from him so soon. He thought he would need some cooling down following their last conversation.

"Your girl's in trouble," the Secretary said flatly.

"What girl?" the VP asked, not liking the tone or the message.

"The mole you have working for WSSN in Iraq."

"Oh, her. What's wrong with her? There's more where she came from, so don't fret. She's not indispensable," he reiterated, thinking to himself that no one was.

"Well, she's got a hell of an infection."

"So what? I could care less," the VP said nonchalantly, glancing out the window.

"It's her arm. There's a problem with the implant."

"What?" Now the Secretary had his undivided attention. "Why? What's going on? Tell me," the VP impatiently demanded, sweat starting to break out on his forehead.

"I'm trying to find out. But she's sick, and she's still reporting, so don't go thinking about disappearing her," which, as a matter of fact, is exactly what the VP was thinking at that very moment.

"I don't have time for this. Call me as soon as you know anything, which should be in ten minutes or less," he said, slamming down the phone and then speed-dialing his Chief of Staff. "Lowell, get me Jones. We need to meet at the bunker in two hours. Make sure he's there."

Jones was not happy to hear from Lowell. "Why should I? Give me one good reason I need to jump every time he says so? He owes me, and until he pays, it's not going to happen."

"He said to remind you of Maria's 'accident,' if you were disinclined to join us," Lowell responded, as instructed by the VP.

"Join you! Give me a break," Jones cried in dismay. "What a joke. You make it sound like an invitation to go camping."

"Up to you, but I don't think I'd like living always looking over my shoulder."

"Here we go with the threats again," Jones said evenly. "You guys are so despicable. I can't come up with enough adjectives to describe you at any one time."

Lowell thought to himself that this sentiment actually seemed reasonable. He waited.

Jones finally broke the silence. "I'll be there, but this better be good. Tell your leader, whatever he wants, I'll have my demands, too."

"Best not to upset him, not these days."

"So many threats, so little time," Jones said disgustedly, as he hung up. He wondered if he should start looking over his shoulder beginning today.

Instead of looking over her shoulder as she should have been doing, Andie gave Nathan a big hug good-bye. Both promised to stay in touch by email or phone. Nathan wanted to know what Andie discovered, and Andie needed Nathan's take on the coverage of the war, especially by DeeDee. He promised to look her up as soon as he returned to Iraq. Andie begged him to be careful and not to take chances. Nathan promised, looking embarrassed, so Andie dropped the cautionary talk and just hugged him one last time. Then she headed quickly to the Metro station. She should have been at WSSN hours ago.

While trudging up the stairs to the third floor, Andie thought she could hear singing. *That would be a new one,* she mused.

The closer she got to the door of the large cubicle-filled office, the louder the singing became. It sounded like . . . she couldn't place it. It was too uncharacteristic for the place. Then she knew. It was a hymn. Suddenly, before she could enter, it abruptly ended. As she entered people were dispersing from the far corner of the room. She saw then that what had been a kind of gathering place with a coffee machine and cooler had been resurrected into a space that had a den-like quality to it. There was a bookshelf, a few cushioned chairs, and what looked to be a new CD system. *Oh, the singing was recorded,* she thought. But . . . then who was playing it? Who was listening to it? She looked around the room. Many of the cubicles were empty, again uncharacteristically. Her colleagues stared at her as she walked to her own cubicle. When she glanced in their direction, they quickly diverted their eyes. She tried smiling and saying hello, but no one really seemed interested in responding to her. She quickly looked over her emails, sending a quick one to Simon to see if he was available.

The phone rang immediately. "Andie, you're here?"

"Yes, of course."

"Come on up," was the hearty reply. "I want us to catch up."

Andie agreed. Walking up the stairs was a totally new experience for her. In less than a week of absence, ratings posters, slogans, photos, and biblical images had replaced the drab green, paint-peeling walls. She couldn't believe the conversion that had occurred.

The War Column knocks the ratings out of the park!

Even RW&B can't keep up!

Join the crowd. Tune in at 6:00 p.m. EST

Support the Leaders Making Those Tough Decisions So

You Don't Have to Make Them

Then there was the photo of the President looming over a huge crowd of apparently adoring spectators giving a standing ovation. The lights behind the President were made to resemble the "stars," as in a planetarium she thought; "heavenly," she decided on second thought.

Then there was the one that actually posed a question:

Are YOU Going to Hell?

Jesus Can Be Your Social Security

She quickened her step as she read these, perhaps because she was trying to reach Simon even faster now, needing to get some answers, or perhaps because they gave her the heebie-jeebies, she didn't know.

As she approached his office, she could hear him talking on the phone. "Ha, ha, ha," he bellowed. "Well, okay. We'll arrange for you to lead the prayer session next Tuesday then. No, we're happy to do it. The staff was asking for you. Yes, you're welcome. And thank you again, Representative."

Andie knocked. A hearty "Come in" was the response.

The poster-laden staircase walls had been shock enough, but Andie now saw that nothing should surprise her anymore. Simon was sitting at a new and huge desk, facing his door, so he was immediately visible, front and center, rather than the three-quarter profile that she was used to seeing upon entering. In the past, his desk had been planted in the corner, more or less. She clearly recalled him saying he liked it that way because he felt it made others feel more at ease. Now, however, it seemed like Simon was thinking mostly of himself. Two tiny chairs were placed in front of this new and apparently improved, humongous desk, dwarfing them and their unfortunate temporary occupants.

"Andie," Simon practically screamed. "Come in," he said, motioning her toward him with his left hand. He pointed to one of the chairs. "Pull up a chair and relax."

Hardly, thought Andie. She sat down. The seat was even smaller than she anticipated. She had to push her back against its back and push her legs forward in an effort to be comfortable. The odor had been present at the door, but now it was overwhelming. "What is that smell, Simon?" She couldn't help but crinkle her nose as she asked.

"What smell? Oh . . . that. Nothing. I've got a bit of a sore on my arm. It's healing quickly, though. I'm putting tea tree oil on it. It's a bit antiseptic smelling, I know," he said, grinning almost sheepishly.

A bit? "What's wrong with your arm?" Andie asked, noting that he had not moved it since she had entered and then recalled him motioning for her to sit down with his left hand.

"Nothing. Slight infection," Simon replied self-consciously, at the same time rubbing the upper outside of his bicep.

"What's the doctor say?"

"Haven't had time to see one. We've been so busy," he said, smiling hugely. "Did you see the posters?" was the next question, asked with great enthusiasm in his voice.

"Yeah, I saw them," Andie said, without the same enthusiasm. "They're interesting. But did you have to paper the entire wall with them? One after the other, after the other, after the other?"

"Oh, it didn't start out that way. The staff did it over time. They're really excited about our innovative War Column. We're the only news outlet that creates so many hallmarks a day about the good things that are occurring in Iraq. Our team is thrilled. We are so popular. Well, you must have seen the ratings by now," Simon concluded, a big smile on his face.

"Simon, isn't that what RW&B does? Don't they tout the war's benefits? It seems that we're duplicating that aspect of the news," Andie replied, rather derisively.

"Oh . . . no, not really. We're actually doing it more often and better," Simon responded, giggling uncharacteristically, not even apparently offended by Andie's tone or question.

Andie sighed. *What the hell was going on?* As Simon chirped on and on about the new series, Andie took time to observe the office more closely. Actually, it had become rather ostentatious, in a trashy way. There were photos of Simon everywhere, faux gold-plated frames and large mirrors. The same posters that were on the stairs were peppered throughout the different wall hangings, competing for attention. Another new addition was a big screen TV on the wall. *How could she have missed that?* she wondered. *Jeez, it must have cost over five thousand,* she thought.

At that moment, WSSN was providing coverage, or so it would seem. A person Andie had never seen before was talking into the camera and pointing to a building behind him. The ticker tape was describing the building in glowing terms and referring to how it had been rebuilt by the good ole U.S. of A.

"Simon," Andie interrupted, "the ticker tape is supposed to inform viewers of other news, not the same news the reporter is reporting," she said. "And who is that guy, may I ask?"

"Andie," Simon said condescendingly, "so sorry for the confusion. I asked you to come to our meetings. We have found that it's too distracting for viewers to listen and read at the same time. True," he continued, noting her blatant look of skepticism. "So we are ensuring that they understand, undeniably, what we're conveying. You know, it's called saturation. We've just taken it to another degree. We decided to provide subtitles, if you will, even though it's the same thing that's being said. It's true, the reporter, his name is Chip by the way, is reading the actual ticker tape. So there's no chance of a conflict in delivery. It's genius," Simon continued. "There's no other word for it. The viewers have spoken. Look at the testimonials from them," he added, as he tossed her a focus group report, glancing back at the screen and smiling again.

"Simon, where's DeeDee?" Andie asked abruptly, irritated with his patronizing and even more upset that a very important human resource to WSSN's whole Iraqi coverage, regardless of how suspect she was to Andie, appeared to have gone missing.

"What? Oh," Simon said, glancing rather distractedly at her but keeping his eyes on the news program for the most part. "She's still giving the nightly news update, the boring facts and figures, attacks and deaths," he said flatly. "It's just not compelling anymore. I need to rethink her mission. But to answer your question, I haven't spoken with her in a couple of days. Actually, the last time we talked, she said she wasn't feeling well. I should check in with her. Thanks for the reminder, Andie," he said dismissively.

Andie stood up.

"You're going?"

"Yes, I've got some work still to do on Claire's tribute. You remember her," she said, sarcastically.

"Of course." He finally stood up and came around to her. "I can't wait to see it, I mean, read it. When do you think it will be finished?"

Andie felt his sentiment sounded rather hallow. "Soon. As soon as I can verify a few sources, I should be able to provide a first draft."

"Okay, but don't spend too much time on source verifications. No one seems to ever follow up on them. Just pick a name out of the phone book if need be, " he boomed heartily.

Andie was shocked to hear this. Simon had instilled in her the need to always verify, verify, verify.

"Some of them are Iraqi names, Simon," she replied, again sarcastically.

"Oh. Oh, yeah, well, check anyway. I'm sure there are Iraqi cab drivers and such here in D.C."

Andie was seething. Just when she thought she couldn't take any more, Simon reached out and grasped her two hands in his soft, pudgy left one. "Andie, there's something else I wanted to mention."

"What?" Andie asked skeptically.

"It's our Bible study session. We are holding them every morning now, 9:00 to 9:30. Please feel free to attend, even if you are working away from the office."

"How did this come about?" Andie asked, genuinely interested in knowing and at the same time shocked.

"Oh, the holidays and such, Claire's death. . . ." Simon trailed off but kept his eyes glued to hers.

Andie looked away, not being able to return the gaze. *God have mercy,* she thought, and then smiled to herself at her own irony.

"Thanks, Simon. I'll take it into consideration," was all she said.

He squeezed her hands especially hard. "Come, you'll enjoy them." He smiled, strangely.

"Thanks, Simon, I'll call."

As she ran down the stairs, fast, headed to the front door, Andie decided suddenly that she should stop by and say hi to Miss Ellie. Maybe she would know what was going on.

She popped back into the newsroom, scanning the tops of heads for Miss Ellie. Turning to go, she bumped into Joel.

"Hi, Joel."

"Hi yourself, stranger. Where've you been?" he asked casually.

"Following up on a story about Claire. How's it going?"

"Not bad."

"Do you know where Miss Ellie is?" Andie asked.

"Oh. . . . " Joel suddenly looked distressed. "Didn't you hear?"

"No. What?"

"She's in the hospital."

"What's wrong?"

"She's got some kind of infection. They're treating it, but they can't find the cause, so it's not getting better."

"Oh, dear," Andie replied, concerned. "Which hospital?"

"George Washington. I think she's in room 202."

"Okay, thanks. I'll try to stop by and see her."

"Yeah, do that, but don't stay long in the building, you'll get sick," Joel said smilingly.

"Yeah, right," Andie agreed, heading toward the stairs.

Walking briskly to the Metro, Andie mulled over the transformation she had just witnessed. She had to admit to herself that she was horrified to discover that her employer and friend was sucking up to someone, who she did not know exactly. She ruefully recalled Nathan's comment. It seemed to make a lot more sense now. No wonder he did not mind returning to Iraq as a freelance photographer, hoping to partner up with a blogger. Where or how could he do his job for WSSN now? The coverage had turned to marshmallow, just like RW&B and all the other media yo-yos out there. Andie was extremely depressed. And now, to learn that Miss Ellie was sick. *What next?* she wondered.

66

Agent Ingram had thought his assignment in the bunker had been concluded, so he was surprised when he was called to return to it this morning. Sure enough, not long after he had stationed himself in front of the door, he heard the men approaching. The VP's unmistakable voice was preceding the actual man.

"Goddamn it! I want answers immediately. We spoke over two hours ago. What the hell is so difficult about finding the cause of her illness?" he was screeching.

Agent Ingram didn't like the content of this question. He was a bit of a hypochondriac and had had misgivings about being down here because of the medical stuff going on. *Who was sick?* he wondered. *What did the person have?*

Just then the VP and his Chief of Staff rounded the corner. The VP was concluding his phone conversation. "Get me the information. Use whatever sources are necessary."

Agent Ingram saw him snap the phone shut. Again he remarked to himself, he had not thought it possible that a cell phone could work down here. Very interesting, he mused, as he opened the door for the two men. As usual, they ignored him totally. After he heard the door lock shut, Agent Ingram remained standing at its entrance. He imagined there were more men to come. Within minutes he could hear the soft shoes shuffling down the corridor. Probably the lanky guy, he guessed. Yep. He was right. The man nodded at him as he opened the door. At least some recognition. Before the door locked behind him, Agent Ingram heard the VP saying, "Well, Jones, you never let me down. Late as usual."

Agent Ingram noted that he was glad the door was soundproof.

Jones sat down without saying a word. The VP looked at his Chief of Staff. Lowell looked at Jones and then back at the VP. "Oh, for God's sake," the VP began. "Jones. We have a problem that's representing a potential crisis. We need your take on it."

Again, Jones just sat there.

"What? You want me to play nice or something?" the VP asked sardonically.

Jones spoke. "Let's just put it this way. I want the rest of my rightful payment. *Now*. Then I'll listen."

The VP nodded to the Chief of Staff, who immediately whipped out a checkbook and started to write.

"Uh, uh. Nada. No. No check. Transfer the money to this account immediately." Jones pushed forward a new number, all the while gritting his teeth.

The VP sighed. He clasped his hands behind his head and just stared at Jones. Jones stared back. Finally, the VP nodded, almost imperceptibly, to Lowell, whereupon Lowell took the piece of paper with the number on it from the table and made a phone call. After some discussion, Lowell hung up. "It's done."

"Confirmation" was all Jones said.

Lowell gave him a phone number and Jones called it to confirm. The money was there, sure enough. *They must have some really big mess on their hands,* Jones thought smugly, not realizing that perhaps the mess involved him, too.

"Okay. Shoot. What's your problem?" he asked cheerfully.

Upon hearing about the woman, Jones's guinea pig, with the arm infection, due apparently to the implant, Jones's recently gained sunny disposition disappeared as quickly as it had arrived. Frowning, he began asking the obvious questions: *When did this begin, what's it look like, is there a fever, are meds working to address it, etc. etc.* But answers were not really forthcoming. The VP and his Chief of Staff had very little to go on. In other words, they had absolutely no answers.

"Well, hell. How would I know what's causing the infection?" Jones finally exclaimed, defensively. "How could I possible know?" he reiterated. "For all I know, it's due to a dirty hypodermic. You guys are so cheap, you probably used the same needle for every hundred recipients of the implant."

With this new thought, the VP turned with a raised eyebrow to his Chief of Staff, but Lowell shook his head no.

"No, we did not use dirty needles" was all the VP said in response.

"Jeez," Jones exclaimed, noting the interchange.

"Anyone else know anything about the implant?" the VP asked cagily, knowing of course that there was another person still working with Jones.

"Well, Maria, but then you know she's not talking," Jones replied darkly. The Chief of Staff sighed. This was going nowhere.

"Well, I suggest you go back to the implant drawing board and try to identify any anomalies related to it. That's all we can go on at this point," the VP snapped. Of course he knew this was not exactly true, since he had everyone he could drum up investigating it, but he didn't want to let Jones off the hook. Plus, he thought there might be something going on that his contacts could not identify. "You know," he continued, looking Jones directly in the eye, "you're responsible for the outcome of this experiment as much as I am. You should be worried. If something's going awry, it's your predicament, too."

"You don't have to remind me," Jones replied evenly. "Believe me, I am concerned. But on the other hand, there's no way you can implicate me in this event, success or failure, it's your show, not mine."

"We'll see," was all the VP said, and with that he stood up. "In the meantime, I suggest you talk to yourself, since there is no one else, and see what you can come up with," he added dryly. "I'll contact you or Lowell here will, tomorrow, to see if you've had any . . ." he paused, "shall we call them insights about this dilemma," he smirked. The two men practically bolted from the room, leaving Jones sitting at the table alone, trying to digest a very bad piece of news. "How many people had been inoculated?" he wondered out loud.

67

Andie decided to stay in town another day before returning to Elliot's house to conduct more research. She wanted to visit with Miss Ellie, and she wanted to examine Claire's personal items that Nathan had passed on to her, alone. She called Elliot from a phone booth in the Metro station, just to be on the safe side.

"That's fine. Everything okay?" Elliot had wanted to know.

"Yes, fine. And you?"

"Okay. I have more research findings I'm excited to show you."

"Okay. Tomorrow then," was all she had said.

"Be careful," was all Elliot had said in response.

No kidding, Andie thought. But a spy she was not, so once again she had no idea anyone was following her. She made it to the hospital late in the afternoon. Fortunately, visitor hours had recently begun. Joel had been right. Miss Ellie was in room 202. Andie was asked to don a hospital mask, "because Miss Ellie is in such a fragile state." *Jeez,* Andie thought. *What was wrong with her?*

She was not prepared for what she saw when she entered the room. Poor Miss Ellie was just lying in bed, staring at the TV on the wall. The volume was muted. She had never been a big person, but now she looked dwarf-like, as though playing a part in a horror movie. Her eyes were sunken and hollow. Her skin was a pale white, and her bandaged right arm was hanging in a contraption that was secured to the foot of her bed by pulleys. It looked as if the bandage was seeping. She looked at Andie without turning her head. Andie thought she could detect a slight smile.

"Miss Ellie, I just found out you were sick," Andie heard herself saying. "I wanted to see how you are doing? How are you feeling?"

"Not bad," was the soft, unbelievable response. Andie approached her bed and asked if she wanted her pillows fluffed up. Miss Ellie nodded yes, appreciatively.

"Have they found out what it's not?" Andie wanted to figure out what they had at least ruled out, if she could.

"Well, they say it's not a virus, and it's not bacterial, but other than that, they just don't know."

"How strange. What's wrong with your arm if I may ask?"

"It's all festered up. I think it's where it began, but then what do I know? Could you hand me that juice, please?" Miss Ellie asked. Andie could tell that she was quite weak.

"So what's next?" Andie asked, rather alarmed that Miss Ellie seemed so nonchalant about her condition.

"Well, I suppose they'll wait to see if I can be healed. I don't talk to the doctors. They just read the charts and look at my eyes and arm and then leave."

"Do you want anything that you're not getting here? I could bring some food in for you."

"Oh, Andie, that's not necessary. I'm not all that hungry, actually. But you could visit as often as you like."

"Of course, Miss Ellie. I will, of course." Andie returned to the chair beside Miss Ellie's bed, and the two women chatted for a while. "Do you have any relatives, Miss Ellie?" Andie asked gently. "Anyone here in the area?"

"No," Miss Ellie said. "You know I never married. My only relative was a cousin, and he passed away a couple of years ago, and although he and his wife always wanted children, it just wasn't to be. I'm so fortunate to have WSSN. You all are my family." Andie smiled and nodded in agreement. After a short while, Andie could see that Miss Ellie wanted to sleep, so she squeezed her hand and promised to return soon, maybe not tomorrow, but soon. Miss Ellie seemed grateful.

Andie left the hospital even more distraught than she had been all day. This was very sad. And Miss Ellis had said that Simon had only visited her once. "He's busy, dear," was her excuse for Simon's absence. It seemed so callous of him, Andie thought. He just wasn't himself these days, or so it seemed. And the fact that Miss Ellie's right arm was infected and Simon's was in a sling may not be a coincidence. Then Andie stopped dead in her tracks. DeeDee's arm was in a sling the last time she saw her, and then Simon said she was just reporting the regular data facts in the evening. Andie had not been watching WSSN lately, but she decided she better ask Simon about this potential coincidence the next time they talked. By the time she left the hospital, she realized that the afternoon had turned into a black, inky night. She headed home; eyes were watching, but no moves were made.

68

Between three and four thousand was the answer from a very calm Dr. Veritos. "You should not vhorry. This is just vhone person. So vhat? Vhat are they all upset about? Vhone person has a problem."

But just then Jones's phone rang. It was Lowell. "Jones? Just an FYI. Apparently there are people all over the D.C. area experiencing unidentifiable infections that seem to be emanating from their arms. We have intelligence gathering this information, so don't tell anyone. So far, it doesn't look like any of the medical community has detected a pattern, but that may not last for long. These guys talk to each other all the time. All we need is for someone to die, and then we're exposed. We've got to get to the bottom of this ASAP. The VP is steaming. Call if you find out anything." And that was that.

Jones could care less that the VP was "steaming," as Lowell had so aptly put it. But he sure as hell did not want someone to die. Maria's death had been too much already.

Jones turned back to Dr. Veritos, who was looking at him quizzically. Now it was more than one, and Jones proceeded to tell him what had just transpired. Veritos became agitated with this news. He went to his computer and began to review his protocols. Jones sat with him. When they got to the implant section, Jones noted that the tiny microchip-sized capsules containing the serum were purchased in bulk. "How did you apply the serum to those capsules?" he questioned Veritos.

"I created a tray holder for them, a hundred per tray, and inserted the serum into each vhone personally, with a very tiny, tiny needle. No funny business."

"But you bought the capsules," Jones continued.

"Of course. I could not make the capsules. No need. They are too cheap to not buy. I got the cheapest vhones, too," he continued, bragging.

"How do you mean?" Jones asked rhetorically, not really caring.

"There vhere three types, the vinyl, silicone, and latex. The latex is very cheap compared to the other two. Very nice and cheap."

Jones slowly looked up from the screen, his eyes resting on the boastful Veritos. *"Are you nuts? What kind of doctor are you?"*

Dr. Veritos jumped out of the desk chair, backing up to the wall. He had never seen Jones this mad before. The transformation had occurred within a split second. "I'm not a doctor. I told you, I'm a scientist. I just know doctoring things."

"Well, you don't know enough doctoring things, apparently," came the snarled response. "Haven't you ever heard of latex reactions, allergies to latex, doctors asking patients if they have had a bad reaction to latex gloves. *Where have you been, man?"*

Dr. Veritos sat down, in a corner chair far away from Jones. "I've been in Austria. I never heard of something like that," he said meekly.

Jones was dumbfounded. But the damage had been done. He'd have to figure out a way to tell the VP and still get away with his hide, and his money. He feverishly began researching the topic of latex allergies, trying to determine what percentage of those inoculated would be affected. Working in percentages was always the best tactic. It reduced the personal nature of events and, more importantly, the size of the impact. He figured if it was twenty percent, for example, he could say that of the two thousand inoculated there would be at most four hundred with some slight reaction. And then they could get down to treatments. It seemed like the best approach, and the healthiest one all the way around.

He did his research. What he found was not reassuring. From a web source titled *Family Doctor Online,* he read that allergic reactions included rashes, hives, bumps, sores, and cracks. Furthermore, being allergic to bananas, avocados, chestnuts, kiwi fruit, or tomatoes could be a precondition to developing an allergy to the rubber. Jones noted that respiratory illnesses were related to the corn starch powder mixing with the latex in latex gloves, but thankfully that was not something at issue here. Another unfortunate connection, however, between those who tended to be allergic was if a person had had a lot of operations, especially during childhood, he or she was more prone to having a reaction. One descriptive sentence scared the hell out of him. *"A latex-sensitive person can also have a life-threatening allergic reaction with no previous warning or symptoms."* Uh, oh. There was simply no way he was going to reduce this group to percentages. There were too many variables. The people who had been inoculated were not some quasi-experimental group. They were bureaucrats and media persons, plain and simple. Jones left Veritos and returned to his apartment. He needed to think.

About the same time Jones was leaving Veritos's home, Andie had finally reached her apartment. It had been such an exhausting day. "My God," she exclaimed when she sat down with a glass of wine, some nice jazz, and Claire's phone. "Okay, let me see what you saw, Claire. Please."

Finding the right password did not take her too long. She tried a few work-related words and then typed in sadie. It was a match. First, she scrolled through the text messages. There were only a few, and they did not seem to reveal much. Andie was surprised, but then she remembered Nathan describing a rather scant number of friends that Claire might have been corresponding with while in Iraq. The last one entered L8R (later) didn't really mean anything to her. The recipient was "unknown."

Andie was disappointed, but quickly moved on to the actual phone calls received, dialed, and saved. There seemed to be quite a few between Claire and Nathan, but what Andie was really looking for was who called Claire to tell her to go to Fallujah. Then, she saw it; at least she was seeing something . . . a 202 area code, indicating D.C. But the number was definitely not WSSN. Claire would have known that, too, Andie mused. She looked to see how many times a call was made to her from this number. Twice. Two days before the day Claire was killed and the day of her death. Andie wondered if there was any way she could figure out who the number belonged to without dialing it.

After a couple of minutes trying to get around the inevitable, she put on her coat and went down to the little convenience store inside her apartment complex, to the pay phone. She made the call and waited. It rang three times before the recorder kicked in. A man's voice stated, "Not available. Leave a message." Andie hung up. She looked around, waited about a minute, and tried again. This time the recorded message did not engage. She wanted to let it ring as long as it would, so she stood there waiting and staring out the door. She then noticed a burly figure standing across the street from her apartment, leaning against a car. It looked as if he was looking up, toward her apartment. Andie was surprised. Why would someone be hanging out at this hour? The traffic had calmed down; there were few pedestrians. In fact, Andie noticed that the Indian woman who owned the store was preparing it for closing, which meant it was close to 11:00 p.m. The ringing ended suddenly, with the well known shrill tone. Andie hung up.

"Have a nice night," Andie said on her way out.

"Thank you. You have a nice night," Gita said, in her lilting accent.

Andie returned to her apartment. She made sure she did not change any lighting. Her blinds were open, however, so she had to approach one of her front windows from an angle so she could look out the corner. Sure enough, the man was looking up toward her window. Andie's heart started beating quickly. Damn! She decided to turn off her lights first and then close her blinds. She had more work to do. But leaving the blinds open, knowing someone seemed to be watching her, would not allow her to concentrate. It gave her the creeps.

A half hour later, she continued to review Claire's phone. There were no more surprises regarding the calls. Then she clicked on the photos. *Oh* . . . Andie began to feel clammy. The photos depicted a city, or what used to be one. Andie clicked through them quickly, mostly because she did not want to view them for too long at this point. They were too disturbing. Soon, however, she was looking at what appeared to be another view of the city. It was also decimated, but this one showed mass graves. Andie put her fist to her mouth at one point. It looked as if a family was huddled around a small pyre, a child's pyre was all she could conclude. Then Andie noticed that Claire must have squatted close to the ground because the next photos were shots of DU. They were all over the place, in and among the leveled buildings, just as Nathan had described.

Andie stopped at this point. She figured she'd viewed about half of the full set. She sat there for several minutes. Claire must have been sickened by all of this, Andie contemplated as she moved to the kitchen to heat some milk, wondering if she would ever be able to sleep now. What Claire was going to do with the photos, Andie could only guess. It was part of the puzzle she was slowly putting together. She was sure she was getting close, especially with Elliot's help, and now Nathan's as well.

When she started to leave the kitchen, she decided to take a peek out of the window again. The man was still there. Andie just shook her head as she returned to her bedroom. Was it the DoD? They had the List, so why would it be them? She decided it didn't matter. The point was she was being followed, and now her return trip to Elliot's was going to be hindered. She decided she would figure out an escape strategy tomorrow. She bet that guy down there wasn't too familiar with the Metro lines. Just as she slipped her robe off before getting into bed, Andie saw the long-forgotten *Candide* sitting on her night stand, the one that Elliot had loaned her. Sipping her milk, she decided to take a look.

69

"I have information that will shed light on your dilemma," Jones said to the VP, implying that *he* owned the problem and not Jones. At that very moment the VP was orchestrating his next exciting event in Iraq for a positive media blitz and hoping it would have the secondary effect of diverting any possible attention from the silly woman with the infected arm.

"Listening," was the gruff response.

"Apparently, the cause is an allergy to latex."

"What's latex got to do with it?"

"The implant is made with latex."

The pause seemed like an eternity to Jones. He could just imagine how this fact was sinking into the VP's knotted brain.

Finally. "So, what's your guess as to how many of our . . . recipients if you will, have an allergy to latex?"

"Probably two to five percent," Jones lied. This was the only strategy he had been able to come up with once he had left Veritos and returned to his apartment. He could do nothing else, he had decided. It was the only way to save his butt. He figured that, by the time the doctors had put two and two together, he'd be long gone. He couldn't afford to tell the VP the truth. But he was totally blown away by the VP's next comment.

"Well, let's go get them," the VP said, matter-of-factly.

"What?" Jones asked, trying to buy time to digest this response.

"I'll have a squad check all the hospitals within the Beltway and track down any complaints. I'll get doctors to remove the microchip, and that will be that. Once I have organized the process for treatment, I'll contact you and we'll oversee the operation, so to speak," he said, laughing hugely.

"Uh . . . " Jones started to protest, but the VP had already hung up.

Jones decided it was time to get out of Dodge. The VP had gone nuts. Forget cleaning up last minute details. He had his money. That was all that mattered. He had already transferred Veritos's share to his account and had provided a good chunk to Maria's family, anonymously, of course. There was just one other thing he had to do, then he would be free. "Yep. No doubt about it. Time to go," he muttered to himself.

The VP was furious, but in his sick way he was laughing. He was thinking about Jones's reaction to his response. *Ha, ha, ha,* he roared to himself. God, he was getting slap-happy due to lack of sleep, he thought grimly, but there was just too much to do and no one but him to rely upon. Now this. What a nightmare. He had been serious when he told Jones he'd contact the hospitals. He hadn't been serious when he told Jones he expected him to join in the treatments. He knew there was no way Jones was going to volunteer his time. He'd just wanted to light a fire under the man and watch him scramble. *Ha, ha, ha.*

He managed the formation of his squad, as he had referred to it, himself. Within an hour he had his team assembled. They numbered in the hundreds and included all of the private contractors, including five doctors, he had employed over the past two years. Unfortunately, he had to terminate all current assignments, but he had no choice. He needed a huge manpower to accomplish what he had in mind. They were told to wear dress suits and spread out in pairs. They would cover all hospitals and infectious disease centers in Maryland, Virginia, and D.C. Their instructions were clear. Eradicate this little irritation before it could become a big one. Take no chances. Find out if any of the "recipients" had visited recently and follow up with them. Get them to one of the doctors *today*.

70

When Andie awakened the next morning she quickly went to her window. *Thank God.* The man was gone. *Thank God,* Andie said again, under her breath. She hurriedly showered, gobbled down some yogurt with coffee while repacking her bag for a stay with Elliot, and then headed off to see Miss Ellie one more time before leaving D.C. She needed to get there before 10:30 in order to make visiting hours.

She entered room 202 without knocking, thinking that Miss Ellie might be asleep, in which case she would just leave the flowers with a note. The man in the bed was certainly not Ms. Ellie. Nor was he a happy camper upon seeing Andie.

"Who are you?" he questioned loudly.

"Sorry," Andie replied with embarrassment, backing into the hallway to leave and also to check the room number again. It was definitely 202. She turned quickly and went to reception.

"Excuse me?" she asked a young woman who was chewing gum and looking at a computer screen. She slowly raised her eyes to look at Andie. "Excuse me, but can you tell me where Miss Ellie, I mean Ellie Watson is?" she asked politely. "She was in room 202."

The woman turned to her computer and typed in the name. A short gasp came from between her lips. She glanced at Andie and then stood up. "I'll be back in a minute. Are you her daughter?"

"No," Andie said, "a good friend."

As she stood there waiting and worrying, Andie noticed two men in suits escorting a man with his arm in a sling to a waiting car. They were chatting easily enough, but the man looked uncomfortable, as though his laugh was forced.

"Uh, Ms.?" Andie turned to see an exceptionally well-built, clean-cut doctor, name tag indicating Neil Turner, M.D., standing next to the receptionist. He was the one who had spoken. "Are you a relative of Miss Watson's?"

"No, I already said I was a good friend," Andie replied, sounding frustrated while looking at the receptionist.

"Well, I'm afraid I have some bad news. Miss Ellie passed away during the night. She was in no pain, I can assure you."

"What?" Andie could feel her heart start to beat faster and her hands shake. "She passed away? I was just visiting with her. What did she die from?"

"Um . . ." the doctor said looking at a chart, "it was sepsis."

Andie was indeed shocked. "Well," she said, not knowing what to do or say. "Well, is she in the morgue? I'd like to talk with my organization and see what we're going to do about a funeral."

"Oh, I'm sorry, but a brother came for her body early this morning. He said she had a burial plot by her parents, and he planned on burying her there." Andie glanced over at the receptionist, who was looking down at the desk. She saw her glance at the doctor for a second and then look down again, seemingly avoiding eye contact with Andie.

Something was wrong. She looked back at the doctor. He was just standing there. "Is there anything else I can do for you?" he asked kindly enough, but there really had been no compassion, no condolences. Andie shook her head and turned to go. She turned back to ask about the brother's name, but the doctor was already gone. The receptionist was looking back at her computer screen. It was as if the entire episode had not even transpired, as if she didn't exist. Andie marched out of the hospital and walked to the Metro station. She remained on red alert as she made her way to one train and then another, getting as close as she could to Frederick. All the while she mulled over the latest incident. Ms. Ellie . . . gone forever. Tears came to her eyes as she considered the thoughtful, selfless woman, alone; all alone, in fact. So who was the phantom brother really? Why was the hospital covering up the death of a patient? Andie wondered what Miss Ellie had really died from.

Once she reached the northernmost station, Andie took a cab to a car rental and got a compact, which she drove the rest of the way to

Frederick, watching out her rearview mirror almost more than her front windshield. Then, once she reached the town, she drove around it for about an hour before heading to Elliot's. It was during this time that she received a bizarre call from Craig.

"Andie, how's it going? Where have you been?" Craig asked sincerely.

"Craig. Hi. Oh, Craig, it's so sad. Miss Ellie died." Andie blurted it out before she could stop herself.

"What?"

"Yeah, can you believe it?" she asked, and proceeded to tell Craig everything she knew that had happened to the poor woman.

"Did you call Simon?"

"Yes, of course," Andie replied. She had called him as soon as she left the hospital. "He was very upset. He and some other staff were on the way to visit her when I called. I'll find out more tomorrow once he's talked to the folks there."

Craig was silent for a few seconds and then he said softly, almost secretly, "Andie, I think Jesus must have had plans for her, so he took her. It's as simple as that."

Andie actually looked at her phone. It was Craig's number showing on the front. "Well, Craig, I'm sure that would be consoling to some, but I doubt Miss Ellie would agree with you. I think she had plans to work for WSSN until she was eighty or older."

"Maybe," was all he said. Silence again. "Well, Andie, I am sorry. I wanted to remind you not to forget that Commerce is having a nice Christmas party, and you are invited, as my friend." Andie couldn't believe how quickly Craig had changed subjects. It was so uncharacteristic. She didn't want to get into it with him though. "Of course," she said. "It's next Friday, right?"

"Yeah. Come to my office around 6:00 if you can, but I'm sure I'll see you before then," he said, as he quickly added that he had another call to attend to.

"Okay. Thanks again," Andie said as she clicked off and started driving again.

About three minutes later her phone rang again. She had just pulled into a package store to pick up a bottle of wine to take to Elliot's. She glanced down, but did not recognize the number.

"Hello?"

"Hi, Andie. This is Tim Walsh," the friendly voice on the other end said cheerfully.

"Who?" Andie couldn't put a face to the name.

"I introduced myself to you at Claire's memorial. I'm the blogger."

"Oh . . . hi, Tim," Andie said, talking as she got out of the car. "How are you doing?"

Thirty minutes later, Andie knew exactly how Tim Walsh was doing, including the Christmas presents he had purchased for his wife and kids. But, most importantly, she learned that he was heading back to Iraq in a couple of days. They agreed to meet to talk about his work with Claire before he left.

Once night fell she drove to Elliot's and parked as before. It was obvious he was glad to see her, and she was just as happy to see him. It just felt right.

She immediately told him about the man she thought had been tailing her. Elliot had already been observing his camera screen, upon Andie's entrance. He now seemed satisfied that, indeed, she was not followed. They sat together in front of the beautiful fire he had started, and Andie proceeded to tell him about her meeting with Nathan and the death of Miss Ellie, remembering to include her concern for Simon's arm as well as DeeDee's. Elliot seemed quite pleased with the fact that Nathan was returning to Iraq to continue Claire's work, at least in some vein, but he was deeply disturbed to hear about Miss Ellie, more so than Andie would have imagined, given that Elliot had never even met the woman.

"Are you sure she died of sepsis?"

"Elliot, I told you, I have no idea how she died. That's what the doctor told me. I planned on checking him out once I got here. What are you thinking? I mean, why are you so interested, not that it isn't kind of you," Andie added, not wishing to sound ungrateful for his sympathy.

"It just sounds peculiar to me," Elliot responded somberly, as he got up to put another log on the fire. "What did you say the doctor's name was again? Neil Trudeau?"

"No, sorry for the misunderstanding; it was Neil Turner."

Elliot stopped suddenly. "Oh," was all he said.

"What?"

"I think I recognize the name, that's all. He may not be employed by that hospital. I mean, if he's who I think he is, and by your description I believe he is, although I haven't seen him for a while."

"Who is he then?" Andie asked, needing to know.

"Well, the last I knew for sure, he'd lost his license to practice."

"Oh," Andie replied. "That doesn't sound good or ethical."

"Yeah," Elliot agreed. "Neither. Let me follow up on this, okay, Andie? I know you're getting close to uncovering just about everything Claire was able to pass on to you, so I'll take on this part of the mystery."

"Of course, Elliot," Andie said. "But I wouldn't be so sure I'm getting close. I think we have more to uncover." She had decided it was a good time to present Claire's phone record and photos and the memory stick that Nathan had given to her.

"Let's get to it," he said smiling.

71

Nathan had been home for less than forty-eight hours, but he was already getting a sense of acute restlessness. It was nice to see his family and visit with friends, but his unfinished business surrounding Claire's death, and to some degree Michael's, made him anxious and despondent. He needed to return to Iraq. He couldn't wait. He was afraid if he waited much longer, he might miss something or someone who had knowledge about what had taken place. Too, he had to admit somberly, he was a bit worried that if he waited much longer, he would not have the resolve to return. It was too easy to sit back, watch "reality" programs with his friends, become distracted from the global realities that were taking place, and pretend, as most news shows seemed to be doing, that life was just grand. There were Hollywood movie stars getting married, getting divorced, having babies, adopting babies, and on and on that his friends seemed to like to talk about, and his mother liked to watch the talk shows on RW&B, which involved a lot of yelling but nothing really substantive.

Yeah, he needed to go. He made his arrangements first and then told his family at dinner. They all simply stared at him, then his mother began to cry. He got up and went around to rub her shoulders. His father and two brothers nodded in understanding, and his younger sister, who was only twelve, didn't really understand what the fuss was all about.

Nathan left for Iraq the next morning.

By two o'clock, the same day Andie found out that Miss Ellie had died, the VP's squad had identified two hundred ten "recipients" with arm infections due to the implant. Stories of other sick people were plentiful, however. The VP didn't like the numbers. Even more distressing was figuring out a way to get the damned implant out.

"You're sure that is the only remedy?" the VP was practically yelling at Dr. Turner.

"You have to remove the latex, which is the source of the problem. There is simply no other solution."

"How can something so tiny create such havoc?" the VP asked, not really wanting an answer.

"Well, the interaction. . . ." Dr. Turner noticed the scowl and discontinued his explanation.

"The old lady has been taken care of?" the VP asked callously.

"Yes, sir. I told you, we took care of the situation." Given the VP's mood, the doctor did not even bother mentioning the young woman who had inquired about her.

"Okay, let's go ahead and set up a clinic to remove the piece. Knock out the patients, tell them it's a new procedure for reducing infection, tell them . . . I don't care what you tell them. Just get the implant out and the infection under control. We don't want the doctors in the area to catch on to this. Thank God you were there last night, and were able to cover up that lady's death. Just think what might have happened. Okay, get out," he ended.

The doctor got up and walked out. He didn't care how the VP treated him. He knew he was a better man.

But Elliot knew differently. Dr. Neil Turner was a former colleague. The two of them had worked in the same NIH laboratory years ago, following Elliot's teaching days and Neil's internship. Both had worked for an independent contractor. Elliot was the scientist, Neil the physician. Elliot had been hired to use his scientific knowledge and experience to experiment with more radical approaches to addressing depression and mood disorders. Neil was there to determine their application.

As often happens, Neil did not have enough self-discipline to avoid self-medicating. He was caught during a random drug test and summarily fired. At that point, the young doctor had fallen on hard times, succumbing to the addiction he had been able to control up until then. Elliot had known him to be pretty wasted during the first few months following his termination. Later, years later, Elliot had heard that Neil was trying to reapply for his license in other states. Now, as Elliot researched his re-emergence, he discovered that Neil was working for a private medical contracting firm, with a license to practice in the District of Columbia. Elliot wondered if he'd really been able to overcome his predilection to drugs. He hoped so, but doubted it.

Once he'd explained this to Andie, she began to see that Miss Ellie's disappearance was indeed intentional. "My only guess is that her death was so unusual that someone did not want it to become known, to anyone," she said to Elliot. He agreed.

"But why would anyone care?" Andie asked, almost to herself. "I imagine they have already cremated her," she added, feeling the tears welling up in her eyes. Elliot got up to get a tissue for her.

"The only thing we can do now is see what else Claire put on her last CD," he said, trying to comfort Andie. They had already looked over her photo logs, and Elliot had begun to track down the phone number with the 202 area code. He had narrowed it down to a mere handful of locations. Finding the person who had made the call was another story.

"I don't know if there is a connection between Miss Ellie's death and what we've uncovered from Claire so far, but the fact that they both worked for WSSN does seem suspicious, don't you think?" Andie asked, looking up after dabbing her eyes.

"It does," Elliot agreed again. "I think there must be a link . . ."

"And the fact that Simon has a problem with his arm," Andie said, snapping her fingers suddenly. "Oh, Elliot, I should have called Simon," noting that it was quite late already. "I'll have to wait until tomorrow."

"Yeah, you can catch him in the morning. You're right, though. Actually, Simon's arm problem is probably more closely related to Miss Ellie than Claire's work," Elliot added.

"I know. I was just thinking that myself," Andie said, standing up. "Well . . ." she said, taking a deep breath, "let's go look at Claire's CD."

The two of them quietly returned to the underground office. After the previous incident with the man who had identified Andie and the house, there was absolutely no question that their research regarding Claire always had to be secure.

During that same evening, the VP was also taking a deep breath. He believed his quick actions and planning had prevented a huge, nasty crisis from occurring. He was relishing his success by having a drink and once again observing his maps. He wished he hadn't bled on the one area, but he was reluctant to exchange the map for another one. He had already made so many notations on it. It was almost like an old friend, he projected. As he looked down on the countries and his newly designed infrastructure, he had a brilliant idea. It was the solution for his "event" that the media would gobble up with glee. He, the VP, would make a visit to the region, and to the war-torn country. Somehow, he would be able to demonstrate that the needs of the country, and the region for that matter, were being met. He, the VP, would show to the world that the people were grateful for his presence, well, the American presence, and that his genius leadership would be held up for everyone to view.

He knew the President would be disappointed, maybe even angry, but it would be too late for him to argue against the visit, and once he, the VP, was received with such adoration and gratitude, then he could not say anything against him. "He's such a lightweight, anyway," the VP sneered, talking aloud to himself and taking another sip of his drink. He needed to get the Secretary in on the logistics for the trip and the choreographing of the scenes. But first, he decided, it was time to quit being nice. The entirety of Iraq needed to be cleaned up, and he would be too old or dead if he left it up to the current administration there to make it right. A few bombs here and there would straighten things out mighty quickly, he determined. They could be called mistakes in retrospect; they'd already used that tactic, and it had worked every time. There would be time afterwards to make amends to some of the more damaged areas, and to make show models out of some of the victims. He would be their savior, as well. He liked the use of that word . . . savior, he nodded to himself, unable to recognize the irony.

In the end, he'd get his plot of land there from where he could direct and control the region and from where he could design the "new world," which he had so cleverly mapped out here in front of him. *If he didn't do it, someone else surely would,* he reasoned, muttering to himself. He wanted to ensure that the history books would be full of him, not some tin horn pretender.

72

Once Andie and Elliot plugged in the memory stick, their lives were altered forever.

"Hello," Claire said calmly, smiling slightly. She was sitting in what appeared to be a small hotel room.

"She's in a different place than before," Andie commented, for no real reason except to break the stunning effect.

Elliot reached over and adjusted the viewer slightly, to make the picture sharper.

"Well, I couldn't seem to provide you with all of the information I wanted to on the previous tape . . . too many spies around here . . . " she said, shaking her head, "just too many. It's really been hard. But I want you to take seriously that this DU is everywhere we've been, here and in Afghanistan. The problem is," she continued, but now it looked as if she might cry, ". . . the problem is . . ." and she looked down for a moment, regaining her composure, ". . . the problem is," she started for a third time, ". . . is that they're trying to wipe us out, too."

Andie and Elliot looked at one another. They didn't know who "us" referred to. "They're trying, and succeeding I must say, to eliminate us with these . . . *these WMDs.* You know, you know how the government is always saying one thing and doing the opposite, you know, like swiftboating . . . well, folks, this is the ultimate. The war on terror is a war we are creating, not the war we're trying to win. The WMD threat is real, but it's our WMDs. And . . . well, they're using them here to wipe us out . . ." she swallowed hard and said ". . . all of the black and brown people of the world, including yours truly. Don't forget, Michael was Lebanese. So, I've got to tell you again, well, you know, I've already said it, it's working. The DU is lethal. So many folks are sick, and their children are really sick. Please don't think I'm crazy, and no, this is not a conspiracy theory. There's too much evidence. Some of the other journalists here and there are beginning to catch on to the government machinations, so, Andie, watch out. If there is a way for them to sway you and your beliefs, they'll find it and use it. They can't afford to let this out, but there are so many people coming here now that it will be hard for them to contain the information. So, really, watch out, they will try whatever it takes to convince you that their movement is the right one. I don't have much time, but I want you to focus on this research from Leuren Moret that I'm going to read to you. It's up to you now to expose this crime.

"The US war in Afghanistan made it clear that this was not a war *in* the third world, but a war *against* the third world. In Afghanistan, where eight hundred to one thousand tons of depleted uranium were estimated to have been used in 2001, even uneducated Afghanis understand the impact these weapons have had on their children and on future generations:

" *'After the Americans destroyed our village and killed many of us, we also lost our houses and have nothing to eat. However, we would have endured these miseries and even accepted them, if the Americans had not sentenced us all to death. When I saw my deformed grandson, I realized that my hopes of the future have vanished for good, different from the hopelessness of the Russian barbarism, even though at that time I lost my older son Shafiqullah. This time, however, I know we are part of the invisible genocide brought on us by America, a silent death from which I know we will not escape.'* (Jooma Khan of Laghman province, March 2003)."

Now, instead of running away as she had appeared to do previously, Claire just sat there, staring out. Then . . . the screen went black.

Andie and Elliot remained seated in front of the screen in silence for quite some time. Andie was strategizing as to how she could expose this truth. Elliot was reminiscing about Claire and what had happened to her, because of her beliefs and her dedication. Neither apparently wanted to discuss her latest and last revelation, however. Finally, Andie spoke. "Elliot, this is going to be really, really hard. This exposure will not be appreciated by, well, by many. But I cannot not try."

Elliot sat in the chair, elbows on his knees, with his head resting on the palms of his hands. He nodded, still staring at the blank TV screen. "I know. We both have to try. It's the only patriotic move we can make."

Andie was surprised to hear him use the word patriotic. It had been so overused by the administration that she could only think of it in cynical terms these days. But he was absolutely right. It was the only patriotic thing to do. It was why Claire had done what she did, even though she apparently knew that she may lose her life. The same could be said about Michael, Andie reflected silently.

"I need to get some rest," was all she could reply in acknowledgment. She was dead tired. She had some ideas, but none of them were laid out well enough in her mind yet to articulate to him.

"Yes, it's late," Elliot agreed, looking at his watch. "Coffee's on at 6:30, just like last time," he said wearily, getting up and observing the camera screen before preparing to exit the underground room. He checked every angle of the surroundings outside before turning out the lights. They headed upstairs.

Early the next morning, Andie was aroused from a very deep sleep by her cell phone ringing. She had forgotten where she was and was a bit disoriented as she fumbled for it by her night stand. The clock by the bed indicated that it was only 4:30.

"Hello?"

"Andie, it's Deidre," DeeDee Morgan's voice rang out.

Andie could hardly believe it. "Where are you Deidre?" Andie asked skeptically.

"Baghdad. You must know it. I'm DeeDee, from WSSN. DeeDee is a nickname, somehow recently assigned to me."

Andie thought she sounded much stronger than when she had communicated earlier. "Are you okay?" Andie asked, truly concerned for her well-being.

"Andie, can I contact you on a land line?"

Andie didn't want to give out Elliot's number, especially before she could figure out what this was all about. "What's your land line number, I'll call you right back. . . . Got it." she said, scribbling it down.

Deidre had hung up.

She called right away, but couldn't get through for over an hour. Finally she made her connection.

Deidre came on with a rather hushed voice this time. "Andie, I have some information that I need to get to you. I realize that you may not trust me, but you're going to have to."

Andie found it difficult to believe this was the same woman, but the familiar, crackly voice was a dead giveaway. "I trust you," Andie said simply. And she did. Suddenly, she felt very close to the woman. Maybe it was seeing Claire and receiving her information, but for whatever reason Deidre wanted to talk with her, she needed to talk with Deidre.

"You asked if I was okay. I presume you were referring to my arm."

"Yes, exactly."

"Well, I had a very bad infection. The doctor I was seeing here in the Green Zone prescribed antibiotics and just kept changing the bandages. He's a really young guy. He told me that he hoped this stint here was his ticket to a private practice back home. I can see why. He really doesn't seem very knowledgeable or experienced. I know he'll be good at dishing out antidepressants. Anyway, it was not getting better. Then, a couple of days ago, I was interviewing a military doctor to see how the military medical teams are holding up. He commented on my arm, and I agreed to show him. He said he thought it looked like it was festering due to some foreign object. He said he could make a small incision to see if he could see anything. Of course, I agreed."

There was a long pause, and Andie thought she had been disconnected. "Deidre?"

"Yes," she whispered. "Please wait a moment."

Another long pause ensued.

Finally, Deidre came back. "Okay, Andie. I'm here," she said rather breathlessly. "I'm going to talk fast, okay?"

"Sure," Andie responded.

"So, anyway, he made an incision, and by using a magnifying eyeset, sure enough, he found something."

"Really? What was it?" Andie asked, clearly surprised.

"I don't know. He didn't know. It's a tiny, tiny capsule. I mean, he showed it to me under a microscope. I laughed a bit, and he did, too, but in the end it remained a mystery. I said I wanted to keep it for posterity sake. And you know what happened next, Andie?"

"No, but I am sure interested in finding out." she replied enthusiastically.

"I started to feel differently. Not because the infection was clearing up, although that did provide me with a great deal of relief. No . . . it was something else. I felt lighter. I felt, and please don't laugh, I felt more balanced. I'm no longer experiencing waves of giddiness that seemed to come and go with certain interactions."

"Deidre, when did he take it out, the capsule, I mean, how long have you been free of it?" Andie asked. Her head was spinning with ideas at this point.

"Ummm, about four days. Time is rather evasive here. Every day seems like the day before. Yes, it was four days ago," Deidre confirmed, whispering.

"So you decided to call me when?" Andie asked, trying to sound casual and helpful.

"It dawned on me yesterday morning that I don't have a friend in the world, especially here in the Green Zone. Then I remembered you, vaguely. Perhaps from some event, but your name kept popping into my head, and I could visualize you from when Simon introduced me. I felt an affinity toward you and finally got the nerve to call you. Andie, I need your help. If you really trust me, and you said you did, can you help get me out of here? I am afraid. Maybe I'm paranoid," she continued, whispering, "but I don't like the way some people are looking at me. I feel like I'm being spied on."

There was the same phrasing that Claire had used, Andie reflected.

"Deidre, I was already thinking that it was time you come home. Why don't you tell Simon you need a break, I'm sure he'll unders . . ." but she didn't get to finish her sentence.

"No . . . not Simon," Deidre whispered defiantly. "Not Simon. He's been asking me to work more closely with Mark, and I just can't stomach that guy anymore. He's too glib, he acts like I should work *for* him. He's very controlling. He keeps insisting that I join his prayer group."

"Okay, okay," Andie said, suddenly putting more pieces together. "Give me until this evening to see what I can do, Deidre. And Deidre?"

"Yes?"

"Guard that capsule with your life."

"You don't have to tell me that. I already figured out that it may not be coincidental or harmless—and, of course, I'm not talking about the infection it wreaked on me."

"Yeah," Andie agreed. "Something is definitely up. Wait for my call. It will probably be quite early your time."

"No problem. Thank you, Andie. Good-bye," Deidre's crackly voice whispered before she hung up.

Andie went to take a shower just as she heard the coffee begin to percolate. She had to catch Elliot up quickly, and then she had some errands to run. This was going to be some day.

73

While Deidre wanted desperately to get out of Iraq, Nathan's return to that country had thankfully gone unnoticed. He "hitched" a ride on a military vehicle from the airport to the Green Zone, showing his WSSN press card to those who asked. As he hunkered down in the tinny jeep, he prayed that he'd make the trip without incident. He really, really needed to get this job done. Fortunately, no IEDs exploded along the three-hour trip, which would have taken twenty minutes under normal circumstances. As he got out, a sergeant commented about the holidays. Nathan said he'd just celebrated them with his family.

"Lucky you," the sergeant said wistfully.

Nathan headed to the smallest set of hotel-like rooms set aside for journalists. Luckily, precisely because of the holidays, there were rooms available. Nathan thought wryly about the fact that many covering the war could leave for the holidays, but those fighting the war obviously could not, although it might appear to viewers in the States that indeed they had. "What a war," he muttered to no one in particular, as he climbed the stairs to his newly obtained room.

As he unpacked, Nathan mentally laid out the activities he planned for the next couple of days. His biggest objective was to remain invisible. But he needed to find a way to get to Fallujah. He obviously needed an Iraqi driver to help him. Claire had been good at obtaining drivers and other contacts. He didn't have the same ability, however, he had to admit. He remembered suddenly that the driver who had returned him to the Green Zone after Claire's death had passed him a sheet of paper with his name on it. He quickly searched through his duffle bag. Ah, thank God. It was inside the flapped pocket. Now he was getting somewhere. And . . . yes, a number was there. He wondered why the driver had given it to him. Maybe Claire had explained her mission, maybe he just wanted to be helpful. Nathan hoped he was still alive.

74

The VP and the Secretary were on civil talking terms again, Lowell noted. They were sharing a drink in preparation for the VP's upcoming promotional event that he'd "designed" for Iraq.

"Let's let bygones be bygones," the VP generously offered to the Secretary. "Actually, I must admit that the Ambassador's kidnapping rescue still turned out some good talking points, so it worked out okay. I mean, I had grander plans, but still . . ." he continued, and then stopped when he saw the scowl cross the Secretary's brow. He needed the Secretary now, so he had to humor him. "I mean, all in all, no harm done, and some good . . . a lot of good. Lowell, you can leave now," he said, turning his back to the man as he motioned toward the door.

Lowell left. Glad to get away.

The VP freshened the Secretary's drink as he ambled to and fro, talking about his ideas and asking about his own security.

"Well, if you want to fly directly into the Green Zone, to make a *big splash* as you so aptly put it," the Secretary responded, smiling as he was starting to feel the effects of the alcohol, "then we'll have to see how to protect you in a Black Hawk from the airport. It may take a platoon of them, but it can be done."

The VP smiled to himself. This was good news. "I was thinking that we can pick two reporters, one from RW&B of course and another from, let's say, an Iraqi news-station."

A frown crossed the Secretary's face this time. "I don't know if you want an Iraqi on board. I mean, it may be dangerous."

"No, no. I don't mean we'll advertise that part of the event. That will be a surprise. I mean when I exit the helicopter, the reporters will follow. It will look like teamwork, and the news going to the Iraqi TVs will indicate that indeed we are on equal footing. We are allies, and the democratic approach to sharing the story will be there for all to see."

The Secretary nodded in agreement, not wanting to rain on the VP's parade by informing him that the majority of the Iraqis did not have access to TV because there was no electricity. Given that this was his first trip to the country since the war began, it was better to let him discover these things once he arrived, if he would even then.

"Okay for the coverage. Who else do you plan on accompanying?" The Secretary was hoping, actually praying, that the VP would not name him.

"Well, you, of course. And I thought we should include a military higher-up, someone from the Command Center at McDill. That will lend credibility to the finality of the event, an olive branch showing, if you will. The military command center will in fact be shaking hands with the Iraqi's military at some ceremony, after our arrival. I haven't gotten that far yet, but you get the picture," he said, taking another gulp and characteristically smacking his lips.

The Secretary did not allow the VP to see his disappointment upon hearing that he was to be included in the entourage. It was his duty. But he knew his wife was not going to like this one bit.

In response he simply nodded and filled his glass a bit more. "It sounds like you've thought this through," he said, smiling like a dutiful soldier.

75

Elliot was quite surprised to hear that Deidre was back in the picture. He looked concerned as Andie relayed their conversation. "It sounds like she's afraid, I mean, really afraid."

"Yeah," Andie agreed. "I got that impression big time."

"What is going on there?" Elliot asked, shaking his head. "It doesn't sound like it's functioning properly. I get the image of a summer camp with a bunch of thugs and bullies on drugs. I mean, who would think that someone would be coercing another person to attend a Bible class for Christ's sake," he asked, chuckling a bit.

"I know. It would give me the creeps. The three people we have heard from, Claire, Nathan, and now Deidre, have all indicated that they are always watching over their shoulders."

"I suspect it's intentional," Elliot said quietly.

"Intentional? You mean creating a corrosive atmosphere? But why?" Andie asked perplexed.

"Divide and conquer. It's one of the oldest techniques in the world, applied socially, economically, politically, you name it. If I had to guess, it's going on in the Green Zone big time. I imagine it's applied to who knows who, how much money you're making, your pay grade, your looks, your school, your parents, your political sponsor. . . ."

"Okay, I get it," Andie replied, suddenly very depressed. "It's not like camp, it's more like high school."

"Whatever," Elliot replied, equally despondent by this point. "The bottom line is that once you're out, you're probably really out. I mean totally ostracized."

"Which adds to the paranoia," Andie commented. "So, Claire gets the cold shoulder first, then Nathan by association, and now Deidre. Not fun, and most likely, not safe."

"That's what I'm thinking," Elliot agreed. "What are your plans now?" he asked.

Andie relayed her ideas, saying that it would be best to get going. "I'll be back this evening, late."

"That's fine. I'll be spending most of the day in the lab."

"What do you do there, if I may ask?" Andie had been putting that question off for a long time because Elliot had never offered to tell her, so she'd assumed he didn't want her to know. Now she had finally just blurted it out.

"I'm still working on mood disorders," he said, easily enough. "I'd like to find some way to address the side effects caused by the drugs that are used to address the disorders, and there are a lot of side effects."

"Pro bono?"

"I told you I had a troubled past. I don't want to work for anyone right now. I'm fine."

Andie just nodded okay. He stood there with his coffee cup in hand, watching her put on her cape and hat. Then he walked over to the surveillance camera and checked it out.

"Be careful, Andie," he said as she left.

"Always," she said smiling.

Following her departure from Elliot's, Andie drove to a coffee shop, The Plowman's Grille, north of Frederick. Tim was already sitting at a booth.

"Thank you for agreeing to meet me sooner than we discussed," she said, shaking his hand as he stood up.

"No problem," he said smiling. "It's coincidental that I live so close by."

Andie barely remembered the man. It hadn't been that long ago, but Claire's memorial had been so emotionally charged that she had not paid much attention. Today he was dressed in a plaid flannel shirt, jeans, and boots. A big, fur-lined suede jacket lay next to him on the booth.

"How are your kids?" Andie asked, since he had gone into such length about their Christmas gifts on the phone.

"Oh, fine. They're very excited about Santa coming," he said, smiling fondly. Andie felt easy with him.

The waitress arrived. Tim asked to have some more coffee, Andie ordered one as well.

"So . . ." she started. "When do you think you'll be going back?"

He frowned slightly. "I'm torn, Andie," he said. "I promised my wife I wouldn't leave before Christmas, but I would like to follow up on some loose ends there. Anyway, I've decided to go after the first."

Andie silently grimaced. She had hoped he'd leave sooner. Nonetheless, she responded by saying, "Wow, what's so urgent?" Tim stared at her. "Oh, yeah, sorry. I forgot that we're competitors," she said, smiling as she continued. "But in all seriousness, you did mention that you wanted to talk with me about Claire."

"True. Yes. I'm not satisfied that her death was accidental. I want to follow up on some of the leads she had there, prior to her . . ." he paused and swallowed, ". . . her being killed." Andie was nodding in agreement while he spoke. "So, you are thinking the same thing?" Tim asked, looking hopeful.

Andie didn't want to tell him that she knew for a fact he was correct, so she said, "Tim, I think there are a number of questions that are still unanswered. I'm glad you're going to investigate. Do you have an inkling as to what she was up to when she died?"

"Well, I know you know," he said confidently. "I believe I gave you the first hint. Well, not me personally. My friend and part-time staff person, Eric, made the delivery for me. He lives in Bethesda. I realize it was probably too cryptic."

Andie looked at him perplexedly. Then it dawned on her: *the man with the envelope!* "Tim, you're right, that was too cryptic. It was not helpful at all. Your friend Eric nearly scared me and my friend to death."

"I can imagine and I apologize. I just wanted to let you know that it existed. DU, depleted uranium. Most have never heard of it, and I was afraid if you came across it, you might not take it seriously. This was like a tip. Given the event, I knew you would recall it, if it came up again. Eric and I figured since we're all three in the news business that we'd run into you sometime soon, so we both carried the envelope with us. He saw you enter the bar that night. I admit, he did not handle it well. I had hoped to call you sooner, but I got distracted with other research. I am sorry," he stated again. "As a blogger, it's harder to get this information out there. We're under the radar, so to speak, which is why we often find ourselves preaching to the choir. But Claire had a chance. She was diligently going about proving its deadly use against civilians. I don't want to lose those leads, Andie. If you have any additional information that would help me, I'd really, really appreciate it," he said sincerely.

And suddenly, just like that, Andie started thinking about switching allegiances, at least in spirit, if not literally. Her mind raced back to scenes of the comfy Bible session corner that used to be the water cooler, the stairway to Simon's office, and the silly man on the TV spouting out the identical ticker tape. While it would be disloyal in one way, she thought glumly, she might be the only person left who could save WSSN from morphing into another tabloid organization. It hurt her heart to think of it like that, but deep down, that's how she thought of WSSN now: a cheap, tawdry, ratings-driven, fake news establishment.

She looked up at Tim, recognizing that she had been lost in thought for some time. He was waiting patiently. She needed him, and he needed her. Why not? Could she trust him? Yes. She wasn't taking chances anymore and had done a lot of research on the man sitting across from her. He was indeed the real deal: a journalist since high school, a sportscaster at one point, a radio announcer in Baltimore, and now a blogger. He apparently wrote bylines for certain local newspapers around the region to beef up his income, and his wife was, fortunately Andie guessed, a CPA. She could support his new avocation, and if his audience could help pay for his trips to the Middle East, as he had mentioned earlier, then she figured they were doing okay.

"I'll help you and tell you what I know," Andie began slowly, "but I need for you to do something in exchange. Is there any way you can go now? To Iraq? I know, I know, your wife and your kids. But what if you return by Christmas Eve? Would that work?" she asked hopefully.

He nodded in agreement, a little. "What is it that you want me to do there?" he asked, sounding worried.

"I need you to help a friend get out of there unnoticed. She's most likely being watched by the authorities, and others, and unusual movements will be observed by them. If you can somehow scope out the situation with her and think of something, I don't care, just something, to get her out, then it will help her, me, and you. She has important information that fits into Claire's research."

Tim looked a bit doubtful. "As you said," Andie continued, "you're under the radar. Authorities have their hands full just keeping the journalists in line. They don't pay much attention to bloggers. Some of them probably don't know what a blogger is," she said.

"Who is she?"

Andie started to say Deidre, but then changed it to DeeDee. "DeeDee Morgan, she works for WSSN."

"I've seen her," Tim said. "Yeah, I've seen her reporting on the evening news."

"That's her. If she leaves under the auspices of the station, it will be obvious, and she may be picked up once she's back in the US. By whom, I don't know, but most likely the DoD. We need to avoid that happening."

Tim nodded again. "It's a tight turnaround," he said, pausing. Andie held her breath. "Okay, I'll do it. As long as I'm back by Christmas Eve, I don't think Edna will be too upset. And this way, she won't be dreading my departure in January."

Andie sighed with relief. "Thank you so much, Tim. Thank you."

"You're welcome," he said. "But don't forget, you and I will be collaborating with shared information once I'm back." Andie nodded enthusiastically in agreement. "I guess we should go over logistics," Tim proceeded. "How, when, etc. I suggest we bring her in either through Mexico or Canada. Canada would be better, but the weather could be bad. Getting her from Mexico, however, will create more airport stops within the US, so I vote Canada," he concluded, motioning to the waitress. "Let's see," he started again, "I'll get there on a Wednesday, Christmas is on Sunday, we'll begin flying back on Saturday, given the time change . . ." he paused, calculating in his head, "we'll be here before Santa," he said, grinning at his little joke. "Will that work for you?" he asked sincerely.

"Absolutely!" Andie loved this man. He was organized, logical, and fast. *What great luck,* she thought.

"Good," Tim said, as the waitress arrived. "Two orders of flapjacks," he said, "and some more coffee for us both."

The waitress quickly turned on her heel, jotting down the order as she started back toward the counter.

Andie protested. "Oh, Tim, I don't think I want any flapjacks right now . . ."

"Andie, this restaurant is famous for its flapjacks. It's known throughout the entire region for them, that and their pecan pie." He pronounced it *Peeekan*. "Honestly, you can't be here and not try one of them."

Andie agreed, reluctantly. As she did, she glanced up, noting the beams in the ceiling. "How old is this place, anyway?" she inquired, suddenly curious.

"Oh, The Plowman's Grille has been here at least since the era of reconstruction," Tim estimated. "I'd say the mid to late 1870s."

"Really!"

"Yes, really. And in this very building, although there have been a number of renovations, and remodeling. I noticed you looking at the beams. I'm ninety-nine percent sure they are the originals."

"I had no idea," Andie said, impressed.

"Yeah, and the same family has owned it the whole time. Charles Winsome's family. The Winsomes were freed after the Civil War, and they began serving food to ex-slaves who were working for a meager living but who were also no longer provided room and board. They made 'cheap eats' for those folks, as the saying goes." Andie had noticed that very phrase on the menu, but had not thought much about it.

At that moment the waitress set down two plates of steaming hot flapjacks. They were already soaking in butter and syrup.

"Forget about the fat and sugar," Tim advised, noticing the concern Andie had on her face. "Just relax and enjoy."

Andie decided to try. She picked up her fork and knife and cut a triangle out of the three-layered mound, noting that it cut like a freshly baked brownie. Placing it carefully in her mouth so as not to burn her lips, she slowly chewed the savory selection.

The senses of flavor and texture arrived simultaneously. Andie decided right then and there that she had never tasted anything so exquisite in her entire life. She thought she must have died and gone to heaven.

76

The first thing the VP did, once the threat of the infection from the implant had been contained, was to reinstate his goons to track down the woman who had had the List, Andie Aaberg.

"We haven't been able to locate her, yet," was the response he'd received. He had no choice but to wait. They'd find her at some point, and then he'd find out what she was doing and if she was dangerous to him.

77

Prior to leaving the Grille, Andie and Tim had decided that Tim would bring DeeDee to Andie, once they returned to the D.C. area. She'd contact him as to where, once they were back in the States. Andie decided Tim didn't need to know where Elliot's place was in advance of his return. Elliot, in the meantime, was prepared to analyze the contents of DeeDee's implant, and Elliot's place seemed like the most logical place to be on Christmas Eve. Elliot and Andie together had decided that even the government would not be out in force during the holidays. They believed they would be safe and able to pursue their research unchallenged from that threat, at least for a while.

Finally, Andie and Tim parted. She wished him luck, both with the trip and his wife and kids. He'd said not to worry. "Everything will turn out okay."

Andie was optimistic as she headed back to her car. She wanted to get to her apartment for more clothes before it got much later. She looked around, trying to see if anyone was watching, but the coast looked clear. As she headed out of Frederick, she decided to stop for some more wine at the same package store she'd stopped at before. Elliot had been so kind as to be preparing meals and making sure the coffee was always available. As she passed through the door, she immediately saw him, Elliot. His back was to her as he was at the register, but it was him. She was surprised, since he had indicated that he would be remaining at his home all day, but she decided he'd changed his mind, obviously. She approached him just as he was turning to leave.

"Hi, Elliot," she said happily, before noticing the earring. Now, it was obvious that the man was not Elliot, but damn, Andie thought, he sure did look like him. He could have been his twin. He had the same lanky build, same intelligent brow, same brownish sandy hair, although she did notice a bit of gray around the temples. He even dressed like Elliot. The man looked directly at her when he heard her speak, then walked around her and out the door. He got into a dark sedan; it looked like a Honda or maybe a Lexus, she couldn't be sure. He was carrying only a bottle that the cashier had put in a brown sack.

"Do you know that man's name?" Andie asked the cashier.

"Never saw him before," the man behind the counter said, as he moved to stack some more cigarette cartons above the register.

She bought her bottle of wine and left. How strange, she thought. She recalled him staring at her when she called him Elliot, almost as though he knew she was talking to him. She wondered what Elliot would say when she told him he had a twin. After dropping off the rental, she got on the Metro and headed to D.C.

On her way, once above ground, she called Craig to see if he wanted to meet for a late lunch. He sounded happy to hear from her and was fine for it. They planned to meet at a restaurant near Commerce, around two-thirty.

After picking up a couple of sweaters and socks from her apartment, Andie called Simon.

"How are you doing?" she asked, the concern obvious in her voice.

"Well, Andie, this has got to be the worst Christmas season I have ever experienced," Simon responded, sounding distraught. Andie had caught him returning from a board review meeting, he said. Even with the ratings skyrocketing, Simon said, he could not be happy. "First Claire, and now Miss Ellie. I just find it so hard to comprehend. You haven't been here for a while, but the morale, which was going great guns for the past couple of weeks, is really low. People cannot understand how Miss Ellie could have died. And they're really upset about not being able to have a funeral for her. We were her family," Simon said sadly to Andie. "We're going to have a memorial for her after the first of the year, I decided. It's too soon after Claire's and too close to Christmas to do it now."

"That makes sense," Andie said. She was really worried about how morose Simon sounded. "By the way, how is your arm?" she asked suddenly, not wanting to forget to find out.

"Okay, I suppose," he replied. Andie didn't think he sounded very convincing.

"Well, make sure you get to a doctor," she recommended. "You can't let something like that go untreated." Even though she thought there might be a connection between Miss Ellie's demise and Simon's own arm problem, she didn't think now was the right time to bring it up.

"Yeah, yeah, yeah," was all he said. "When do you think you'll be coming back to the office?" he asked.

"Well, Simon, it's almost Christmas, and I do have a lot of loose ends to follow up on in order to finish this tribute. If it's okay, I'd rather keep working from home so I can concentrate. I can be back on the second, unless you need me sooner," she added, hoping he would take her up on the suggestion.

"No, no. I think the tribute is extremely important, especially for starting off the new year. Make it really, really good, Andie, I'm counting on you."

"You won't be disappointed," Andie assured him, thinking how very powerful her piece would be, indeed; powerful, telling, and most of all incriminating, she thought after hanging up. Some people needed to be held accountable to make sure Claire had not died in vain. Some big people.

Andie looked out her apartment window before leaving. "Dammit," she muttered, as she noticed the man standing by his car about a block away. Same big guy. What do they want? she wondered for the umpteenth time. They have the List. What more? She didn't think they were aware of Claire's CDs. Those folks were different. Or were they? She thought back to when Elliot had explained to her that she was now in danger, simply by affiliation with Claire, and with the List, and who knows what else. She realized sadly that she was, and it wasn't going to change until she exposed these creeps. Soon. Okay, she'd drive to Craig's but leave her car in the underground parking. She'd have to find another way back to Elliot's.

By the time she'd parked her car, she knew the guy had followed her. Now he was lurking around the corner from the garage. *So what?* she thought. She made her way on foot through the traffic, noting that the cold, windy weather was supposed to become even more intense as the holidays approached. The weather stations had already predicted a white Christmas for the northeast. Somehow, she sighed, it did not make for a nice Christmas this year. There had been too many "incidents" for this to be a cheerful or even a religious celebration, she thought sadly. She saw Craig approaching from the other side of the street, so she slowed down and waited. They were almost to the restaurant. Something looked different about him, she thought immediately. Then she saw it. "Craig, you cut off your ponytail!"

"Yep, I decided to become an adult. Well, sort of," he said, grinning.

"I like it," Andie replied, and she did.

"Really?"

"Yes, really. You actually look more youthful."

"Others have said that, too. It's a funny phenomenon, but I guess it's true. You wear the same haircut you had since high school, thinking that you don't want or need to change it, and then it actually dates you. It was time."

"Time for what?" Andie asked, as Craig held the restaurant door open for her.

"Time to grow up, like I said. It's time to start making some commitments," he said seriously.

"Oh . . . you sound so declarative, like you're going to change your entire life's goals."

They sat down by the window in the now almost empty restaurant.

"Let's just say that I take God and country more seriously," Craig said, as he picked up the menu. Andie didn't necessarily like the sound of that statement, but she picked up her menu, too, without saying anything.

"I'll have the chili and hot tea," Craig said to the waitress. Andie wasn't too hungry after the flapjacks, so she just ordered a tossed salad. Soon, a basket of assorted breads arrived.

Craig asked how the tribute to Claire was going, and Andie replied with mostly ambiguous comments, trying not to be evasive, but not wanting to let Craig know that she was spending time out at Elliot's. She wanted to protect his privacy. She did mention, however, that she had talked with DeeDee and that the woman was scared.

"She's the one who was calling me," she said, rather nonchalantly.

"Really?" Craig was surprised to learn that DeeDee was the mysterious Deidre. "Why the two names?" he asked.

"DeeDee's a nickname. I think she prefers Deidre," was all Andie said.

"What's she afraid of?" Craig asked, while dropping crushed saltines into his chili.

"I don't know exactly," Andie said, although of course she did. "She wants to come home, and I told her I'd try to help."

"Hmm," was all Craig said, as he looked out the window. He assumed Andie meant that she would be sweet talking Simon to bring DeeDee home. "You know, Andie, I think with the new war coverage, the War Column that WSSN is doing is quite good," he said, out of the blue.

"You're kidding!" Andie replied, surprised. "I think it's just like everyone else now. We've become the Stepford Newscasters."

"No. It's good really," Craig continued, smiling. "There ought to be some positive highlights about the war, and WSSN tackling that was a good approach. I watch it every night," he said, grinning again. He motioned the waitress for the tab. "I'll get this," he said. "I've got a lot of fun holiday festivities planned for our department, so I don't have much time this afternoon," he apologized. "You won't forget the Christmas party on Friday?" he said, again.

"I'll be there," Andie said, again, wondering why he kept putting so much emphasis on it and on her attendance.

After paying, he handed Andie her cape, and they walked out together.

"By the way," Andie said, "don't look now, but I'm being followed."

"Really? Why, by whom?" Craig asked, rather alarmed.

"I don't know; it all started with the List."

"Are you in danger?" Craig asked, concerned.

"I hope not. I don't think so, but it's unnerving. Maybe they'll leave me alone once the holidays begin."

"Well, call if you need anything," Craig said sincerely. He gave her a peck on the cheek as they parted at the next corner. Andie headed toward the Metro. She decided to use the same tactic as before, since it had worked and since she didn't know what else to do. The wintry skies were already turning dark.

As Craig headed back to his office, he decided Andie had become a bit kooky and hoped that after the pressure from developing Claire's tribute was gone, she'd snap out of it, especially the paranoid aspects of her behavior. He liked Andie, but the conspiracy-theory part of her thinking was driving him crazy.

78

The VP had locked his office door in order to remove his precious map. He was in the process of writing out the plan for his entrance into Iraq, Baghdad, and on into the Green Zone for the Defense Secretary to review. He looked longingly at the dotted lines on the map, indicating a yet-to-be-built tunnel between the airport and one of Saddam's palaces, in the heart of Baghdad. If only he could have gotten the contractors to focus specifically on that construction, it would have been done in time for him to use. But as it turned out, they had complained that delays in the delivery of materials were preventing them from staying on schedule. Oh, well, he sighed slightly, there would be other opportunities for him to make grand, televised entrances into that edifice. For now, he would be satisfied to enter the Green Zone amidst a swarm of Black Hawks. That would be grand, he reasoned, and deserved. After all, the whole plan had been his idea. It was time for him to get his due credit.

He observed that the map was taking on an almost three dimensional appearance. Over the past week, the VP had added new, bold, black lines indicating where walls had been erected around the city, and two big border walls were now completed between Syria and Iraq and Iran and Iraq, both in strategic transportation locations. Then it happened; rather suddenly, he noticed that the room had become a bit darker, and colder, he thought. He looked around as he rubbed his hands together, to warm them. What he could not perceive were the ghosts of war that had come out of their crevices to watch him, as they often did. They lurked nearby, saddened, and ashamed of this powerful man so full of folly. The VP looked out the window to notice that the afternoon was waning. He decided it must have been his imagination. He simply pulled the desk lamp closer, as he returned to studying the map and his handiwork with admiration. The border walls were made of cement, steel, and wire. The VP used his wife's nail polish to indicate these two constructions. Border walls deserved the most dramatic demonstration, because of what they represented: his control, his power. It would be a while before he could add to these, but so far, so good. The press pretty much ignored complaints from those two countries, and the money going to the Iraqis in charge was too good for them to complain, to anyone. His plan was going mighty well indeed, he surmised.

While the VP was gloating over his map, Nathan was actually on the ground in Iraq, and the sight was not a pleasant one. He had been able to locate the taxi driver, whose name was Yasin as he had learned, and had promised to compensate him generously, at the onset of the trip, in case anything happened. Yasin had agreed. He was not a bad person by any means, he explained to Nathan when he picked him up, in the dead of night, on a corner directly outside the Green Zone. He reminded Nathan that he knew Nathan could not pay him the last time, but now things were worse, much worse, and Yasin had to have some money for risking his life. His father and brothers had been killed in the civil war that had ensued, and he expected he would be next. He was trying to save money for his wife and children, before his almost guaranteed death.

Nathan understood, of course, but the sheer madness and senselessness of the reality in Iraq, for these people, was enough to make you go crazy. He couldn't believe anyone was still trying to survive, much less in such a noble way. He was glad Andie was following up with Claire's self-assigned mission and that he was a part of it. Somehow, this insanity, this lunacy, had to end.

He arranged to have Yasin return to pick him up in two hours. That would give him enough time to find what he needed without rushing. If he rushed, he might kill himself.

They arrived in the city around dawn, as Nathan had planned. Just before he swung the door shut, as he tried to discreetly slip out of the taxi, he said, "I'll see you in two hours, here."

He heard Yasin's whispered reply, "Insha'allah." For the first time in his life, Nathan felt like he truly understood the phrase so often used by the folks here, "God willing." He wished he'd thought to say the same to Yasin.

Fallujah was no more, Nathan observed grimly, as he darted carefully from one rubble pile to another. There appeared to be very little life left here, but he could hear distant shooting, so apparently something was worth fighting for, though he could not guess what it could be. He kept low and tried to look for the shiny stuff. It seemed it was everywhere, but he needed abundant choices to choose from, so he looked for clumps of the deadly material. He saw some near a burned-down building and slowly made his way there. He remained in the shadows of what used to be an office building, he surmised, after noting the remains of a metal desk and leather chair, and what looked like a filing cabinet. Then he saw a hypodermic and realized it must have been a medical building, maybe even a hospital. He put on the gloves he'd tucked in his jacket after taking out the sterile packing case. Then, with the large, oversized tweezers, he looked for what he felt were choice specimens.

Because he was trying to make a design, he looked for the shiniest, smallest, and most colorful DU-tipped shells. Most were gold-colored, some were emerald green, some were yellow-bronzed. He collected two that were the same gold color and then a longer, emerald green one.

They were attractive, unique, colorful, and Nathan thought, hopefully convincing. He placed them gingerly, very gingerly, in the sterile packing case. He looked at his watch; he had thirty-five minutes remaining before Yasin was to return. He was not far from the drop-off, but there was no place to hide by that road, so he sat in the shaded cover of the demolished building and waited.

It was hot, but there were no bugs. There were no birds, no wind, no anything. There was nothing. The shooting had stopped. The only thing that could be deduced by the five senses was the odor. It was not nice. Nathan looked again at his watch. It was time to get moving. He tried to retrace his steps, carefully, across the same stretch as before. Now he was exposed, but it appeared that he was alone, totally. Then, he saw Yasin's Mercedes coming toward him. He veered a little bit here and there to avoid debris on the road and pulled up beside him. Nathan jumped in, and the two took off. Yasin said nothing. He never asked what Nathan was doing. He probably didn't want to know, Nathan guessed. The trip back to Baghdad was uneventful, but took much longer than either man had anticipated. Now it was just past noon, so it was now going to be hard for Nathan to sneak back in. He wanted to stage a drop-off where Yasin would throw him out of the car, but that would endanger Yasin. So in the end, he just got out a block away and walked toward the heavily guarded entrance. The guards recognized him, thankfully, and upon showing his ID, they let him in. Too easy, Nathan thought, but realized that everyone was too tired anymore. Fatigue was taking its toll on everyone, but especially the military. This is how mistakes had been and would be made.

Nathan entered his room, took out the sterile case, his gloves, and tweezers tool, setting them carefully on his dresser next to the velvet jewelry case, and then collapsed on his narrow bed. The sun was shining through his only window, casting shadows on the walls and across his bedspread. He was truly exhausted. The jet lag, coupled with the previous night without sleep, and then the stress and tension from the trip to and from Fallujah, as well as his "collection exercise," had wiped him out. As he drifted in and out of sleep, he pondered his departure from Iraq and re-entrance to the States. He hoped it would work.

While Nathan was sleeping through the day, Tim Walsh arrived. He happened to find a room in the same hotel that Nathan was staying in, although the two did not know each other.

79

Andie heard the door click open upon arriving at Elliot's. She entered, thinking he would be working in the lab or reading or whatever. She was not prepared for what she saw upon entering the living room, however. Elliot and another man, looking quite similar, were sitting across from each other, glaring at each other, it appeared. The coffee table was cluttered with bottles of Old Dominion beer and a bottle of Absolut Vodka.

"Andie, meet Kirk," Elliot said, not taking his eyes off the man.

Kirk turned slightly to glance at Andie and gestured a quick nod before returning his gaze to Elliot.

"Hi," was all Andie said, taking her bottle of wine to the refrigerator and her clothes to the nearby room where she stayed.

"Come on in, Andie," Elliot shouted. "Bring a glass and pull up a seat."

Andie did just that, wondering what was up.

The man she was introduced to was the same man she had seen this morning, in the package store.

"Elliot, please let me make amends," Kirk said, pouring more beer into his glass.

Elliot poured a shot and downed it. "I've told you, Kirk, I'm not going to get into this anymore. You have hurt me too much. You have no conscience."

"That's what I'm saying, let me help fix it. I can give you the formula so you don't have to reinvent it. It will save you a lot of time."

"I don't think I can accept anything from you. I'm so disappointed in what you have become. You are a despicable human being. Just get out!" Elliot said, suddenly raising his voice and pointing at the door. "And don't you dare tell anyone, no one, do you understand me, where I am. Get out, Kirk. You're dead to me."

Kirk stood up slowly, and with slumped shoulders turned to pick up his parka, which had been lying beside him, and then walked out the door. It slammed behind him.

Elliot turned to look at Andie and then leaned back against the chair, sighing. "My brother," was all he said.

"Oh," was all Andie said.

She poured herself a small vodka and drank it quickly. Well, this was new news, she thought. She picked up the empties and wiped down the table a bit. All the while, Elliot just sat. Finally, she returned to her seat and asked, "Do you want to talk about it, him?"

Elliot remained sitting still for another minute or two and then got up and went to the kitchen. Andie could hear him chopping something, so she joined him.

"Thanks for the wine," Elliot said, as he uncorked it. Two wine glasses sat on the counter. He had placed chunks of cheese and apples on a plate. "Let's go in the other room, and I'll tell you about it," he said.

They sat down again, and Elliot began with, "I'm sorry, Andie."

"Why tell me you're sorry? What have you done?"

"It's a bit of what I've done and what I have not done. Kirk is my younger brother, by about a year only. We were very close when we were growing up. We both majored in Chemistry. But Kirk is lazy. He's always been lazy. Maybe it's because I cleaned up after him, who knows. But while I was working at NIH, he called to ask if he could stay with me for a while. He hadn't been able to find work, although I often wondered if he actually even looked.

"Anyway, he moved from California where he'd finished graduate school, and just plopped down in my apartment. Every day, he did nothing except wait for me to get home. I mean, he did the errands and fixed great meals, so he was earning his keep, so to speak, but he wasn't working. When I'd get home, I'd talk about what I was doing at work, my experiments, my colleagues, including Neil Turner, and so on. I was trying to get him excited about working, about finding something. He'd been there for over a month and still hadn't ventured out to make inquiries. Whenever I talked about my mood disorder work, he'd perk up. He'd take notes, and sometimes he even helped me solve some roadblock I'd come across. I was trying to develop a formula that would make folks feel more happiness, an antidepressant, of sorts, that had no side effects. Well, one day he said he'd found something downtown, in D.C., and that he'd be moving out soon. And he did.

"What I didn't know is that he was working for the Pentagon and that he'd taken my formula with him when he applied for work there, as though it was his work. I don't know if anything ever came of that particular formula, but I do know that he met a lot of people who now make up this administration, which is why I decided to build this place. As long as my brother was keeping bad company, I was fair game. So, I've been waiting to see what he'd do. We haven't communicated really since he started hanging out with people I consider to be, um . . . morally challenged, you might say. And I don't mean that lightly. Anyway, he got an offer he could not refuse recently, and he's, in part, behind the strange behavior changes that you have begun to notice. I suspected . . . let me say that I was ninety-nine percent sure . . . he was behind it, but tonight he told me everything. He regrets his role in what has become a huge, illegal, unethical, and medically unsound experiment using many of the civil servants working for the US Government, and . . ." and here Elliot paused and poured more wine into Andie's glass. She noticed he was not drinking. ". . . and some of your media colleagues."

"Oh, Elliot. So . . . Kirk is responsible for this . . . brainwashing?"

"Yes."

"And Claire knew it was in the works?"

"I don't know about that," Elliot said, shaking his head. "She just knew that they, the government, would do anything to prevent the citizenry from finding out about the DU's effect on millions of people, millions of second class people, I should say, rather, millions of minorities, including our own citizens. As we found out from Claire's evidence, the DU's poison doesn't just reside in the person exposed, like Agent Orange did. It's passed on through contact with other people, such as a spouse, and it creates genetic nightmares. It's a true WMD."

Andie nodded, her mind racing. "So . . . well," she started again. All of the loose ends were starting to come together now. "So . . . your telling me 'the leak was a plant' means you knew what was going to happen."

"No!" Elliot said emphatically, getting up and starting to pace. "I knew that Kirk was involved in something nefarious and that he'd lost all integrity. I mean, he lost a colleague because of this!" Elliot exclaimed angrily. "Maria Stone was a beautiful woman and wife and mother, and because of her involvement with Kirk, the government took her out. She was killed on the Beltway only last week."

"Oh my God," Andie cried, suddenly realizing how much danger she really was in.

"So, no, I didn't know the specifics, but I knew something was happening, going to happen. I realized it was happening once you started telling me about the strange behavior you were seeing from people at your office. Then when you told me about Miss Ellie, I realized that, by God, they had actually done it. They had actually violated people's personal and physical rights by injecting them with something. I've been trying to backtrack to see what and how, and I thought I was getting close. I figured once we had Deidre's evidence, I could complete the analysis. I just wasn't sure how they actually injected it. But Kirk told me. It's in a micro implant. It's set up to coincide with some kind of visual presentation that people are watching, which includes a lot of pep rally enthusiasm and word repetition. You know, the one your friend Craig was going to attend before we stopped him. They administer the micro implant in the guise of a bird flu preventive."

"Jesus," Andie said, alarmed. "I honestly can't believe this, Elliot."

Elliot sat back down, saying nothing.

Andie shook her head as if to shake off a cloud of weighty dust. "Elliot, we have to make our plan work. It's imperative now. We can't let Claire and Michael down. We can't let decent people in this country down. They have been betrayed."

"I know, Andie, I agree with you totally. How did you plan to go about getting Deidre out of Iraq and back here?"

"The blogger will do what he can." Andie had called Deidre from a pay phone near the car rental store to let her know that Tim would be arriving in a day. "I don't want to tell you his name," she continued, speaking to Elliot, "just because I don't want him exposed. He's a really nice, dedicated guy. We're going to work together, afterwards, hopefully . . ." her voice trailed off as she wondered how this travesty would ever be resolved.

"Good," Elliot replied, standing up, starting to pace again. "Have you heard from Nathan?" Andie had told Elliot about that part of the plan after she'd met with Nathan at the Smithsonian.

"No," Andie said, "but I didn't really expect him to contact me. I guess the best light to put on it is 'no news is good news.' I trust he's doing okay."

"Okay," Elliot said.

"Okay," Andie replied. "I guess for now we wait until we have the proof."

"Exactly," Elliot agreed. "Let's wait and stay organized."

"Elliot?" Andie asked suddenly, "I didn't see a car out there. How did Kirk get here?"

"He said he'd parked it down the street and walked."

"Well, that was decent of him."

"I don't want to talk about him anymore."

"Okay," Andie said, understandingly. "Okay. Well, I need to get my computer from the trunk of my rental, so let's check the system," she said suddenly, not wanting to leave it there overnight. "I have been followed today, so I did everything I could to lose them, but you never know. I'm almost a hundred percent sure that no one could keep up with me changing at different Metro stops."

Together they looked through the surveillance camera. Everything was quiet. "It's so still out there," Andie said, crossing her arms to rub her shoulders.

"Yeah, it's okay to go get it," Elliot said. "I'll keep watching just in case. The good thing about being hidden is that you can't be seen; the bad thing is that sometimes you can't see anything yourself."

Andie laughed a little and walked quickly out the door. She circled around behind the house toward the garage where she had parked. She popped the rental's trunk with the remote as she headed toward it. A small light came on inside the trunk. She grabbed her computer and slammed the door shut. That's when she saw it. There was an envelope under the windshield wiper. A bright white one. She walked around to the front of the car and pulled it out from under the wiper. She could tell it contained a CD. She got in the driver's seat of the car and looked at it. Both sides were blank, so she ripped it open. A note dropped out with the disk.

"Dear Elliot." *Oops,* Andie thought; she shouldn't be reading this, but she already had.

> Dear Elliot,
>
> I know you are angry. Don't worry, you'll never see or hear from me again. Please use the information on the disk. It will save you time and trouble.
>
> Your loving brother,
>
> Jones.

Andie quickly got out of the car and locked it, looked around, then headed back to the house. Elliot was waiting, still watching the camera. "What took you so long?" he asked, anxiously.

"This," she said, as she held up the envelope, with the contents re-placed in it. "I'm sorry, I didn't mean to read it, but it's so short," was all she could say, which was honest. Then she added, "Why Jones?"

Oh, that's the name he's gone by for years and years among friends, and foes," he said, after glancing at the note. He reached in for the CD.

"Will you use it?" Andie asked, curiously.

"Yeah, I probably will, now that I have it here in my hand. Why not?" he asked rhetorically. "Why the hell not? He owes me. I may as well take what I can get."

"Good," Andie said, knowing that it must be of some relief for Elliot, but it was also a relief for her. The sooner she could get the proof of such machinations exposed, the sooner Americans could become aware of what was going on and the sooner crimes could be investigated. Deidre would hopefully be here soon. Elliot could corroborate his analysis of the implant with the actual formula, although one sample alone was problematic, but she'd have to deal with that later. For now, it appeared that things were on schedule. She hoped.

Meanwhile, Tim was sitting with Deidre in his small hotel-like room. She was obviously scared, he noted. Scared of a lot of things, he imagined; scared of him, scared for herself, and scared of their upcoming flight, or at least their effort to do so. They had less than three hours before leaving the Green Zone. It could take them several hours to get to the airport. Tim had been lucky enough to secure a ride with a military unit head-ing out, so they would be in a cargo plane. The fact that he promised to get gifts from the three soldiers to their families before New Years had done the trick. And Tim planned on fulfilling his promise. These poor guys were on their fourth tour. One of them hadn't seen his newborn yet, and another one had missed his kid's high school graduation last year. It was heartbreaking. Now they were headed to Saudi Arabia for some brief R&R, but that was so insufficient. It didn't get them back to their families or their lives. They said they would help Tim out of Saudi Arabia as well. Apparently, there were frequent commercial flights out, but it would cost. Andie had given Tim plenty of money, exactly for this purpose, so that was not a problem. He wondered how such a young woman, a journalist, could have so much money, but he had decided not to ask questions. It wasn't any of his business.

"Okay, Deidre, I think the best bet is to go ahead and blend the baby powder into your face, neck and hands. Just don't expose any other part of your body and wear a scarf, of course. Once we've reached Saudi Arabia, you can use the restroom and reapply it. Then always, always drink the cough expectorant right before we get into any line, whether it be security or boarding. Once you get close to any attendants, cough as often as you can. Oh, and here, sorry, but I want your big, beautiful brown eyes . . ." he said, noticing that she smiled a bit upon hearing this compliment, ". . . to be as bloodshot as possible."

"How am I going to do that?" she asked.

"Well, sorry, but I've brought an irritant for you to use. It's a small amount of shampoo in water," Tim said, as he held up a tiny plastic bottle. "It will sting, of course, but it will also work, believe me, I tried it myself."

Deidre took it from him and put it in her satchel, along with the powder and cough medicine. "Okay," she said resignedly.

"Any questions?" Tim asked cheerfully.

"No. I just want to get out," she said. "I feel so betrayed."

Tim wasn't savvy yet to her relationship with Andie and, therefore, indirectly Claire according to Andie, but it didn't matter. Now that he'd met Deidre, he felt obligated to help her. She was in way over her head, he could tell.

"We will, I promise you, we will. I promised my wife I'd be back for Christmas Eve, and believe me, I cannot break that promise. She would be so disappointed. So . . . let's get ready. I'll meet you downstairs at four o'clock."

Deidre nodded. "Thank you, Tim. I do appreciate everything you are doing for me."

"Not a problem," he said, "I assure you. And after we get back, maybe you'll want to start blogging with me," he added, trying again to cheer her up.

"That's a definite possibility," Deidre said, before closing the door as she exited.

After hunkering down in the Humvee, Deidre and Tim did not speak. She had powdered her face and hands, put drops in her eyes, and drank the cough medicine. The ersatz sickness appeared to be working. The soldiers would look over at her from time to time, but they stayed as far away from her as possible. One of them had asked Tim what was wrong with her, as though because she was sick she couldn't speak.

"She's got an upper respiratory infection is all. It's not contagious, believe me," he added, noting the concerned looks on their faces. "If it was, I'd have it for sure," he said, scooting a little closer to Deidre and patting her on her back the next time she coughed. She leaned against him as though for support, like they had discussed. The image was effective.

Once they landed in Riyadh, one of the soldiers, Jim, said he'd help them through to the next stage. Tim was grateful. The plan began to work. Deidre leaned on Tim in line, in a needy kind of way. As she reached the security gate, she began coughing uncontrollably. The woman getting ready to frisk her backed away momentarily. Once Deidre had gotten the cough under control, the woman gingerly checked her out and motioned her to continue. Tim, looking unassuming and stating his profession as blogger, was waved through as well. The Saudis were not big on bloggers as of yet, so they could care less.

When they stood in line to board, Deidre coughed a bit now and then. As she reached the individual checking her ticket, her red, bloodshot eyes combined with her cough forced the person to unconsciously give both Deidre and Tim a wide berth. They boarded the plane and buckled in. Apparently, they were well known by now, as no one made eye contact, and no one stood too close for too long. Tim imagined the airline attendants were hoping Deidre would not need their services. *Not a problem,* he thought. Now if they could just get through two more international stops before Deidre's absence was noticed, they would be home free.

Frankfurt was a piece of cake. The lines were well organized, and the two of them looked like they belonged together. Tim would help Deidre along as they walked, and she coughed, and periodically they would sit together so she could sip some water from a bottle that Tim would hand to her after taking off the cap. If anyone viewed it from a surveillance tape, the two of them would simply look like a sweet couple, with one of them in need. Otherwise, they were indistinguishable. They cleared immigration, customs, security, and obtained their boarding passes without incident. Next, and hopefully last, was Ottawa. Tim had selected that destination because of its smallness and friendliness. He figured Toronto could have more screeners, and Vancouver was too far out of the way. Last time he checked the weather, it was holding. A huge snow storm was due on the East Coast by Christmas Eve, but it had stalled in the Rockies for the time being. He hoped they could reach D.C. before it did.

"Happy holidays!" the customs official said with a Canadian mid-western drawl, smiling at Tim. "Your little lady under the weather?" He had just stamped Deidre's passport and was getting ready to do the same to Tim's.

"Same to you, sir," Tim said, relieved. "Yes, I think she's got a pretty good cold going on, but it should be better in the next day or two," he said genuinely.

"Well, good. Have a great Christmas," the agent said, smiling.

"We will, and you, too," Tim replied, joining Deidre. Now, on to the car rental and they were out of there. But first, Tim planned on calling Andie.

He had almost hung up when she answered on the sixth ring. "Andie, Tim here," he said, somewhat enthusiastically.

"Where are you?" Andie asked urgently, and rather breathlessly.

"In Ottawa, about ready to pick up the car you reserved for us. What's up? You sound upset."

"Have you seen any TV there?" she asked.

"No. We've been kind of incognito," Tim replied, looking over at Deidre, who was sitting quietly with the head scarf on and her head down.

"Keep it that way. They have just at this very moment plastered DeeDee's photo all over the airwaves," Andie said. "You've got to get her here fast," Andie said. "Please, Tim, you're so close."

Tim looked up just in time to see what Andie was talking about. RW&B had *Breaking News* flashing below its screen. The text was on so he could read what the talking head was saying:

"If anyone has seen this woman, please call the number below. The US Department of Homeland Security is telling us that she may be on the run. She is a member of the WSSN news team and has disappeared from the Green Zone. No foul play is suspected. But she has had access to classified information and may in fact have taken materials before heading out of Iraq. She could be dangerous. If you see her, call the 1-800 number below," the talking head concluded, looking worried. Then he followed this statement with a huge smile, showing perfectly straight, snow white teeth and saying, "And we've just learned there might be a reward in it for you!"

"Shit," Tim muttered under his breath. "Okay, Andie, I'm seeing it now," Tim responded. "Not to worry, I'll get her there. I'm meeting you at The Plowman's Grille at 10:00, correct?"

"In front of it, at least," Andie said. "It will be closed, I'm sure. I'll be there waiting."

"We'll see you soon," he said optimistically, wondering what the sentence would be for aiding and abetting a faux criminal.

He sat down next to Deidre and explained to her what was going on, leaving out the suggestion that she had committed a crime.

"So they've already noticed that I'm missing?" Deidre asked, worried.

"Yes, and they're looking everywhere apparently. You're going to have to use the powder and the drops and expectorant again, I'm afraid. We don't want to take any chances until we get out of here and through the border. So far, these folks are pretty relaxed, but since your photo is on the tube. . . ." He was interrupted.

"What?" Deidre had put her artificially paled hands to her pale face with alarm. "But why?"

"I don't know. You must know, however."

Deidre did know, now. It was the micro implant she had with her. "Oh God," she said with recognition.

"Listen, let's just get the car and go. No one is going to recognize you. You look different. I'll wait while you use the restroom," Tim said soothingly.

Deidre obediently got up and went in to touch up her disguise, such as it was. She did it in the stall, to avoid having anyone watch her.

When she came out, she saw that Tim was at the rental counter, so she sat down again to wait. Then she saw it. The same clip Tim had seen. And . . . she saw that she was being accused of lifting classified information. "How dare they?" she muttered. She was furious. Suddenly, she was no longer a victim. Tim approached her with the keys, glancing up to see that she had watched the report. He took her by the arm, and they walked out. No one really paid any attention, as far as he could detect. The hardest part was over. Now it would just be the border, gas, and food. They'd have to drive straight through instead of resting anywhere, he had decided. It was going to be about a seven-hundred-mile trip. Deidre would have to do her share of driving. He glanced over at her. She smiled when she saw the black Lincoln Town Car. "Is this it?"

"You bet," he said, glad that she was pleased.

She took a deep breath. "Okay. Let's go."

80

"What do you mean she's gone?" The VP was shouting at the top of his lungs by now. "She can't be gone. She couldn't have just disappeared. I told you, don't let that little bitch out of your sight. She's gone? *Find her!*"

The Defense Secretary explained again that he'd contacted DHS to search for the woman.

This time the VP screamed. "Not Homeland Security, for God's sake. Don't you know they're a facade? They're the two-sided coin, fear and security, fear and security, fear and security, but they don't really do anything. They can't. They're literally incompetent. You need to get on this immediately. Call the international agencies as well. Interpol, and God knows who else. She's out there somewhere, and she's trying to make a fool of me, right before my glory is unveiled. Don't let me down. Oh, and inform your staff, all of them, no Christmas until she's located. This is a 24/7 exercise . . . including yourself," he added, before slamming the phone down.

The Secretary of Defense was alarmed. His good friend appeared to be coming unhinged. He had begun to wonder about his judgment over the last few weeks. Now this. The woman, DeeDee Morgan, simply could not be that big of a threat to them. Sure, her arm had become infected, but it was cleared up now. The only thing that might be lost was her unwavering loyalty, but he was sure they could live without it. She was no longer needed by them, anyway. The entire crew at WSSN was altering their broadcasts and delivery, be it print or visual. They were right in line with the other stations, and the RW&B was still in the lead, despite some increased ratings for WSSN's new program, *The War Column*. The Secretary picked up the phone, swallowed his pride, and contacted the head of Interpol. Now the French were going to be laughing at them, after all of the anti-French hype they'd generated at the beginning of the war. But the Secretary did not want to be spending Christmas with his staff, so he had no choice.

While the VP and the Secretary of Defense were hastily getting all of their ducks in a row to hunt down DeeDee, Tim and she were fast approaching the Canadian-American border. Tim was nervous. "Deidre, please drink the cough medicine now," he suggested.

"Tim, my lungs are killing me," she replied. "I honestly don't think I can take it for much longer." Tim could hear how raspy her voice sounded.

"Okay," he agreed. "You look sick enough."

"Gee, thanks," she said, smiling but feeling very tired suddenly.

"Okay, here we go," Tim said, a few minutes later. The border buildings were all adorned festively with Christmas and Chanukah holiday decorations. Music was coming out of the speakers that were supposed to be used for alarms and verbal warnings. The agents were dressed like elves. Tim handed their passports to the agent, who conducted a cursory glance at both the passports and the occupants of the car. While Deidre's passport indicated just that, DeeDee could obviously be a nickname. Morgan was a common name, however. Tim realized it was going to be just a matter of luck if the news had reached the agent they got and if that agent was going to be in the mood to pay a lot of attention. But she handed back the passports and waved them on through, after issuing a hearty "Merry Christmas, Happy Chanukah." Tim and Deidre said nothing for the next several miles. They had made it.

As the stormy snow clouds began to move east ever so slowly, Nathan was making his way west. In contrast to Tim and Deidre, who had snuck out of Iraq, he had had no such problem. His clearance was good for another six months under the auspices of WSSN, and he could move freely.

"Please show me what's in that black case," a Frankfurt security agent said, pointing to Nathan's black jewelry case. He'd just been flagged at the x-ray station. He knew it would happen. He just didn't know how the episode would end. He'd said his prayers, naturally. He opened it ever so carefully to reveal the three items, lying symmetrically on the black velvet. Nathan had placed a thick gold chain behind them, as though they were already a necklace.

"That's beautiful," the woman said. Nathan had gotten in a line with a female security agent intentionally.

"It's a gift for my little lady," Nathan said, in his best "aw shucks" West Virginia accent.

"Very pretty," was the only and final response. Nathan smiled genuinely. She motioned him on and turned to screen the next passenger. He sighed, imperceptibly, as he left the screening area. Now he only had to get through BWI in Baltimore, and he was home free, or at least he thought so.

As he turned to walk toward his gate, he noticed the TV screen. A photo of DeeDee Morgan, WSSN, was being displayed. Under her photo was the label, AWOL. The next thing he knew, a reporter was saying she had stolen classified material and was on the loose, somewhere in the world. The US and its Coalition of the Willing were fast in pursuit of the young woman, who was believed to be armed and dangerous. Nathan had not had the inclination, or the chance for that matter, to meet her. He had decided against trying to do so after observing the transformation that was occurring under Simon's leadership at WSSN. The whole thing had given him the creeps, as did anyone related to the organization, although he knew he was still employed by them, at least formally. He planned on resigning once he returned home. But, what the hell was up? he wondered. He thought about contacting Andie, but figured she had already seen this, so no point. He'd talk to her as soon as he arrived, anyway, so he decided to let it go. He pulled out his ticket as he reached the boarding agent, and was ushered onto the plane. Once they were in flight, the captain indicated that there was a huge snow storm on its way toward the East Coast, but they would be arriving at BWI well ahead of its arrival. He wished everyone happy holidays.

Andie and Elliot were ready and waiting for Deidre's arrival. For his part, Elliot had reviewed the formula submitted by his brother, Kirk Jones, and had found that he was close to replicating it, but he certainly would not have been able to do so as quickly as they needed at this juncture. The one piece of information that he found to be extremely important was the notation that the implant material was embedded in latex. *Ah, ha,* Elliot had thought. *That explains it.* He quickly informed Andie of this finding and explained that a small percentage of people were allergic to latex.

"It can become quite serious, as you discovered with Miss Ellie," he told her.

"Poor Miss Ellie," Andie said, "she could have been saved if they'd realized what was wrong."

"Perhaps," Elliot said, "during the early stages for sure."

Once he could examine DeeDee's implant, he could conclusively identify its makeup. Since it obviously had been placed inside her without her knowing it, the question would have to be resolved as to how it got there. He explained to Andie that Deidre may or may not begin to remember what happened to her. His best guess was that her memory would come back to her in snippets, a bit here and a bit there. She may get it back in time to be helpful, but otherwise they'd have to make a case for the fact that only the DoD, or in more general terms, the government could have implanted the object. They'd have to see who else might be able to corroborate this assumption. Elliot was sure his brother was long gone by now, so his testimony was not an option. At this thought, Elliot scoffed to himself. His brother never would have provided any direct assistance, no matter how much he or his country had needed him.

"Andie, when are you going to The Plowman's Grille?" Elliot asked alarmed, noting the time.

"Oh my God," Andie said, jumping up. She had been watching more of Claire's CDs, while Elliot had been examining the formula. The two of them were in the bunker, the former underground hideaway. "I hadn't realized it had gotten so late," Andie said, regretfully. "Let's check the periphery; I'm ready to go now. You know, I might be some time," she added. "I haven't heard from them, and their arrival time could be delayed. I know they did not want to stop to call. They're well aware of the risks," she added, glancing over at the non-stop APB-hype on DeeDee Morgan the media had been playing since she was discovered missing.

"Yeah, okay. I've got more writing to do, so I'll just be here waiting. I'm looking forward to meeting her. She's been through a lot, and I think I can help calm her mood swings, which must be occurring, based on what I now know of the formula," Elliot said, smiling. He got up and went over to where Andie had just stood up. "I think things are beginning to come together," he said happily, looking intently at her.

"I'll be happy when we have all of the details ironed out, but, yeah, I am feeling better about our ability to expose these criminals," she said.

Elliot nodded. "Come on, I'll walk you up and watch to make sure its safe," he said, taking her hand. Andie felt warm and very secure suddenly, and very happy.

Just after leaving Elliot's, her cell rang. She glanced down and saw it was Craig. *Uh, oh,* she just realized that she had totally forgotten the Christmas party. She was supposed to go there this evening! She almost didn't answer it but felt badly for even thinking that way. Craig was a good friend. She'd just have to admit that she'd forgotten about it. It was too bad, but it couldn't be helped. Things had changed drastically since she had agreed to attend it.

"Hi, Craig," she said, trying to sound harried.

"Andie. Hi. Just checking to see that you're still planning on coming this evening."

"Oh, Craig, I'm so sorry. I'm not going to make it after all," she said sorrowfully. "I know I'm not going to be able to apologize enough for not letting you know sooner that I won't be able to come. How's it forming up, anyway?" she asked, trying to deflect the conversation.

"Everything's set up really nicely. I wanted you to come and meet a lot of my staff and have a good time. I'm very disappointed," he said, and sounded it.

Andie winced upon hearing this admission. "Please don't make me feel worse. It's just that work is really demanding right now."

"Okay," Craig said. She knew he couldn't remain mad for too long. "Hey, Andie," he said, continuing, "I was wondering, do you know where DeeDee is? I mean her face is broadcast everywhere now. She must be the most popular person on earth at this very moment. You said you were going to try to help her, I hope she's okay," he added, sounding sincerely concerned.

"Yes, Craig, don't worry. I'm continuing to help her. She's safe. It's nice of you to ask."

"Are you at your apartment?" he asked innocently enough. "I could come over after the party and visit, keep you company if you're waiting for her or whatever," he said.

"No, no," Andie said smiling, thinking again about what a good guy he was. "It's not necessary. I'm not there anyway," she added.

"Where are you then, are you sure you are going to be safe?" he asked.

"Yes, don't worry. I'm with a friend," Andie added. She turned into the Grille's parking lot, noting with surprise that indeed it was open. "Okay, Craig, thank you for your understanding," Andie said, wanting to bring closure to a rather uncomfortable conversation. "Merry Christmas, and I'll talk with you soon."

"Okay, Andie, just call if you need anything," Craig said, sounding like he didn't want to hang up.

"Bye, bye," Andie said, clicking off her cell and thinking that it had ended rather awkwardly.

She looked around to see if there was anything or anyone suspicious that she could see. Nothing. She entered the restaurant and noticed it immediately: the place smelled great! She could detect roasted turkey and sweet, nutty desserts. She hadn't thought about it in a while, but she really was hungry. She sat by the window, as before, noting the darkening clouds and wisps of icy snow beginning to drop. An elderly black woman came to take her order. No one else was in the restaurant.

"I didn't think you'd be open today," Andie said, smiling.

The woman smiled back, showing a row of beautiful white teeth. Her name tag indicated Wenona Winsome. She was wearing a mid-calf skirt and soft sweater, covered by a chef's apron. "Aw, missus," she said in a gravely voice, "we've been open every Christmas Eve since my husband's family started this here place. We don' want no poor soul out alone this time of year. All's welcome. We aim to make sure everyone's got someone, if you know what I mean," she said, smiling again.

Andie's emotions jumped to her heart. She felt like crying. She hadn't realized how tense she had become, and here was this nice lady offering her establishment to anyone who needed some company and a warm place to stay for a while on Christmas Eve. "Well, thank you so much," Andie said, sincerely. "Something smells so good, what is that sweet baked odor?"

"That there's pecan pie. It's mighty good with some real whipped cream on it, too, if I can suggest," she said.

Andie had forgotten that Tim said they made the best pecan pie in the region as well. "Please," Andie said. "And I'll take the whipped cream, too."

"Real whipped cream," the lady said, smiling again as she took down the order. "How 'bout a cup of just-perked coffee, too?" she asked. "It's on the house."

"Yes, and thank you," Andie said.

As Wenona Winsome walked off to the kitchen, Andie looked up at the TV in the corner. She couldn't believe it. Now, one shiny-faced male talking head was telling the beautiful blonde with a V-necked cashmere sweater framing her deep cleavage that: "Sure enough, some people are saying that this DeeDee Morgan from WSSN actually took out two personnel with a semi-automatic rifle as she fled the Green Zone."

"Yes, Greg, that's what our sources are telling us. This is truly a tragedy. What a sad thing for the family members to learn during this time of year. Our prayers are with them," she said, turning to smile largely and directly into the camera.

Andie felt sick. Soon the piping hot pie with melting whipped cream was sitting in front of her along with some deliciously smelling coffee, but she'd lost her appetite. *Poor Deidre,* she thought. She wondered if she'd ever be able to get her life back, or any life for that matter.

She picked at the pie as she waited anxiously, keeping one eye on the parking lot and the other watching the sickening, unfolding, over-dramatized, and downright untruthful news story about Deidre. At one point, the waitress came to check on Andie. She looked up at the TV screen and just shook her head. What she meant by it, Andie couldn't guess.

As the storm rolled slowly in, Andie began to see sleet hitting her car's windshield and then the restaurant's glass windows. Suddenly her cell rang.

"Hello," she said anxiously, expecting to hear Tim's voice.

"Andie?"

"Nathan?"

"You bet." Andie could feel tears of joy accumulating as she smiled into the phone. "Nathan, you're here?"

"BWI. Merry Christmas, Andie," he said. "I have a great gift for you."

"Oh, Nathan, thank you!" Andie said.

"No problem," he said, chuckling. "How and where?"

"I'm in a bit of a pinch right now. Can you head to Fredrick? I'll meet you at City Hall. How long do you think it will take you?"

"Well, the weather's getting bad, but I should be there in a couple of hours, I should think," he said casually.

"Okay, Nathan. Drive carefully," Andie warned sensibly. "And, Nathan?"

"Yes?"

"Welcome home."

"See ya soon," was all he said.

Just then, while she was returning her cell to her bag, Andie saw the Black Town Car pulling in. "Oh, thank God," she muttered under her breath. She looked over at Wenona Winsome, and put a twenty-dollar bill under the sugar jar.

"Okay, I'm leaving," Andie said, on her way out. "I left the money on the table," she added. "Hope it helps some other lonely soul. Thank you so much for your hospitality, and Merry Christmas."

"You have a good one," Wenona said, as she headed to the booth to clean up the dishes. "And, missus?"

"Yes?" Andie said, turning to look at her again

"Don' let nothin' get in the way of your mission, ya here? I got a feelin' 'bout you. You be careful."

The hairs on Andie's neck rose quickly before being damped down by the cold blast of wind that hit her on exiting the establishment.

She looked around as she got into the back seat of the Town Car. Tim turned to smile. Andie looked at Deidre. She looked simply awful.

"Thank God you two made it," she said, a bit too loudly.

Tim continued to smile, motioning to Deidre with his eyes and raising his shoulders at the same time, as if to say, *I did my best, but she's not doing so well.*

"Well, it was an adventure," he said. "Deidre is good company, I'm pleased to say."

Deidre looked at the two of them and smiled slightly. "I'm just glad to be somewhere safe. The fact that my country would abuse and betray me is just unforgivable." Andie wondered what she'd say if she'd seen and heard the recently escalated tales.

"You'll be safe," Andie said immediately. "You can count on that. You'll feel like a new person in a few days, and while you recuperate from this ordeal, we can figure out what to do next, so you'll continue to be safe. Believe me, you're going to love where we're going. Security is *not* an issue."

"Thank you," she said meekly. "And thank you, Tim. You've been so good, thank you again."

"It's my pleasure," he said, winking at Deidre and then turning to Andie. "So, I'll drop off the car and head home now."

"Yes, that would be super." Andie said, smiling. "Deidre and I will head home, too."

"Okay, Andie," Tim said. "And we'll talk after the first of the year?"

"Absolutely, Tim. We're partners now. I'm looking forward to working with a blogger, I mean really working with you. I think we can ensure some very newsworthy stories coming up. And factual."

Even Deidre laughed with that comment. "I might want to work with you two, too," she said, trying to snap out of her malaise.

"That's right," Tim said. "Deidre is considering blogging now, too. So . . . have a great Christmas and Happy New Year, and we'll get together soon."

"Okay," Andie said.

"Deidre, let's move to my car, quickly," she said, looking around carefully at their surroundings. The streets were totally, totally empty. Not a moving headlight could be seen.

The two of them got out of the Town Car and into Andie's car. They waved good-bye to Tim, and the two drivers drove off in separate directions. Andie looked at her watch. She needed to get Deidre ensconced at Elliot's and then get back to City Hall pronto.

Andie's hard work was paying off for her, but unbeknownst to her, it was making some people reel. The DoD was combing its records and surveillance tapes to find out just how and when DeeDee Morgan left the Green Zone. They were stumped. There was no apparent sighting of her anywhere. The people were working around the clock to find something, anything, so they could go home to their families and celebrate the holidays; even if they ended up sleeping through them.

In the meantime, the VP had taken things into his own hands. He was having another, special group look into the disappearance. He had instructed them to go to the sources. Check out government employees and find out what anyone might know. "She can't have lived in a vacuum," he shouted. "She had to be communicating with friends, family."

"Sir, she has no family. That's one of the criteria you insisted upon for identifying her as our possible WSSN insider."

"Okay, okay. Whatever," he said, exasperated at the inadequateness of the intelligence. "Find her yesterday! I need to move on." And with that he stomped off to his office and his secure phone.

"Are you finding anything?" he asked the Secretary of Defense with his usual gruff mannerism and lack of respect.

"We're doing everything we can. . . ."

"Blah, blah, blah," the VP interrupted.

"Look, what do you want? My entire department is giving you everything, including their blood, sweat, and tears. There's nothing more we can do at this point except stick with our strategy . . ."

"Which is?"

"Which is to leave no stone unturned. We're going after her systematically."

"Why don't you go after her realistically instead?"

"Meaning?"

"I've got my men working on this, too. You need to do what they're doing and apply some pressure to those around her. Find out who knows what."

"We are," the Secretary said tersely.

"Okay," the VP said, just as tersely. "Now listen. The plan for my departure remains. Do you have everything prepared for that and for our arrival in Baghdad and then on to the Green Zone?"

"Of course. I was working on that 24/7 before I was put on this assignment 24/7. I guess you could say I now work 48/7."

"Stop with the comedic role," the VP said under his breath, clearly angry at being mocked. "Are you prepared as well to accompany me?"

"I am."

"And you have at least a three-star general from Centcom, in Tampa?"

"I do."

"And an Iraqi?"

"Yes."

"Okay. Very good. Let's plan to stay on schedule. As soon as DeeDee Morgan is contained, let's go. I need to get there as close to Christmas as possible. I want to play on the religious timing of it all, you know, the Middle East, the birth of Christianity, and now the birth of a new region."

"Will do," the Secretary said, sighing. There was a click, and he knew the man on the other end of the line was gone.

The VP may have hung up, but he wasn't finished. His next call was to Bobby Puckit at the FCC.

"How's the big man?" Bobby asked with a boisterous voice, always happy to hear from his benefactor. Since he'd become Chairman of the FCC, land deals were occurring faster than he could keep up. His company was simply non-stoppable, and as CEO of it, his wealth had more than tripled since he'd incorporated, at the recommendation of the VP, who was also getting a percentage, naturally. Of course, part of the reason he was able to make so much was the very cheap labor he used to clear the land and build on it. The little brown men were a dime a dozen. "What kin I do you for?" he asked, before adding that the multi-channel media blitz he'd created for the President's *Operation Rehab for Iraq* had increased his approval rating to seventy-five percent.

"The blitz was my idea," the VP said quietly.

"Sure was, and a good one, too, I might add," Bobby gushed quickly, noting the displeasure in the VP's voice.

"I'm getting ready to make a trip to Iraq. An unannounced one. In other words, it's a secret."

"Roger that."

"I need coverage, nonetheless. Can you get your stations ready to broadcast non-stop, just like for the *Operation Rehab* presentation? I mean, I want to be on every station, simultaneously, around the clock. I will be talking about the end of the war and a new direction for the Middle East. It will be impressive, believe me."

"No problem. They'll be ready and waiting. When do you think you'll be announcing, just so I have a ballpark time frame in mind?" he asked carefully.

"Christmas Day, if I'm lucky. Wait for my signal of departure and ETA and then go for it," the VP ordered, before hanging up on Bobby as well. He looked at his watch, realizing he needed to get home to his family to keep up good impressions, given that the holidays were considered a family event. God, he hated this part of the job. He looked around his beloved office on his way out, glancing over in the direction of the hidden safe. He wanted desperately to look at his map again, but . . . later. Duty called.

81

"Deidre, meet Elliot," Andie said, ushering Deidre into Elliot's cozy living room. Elliot stood there quietly, with his hand outstretched to shake Deidre's. She took it appreciatively, looking around at the same time, her huge brown eyes turning into saucers. "This is beautiful," she said, then turned back, quickly catching herself. "Hi, Elliot, it's nice to meet you. Thank you for having me."

The three of them laughed. Deidre apologized for gaping, but said she hadn't seen such nice surroundings in a very long time. Elliot took what little luggage she had and showed her to her room. It was next to the one Andie was using, but further from the kitchen. Then they returned to the living room. He offered her a glass of wine, noting that, although it was still afternoon, it was Christmas Eve as well.

"I would love a glass of wine," Deidre said happily, "but could I take a shower first? I'm absolutely filthy. I have ten layers of baby powder on my face and hands," she said, explaining Tim's trick for getting her safely out of Iraq and all the way here. Andie and Elliot listened attentively, both of them impressed with their new buddy, the blogger.

"Of course you may. It's across from your room. Towels are laid out for you," Elliot said graciously.

"Thank you again," Deidre said, heading toward the bedroom again. "This is just a gorgeous house," she said again, glancing around.

Andie and Elliot waited until she was out of earshot before talking.

"How's she doing?" Elliot asked, concerned.

"Okay, actually," Andie said quietly. "She's scared. All in all, though, I think she's stronger mentally than when she left for Iraq. At this point she's depressed, at least that's what she told me. She said she can't believe that the government would use her so blatantly, and then turn on her, without blinking an eye. So I'm guessing she'll be wanting to get even, which means fully cooperating with our efforts."

"That's very good to hear," Elliot said, nodding affirmatively.

"Oh," Andie said, looking at her watch. "I've got to go."

"Where?" Elliot asked, surprised.

"I haven't had a chance to tell you. Nathan called. He's here. I mean, he's on his way here. He just arrived at BWI when he called me. I'm meeting him at City Hall. He has the proof, Elliot," she said, lowering her voice. "The real proof. Can he stay here, even though it's premature? I don't think he should be out driving tonight."

"Yes, of course," Elliot said. "Wow, Andie, things are starting to come to fruition, aren't they?" he said, smiling fondly at her.

"They are, Elliot. They truly are. Okay, I've got to go."

"Wait, let me check the surroundings," Elliot said.

"Believe me, Elliot, there is no one out. A big storm is coming, on top of it being Christmas Eve."

"Andie, don't let your guard down. Not for a minute until we've got the evidence lined up and the report finished. Please. These people will stop at nothing," Elliot admonished.

"Sorry, Elliot, you're right."

He nodded. They both went to look at the camera, and then he motioned for her to go ahead. "I'll be right back," she said.

He grabbed her arm as she turned to go. "Please be careful, Andie," he said, looking into her eyes. "Please."

"I will, I promise," she said. And then she was gone.

Wow! she exclaimed to herself when she got to City Hall. Nathan had described his rental when he called, and sure enough, there he sat.

She pulled up to the driver side and waved. They lowered their windows. "How long have you been waiting?" she asked, concerned.

"Not long, actually. There's no one on the roads. It took less time than I had thought," he said, sheepishly.

Andie nodded, sure, knowing he must have speeded to get here this quickly. She looked around. All they needed was a highway patrol tracking Nathan. But . . . no one.

"Okay, do you want to follow me to a friend's house?" Andie asked excitedly. "It's Christmas Eve. It's a nice place to stay."

"Sure," Nathan said, with a gleam in his eye. "You mean party time, right?"

"Kind of," Andie said, laughing. She wondered what Nathan would say when he saw Deidre. He must know by now that she was "on the loose."

Upon reaching Elliot's, Andie motioned Nathan to park behind her, out of sight as well. They got out of their cars practically in unison. Nathan grabbed his duffle bag and quickly followed Andie inside. "Whose place is this, anyway?" Nathan was asking as they entered. He stopped dead in his tracks. There sat pretty Deidre with a glass of white wine in her hand and a huge smile on her face. "Well . . . how . . . you!" he sputtered. "How did you get here? You're okay? I've been watching your story all the way from Iraq. Well . . ." he looked around at Andie, who was standing next to Elliot by this time. "Well . . ." was all he said again, as he dropped his duffle bag and went over to Deidre. "I don't believe we've met, at least formally, but I'm happy to have the honor," he said, reaching out to shake her hand. "Nathan McCabe. I believe you are the now infamous, and from what I hear, rather criminal, DeeDee Morgan." Deidre smiled and shook his hand.

"It's a pleasure, Nathan, I've heard a lot of good things about you from Andie." Andie had told her about Nathan's closeness and assistance to both Michael and Claire.

Now it was Nathan's turn to look a bit embarrassed; he was a very modest person. He turned to look at Andie. "Nathan, let me introduce you to Elliot, Elliot Jones. Elliot's a good friend," Andie continued, "and was a very good friend to Claire."

Nathan reached over and shook Elliot's hand as well. "Pleased to meet you. Anyone who was a friend of Claire's is okay in my book. Claire was one of a kind," Nathan added, solemnly.

"Agreed," Elliot said, as he motioned Nathan to the couch. "Can I get you something to drink?"

"Do you have any scotch?"

"Of course," Elliot said, walking over to the dry bar, stopping along the way to throw another log on the fire. "I guess it's picking up out there," he said over his shoulder.

"I was lucky to get into BWI," Nathan replied. "They started to shut down the airport while I was in line for the rental."

At that moment Andie's cell rang. She got up and went into another room to take the call. "Simon?" It was Simon, but he sounded terrible. "Simon, what's wrong?" Andie asked, alarmed.

"Andie, I'm so sick. You were right. I should have had this arm looked at. It's gotten pretty bad. I don't know what to do."

"Well, go to the emergency room," Andie demanded, surprised that he hadn't already had it looked at.

"*No!* I'm not going there. Remember Miss Ellie? That's where she went to begin with, and look what happened to her. No. They kill you there. Oh, Andie, what am I going to do?" he asked, practically sobbing.

Andie tried to think fast. She considered the crowd here, and although Simon was not part of this group, he could be brought up to date. And . . . now she was really thinking, and now Elliot could not only take care of Simon, by cleaning his arm, he could clean is arm out, and in doing so, remove any foreign object that might be implanted in it. They would have the necessary corroborative evidence with the chip from Simon's arm. She felt badly thinking this way, but. . . . "Simon, I'll come and get you. I have a friend who can help get your arm cleaned, and it won't be threatening, I promise you. Where are you?"

"At my home."

"Oh." Well at least he was north of D.C., Andie thought. Simon lived in Rockville. "Okay, I'll be there in an hour, maybe a bit longer. I'm out of town right now," she said, remembering that a storm was rolling in.

"Oh, Andie, thank you. I really feel terrible."

"Take some aspirin, Simon, and put a warm compress on your arm. We're going to have to get it cleaned out."

"Okay, Andie, thank you."

Andie walked out to the other room to hear the folks conversing and laughing. It made her feel good. It had been so long since she had felt this light, although she was concerned, understandably, about Simon.

Nathan was just taking his first sip of scotch when Andie told them that it was Simon on the phone and he was really sick now from an arm infection. Andie glanced over at Deidre while she was saying this. Deidre frowned and rubbed her own arm. "If it's from the same source, it gets really serious if it's left unattended, believe me, I know."

"Yes, we know now," Andie said, agreeing. "Miss Ellie died from it. I know you didn't know her, Deidre, but she was an older woman who had worked at WSSN for a very long time."

Nathan looked quite shocked upon hearing this news. "I didn't know," he said, shaking his head. "What did you tell Simon?"

"I told him I would bring him here," Andie said, "if it's okay with you, Elliot. He doesn't have anyone close to him here and, well, I thought you would be the best person to take care of his arm. He's scared to death of going to a doctor, given that Miss Ellie was in the hospital when she died."

"Of course," Elliot said, agreeing enthusiastically. "I know exactly what to do and what to look for," he added, glancing over at Deidre. Deidre nodded affirmatively as well.

"I'll go get Simon," Nathan said, standing up. "You shouldn't be out Andie. I'm buzzed from the trip, so it won't bother me, and no one is looking for me, as far as I know."

"He's right," Elliot said. "And we have some work to do here."

"Are you sure, Nathan?"

"Absolutely."

"We'll catch you and Simon up when you return."

"No problem," Nathan replied.

"Okay, well, thank you," Andie said. "I'll walk you out."

"Right," Nathan said. He grabbed his duffle bag, and the two of them started toward the door. Elliot followed to check the surveillance camera.

"Oh, by the way, Andie," Nathan said, reaching into his duffle bag, "here's the gift I promised." He looked over at both of them.

"Ooooh," Andie said. "Thank you, Nathan!"

"Again, as I said, no problem."

"For the life of me, I don't know how you got it here," Elliot said, shaking his head.

"Well, Andie and I both reasoned that I'd have to go through x-ray machines, but there were no Geiger counters," he replied, grinning.

"Good point," Elliot said, smiling.

"I gather from what you told me, Andie, that Elliot is going to be the one examining them," he said. It was more of a statement than a question.

"Yeah, you've got that right. I have a lab downstairs, in a safe bunker," Elliot said.

"Fantastic," Nathan exclaimed. "I can't wait to see it. I can't wait to know the results, given that the Pentagon keeps denying the existence of any harm to anyone from these wretched weapons. This is what Claire died for," Nathan said sadly.

"We know," Andie said. "And we're all going to do right by her, believe me. You just be careful, Nathan. Call Simon when you get there and let him know I sent you. If I do it in advance, he may get squirrelly. He's quite a mess by the sound of his voice. Try to calm him down. He should be happy to see you," she said.

"I feel badly for him. He's been . . ."

"Brainwashed," Andie filled in for him.

"I guess so," Nathan said, sighing. "It's unbelievable that this could be happening. Thank God for Claire and Michael," he said again, "They're the true patriots in this God awful war. See ya soon," he said, heading out after Elliot gave him the go-ahead.

"Well, that's one hell of a young man," Elliot said to Andie after Nathan drove off. "I wish I had been so clear-headed and centered at that age. I might not have been responsible for so much turmoil and deceit if I had been," he said regretfully.

"Come on, Elliot. You're the one who is always saying let's keep focused. You didn't cause what has happened," Andie said, comfortingly. "It's happened for a number of reasons, as you told me, the first day I met you. Let's go see what kind of gifts Deidre and Nathan have brought us," she said smiling, looping her arm into Elliot's.

Elliot nodded slightly, and they moved back into the living room. Deidre was sitting, happily sipping her wine. Andie observed that, although she was not a child, she sure seemed as innocent as one right now.

"Do you feel well enough to discuss your situation and what's happened to you?" Andie asked.

"Yes, of course." Deidre said eagerly. "I want to tell you everything and to give you the piece that was taken out of my arm," she said, reaching into her purse and pulling out a prescription medicine bottle. She shook it slightly. They could hear a slight, tinny sound inside it.

"May I?" Elliot asked, reaching out for it.

Deidre gladly handed it over. "Do you know why it made me sick?" she asked.

"Yes," Elliot said. "The people who developed this implant made a mistake and embedded it in latex. Do you know if you're allergic to latex?"

"I am," Deidre said. "It was discovered in college when I was having a physical and latex gloves were being used. Unbelievable," she said. "It was sitting inside me the whole time, making me sicker and sicker, and I didn't even know it was there."

"What do you remember about the lead-up to your assignment at WSSN?" Andie asked. "I've been dying to know what you experienced."

Deidre proceeded to describe what she could remember. She had been quite happy at the DoD, working as a media specialist in their press department. "I was promoted suddenly. It was strongly suggested that I take this job, or rather the job I used to have," she said, becoming subdued for the first time since she arrived.

"But something happened between the time you left the DoD and the day you came to WSSN," Andie said impatiently.

"I know. That part is very fuzzy. I do remember calling you, Andie. I still know your cell number. It was like it had been etched in my brain. I remember, sometimes, rather stark sleeping arrangements. Stark and cold. But I don't know why I wanted your help. I felt pretty good once I arrived at WSSN, although at times I had some nasty thoughts, which is uncharacteristic for me."

"Any other uncharacteristic behavior or thoughts that come to mind?" Elliot asked.

"Actually, I felt very pro-government. Very pro-war. I was excited to be going to Iraq, even though I was scared. I felt good about representing the government there. Then it turned out to be pretty easy. I was just asked to read stories in front of the camera. I didn't mind, although," Deidre paused for a moment, "although I don't consider it to be journalism. Now I feel rather ashamed that I did it. At the time, it seemed like the right thing to do."

"Do you know who wrote the stories?" Andie asked. "I mean, were they coming from WSSN?"

"No . . . I'm pretty sure they were from the DoD. I don't know why, but I'm pretty sure they were."

"Do you have any of the hard copies that you read from?" Andie asked, suddenly thinking that they might provide a clue.

"I might," Deidre said, getting up to look. She returned with a white sheet of paper in her hand, and a big smile on her face. "Here's the last one I read from, before my arm made me too sick to get out in front of the cameras."

Andie took the paper from her. It was of high quality. She held it up to the light, just on a hunch. It had a watermark on it. "Look at this," she exclaimed.

Office of the Vice President
United States of America

"Oh my God," Deidre said, slouching in the couch and covering her face with her hands. "I was just a talking head for the government, literally."

"It's okay, you weren't yourself," Andie said.

"But the shame I've brought to the profession is heartbreaking to me."

"Don't worry, you're not the first and certainly not the last," Andie said, "but most of them don't have a problem sleeping at night," she added sarcastically. Deidre seemed to appreciate this comment.

"It's interesting it's on the VP's paper. It proves what Kirk told me is certainly true. This scheme is being orchestrated by the VP."

"Who's Kirk?" Deidre asked.

"My brother."

"Oh." Deidre didn't pursue it any further, given the dark shadow that crossed Elliot's face when he answered her.

"So, this is coming from the VP's office," Andie said, getting back on course. "That will help a lot when we get down to providing direction for investigators."

"Investigators? How are you going to go about it?" Deidre asked, perking up. "I'd love to nail someone for this. I don't know who, but someone."

"There are a lot of folks that need nailing, so to speak," Elliot said. "You'll be involved, don't worry."

Deidre looked pleased.

"Now, let's go look at this implant."

Deidre was even more pleased to visit the lab and the underground bunker. "I told you you'd be safe," Andie said reassuringly.

Although Deidre might have felt safe, Simon did not. He was in a lot of pain, and the way that Nathan drove was adding to his sense of panic. "Please slow down," he moaned, as Nathan zoomed onto the Beltway. "You're crazy," he yelled, about ten seconds later as Nathan passed a semi that was obviously speeding. "What's wrong with you?"

Nathan tried to slow down, but it didn't come naturally to him. He just liked fast. Plus, he was looking forward to returning to Elliot's comfortable retreat, looking at the bunker, and having his scotch. It'd been a long week. "Simon, relax, there's no one on the roads. There's no traffic."

Simon sighed, resting his head on the seat headrest and closing his eyes. He had no control over the situation. "So, who is this guy with Andie, anyway?"

"I just met him, actually," Nathan replied. "His name is Elliot Jones. He seems like a nice guy. I think he's a scientist. He knew Claire."

"Really?" Simon was intrigued now. "How did he know Claire?"

"I don't know," Nathan said, exasperated. "I told you, I just met him. You must be delirious, Simon. You don't make sense." Nathan reached over and touched his forehead. *Ouch!* The man was burning up. Nathan sped up just a little bit. He didn't want his boss to die on him, here and now, even if he was going to quit. "How long have you been sick, anyway?"

"Too long. It's been getting worse by the day, but today, it started getting worse by the hour. Are we almost there?" Simon asked weakly.

"Just about."

"What's the guy's name, the scientist? I sure hope he can help me."

"He'll help you, Simon. I promise," Nathan responded, though he was beginning to wonder if Simon might be beyond helping.

"How did DeeDee get there?" Simon asked a few minutes later. He had been startled to just now learn from Nathan that she was with Andie. DeeDee worked for him, and he'd been trying to find her ever since she'd gone missing. God, how the Feds had been questioning him. Night and day, night and day. Simon thought that perhaps the late night phone calls had exacerbated his current condition. He couldn't sleep. Oh, he felt so badly, and his arm was really throbbing now.

By the time they arrived at Elliot's, Simon had fallen asleep. Nathan called Andie to let her know they were pulling into the driveway. The automatic door snapped locked behind them after they entered. Simon was leaning heavily on Nathan's shoulder. Elliot and Andie helped to make him comfortable on the couch. "Boy, this neighborhood must be anti-Christmas," he said. "There are no decorations, no lights in the houses, nothing. It's deserted."

Andie agreed. "I noticed that, too," she added, putting a blanket over Simon.

"I know it seems that way," Elliot said, as he began to examine Simon and his arm. "Just about everyone here goes south during the winter. They don't like the winters. They're all very wealthy."

"Must be nice," Nathan said, as he left for a quick shower.

Deidre had described how the doctor had removed her implant, so Elliot was prepared to do the same. It went pretty well, considering that Simon was not in the best position, nor was he the best patient. He kept squirming and moaning. Elliot had some sedatives and strong, wide spectrum antibiotics available as well. He administered them quickly, hoping the infection had not penetrated so deeply as to cause additional, secondary infections. Finally, the man was resting comfortably, even snoring slightly.

"Will he be okay?" Andie asked worriedly.

"I should think so, his vitals all seem good. In part, he's just exhausted," Elliot said, as he carefully examined the tiny implant between the tweezers. Yep, it was just like Deidre's. What a lucky coincidence. Simon had arrived just in time to be saved and to help them tremendously.

"Wow, I guess that allergy to latex really does a number on people," Deidre said, entering the room. She had remained in the other room so as not to distress Simon.

"No kidding," was all Andie could say. "What a travesty. I can't believe our own government is going around implanting people with potentially lethal material."

"You haven't seen lethal," Nathan said, joining the group following his shower. "If you think that's bad, look at the effects of the DU."

"The what?" Deidre asked curiously.

Andie quickly explained what they'd discovered from Michael and Claire's investigative reports, adding that Nathan had brought samples so that Elliot could analyze them and determine the effect they have on humans. "It will be an unbiased analysis, compared to the crap disseminated by the Pentagon's scientists," she added.

Deidre seemed horrified by this new news. "You mean I was exposed to DU when I was in Iraq?"

"No, not you personally," Nathan said. "But people all around you were and are. It's everywhere. If you happened to have slept with someone who was exposed, and I'm not saying that you did, obviously, but even that can result in exposure to you. It's a nasty WMD—the gift that keeps on giving," he said sarcastically.

The conversation was taking a macabre turn, and Andie didn't want to get into it right now. "Let's let Elliot examine the samples and tell us the truth about it," she said, trying to change the subject before Deidre became even more depressed. "Let's go look at the bunker and the lab," she suggested cheerfully, glancing over at Simon. "I think he'll be resting for another hour or so . . . maybe more."

Elliot agreed, and the four of them headed downstairs for a little tour. "Watch your head," he said to Nathan. The stairs were so steep that they all had to turn sideways a bit to feel as though they wouldn't tumble down them. Once they reached the bottom and could see the layout, Elliot explained the history of the place in an engaging way, so as to give it character, only. He didn't want to contribute to any more ghoulish descriptions, given the tone Nathan had set.

At the same time that the group was checking out the security of the underground bunker and lab, Craig was trying to locate Andie. He was concerned for her, but more importantly, something inside him kept eating away at his conscience. He felt as though he had a duty as a citizen to let authorities know that DeeDee could be located. He needed more information, though. More importantly, where she was located now. He sat at his desk, wondering if he should actually try to locate her on behalf of the government. He knew he could find Andie, so he decided to take a gamble and make the leap from her location to that of DeeDee.

Once he'd made up his mind, he moved quickly. Jumping up, he walked over to his GPS screen and typed in Andie's cell number. What the hell? What was she doing in Frederick? For the life of him he could not recollect anyone they knew who lived in Frederick. He zoomed in on the exact location. Good God, the physical location was barely visible due to all of the trees. The land around it was immense. All of it was covered in trees. Tons of trees. How strange, Craig thought. So much acreage in what appeared to be a normal type neighborhood. An upscale one, but all the same, a neighborhood.

He tried to zoom in more, but this created a loss of resolution at some point. Craig sat back down. What was Andie doing there? Scenes of their meetings, discussions, phone calls over the past week quickly passed through his memory. And the fact that the DoD was most likely responsible for ransacking her apartment in search of the List could not be forgotten, nor ignored. He realized suddenly that he had been feeling guilty about giving that huge document to her for quite some time now. It had been the wrong thing to do. No doubt about it, he finally concluded. Andie had gone nutso. She needed saving now as much as DeeDee Morgan did. Craig picked up his office phone and called his boss, the Secretary of the Commerce Department. He had some news the man would need and want to hear, Craig figured. What he did with it was none of his business. Craig would have finally served God and country, which is what he cared about lately. It had almost become an obsession, he reflected momentarily.

"Mr. Secretary," he said briefly, "I have news that may interest you." In quick, short, staccato sentences, primarily in response to the abrupt questioning from the Secretary, Craig informed the man that he believed he had a pretty good idea of the whereabouts of the woman DeeDee Morgan, who had only recently disappeared from the Green Zone in Baghdad. "And," he added, "I have some news about a document that had inadvertently ended up in the wrong hands, the hands of Andie Aaberg, a journalist working for WSSN. I believe the DoD was looking for her as well. The two are together, Mr. Secretary," Craig informed the man.

"Is Morgan holding folks hostage at that location?" the Secretary wanted to know.

Craig said he didn't believe so, but could not verify this one way or the other.

"How heavily armed is the woman?" was the next question.

Craig couldn't answer that one either.

"How do you know then, that she is there, or that the other woman, the journalist, is there, if you don't know anything about their surroundings?" the Secretary asked, frustrated.

"I just have a hunch, a scientific one I might add, that the address I have given you is where you will find them," Craig responded. "Between you and me, sir, I am one hundred percent sure. If you want to state it differently to anyone else, please feel free."

The Secretary knew that Craig was young, but competent. He decided a feather in his own cap for the capture of this young lady could not hurt, especially if it came with a bonus. Yeah, he could use a bonus, and, he calculated, even if the information was wrong, he would not be tarnished too badly. There was really no one else on the horizon that the President could get to replace him. He knew too much already.

"Thank you, Craig," was all he said, before hanging up.

Craig went to the back of his door to take his blazer off the hanger. He put it on slowly, looking all the while at his reflection in the long mirror attached to the same door. He felt good about himself, and what he had just done. He turned to leave, thinking it was now time to go praise the Lord with his Christian staff and help them celebrate the baby Jesus's birth at their Christmas Eve party.

"Mr. Secretary," the Secretary of Commerce said deferentially to the Secretary of Defense.

"Yes," the Secretary responded wearily.

"I believe we have received a tip as to the whereabouts of the missing DeeDee Morgan, as well as another journalist, Andie Aaberg, who may be her accomplice," he said, embellishing the information.

"What?"

"Yessir," the Secretary of Commerce replied with confidence. "Merry Christmas," he added.

"Where, when, who?" The questions came flooding faster than the Commerce Secretary could respond.

Their conversation was short and succinct. The Secretary of Defense took down the information as rapidly as he could write. He started feeling a sense of relief just as he thought everything was lost. He did not want to spend day and night looking for this woman. Now he'd have to accompany the VP to Iraq, but that couldn't be as bad as this task, which had seemed fruitless until now. How the hell that woman got back to the States under his nose, he'd have to learn later. Perhaps the other woman, Andie Aaberg, had played a role. The main point was to let the VP know that the Morgan woman had been located and allow that man to continue with his plans. The Secretary of Defense was hoping that this next year would be better than last year. He was counting on it.

"Okay. Thank you," the Defense Secretary concluded. "I'll be sure to let them know the role you played in this . . ." he paused, ". . . in this retrieval. I'm sure you'll be in for a big promotion after all this is over," he added.

The Secretary of Commerce beamed on the other end of the phone. "Yessir," he said, as they concluded their conversation.

Immediately upon hanging up, the Secretary of Defense contacted the VP. "I've located the woman!" he practically shouted.

The VP was relieved, but he did not allow this to be expressed. "Where is she?" The Secretary of Defense quickly provided the location, adding that there was another female with Morgan, an Andie Aaberg, who was her accomplice.

"It appears to be a house in a neighborhood, so I am suggesting that your men try not to make a scene. Remember, we don't want, we can't afford," the Secretary of Defense added, "any press. Not until we have her, or them rather, under our control. Are you sure you do not want me to delegate this within the DoD?"

"I'll advise my team accordingly," the VP said quietly, not liking to be lectured. "Now, given that this is resolved, I'd like to suggest that we get our butts into gear and arrive in Baghdad on Christmas, or as close to it as possible. We can make an even bigger splash if we show up engulfed in fireworks."

Instead of commenting, the Defense Secretary was thinking about his wife's disappointment when he informed her that he would not be able to be home for Christmas.

"Hello? Are you listening?" the VP asked rudely, bringing the Defense Secretary's thoughts back to the issue at hand.

"Yes, of course. I was just thinking about how to get the fireworks there, but I imagine we can bring them ourselves in the plane's cargo. The embassy must have some as well to celebrate July Fourth, there in the Green Zone."

"Good point," the VP said, agreeing. "Okay. I'll let you take care of it. But hurry, we're running out of time."

"Got it," the Secretary said. "Anything else?"

"Not at the moment." *Click.*

The Secretary shook his head. The man was crazy, he concluded. Fireworks of all things, what was he thinking? But then he reflected on the huge success *Operation Rehab Soldiers for Iraq* had been and still was. His recruitment numbers were higher than at any other time in the modern history of the US. The savings from the money was allowing them to build, secretively of course, more bases in Iraq, plus they were able to put additional funds into more prisons there as well. It was good that the country was pretty much off limits for the majority of Americans. They'd be shocked to see what was really happening there on the ground. And the ability to get the press to be as compliant as it was had been another fantastic move by the man. Geniuses must just be naturally crazy, the Secretary concluded.

As soon as the VP hung up, he called his main man, the one in charge of his shadow soldiers. "We've ID'd the target's location. Actually, there are two of them, the target and her accomplice, another female. You've got a twofer. They need to be taken out. Tonight."

"Yessir!"

"Be careful. It's in a neighborhood, so you're going to have to be creative. We don't want any press, no attention. Do you understand?"

"Yessir!"

"Remember, given what I pay you, you have no room to fuck up."

"Yessir!"

And with that the VP provided the coordinates for DeeDee Morgan's and Andie Aaberg's demise.

82

As the tour of the downstairs bunker continued, Deidre gravitated toward an object against the far wall. "What is that for?" DeeDee asked, pointing to a large box-like container.

"That's to examine the DU," Elliot said, walking over to it and switching on a light to illuminate the inside of it. Andie, Deidre, and Nathan followed him over. All of them peered into the container. There lay the three specimens Nathan had brought. They were suspended in a liquid substance. "That's to keep them from being affected by any physical disturbance that could set them off, which would be unlikely, but every precaution is necessary. I've begun to extract the substances from within them, from the small tubes that you see. In fact, I'm almost finished. So is the report," Elliot explained.

"Why did you decide to take the chance to analyze it?" Deidre asked.

"For Claire," was all Elliot said. Then added, looking over at Andie, "She asked me one time if I thought the use of chemistry can ever be construed to be a benign science? Or was I of the opinion that it is used for either good or evil? Here we see it being used for both. First the evil, and now, from the readings I'm getting, it's clear that the contents are lethal to humans, animals, the environment, and well, let me just say, Mother Earth. Now if we," he said, looking over at Andie again, "can get the information to the right people, and if an effort is made to clean up the mess, then this potentially evil tool will have been used for good. It was a good question," Elliot concluded.

"I see," was all Deidre said.

"So, are we ready to get the results out, then?" Andie asked eagerly.

"Yes," Elliot said. "Let me wrap up the last paragraph, and we'll have what we need."

"Hey, Elliot, do you have a generator to run the electricity if it goes out?" Nathan asked, looking around.

"Yes. Its controls are over here." Elliot moved to show him the switches behind a metal two-foot door. "The supplies are over there," he said, continuing to show Deidre and Nathan around. He indicated the batteries for the flashlights and torches, the water jugs, and the canned goods. "It's a good six weeks' worth."

"Wow, it's like having two houses," Nathan said, grinning. "Do you ever just come down here and hang out for a few days, like you're on vacation somewhere, eating beans and franks?"

"No . . . hadn't thought of doing that," Elliot said, chuckling.

During this time, Andie had walked over to the surveillance camera, curious to see what the weather was doing. The background was a dark gray. White stuff was falling like rain, angling sharply, almost blowing horizontally. Jeez, she thought, it's not even snow. It truly is a blizzard, just like they predicted. She shivered slightly, wrapping her arms around herself and rubbing them vigorously, even though there had been no change in the temperature. Suddenly, she saw a flitting object. *What the?* . . . She got closer, gazing deeply into the dark morass. She was sure she had seen something. There it was again. Then another one. She tried to zoom in to where she had seen it, by the corner of the house. Her gasp caught in her throat. "Elliot!" she half whispered, half yelled. "Elliot come here, fast." She was trying not to be alarming, but it didn't work. The three of them were at her side in seconds. "What is it?" he asked concerned

"Look, watch closely. You tell me. There, did you see that?" she asked, pointing to a spot on the screen.

"You bet I did." Elliot responded.

"How many are there?" Nathan asked.

"Enough," Elliot said, quickly stepping into high gear. "Nathan, can you get Simon down here? Fast? There should be no shadows visible from the outside, all the shades are drawn, but you'll need to be fast, very fast. I imagine they are going to get through the door in no time."

Deidre screamed softly, putting her fist in her mouth, practically sobbing.

Nathan headed up the steep stairs, two at a time.

Andie had already anticipated the next move. She rushed quickly to the laptop that Elliot was using to write his report. Elliot was right there next to her. "Go ahead and send it. It doesn't need the conclusion. Somebody would have to be an idiot not to be able to surmise the message," he said grimly. "Go ahead," he urged. Andie didn't need any urging. Her fingers were typing as fast as possible. "Make four copies on the memory sticks and four more on the discs. We'll do our best, that's all we can do," he added, somberly. Andie complied immediately.

"Done!" she said, hitting the send button. "We did it, Elliot," she said, grabbing him. He wrapped his arms around her and pulled her to him, hugging her tightly. "We did it," she said again, "it's in good hands, even if we don't make it." Unfortunately, she hadn't seen that Deidre was within earshot of her making this statement.

"Oh my God," she said, dropping to her knees. "We're dead. We're all dead."

"Stop it, Deidre," Andie ordered, going over to her and trying to console her. "Nobody's going to die."

"But you just said 'if we don't make it.' "

"It was just a . . . figure of speech," Andie said, trying to soften what she had in fact just said. "I just meant that we may not be able to send the material if we are arrested or detained. This way, it's been sent."

Elliot interjected at this point. "There is no way this room can be detected," he said, exuding confidence. "It's seamless from any detection within and outside the house. After they have made a thorough search, they will undoubtedly leave. They're not going to blow us up in such a public place. We can keep an eye on them from here. We'll know when they've gone."

By now, Deidre's waterworks were slowing up a bit, and she was only sniffling. "Oh. Oh . . . okay, but who is out there?" she asked, motioning toward the surveillance camera.

"Goons," Nathan said loudly, as he practically dropped Simon onto the couch. "Our government's goons. I recognize them. They're contractors. The company's name is DARKSAND."

"How do you know them?" Elliot asked, kneeling to put a pillow under the now conscious but bewildered Simon.

"They're all over Iraq and Afghanistan. They put the fear of God, or Allah, in everyone. Those guys do not live by the normal rules. They are crazy. They'll do anything, and they get away with it because there is no US or international law that regulates them. I was always more afraid of them than any Iraqi, Afghani, or insurgent for that matter," he added, as he stared into the surveillance camera. "They're mercenaries," he concluded.

"Who hires them?" Andie asked, now joining Nathan to watch.

"I told you, the government. Some say they work directly for the Defense Secretary, but the actual truth of the matter is that they work for the VP. It's an unspoken truth, because everyone who knows of DARK-SAND is afraid. Look at how stealthily they are combing the perimeter of the house. They don't want to be seen by anyone. I guess that is to our advantage, or they would have just blown us up," he commented, whereupon Deidre began to sob again.

"Jesus, Nathan!" Andie said.

"You asked," he said, raising his shoulders as if to say, *What did you want, a lie?*

Suddenly, it occurred to Andie that their belongings and ID remained upstairs. "Come on, Deidre, let's go get our stuff out of the rooms. Come. Quickly," she added, as Deidre slowly moved toward the stairs. "Nathan, did you leave anything personal up there?" she asked, offering to grab it.

"Nope, it's all here in my duffle bag," he replied. "Thanks though."

"Hurry," Elliot said, noting that the shapes were getting closer to the house.

Upon their return to the bunker, Andie and Deidre put their small satchels and suitcases in the corner closet. Elliot and Nathan were continuing to stare into the surveillance camera. Andie had been thinking about these men showing up. She was confused.

"I wonder how they knew we were here," Andie asked out loud, looking over at Elliot. He shook his head, having been unable to figure it out.

"Well, no one followed us back. No one knows me," Nathan said a bit defensively, given that he was the most recent person to have returned from outside of the house.

"Did anyone here mention anything to anyone who's not here, besides our blogger buddy?" Elliot asked, trying to problem-solve.

Silence overtook the group as they thought about Elliot's question and continued to watch the DARKSAND members encroach closer and closer toward the house.

"Uh, oh," Andie said suddenly.

"What?" Elliot asked, obviously worried.

Everyone now turned to look at her, even Simon who had become fully conscious and was now sitting in an upright position staring dumbly at Andie, not knowing what was going on.

"I mentioned to Craig that I knew where Deidre was . . . just today," she added lamely.

"So," Elliot responded. "He wouldn't have told anyone. He's one of your best friends."

"Craig?" Nathan asked, somewhat incredulously. "Craig from Commerce, that Craig?"

"Yes," Andie said, "why, what do you know about him?"

"I know he's got one of those . . . those thingamajigs in his arm," he said, pointing to Simon. "He's been through the program in other words."

"No!" Andie said. "No! He does not. Elliot and I both told him not to go to that seminar. That's the only place he could have received an implant, well practically," she said, looking over at the very visibly scared and unhappy Deidre.

"Well, sorry to disappoint you, Andie," Nathan said very sincerely, "but it is true. I was in line ahead of him when I decided to leave. We chatted for a few minutes on my way out. He stayed."

Andie shook her head sadly, reflecting on the rather strange changes she now recognized occurring within Craig. And though denial continued to grip her, she had to admit to herself now that he had seemed too damn curious about her situation when she last spoke to him. What was it he had said earlier at one point that had sounded so uncharacteristic? Oh, yeah, he'd stated his desire to serve "God and country." She should have realized something was up.

"But," Elliot said, "he wouldn't have known where we are, I mean, you didn't tell him where you were, right?"

"Of course not," Andie said, trying to figure it out. "Oh, oh, folks, I'm sorry," was all she could say for a moment as she sat down on the office desk chair. "Craig has a huge GPS capability. He must have tracked my cell."

"That's got to be it then," Elliot said.

"What do they want?" Deidre asked quietly.

Everyone turned to stare at her; even Simon was catching on by this point. "Well," Andie started, as gently as she could, "I am sorry, Deidre, but I think it's about you. The fact that the Feds have been looking for you for the past seventy-two hours suggests that you're their target . . . oh, please don't cry, Deidre," she said, as she walked over to put her arm around the woman's shoulders, which were now shuddering.

"There's no way these creeps will get you," Elliot said calmly but sternly, reiterating that the place was absolutely impenetrable.

Nathan had returned to the monitor. "Hey, everyone, they're about ready to enter the house. This should be interesting." The group, including Simon, who seemed to be catching on to the situation at hand, gathered around the surveillance camera. They watched as two of the men dressed in what appeared to be army fatigues, including flak jackets, attached a device to the door.

"Get ready," was all Elliot said, as they witnessed the door imploding inwards, but not before they heard the soft explosion. A puff of smoke rose up from where the door had been. The men entered. Four more followed. They were heavily armed, and night goggles were hanging around their necks. Big tufts of snow and ice fell from their clothing and boots as they spread out across the room. Within seconds, the floor at the entrance was drenched, and the snow outside just continued to pour in freely with the continued strong wind. For a brief second, two of them looked up, directly into the surveillance camera.

"Jesus," Simon said. "They're just like out of the movies."

"No kidding," Nathan added. "Honestly, folks, this is how they behave in Iraq. I've seen them do this to one family after another. Usually they haul off the men and boys. The remaining women scream, cry, and moan, but these assholes are impervious to their distress. Well, you don't need me to tell you that. I'm sure you've seen it on TV as well, especially since Claire would report on it from time to time and so did Michael."

"Yeah, and it got them murdered," Andie added.

"What?" Simon asked incredulously. "What do you mean?"

"That's what I've been working on, Simon," Andie said, "but I don't have time to go over it now. Later," she said, as she turned back to gaze at the surveillance camera. "Oh my God," she exclaimed, pointing to one of the men who had entered the house. "I know that guy. He's the one I told you about, Elliot, the one hanging out below my apartment. Wow. Look at him, he doesn't care about anything, does he?" she commented, as the man began systematically dumping the books off the bookshelves. "Aren't they getting close to this door?" Andie asked Elliot, becoming a bit concerned.

"Yes, but there's no way they'll find it," Elliot replied calmly. "Please believe me. It's not only invisible, it's airtight. Did any of you see it before I opened it?" he asked, trying to make his point. They all answered no.

By this time the men were in every room, going through all drawers, turning over mattresses, emptying containers of any kind, and all of them at one time or another would glance at the camera. It made Andie kind of dizzy trying to keep up with them all.

Then one of them entered Elliot's bedroom. He immediately went over to his dresser, whereupon he quickly opened a small jewelry chest. He lifted up the tray and dumped its contents into his hand and then into his pocket. Elliot just stared as the others stared at him for a moment. Next the man seemed to have located an envelope in one of the drawers. He ripped it open at the end and pulled out a fistful of bills, again stuffing them in his pocket. "My emergency cash," was all Elliot said.

After shaking the contents out of all of the other drawers and apparently not finding anything he was interested in, either for this assignment or personally, he went to the closet. He started heaving the clothes inside it onto the bed, occasionally reaching into a blazer's pocket or rummaging through a pair of slacks. His actions were both meticulous and ruthless. At one point he seemed to have located another item of interest, because he held something up to the light and then put it in his coat pocket. Andie looked over at Elliot again, but he just raised an eyebrow, as if to say he didn't know what the hell that was. Even the pictures on the walls did not escape the man's apparent desire to ensure that every item was touched. On his way out of the room, the man looked one last time at the camera and then, without warning and with lightning speed, he pulled a handgun out and shot it.

As one of their windows into the activities above blackened, the group gasped. "That was spooky," Nathan said, somewhat casually. For Elliot, it was more than spooky. He had begun to have a sinking feeling from the first time he saw the men look blatantly into the camera. He knew they knew they were there. But this behavior was so extreme, so "in your face." Now another room's camera had been shot, and the rest were going to go quickly, he was sure. There now existed an uncanny silence in the bunker. The fear of the unknown was starting to sink into the group. Elliot was pretty sure he knew one thing. These men did not plan on letting anyone who had seen them survive. But the tape was down in the bunker, Elliot reasoned, so how could they be sure that they would get it? In a split second, he knew the answer. The generator kicked on just as the electricity in the bunker had gone off. All of the men in the house were now standing in the living room, staring at the last camera, all six of them. The team leader then motioned for them to head out. They began to put their night vision goggles on as they departed. The leader looked back at the camera and shot it.

Elliot knew that they would be able to locate the generator in no time, even though he had taken great pains to camouflage it. If he turned it off now, they would just wait until he turned it back on again. Sure enough, as Elliot, Andie, Deidre, Nathan, and Simon watched, two men from the team were quickly on their way to locating the whereabouts of the generator. "There it is," Elliot said, when the men reached it. Within minutes they had disabled it and with it, the bunker's air.

While Elliot and Nathan were gathering the battery-operated torches and setting them in strategic places around the bunker, Deidre's sobs were starting to sound like a continuous drone. "Please, Deidre, stop crying," Andie entreated. "Simon, maybe you can spend some time with her," she said, noting that he was just sitting and staring.

"Wha? Oh, okay," he said, moving over on the couch next to the inconsolable Deidre. He awkwardly put his arm around her. She put her head on his big, wide shoulder and tried to stop crying.

"How much time is there, Elliot?" Andie asked, while both he and Nathan were in the storeroom. They both knew she meant time, as in how much oxygen was left.

"Maybe a couple of hours. It depends," Elliot said, sighing. "I'm sorry, Andie," he added, looking over at her affectionately, but with concern.

"It's not your fault, Elliot," she quickly said, trying to console the terrible guilt he must feel.

"It sure isn't," Nathan said, agreeing. "I told you, those guys are ruthless. Most are ex-military, so they have all of that training, plus they get to Iraq, and suddenly it's either them or the enemy. It does something to your head. They've become like animals. Plus, there's no accountability. They do not fall under any militaristic rules of law. They cannot be punished for blowing someone away there. And it doesn't hurt that they're paid for acting this way. It's your tax dollars hard at work," he added, trying to make a joke.

"Not funny," Andie said, although she smiled at Nathan when she said it. He was trying so hard to be a calming element, she noticed. But deep down, she figured they were all a bit panicked. "Let's go sit in the common room with Simon and Deidre and talk," she suggested. "There must be something we can do."

Elliot agreed, and the three of them joined the two. It looked like Deidre had actually fallen asleep.

"Hey, Simon, we're trying to problem-solve, so put your thinking cap on," Andie said, jokingly.

"It's always on," Simon said. "So what's up, and what are we going to do? I know the air will run out eventually."

"Glad you're back with us," Nathan said, patting Simon's shoulder as he sat down.

"Can we call anyone?" was Andie's first question, knowing they all had cells with them.

"These guys are assuming someone is here, so they'd pick up on a call in a flash," Elliot said grimly. "Basically, they need a body count to match their mandate, their assignment. They're going to wait."

No one said anything for a couple of minutes. "So, let's think," Andie continued. "This was a former underground. It's where people came to stay or hide, until they could move on."

"Right," agreed Elliot.

"I wonder what they did here while they waited," piped in Deidre. Everyone stopped to look at her. She had awakened and was sitting up, looking a bit better, Andie thought.

"They waited, they talked maybe, and maybe they slept," Nathan said.

"I bet they were scared, too," Deidre said, looking around the place. Others followed her gaze. The bunker had definitely taken on a significantly different air, given the spot lighting from the torches; shadows loomed, items were no longer distinguishable.

"I mean, we're trapped just like the slaves were trapped," Deidre added, beginning to sniffle again. "People out there want us to die."

Andie had to secretly admit that she was right. It was pretty revolting to think that they were hiding in here just like the slaves must have hidden, a century and a half ago. For everything Claire and Michael had tried to uncover about the government's deadly targeting of minorities, here they sat because they had tried, or were in the process of trying, Andie corrected herself, to expose their unlawful use of DU, among other crimes. As she looked around again at their surroundings, Andie began to envision a much more sinister place. Bottom line, this hideaway was no longer cozy and hospitable. It held persecuted people long ago who were considered dispensable, and now they, too, were being viewed in the same light. It was even more reprehensible given that it was Christmas Eve. "You know," she said, talking out loud, "if this place could talk, the stories would be huge."

"It used to be even scarier," Elliot said. "You should have seen it when I first started to excavate. I'm sure there were some things that I saw that an archeologist would have wanted," he added.

"Like what?" Nathan asked, curious to know.

"Rope," Elliot replied immediately. "Lots of pieces of rope kept popping up. And also a lot of candle bits. We should count ourselves lucky," he added. "Just think, we could be using up even more oxygen if we had to use candles."

"Well, now that you mention it, I wonder how they ventilated the place?" Nathan asked, standing up and walking toward the back of the room. He took one of the torches with him, so the shadows on everyone else became more pronounced, helping make each person less distinct. Andie felt a chill come over her that started at the top of her head and quickly descended down her spine. Instinctively, she stood up quickly to shake it off. Elliot stood up at the same time.

"That's an interesting question," he said, as he crossed the room to join Nathan. "It's at this end that I saw more of the previous dugout, but decided to close it off anyway. The underground had become large enough for my needs, although I did install this door here in case I ever wanted to expand."

"What's behind it?" Nathan asked, trying to contain his hope.

"Nothing. Just earth, basically. I don't even know if the builders reinforced the area. Why, what are you thinking?" he asked Nathan.

"I'm thinking that when these folks finally got the chance to move on, after a day, two days, maybe even a few hours only, that they would not have left by a front door. They would have needed to pop up somewhere not close to the safe house, to protect those trying to protect them."

Andie had joined the two by now and was intrigued by Nathan's logic. "That makes sense," she said, looking at Elliot, who was already nodding in agreement.

"So, let's open up the door," Andie urged. "We have nothing to lose," she whispered, looking over at Deidre. Simon was staring at them.

"Okay," Elliot said, "but there's one small hitch. It's locked electronically."

"No problem," Nathan said. "If you have an ax, a shovel, anything, I can break through this. Believe me."

Elliot went to the storage room and brought back both, plus a pitchfork and a small hoe.

"Why would you have these in here?" Andie asked, incredulous.

"Actually, I used them one day and was too lazy to return them to the shed outside because the weather had gotten so bad. So I just put them down here until I had the chance to use them again, then I thought I'd put them back. Lucky for us," he said, grinning.

"Let's hope so," Andie said, smiling back at him. She could already tell that the air was thinner. She was having just the tiniest bit of difficulty breathing.

Nathan took the ax and examined its head, then carefully scrutinized the butt of the head. Then he ran his forefinger across the edge to determine its sharpness. Finally, he looked at Andie and Elliot and said, "Get back, way back." They did as they were told.

Nathan backed up himself and then took a kind of running start, with the ax held cocked, behind his right shoulder. As he reached the metal door, he slammed it as hard as possible directly between the crack and the door jam, right where the locking device was situated. The ax stuck for a second and then fell to the ground along with pieces of the lock. The door swung open slightly, emitting a combination of cold with a very musty, earthy odor.

"How the hell did you do that?" Elliot asked, absolutely flabbergasted. Andie was awed as well.

"You must have forgotten," he said, smiling, "I'm from a coal mining family. We know how to handle ourselves underground, in the worst of circumstances. If you know how to use an ax, it can save your life."

By now Deidre had joined them, while Simon continued to rest on the couch. "Is this a way out?" she asked hopefully.

"We're about to find out," Nathan said, as he and Elliot pulled the door toward them. "Give me the shovel," Nathan said to Andie. It wasn't much, but it could dig. He took it and gingerly poked into the dirt that surrounded the door. Some pebbles fell down and rolled into the room. He jabbed at it again, but the same thing just happened again. He then poked at it directly across from the door jam. He hit something hard. He tried on the opposite side, across from where the door opened. Again, he ran into something hard. "I'm going to have to dig for a while," he said to Elliot. "It means a lot of this dirt is going to be coming in here."

"Don't worry," Elliot said, as he grabbed the pitchfork. "Let's have it."

Twenty minutes later, the two men were resting against the walls inside the bunker. Andie had been handwriting up some ideas regarding Claire's reports, and Deidre and Simon were sleeping against each other, trying to stay warm. It was getting colder, especially with the door open. The air was continuing to thin. Andie went over to them to find out what was up.

"There doesn't seem to be anything but dirt," Elliot said, obviously unhappy.

Nathan just kept shaking his head. "Something has to be keeping the dirt from just flooding in though. Hey, wait a minute," he said suddenly. "Elliot, we've been digging in the wrong direction!" He returned to the small alcove they had been able to chisel out and jabbed his shovel upward and outward, knocking large chunks of the earth out. After a few minutes, his shovel hit something hard. He tried again, *tap, tap, tap*. He turned quickly to look at Elliot and Andie. "There's something there," he said excitedly.

By now it was nearing midnight. The two men were tired and hungry. Andie brought out crackers and peanut butter and some semi-warm soft drinks. "What do you think is up there," she asked, not wanting to become too hopeful, but hoping beyond hope nonetheless. The bunker was becoming a coffin. The air was hard to breathe, and the cold was starting to penetrate to the point of being unbearable. Deidre and Simon continued to sit on the couch under a blanket, although Andie could tell that Simon was becoming restless and wanted to help. She shook her head *no,* when he had looked in her direction. She preferred that he stay with Deidre, who was remaining relatively calm because of his presence.

"We're about to find out," Nathan said, as he and Elliot got up from the small table where they'd been eating. They pulled up two chairs under the dirt ceiling and began to hit away at the dirt, tapping the obstruction each time. After another ten minutes or so, Nathan held up the battery-operated torch. "It's a trap door of some sort," he said excitedly. "We've got to get past it." He hit it hard with his shovel, but it didn't budge. "Elliot, give me your pitchfork," Nathan demanded, handing the torch to him at the same time. He took it and stuck it into the edge of the wood. They could hear it splintering as he pulled hard on it.

"Be careful," Elliot warned, "we don't know what's on the other side."

If Nathan heard him, he ignored him. Suddenly, it gave way. With a whoosh, the entire area was filled with dirt, burying Nathan.

"Oh my God, we've got to dig him out," Andie cried. Elliot was already doing so with his hands. Unexpectedly, Nathan's arm shot out from beneath the dirt. Elliot and Andie and Simon, who had quickly lumbered over, grabbed what they could and pulled. He came sputtering out within seconds, gasping for breath.

"What's up there?" he asked between breaths, "what's up there?" No one had looked yet. But Andie could certainly feel cold, cold air coming in. Unfortunately, it was stale and not that robust, she noted.

While Simon and Elliot brushed Nathan off, Andie took the torch and climbed up on the chair. She pointed it into the abyss. She could barely make out the indentations in the steep passageway, the imperceptible stairs that allowed people to winch themselves forward hand over hand, pushing with their feet. The tunnel appeared to be built at a forty-five to fifty degree angle. How far it went or what happened at the end was unknown. Andie stepped back down off the chair. Elliot was looking at her quizzically as Simon handed a glass of water to Nathan. She opened her hands, indicating that it was a mystery. Elliot nodded, understanding. They had no choice.

83

The VP's Christmas Eve dinner with his family turned out better than he had anticipated. The meal was absolutely delicious. His wife knew his favorites, and although everyone knew he shouldn't eat the rich, caloric food, everyone did whatever they could to make sure he was in a good mood so as to keep his temper in check. "Everyone" included his two sons, their wives, and the three grandchildren, so far. All of them girls. He wanted one of his sons to have at least one son, so he hoped they'd get their wives pregnant again soon. Both women were mousey and as uninteresting as their husbands. They sat at the dinner table quietly, trying to keep their children engaged, while the old man had his third helping of the roasted pig, mashed sweet potatoes, stuffing, and green beans, and the piping hot rolls with melted butter. Dessert was going to be his favorite as well, ice cream pie.

The kids were wound up with thoughts of Santa coming down the chimney and were worried that the fire in the fireplace would prevent him from delivering the goods. The moms reassured them over and over again that the fire would be out well before Santa's arrival. Finally, they excused themselves and took their children upstairs to read some stories. The sons tried to engage their father in discussions about the upcoming Winter Olympics, but he was uninterested. After his dessert, he excused himself to his office. In there he finally had some peace and quiet to contemplate his upcoming trip. He flipped on the TV and noted that RW&B was no longer showing the photo of the woman, DeeDee Morgan. He imagined she had been terminated by now. He smiled slightly to himself with this thought, as he replayed all of his planning and knew that she had been the one potential flaw that could have ruined everything. But now everything was on track. He was going to be legendary, he was sure of it. His bags were already packed.

84

The group sat around the small coffee table and discussed their plan. "We're going to have to go. It's our only way out," Andie explained.

"Why doesn't someone go first and then come back and tell us what it's like and if it's safe?" Deidre asked.

"It's not that easy," Elliot said. "We're going to need to help each other out as we go. We need to pull and push one another. One person may not make it alone. I'm sure that's why they carved those steps the way they did."

"But where does it go?" Deidre asked, for the umpteenth time.

"We don't know, but we know it's been used," Andie said, "and that's good enough for us. We've got to get out of here, and we believe that it will come out in a good place. We have to believe it. So, everyone bundle up and let's get ready to go. Elliot will lead and Nathan will bring up the rear. Deidre, you follow Elliot, and I'll follow you. Simon, you come behind me, and Nathan will help from below."

"I don't think I'll be coming," Simon said, stoically.

"Don't be absurd," Andie replied. Nathan looked irritated, Elliot sighed.

"I'll just be a burden," he continued, ignoring Andie's comment.

"Simon, we're not going to beg," Elliot said, calmly but evenly. "We'll be tying a rope around each of us, linking us like climbers. I know, it can be dangerous," he said, noting the look of skepticism on the man's face, "but it's what they must have done as well. We don't want anyone slipping and falling. I'll keep the ax digging into the earth, like we're climbing a mountain, so as to secure the group at each new step. Nathan can help push you from behind. If you don't like the plan, then, yes, you can stay. But you will certainly die. The oxygen is almost gone," he said, gasping a bit when he did, perhaps to make the point. He didn't need to, however, as Simon was already having the most difficulty of all of them catching his breath. His chest was noticeably heaving in and out.

"I'll do my best," he said resignedly.

"We all will," Nathan said, zippering up his jacket. "Let's get moving." He held out the rope, which had already been slip-knotted in five different locations. After Elliot put it over his shoulders, he dropped it to his waist, tightened it and then helped Deidre, who had become visibly terrified to pull it on, then he handed it to Andie, who did the same. She and Nathan helped get it over Simon's substantial bulk, and then Nathan put the last link over his head and pulled it tight around his waist.

"Let's go," Elliot said, as he headed toward what they all hoped would be their safety route.

Deidre was the only one of the group who had not seen the tunnel. Elliot led, grabbing the first step and then hoisting himself up to the next; Deidre entered the darkness. "Oh, no," she sobbed, "no, no, no." The darkness and closeness suddenly brought back repressed memories of being alone in a dark, cold cell.

Andie was right behind her. "Shut up, Deidre!" Andie said sternly. "Shut up, or I'm going to knock your block off myself."

Deidre's next sob was more of a gurgle.

85

The team leader was sitting in the van, smoking a cigarette while he contemplated what to do next. He looked at his watch. *Jesus,* it was past midnight already. His little girl had surely gone to bed by now. She'd been so excited about Santa coming that he and his wife couldn't get her to calm down. His wife was so happy to be pregnant again, too. The baby was due around New Year's. Yes, indeed; it was going to be a great Christmas, *if,* the man thought angrily to himself, *if* he could finish this assignment and get home.

His men were making the rounds and trying to figure out what the generator had been used for, where the room or rooms were located, while making sure no one escaped. Unfortunately, they weren't making any progress. Just then his lieutenant radioed in: "No targets identified. Do you want us to repeat last directive?" he asked.

The team leader thought for a moment and then said, "No, I'm coming there. We need to complete the mission." He knew he was being impatient, but he didn't care. He was so glad to be stateside finally. The last three years had been spent in Iraq, and some of it in the bloody battle of Fallujah. He didn't want to miss another Christmas.

"Roger that," the lieutenant replied crisply.

The Team Leader got out of the van, flicked his cigarette into the nearby three-foot snow bank, and zipped up his down parka. *Shit!* It was freezing out here. It wouldn't be so bad except the wind was horrendous, the man thought, as he reached into the back of the van and pulled out a heavy metal box, then headed up the driveway. He noted the two cars again, or at least their silhouettes, given that over two feet of snow had covered them. On a hunch, he wiped it away off the back windows to see if people were hiding in there. Nothing.

Once he reached where his men were congregated, he laid out his plan. "Let's torch the place," he said calmly. "We'll place the explosives twenty yards apart around the perimeter of the foundation," he explained. "Then we'll ignite them simultaneously. It will go up rapidly, and with this kind of material," he said, pointing to the box of explosives, "there will be no telltale residue as to what caused the fire. Any questions?"

One man raised his hand. "What about the neighbors?"

"What neighbors?" the Team Leader asked derisively, looking around. "Just because there are houses, doesn't mean people are here." He had noticed the minute they'd entered the street that it appeared deserted. He felt the man on his team should have been just as observant.

"I have a question," the lieutenant said.

"Shoot," the team leader responded, smiling at his little pun. He and the lieutenant had been friends since they were in the Marines together.

"What about proof? We need to make sure that we get them," he said, referring to DeeDee Morgan and Andie Aaberg.

"They're here all right," the Team Leader responded with confidence. "We'll let the local police department and their medical staff match the dental records. It's Christmas Eve, for God's sake," he said impatiently. "Well, now actually it's Christmas," he added, looking at his watch. "Merry Christmas, everyone. Don't you want to be home with your loved ones?"

They all eagerly responded yes.

"I thought so," he said. "Let's get going. We'll reconvene here as soon as you've set up the explosives. We detonate after we pull away, obviously. Okay, men, you've got your orders. Let's go," he said. The team quickly dispersed, laying out the ammunition.

Within twenty minutes, Elliot's house was an inferno. It lit up the night sky for hours, even though the fire department did everything it could to quash the flames. By the end, there was only a foundation remaining. The appearance was ghostly. While the storm raged on, the ashes were quickly covered in white, except where one of the firemen would step, creating a black streak within the white blanket. Once the foundation became covered with snow, it looked more like an ancient ruin than a recently lived-in homestead.

"I sure hope no one was home," the chief fireman remarked to the detective.

"Me, too," the other man said, "but it looks like there were two cars here," he said, pointing to the smoldering tires.

"Yeah, I noticed," the chief said, sighing. "It's too bad."

If Elliot could have known right then and there that his house had just been set on fire, he could have cared less. Right now, he and the rest of the group were fighting for their lives. What little air there was in the tunnel was spoiled. The dampness and overall tightness of the space made it almost impossible to take in a good, full breath, Andie noticed. Most of the time she could only take in a shallow one, or sometimes none at all. Added to not being able to see much ahead, except for Deidre's feet and a wall of darkness, claustrophobic panic was a very real possibility. And the steps, which had not been used in well over a hundred years, Andie imagined, were difficult to find, and once she located them, it was hard to keep her feet from slipping. Every time this happened, Deidre screamed out because she felt the pull on her waist and thought she was going to fall.

Then there was Simon, who was coming up behind Andie. He was having even more difficulty, Andie could tell. She could hear him struggling for every breath, almost as if he were being strangled. His weight and crippled legs created a greater problem because when he slipped, like Andie did, the pull on her was huge. They should have thought this through more carefully, Andie reasoned now. It would have been better to have Simon at the lead, maybe. But no, she thought again, that would have made it more treacherous for all of them. Thankfully, after Simon slipped a few times, she realized that Nathan was trying to anticipate it, and he would push up on the man, attempting to alleviate the impact his pull would have on Andie.

So far, no one had spoken a word. Probably because no one could, Andie thought to herself wryly. She wondered what Elliot was seeing, if anything. She wondered how much further it was until they reached the opening. This was just terrible. She couldn't imagine what it was like for the slaves. Persecution was a horrible human characteristic, Andie contemplated as she struggled to secure her next footing, especially when it was government-sponsored.

Just at that moment, Simon slipped hard. Andie felt herself airborne, dropping back. Deidre screamed loudly. And then, after what seemed like minutes, Andie jerked to an abrupt stop, hitting hard against the earth as she slammed into it. Deidre's feet were on her head. She no longer felt Simon's weight below her, but she dared not look down. Finally, she heard Elliot ask if everyone was okay. Simon and Nathan did not answer. Elliot caught his breath as best he could and then yelled out as loud as he could, "Nathan?" The name echoed for a couple of seconds.

Nothing.

Andie finally got up the nerve to turn to look. She could barely make out the bundle several yards away. It appeared that the two men were together. Finally they heard Nathan.

"I cut the rope to stop your fall," he said to the group. "We'll have to follow as best we can. Simon's okay, but he can't breathe very well." Nathan stopped speaking for a minute to catch what breath he could. Then he continued, "I've got everything under control. Go ahead."

Elliot did not respond immediately. He was wondering if there was a safer alternative to Nathan's plan. Finally, unable to come up with anything better, he agreed. "We'll see you at the opening. We'll wait for you, wherever we come out. We'll wait there. Good luck," he yelled. Then he calmly and quietly said to Deidre and Andie, "Let's go." For the next ten minutes they retraced their steps. They were moving much more quickly now. Andie was wondering how the two men below her were doing. If they could move this quickly, then it should be easier for Simon and Nathan, she thought. She hoped so, but something told her that things were not going well for them. After another twenty minutes or so, Andie realized that she was nearing exhaustion.

"I'm feeling some colder air," Elliot yelled suddenly. "I feel more air!" he said, even more loudly. Andie heard Deidre start to cry. "Jeez," Andie muttered to herself, *she cries when she's sad, when she's scared, and when she's happy, what a nut.* Then Andie could feel the air Elliot had alerted them to. It was so refreshing. Even though it was cold, it was abundant. Andie started feeling better immediately.

"I'm coming up to something," Elliot reported. "It's an opening, but . . . uh, oh," and he stopped talking.

"What is it, Elliot?" Andie asked. "What are you seeing?" They had stopped moving.

"There's a barrier," was all he said.

"But we're feeling the cold air," Andie argued. "We're getting oxygen."

"I know, but it's through a crevice only. Both of you secure yourselves," he said next. "I'm going to try something."

Andie hugged the earth as best she could. She imagined Deidre was doing the same. She could hear Elliot pounding on something. Then she heard scraping; it sounded heavy. Then more air than she could have ever dreamed of rushed in. It felt like her lungs were going to explode. She didn't think she'd ever had such a wondrous feeling in her whole life.

"Okay, got it," Elliot said. "I'm going to cut the rope now, so hang on again."

With this announcement, Deidre began to protest. "No, please don't cut it, Elliot. What if I slip, what if I can't hold on, what if something happens to you and you can't pull me out?"

"Deidre, I'll take care of you," Andie said calmly. "You're not going to fall." Inside she was tiring of this woman's histrionics. Then she felt badly, remembering that Deidre had had a hell of time during the past week. She should give her a little slack.

Elliot had already cut the rope. Next he hoisted himself up and out of the portal he had created by pushing up on the cement, first with the butt of the ax, then by prying it from where it had been resting. *Nathan was right,* Elliot thought. *An ax could save your life.*

As soon as he got up and out, he turned to help Deidre and Andie, still not taking the time to assess where they were. All he knew was that it was dark, and apparently deserted. There wasn't a soul around as far as he could tell.

"Now, Andie, cut the rope so I can get Deidre out," Elliot said. She did as she was told, the problem being now that she would have to move without the security of anyone above her. She hung tight, though, knowing she was going to have to move when Elliot told her to come.

"Okay, Andie, push yourself forward. I'll grab you as soon as I can," Elliot said. "Take it easy, it's not too hard. Just secure your footing."

Andie took a deep breath and pushed with all of her might, trying to create the necessary momentum to scramble up and out. Suddenly, she felt Elliot grab her forearm and pull. Then, with little warning, she was out, standing in the freezing cold and looking at Elliot. She hugged him tightly, and he did the same. Both of them forgot momentarily that Deidre was there. After a couple of seconds, Andie pushed back from Elliot to take in their surroundings. She immediately noticed that, while she could see it snowing, it was not snowing on them. "Where are we?"

she asked, still taking in the wonderful feeling of being safe in Elliot's strong arms.

"I don't know yet," Elliot said, grabbing the torch. He held it up so they could look around. "Oh my God," Deidre gasped. Andie had just done the same thing.

"Can you believe this?" Elliot asked. "What are the chances of this happening?" he asked, looking around in all directions with dismay and shaking his head.

Just then they heard Nathan. "Help!" he cried. "I need help." Elliot and Andie rushed to the opening. Nathan was dragging Simon, face down, up the tunnel. "I've got him, pull me out," he said, as he held his arm up out of the portal. "I'll hang onto his ankle. I don't know if he's still alive. This is all I could do," he gasped, as Elliot pulled. Andie tried to steady Nathan so he would not lose his grip on Simon, who appeared very limp. As soon as Nathan was out, he and Elliot pulled Simon out and laid him on his back.

Nathan felt for his pulse, which did not register as he listened for breathing. "I don't hear anything," he said rather frantically. Elliot moved in. He tilted Simon's head back and opened his mouth. Then he reached in it with two fingers and pulled out significant amounts of dirt. Holding Simon's nose, he began CPR. "Nathan, push on his chest when I tell you to," Elliot ordered, "No, higher, put one hand on top of the other. Okay, now push rapidly and count." Following fifteen compressions by Nathan, Elliot breathed into Simon's mouth. After a minute or so, Andie saw Simon's chest rise; Elliot quickly turned him on his side so he could cough the dirt out. It worked! Andie realized that she had not been breathing herself during the exercise. The sense of relief was overwhelming. They sat him up and helped to lean him against one of the many tombs surrounding them. The portal had led them to the inside of a mausoleum.

Deidre was sitting against another one, hugging herself and gently rocking back and forth. Andie decided she might need some heavy duty counseling if they ever got out of here.

"Does anyone have a charge on their cell?" Elliot asked hopefully. Everyone looked, but they were all dead. It seemed as if the inclement weather had knocked out the signal.

"I don't think the ax is going to be able to get through that lock," Elliot said to Nathan, as the two stood and looked at the iron gate imprisoning them.

"Agreed," Nathan said somberly. "I didn't even know they could make locks that big," he said, staring at the ancient padlock that resembled a large platter.

"I guess someone really wanted to protect this place," Andie said, looking around. "There must be twenty tombs in here," she said, amazed.

"At least," Elliot said, uninterested. "The point now is how to get out. We're going to freeze to death if we don't do something, and soon."

The dawn light was just beginning to show itself, even though the blizzard continued to rage. The temperature was well below freezing, and the clothing they had worn would not be suitable for a long stay in an open confinement.

"Let me look around for a place where we can all huddle to share our warmth," Andie said. "Maybe we can figure something out."

"Maybe we'll have to go back to Elliot's bunker," Deidre whispered.

"I don't think so," Elliot responded. "It will be the same as we left it, we won't be able to breathe."

"I heard it's not so bad to freeze to death," Deidre continued. "You just go to sleep."

"No one's going to freeze to death," Andie said, trying to sound re-assuring, although she thought her tone was rather hollow. She wished Elliot had not mentioned it. As she looked out at the great expanse of the land surrounding the tiny cemetery, she figured it would be a while before anyone came this way. Who knew when someone would visit a loved one near this mausoleum? As she made her way around it, looking for a nook to stay warm in, Andie suddenly remembered where she'd seen the name that kept popping up on all of the tombs: *Winsome*. Those were the people who had started The Plowman's Grille. She then began to observe the dates—they went back to the late 1860s. So . . . they were living here right after the Civil War and maybe during it, Andie mused. It was then that she saw them. She realized she had missed them earlier because they were no longer recognizable. There were flowers, or what used to be flowers, strewn all over the place. The wind had blown them, but someone had brought them here. Someone visited this place. There was the tiniest bit of hope.

Andie didn't want to huddle too far away from the iron gate for fear of missing anyone who might happen to pass by, but on the other hand the iron gate allowed the incessant wind to penetrate what shelter they had.

She quickly located three tombs, on the east side, not far from the gate that were situated in a U. Andie read one of the names: Viola Winsome, fond wife of Samuel Winsome and mother of Abraham Winsome. This mausoleum was in tribute to the people who had started The Plowman's Grille, Andie realized. The dates ranged from 1874 to 1941. It looked like Abraham had lived the longest life, being born in 1880. Dead flowers were also in this corner, Andie noted. She called the others over, and they all grouped their belongings together to figure out a way to make the most of any warmth. Deidre looked like she was going to fall asleep standing up and Simon looked ill.

"Why doesn't everyone try to get some sleep, while I keep watch," Elliot offered. "I'm sure everyone's beat."

"I'll stay awake with you," Andie said, wanting to spend time with him.

"Okay, sure," he said, smiling.

Nathan nodded okay, too, having started out tired from jet lag and the exertion it had taken to save Simon. He was asleep in no time. In fact, within an hour they all were. Andie had fallen asleep on Elliot's shoulder and he on hers.

Fortunately, the owner of the horse had laced a string of bells around its neck, which jingled loudly enough to awaken Andie and Elliot. They looked up to see what had made the noise and observed the animal, steam flowing freely from its nostrils like a locomotive, coming across the field. As they watched it, the wagon it was pulling, and the person driving it approach them, they could not believe their eyes.

"Am I dead or dreaming?" Andie asked Elliot, rubbing her eyes for the second time.

"If you are, then I am, too," he said, starting to stand up.

"Wait," Andie said, "maybe we better see who it is before we allow him to see us."

"I can tell you it's not DarkSand, if that's what you're worried about," Elliot said jokingly. "They tend to be a bit more modernized."

"I guess you're right," she agreed. "I've become more paranoid than you now."

"I can understand why," was all Elliot said in response.

By now it was obvious the wagon was approaching the mausoleum. Andie had stood up, too, and they both were leaning against the bars, looking out. They could see now that it was an old man who was driving the wagon, an old black man, an African American, Andie saw. "Thank God," Elliot whispered. Andie felt the same way. DARKSAND he was not.

Finally, after some time crossing the field through the blizzard, the wagon driver and horse were nearing the burial chamber. He looked up to see the two figures of Andie and Elliot standing at the gate, with the wind blowing their clothes skin tight against their frozen bodies and matting their damp hair to their skulls. Their bare hands were white-knuckled around the bars as the snow on the outside swirled around. All in all they presented a picture to the man of apparitions trapped in his family's old mausoleum.

"Good Lawd Almighty," were his first words, as he brought his horse to a stop. "What you two people doin' in there?"

Andie and Elliot didn't know what to say.

"We're trapped, kind of," Andie finally said hesitantly.

"Good Lawd," was all the old man said, shaking his head as he walked toward them with a large key in his hand. "Good Lawd. And on a day such as this. It's Christmas, you know?" He was tall and lean, maybe in his late sixties or early seventies, Andie couldn't tell. His top coat was suede, and the oversized hat he wore looked to be almost as old as him. It was catching the snow in its brim.

"We know," Andie replied, smiling as best she could.

As the old man put his key in the large padlock and turned it, he said, "This here is my family's plot. My name's Charles Winsome."

Oh, Andie thought, *Tim had told me the current owner's name of The Plowman's Grille was Charles, Charles Winsome. Here he was.* She didn't have time to think it through; it was just too damn spooky. She hugged her body again, feeling a brief chill unrelated to the storm.

"We're sorry to have trespassed," Elliot said, not sure where the conversation was going and not wanting to be disrespectful.

"Nah, that ain't a problem. They are all dead, if you hadn't noticed. I'm just worried that you might be freezin' to death. You might have been joinin' 'em if you get my gist," he said, chuckling softly to himself.

Just then Nathan sat up from where he had been curled up behind one of the tombs.

"Oh my Gawd," Charles Winsome said again. "You got more people in here?"

"Two," Andie said flatly. "Two more."

"How'd you get in there?" he asked, looking at Elliot.

"There's a door in the floor. We were trying to get away from some danger and found a tunnel that led to here," Elliot said simply.

The old man shook his head again and went back to his wagon. He let down the back and began rolling up the covers that were lying on the bed, on top of something that Andie and Elliot could not see.

"Come here and get yourself one of these," he said, handing the blankets out to Andie and Elliot, who had now walked out of the crypt. They quickly did as he said, wrapping the warm flannel around themselves. "Here, take the rest for your friends," the old man said, shoving more blankets at them. The cold wind whipped the corners of the material up into the dark sky, almost forcing it to seemingly take flight. Elliot grabbed a tail quickly and hugged it against his body, turning to take the rest to the group. Andie pulled hers tighter around her neck, catching a whiff of a sensuous odor.

"What is that smell?" she asked.

"That's the fine scent of roses," he said, motioning toward the bed of the wagon. "I bring them twice a year to my family here, Christmas and Easter. I never missed doin' either," he added proudly. "Here you go, missy," he said, handing her the most beautiful white rose she had ever seen. "Merry Christmas."

"Oh, why, thank you, Mr. Winsome," Andie said, feeling tears welling up in her eyes. "Thank you."

"Here come your friends, little lady," he said, smiling at her, looking at the four people coming toward them, all wrapped in the blankets. He noticed one man having trouble walking. "Let's get these flowers to my family in there, and then I'll take you out of here."

Andie nodded obediently, like a child, and began to collect the flowers from the bed with him.

"Now, y'all," Charles Winsome said, motioning to Elliot and the rest of the group, after he and Andie had gathered up the flowers, "y'all get in there and stay warm. I'll take you where you need to go directly."

Elliot quickly joined the two as they entered the mausoleum. "Mr. Winsome," he said in a soft voice. "I want to tell you that we appreciate your offer to take us somewhere, but to be frank, you do not want to be affiliated with us. We may be being chased by the government, or at least a government arm." The old man listened thoughtfully as he took the flowers from Andie and laid them carefully on the floor in the center of the crypt. Then he turned and looked intently at Elliot.

"Oh, come on. No one from the government is chasin' anybody, not on Christmas. I guarantee you that," the man said sincerely, as he picked up one of the roses, walked to a tomb, knelt, and put a flower on it. "You two best go back and get in that wagon and get warm, I got some prayers to say now."

Andie, still clutching her white rose, turned to go back to the wagon. Elliot followed, concerned that the old man was not hearing him correctly.

All five were huddled in the bed of the wagon, one in each corner, with DeeDee sitting curled up in the middle. She was still shivering, but the flannel blankets were doing their trick and starting to trap the heat. The snow had stopped, but the wind was still blowing fiercely. Finally they heard the man coming. He approached the bed.

"I've been thinking 'bout what you said," he said slowly. "You best come home with me. Me and my wife ain't got any children with us this Christmas, even though my misses has been cookin' like we do. We could use the company. Come home, have a meal, and we'll decide what to do. I won't take no for an answer," he added. "Now you best cover up, *allll* up, so as not to get more chill," he said, emphasizing the *all*. "I mean cover everythin', every lil hair." The tired group did as he said, basically submerging themselves under the multitude of rose-scented flannel blankets.

They felt him get on the seat and then heard him clucking his tongue in such a way as to turn the horse around. Despite the bumpy ride, and the incessant jingle from the bells, they all fell asleep in the rickety old wagon.

86

"Are you ready to go?" the VP asked the Secretary of Defense.

"Yes," he said, still regretting that he was going on this dreadful trip with the man he hardly recognized anymore.

They were standing in the VP's office. As he was going through his checklist, the Secretary had arranged for everything, he confirmed. "Okay, let's go," he ordered. "I'll meet you there in two hours," he said, looking at his watch, referring to Andrews Air Force Base. "Don't be late."

The Secretary of Defense was tired of the man's attitude and manner, but he was also too tired to care. He couldn't wait to get back and spend time with his family. They planned on having a nice New Year's Eve party.

After the Secretary had left, the VP walked boldly to his secret safe, opening it quickly so as to remove his treasured map. He pulled out the document carefully and then opened it to the map, lifting it out gingerly, and spreading it for the umpteenth time on his desk to observe and admire it. Ghosts watched and waited helplessly, wondering what evil was to be executed next.

The man picked up a magnifying glass and placed it over Iraq. He squinted slightly, noting the airport, the road into Baghdad, and the palace within the Green Zone. He felt like a kid who couldn't wait to receive his trophy for winning the game for the team, for the whole school. For that reason, he reached in his desk and pulled out the razor. Without ceremony, he deftly scratched off the Green Zone, making sure he did not nick himself like he had before. Damn that blood on there. He hated to see it. But he could do nothing about it. He then ambled back to the safe and returned the document, sans the map. He folded it carefully and put it in his briefcase, which closed automatically with a loud snap, indicating the lock was engaged.

With that, he looked around his office, sighed happily, turned off the light, and started to exit. Suddenly, without warning, he felt the need to turn and look; at what he did not know, but the opportunity allowed him to see his office from a different perspective. The muted darkness created the sense of cobwebs in and among his books and memorabilia. It seemed that the room's temperature had taken on a life of its own. It had dropped ten degrees. Though the light was minimal, coming in from the outside only, there actually appeared to be shadows throughout the room, but . . . they did not belong. The powerful man hurriedly closed the door, dropping his briefcase as he did so. He leaned to pick it up and realized he was shaking.

The Secretary of Defense had already had Air Force 2's cargo loaded with the fireworks desired so highly by the VP. The staff had boarded. The pilot and co-pilot had just introduced themselves to the Secretary over the intercom and were checking out the controls. Now all they needed was a VP.

He eventually showed up, walking calmly from the limo to the plane. The Secretary was at the top of the steps to greet him. He reached out to take the briefcase from him in a helping manner as he approached the top, but the VP shook his head no and pulled it closer to him.

"What's wrong with you?" the Secretary asked, looking concerned. "You look spooked." And he did. His face was white and sweaty, and his eyes conveyed a kind of wildness, like fear.

"Move," was all he said as he brushed past the Secretary and entered the cabin.

Soon, the two men were buckled in and had a beverage in hand as the engines started up. At that moment, the Secretary happened to look out his window. He saw who he thought to be the co-pilot walking back into the hangar. He decided his eyes must be deceiving him, however, because at that very moment the jet began to back up with the help of the agent on the ground, motioning with the lighted batons. They were soon airborne.

"Did you let *him* know you were going?" the Secretary asked the VP after twenty minutes or so.

"No. He doesn't need to know quite yet. He's doing the Christmas thing with his family and the public. The news might be disruptive to his agenda," the VP replied flippantly.

The Secretary thought this was an understatement. Ever since he could remember, the roles the two men played had seemed reversed. The President was constantly doing the cheerleading, while the VP was doing the hard work, albeit behind the scenes. He'd never quite understood it, but he figured the two men had come to some understanding. Now, however, the VP was not only acting behind the scenes, he was acting behind the other man's back. This did not seem like a good idea, but, hey, he was just the Secretary of Defense.

"What are you going to do, let him see it on TV?" The Secretary was just curious.

"Maybe," was all the VP said, as he got up and went to the back of the cabin to lay down.

The Secretary shrugged and ordered a meal. He was hungry.

87

"Okay, folks, here we are," the old man said, as the horse and wagon came to a halt. Everyone slowly woke up and began to pull the blankets off. Andie did not know what she expected, but it was not this.

The wagon was sitting in front of a veritable mansion. The house was palatial. The porch surrounded it in the antebellum style seen in movies about the Civil War. That was it, Andie thought to herself suddenly, it was a southern style mansion. How ironic she mused, as she stood up and shook the flower leaves and stems from her clothes. She started to jump off the back of the wagon when Mr. Winsome took her hand and helped to lift her down. Andie was surprised at how strong he was, especially given his age. "Thank you," she said, turning to look once again at the majestic house.

"Get on in," he said, motioning to the front door. "Y'all get on in. It's freezin' out here, if you hadn't noticed."

The motley crew headed in, with Nathan helping Deidre and Elliot helping Simon. Andie followed, looking around at the grand expanse of the land and home, the three-car garage, the adjacent greenhouse, vast field, the smell of a fireplace burning, and the beautiful pond off to the west. It was just gorgeous.

Then they were inside the house. The smell of roasting meat and baked desserts wafted everywhere. The Christmas decorations, both secular and religious, were stunning and had been placed all over. There were two trees in different rooms fully lit and a dinner table set for them all. Andie wondered how this had come to be, but decided not to ask. Just at that moment, Wenona Winsome came walking out from around the corner to greet the company. Charles Winsome simply said, "Here they are, darlin', just as I promised. Now I got to get Ginny into her warm barn. I'll be back in few minutes."

Wenona looked like a different woman from the one Andie had met as a "waitress" in The Plowman's Grille. She was casually dressed in a very becoming green and red skirt and sweater outfit. "Merry Christmas, everyone. Just call me Wenona," she said, nodding knowingly at Andie. "Anyone wants to take a shower, follow me. We've got plenty of bathrooms and bedrooms, so don't be shy," she said, smiling. "I've got some fresh clothing for everyone. Our children always leave behind two or three outfits so they don't have to pack so much when they come for visits, which ain't often enough, believe me," she said genuinely.

She took special interest in Deidre, putting her arm around her as they walked and talking to her in soothing tones. What she said, Andie did not know. Andie was bringing up the rear and entered the last bedroom that Wenona was pointing to. But to her surprise, Wenona followed her in, closing the door behind her.

"Well, missus. I told you I had a feelin' 'bout you, remember that?"

"Yes, ma'am," Andie replied, quite taken aback.

"You're Andie Aaberg, right?"

"Yes, but . . ."

"And the other young lady is DeeDee Morgan, correct?"

"Yes. . . ." Andie was beginning to have a bad feeling about this line of questioning. How did she know?

"Y'all are all over the TV. They've got you doin' some big misdeed. And now they've added to the story that y'all are dead."

Andie's heart was in her throat. "I don't know what to say, Mrs. Winsome. . . . We told your husband that it was not safe for him to help us, but . . ."

"Call me Wenona, dear. You don't have to say nothin'. I'm just tellin' you that you're in big trouble. Charles and me, we want to keep you safe. Now, are the rest of these folks with you trustworthy?" she asked, with a quick nod of her head in the direction of the others.

Andie felt a great deal of relief upon hearing this from the woman. "Yes, ma'am, I mean yes, Wenona," Andie said.

"Okay, then. Let's carry on. After supper, we'll go watch a bit a TV news and see where their storytellin' is headed." And with that she turned on her heel and left the room.

Andie had never taken a shower that felt so good. The water was hot and strong and the soaps plentiful. She washed her hair twice.

An hour later they were all at the table. Andie was famished. So was everyone. They held hands and prayed together. Then the meal began, and it was a feast. There was turkey and ham, sweet potatoes, mashed potatoes, gravy, fresh bread, fresh fruit, a gorgeous green salad. All of the vegetables were from their greenhouse, but in the spring, summer, and fall, they had a garden and orchards, full of vegetables and fruits, Charles explained. He said the spring, summer, and fall gardens were even better. The desserts began, after they were all full, but it didn't stop them. They were having a great time to boot, as they described their situation to their hosts, and now could even laugh at some of their mistakes.

Even Deidre was talking and laughing. Simon was looking much better as well. They had all been through a terrible ordeal, but they had made it, Andie thought to herself; at least so far. From what Wenona had told her, it seemed that now she was implicated as well. She couldn't imagine where the story about their deaths had come from, but nothing surprised her these days. *If it was on the news, then it must be true,* she thought sarcastically.

At the same time the group was consuming the dinner at the Winsomes, Tim Walsh was looking at Andie's email and downloads. The research was thorough. The data surrounding the DU were undeniable, and the information was presented in a format that every layperson could easily understand. The facts surrounding the death of Claire Thompson were also compelling. And then there was the analysis of the implants from Deidre Morgan's and Simon Feldman's arms. Simon was head of production for WSSN, for God's sake, Tim thought to himself. This was really too much to digest. The information condemned, overwhelming, the government's role in some very, very ugly business. And all of this had occurred right under the American people's noses. How could they have been hoodwinked so completely, so convincingly? he pondered. He knew that as a blogger it was his responsibility, and others like him, to get the information out. The mainstream media simply did not provide news anymore. Without the Internet and the bloggers, people would not be able to find out about the conspiracy he was looking at right now. He was proud to be part of a changing modality for ensuring that people in the US had informed choice. At the same time, he was a bit overwhelmed. He could hear his wife playing with their kids and their new toys and was alarmed at what kind of future they may have if he did not succeed.

88

"Does anyone want more pie?" Wenona asked her weary guests. They were all so full and content by now, that another piece of pie was an impossible feat. "Okay, then," she said, standing up, "how 'bout we go watch some entertainin' news?"

"Oh, darlin', please, let's not," Charles said, looking a bit distressed. "Not on Christmas."

"I know, honey, but these folks have got to see this. You know, but they don't, and they need to see it. I'm bringing in some hot coffee to help with the fatigue."

Andie and Elliot stood up first and headed to the living room where Wenona had pointed. There on the wall was a huge TV screen. Charles followed and flipped it on for them. Nathan, Deidre, and Simon followed, wondering what was going on. They had all been so content, but now their interest was piqued. They sat down to watch. Wenona came in quickly with a tray and cups and saucers. She returned a few minutes later with a pot of coffee, as promised.

Charles picked up the remote and pointed it at the screen. "Let's watch 'em all," he said, looking at his wife, who nodded her approval. The RW&B channel popped up first.

"Whoa," Elliot said, as Nathan whistled. The split screen showed both Deidre and Andie, which quickly flipped into a smaller inset allowing the pretty talking head to continue with her delivery in person. "What do we know about their demise, John?" she asked, smiling into the camera.

"Thanks, Wendy, and a Merry Christmas to you as well," John replied. He was outside somewhere, apparently, because he had a scarf and hat on. "While the DoD isn't talking, we've heard rumors from the local police in Frederick, Maryland, that they were holed up in a residence there. We don't know if there were hostages at this point."

"Who was responsible for taking them out?" Wendy asked, continuing to smile. The camera switched back to John.

"We're told that the CIA was involved in their eventual termination."

"The CIA?"

"Yes, Wendy. The CIA was involved because the woman DeeDee Morgan had fled the Green Zone in Iraq after killing two persons there during her escape. She apparently had classified information and was trying to sell it to our enemies."

"Sell it to who, John?" the pretty woman asked, either because she could not hear his response or because she thought the audience might like to know.

"We're still not sure, but it could have been to any number of countries in the Middle East, perhaps to North Korea, or maybe even to some in Indonesia. It's just not clear."

"Interesting, John, let's go back over the troubled woman's history, and then we'll talk about the other woman, her accomplice, Andie Aaberg. I understand both of these women worked for one of our competitors," Wendy said, grinning.

"Yes, that is correct," John replied, chuckling.

"Change it," Andie yelled. "I can't take it anymore. Aside from the fact that none of it's true, they should be discussing the shame of this war," she said angrily, looking around the room. Elliot and Nathan were both sitting straight up in their respective chairs, breathing heavily as though they could hit someone; Deidre looked over at Andie with a mournful expression on her face, and Simon appeared to be totally bewildered as he continued to stare at the TV.

The next channel had a similar format going, only this time the anchor was a nice-looking older man talking into the camera.

"And now an update on that double extermination by the CIA of the two women involved in traitorous espionage. What new information do you have for us, Cindy?" he asked, smiling into the camera.

A woman in a leather jacket, blonde hair blowing, standing somewhere outside, again, smiled and began. "Well, Robert, we know that the two women had apparently been friends for quite some time, and, as some say, they may have been more than just friends. Whatever their relationship, they were taken out by agents early this morning after being discovered in a home in Frederick, Maryland. It is still unknown if they had hostages and, if so, whether they murdered them prior to the agents' intervention."

"Did the agents try to take them alive?" Robert asked, obediently.

"Yes, of course, Robert, but they were unable to do so, as we have all learned now. The two women apparently put up a fierce fight, and they had plenty of ammunition. It was the best thing for the agents to do, to protect themselves and their lives. I'm sure their families are happy to have them home safe and sound on this white Christmas," Cindy said, smiling.

"I'm sure you're right about that," Robert replied. "We'll check back with you when you have more on this breaking story. And a Merry Christmas to you, Cindy."

"Same to you, Robert, you and your family," Cindy replied, smiling brightly.

Grinning, Robert turned to the weather woman, who was dressed in a type of party outfit that made her look more like a game show host than a meteorologist. "And a white Christmas it is, Jill. You want to give us an update?"

"I know," Charles said, as Andie started to ask that he switch channels again.

"Why don't you switch it to WSSN?" Simon asked, still perplexed. "We report the news. Not this BS, excuse me, Mrs. Winsome," he said, looking over at her. She pretended not to have heard him.

Charles had already done it. The WSSN reporter was unknown to Andie. "Who's he?" she asked, looking at Simon. He just shrugged. "I had to turn over hiring to someone else because I got so sick with my arm and all and so busy with . . ." and he paused, ". . . with the Bible classes," he said, his voice trailing off.

Andie rolled her eyes.

"We're sorry to report that our former colleagues Andie Aaberg and DeeDee Morgan were somehow involved in this un-American and un-patriotic scheme to steal and then sell classified documents to other countries. Joel, what are you hearing?" the man asked.

"What's Joel doing reporting?" Andie asked, alarmed to see him on the screen. Joel had always wanted to do the research behind the scenes.

Simon shrugged again.

Andie sighed loudly.

"Well, Wayne, we've got conflicting stories at this point."

"Finally," Andie said, expecting that there would be accurate information provided. Unfortunately, she was soon to be disappointed.

"We're not sure if Andie and DeeDee were killed together or they had split up in an effort to ambush the CIA . . ."

"Just turn it off," Elliot said, which Charles did happily. "We get the picture. Now we have to decide what to do. Let's not get too emotional about it."

An eerie silence overtook the room.

"Maybe it's not bad that you're both dead," Nathan said simply.

Andie looked over at him and started to laugh at this brilliant observation. "Maybe you're right," she agreed. She looked at Deidre. "What do you think, lover, are we better off dead?"

Deidre started to laugh. "I sure feel better dead," she said. Then they all laughed.

Another person who felt better that they were dead was the Secretary of Defense. He, too, was watching the news as it was unfolding. His quick notes to the RW&B had been conveyed accurately, he observed, and the rest of the stations were falling all over themselves to jump on the bandwagon. He started to relax a bit and was drifting off when his phone rang. The VP was still in the "bedroom" taking his nap.

"Mr. Secretary," his Chief of Staff stated, "I have a request from the Frederick Police in Maryland to talk with you. I told them you were out of the country, but they said it was extremely important that they speak with you, immediately," he added.

"Set it up," the Secretary said, sighing. He had contacted the police department there before leaving to inform them that he was extremely knowledgeable about the cause of the destruction of the house and that it was classified, but for them to let him know what they found in the way of persons killed in it.

"Mr. Secretary," the man said, his voice deep and gruff. "This is Captain Butler of the Frederick Police Department."

"Yes. Go ahead. This is a secure line," the Secretary stated.

"We have received the preliminary report from the medical examiner, and I stress the word preliminary."

"Go ahead."

"It appears, from the evidence collected so far, that there was no one in the house at the time that it burned down."

The Secretary was speechless.

"Excuse me, Mr. Secretary," the man continued, "I am concerned about what I'm seeing on the TV news."

"Yes, I can understand," the Secretary responded, his mind racing. "At this point, it's not your concern, however," he said sternly, trying to regain his status through articulation. "You must do everything in your power to keep these findings confidential. Who else knows besides you?"

"Just the Medical Examiner."

"Good. Tell him not to tell a soul," the Secretary emphasized.

"She's not allowed to speak about her results," the man said simply.

"Okay. Good. I'll be back in touch when I return to the country."

"Thank you, Mr. Secretary," the man said.

"Thank you," he responded and hung up.

Damn the VP's men, the Secretary thought. They appeared to have failed miserably. The women had escaped. How, he had no idea, but it didn't matter. What did matter was where they were now. He decided to keep this news to himself until he could get more information and design a course of action. Anything short of figuring out a strategic, finite approach to quash any news from the two females would blow up in their faces, and this last effort had the potential for doing just that. And so he stewed. He was still stewing when the jet began its descent into Riyadh.

89

Tim looked at his message to his readers and fellow bloggers. He felt it was the best he could do on behalf of Claire, Michael, and, now it appeared, Andie and poor Deidre. How sad and how unfair, he reflected. They were the true patriots, and look what had happened. Even given these circumstances, he had tried to be as unemotional as possible. If people got angry, they would be unable to deal with the realities on the ground, where the very real threats lay.

www.INFORMED CHOICE.com

Tim Walsh

Remember, it's up to you

Dear readers and fellow bloggers. Today is Christmas. I do not like to be the bearer of bad news on such a day, but time is of the essence, and we all need to remain vigilant in the fight to ensure that we can always obtain accurate information, no matter how hard it is to swallow sometimes.

You may be seeing on the MSM that Andie Aaberg and DeeDee Morgan were killed by the CIA because they were committing treasonous acts. They did no such thing. Do not believe it. I have firsthand knowledge that it is not true, and now you will, too. Please read on.

And with that he laid out the information regarding the DU, the government's effort to brainwash members of the press and others, although
he did not have any evidence as to who the others might be, and the fact
that if the press did not cooperate, then the government was resorting
to murder, and here he pasted in photos of Claire, Michael, Andie, and
Deidre. It was lengthy, comprehensive, and startling, to say the least.
Then he did what he and Andie had discussed and had decided was
necessary. He cc'd all members of Congress. All of them.

As he hit the send button, he realized that his life might never be the
same. But he could not not do this. The blogging community, at least
those who held similar values, would be supportive.

90

Following the decision by Andie and Deidre to "stay dead," the group
sat around the fireplace, enjoying its blazing warmth and talking about
what they were going to do to get on with their lives.

"I'm heading back to Iraq," Nathan said quietly. "I'm going to link
up with Tim there, if he'll let me, and we'll do the real stories. You know
what they say, a picture is worth a thousand words, and I believe I can
make a difference with my camera. I really do." Andie had told Nathan
about Tim earlier, at the dinner table.

"You're brave," was all Deidre said. It was all anyone said to him.

"What will you do, Miss Deidre?" Wenona asked sweetly.

"I think I'm going to move to Scotland," Deidre replied slowly. "I like
it there, and I can disappear there. I might try my hand at writing news
articles. I do enjoy it. I may be able to find some work along those lines.
I can do that without showing my face. I mean, I don't think anyone will
even recognize me. If they quit showing my photo. Maybe I'll dye my
hair for a while. I've always wanted to be a blonde."

"That would look nice with your big brown eyes," Nathan said en-
couragingly.

"Thanks" she said, looking over to him and smiling shyly.

"I'm going to go back and reclaim WSSN," Simon said defiantly. "I've
spent a good part of my career ensuring that it is an upstanding news
organization, and to have let it collapse so quickly, so far, I'm ashamed.
We need to be the leaders, since no one else will do it. And now, Andie,

what is going to happen? I mean, since you're dead. You're not going to be able to help me, are you?"

Andie looked at Elliot, who was sitting next to her on the couch, and then back at the group. "I don't think so, Simon, but you can still print the tribute to Claire, if you don't mind. Just don't put my name on it. I've lost all credibility. And although I've got to keep low for a while, I don't think Deidre and I will have to be anonymous forever. I believe things have a way of being resolved. But first things first. It seems from the news, or whatever you want to call it, that we have some cleaning up to do at Elliot's." Elliot nodded. "Then I guess I'll figure out what's next."

Elliot put his arm around Andie at that point and said, "We'll figure out what's next." She squeezed his hand.

Simon nodded understandingly, and Wenona said, "That's great. It's good somethin' good is coming out of this travesty. I mean, Charles and me can hardly believe what y'all been tellin' us. It's a cryin' shame."

"Well, thank you for taking us in," Nathan said appreciatively. "I really didn't relish the idea of spending Christmas in a mausoleum, no offense 'cause I know it's your family and all," he trailed off. Everyone just laughed.

"No offense taken," Charles said, getting up and putting more wood on the fire. "Y'all just relax. Tomorrow's another day." And soon they all said their goodnights and retired to the many rooms Wenona had set up for them. Nathan remained on the couch, as they were one bed short.

91

Upon landing in Riyadh, the Secretary watched as the cabin crew politely said Merry Christmas to him and good-bye as they filed off the plane. He looked out the window to see men refueling. The whole scene was uncanny. He felt a chill run down his spine as he looked around the cabin. The VP was still napping in the back, so he was alone. All alone. He could see the men on the tarmac speaking to each other but, of course, could hear nothing. The silence was palpable. Something seemed wrong, but what it was he could not detect. Just at that moment he felt the jet's engines start up and realized they were about to take off again. He felt better, or did he? He wished he could run away.

Since it was only about six hundred miles to Baghdad, he figured they would be in the air for less than an hour. That was good. He wondered if he should awaken the VP, but didn't have to as the man was just then coming down the aisle, hugging his briefcase to his chest. He actually looked pretty good, the Secretary noted. He had apparently just showered and was dressed exquisitely in a very expensive suit and tie, and new designer shoes. His French cuffs were expertly clipped with diamond and gold cufflinks. He wore what had become the obligatory American flag pin on his lapel. Yeah, he probably was looking the best he ever could, the Secretary surmised.

He sat down across the aisle from the Secretary. "How much further?"

"I imagine about an hour until landing," the Secretary responded.

"Good, I'll have enough time for a bite." He hit the button in front of him that solicited the aid of one of the cabin crew. The Secretary looked at him quizzically.

"What?" the VP asked, looking annoyed.

"There's no one here," the Secretary said, confused. "I mean, they all got off in Riyadh."

"What are you talking about, no one here. They're always here. They are required to stay on this jet with me. Where are my bodyguards? Where are yours? And where are those reporters you were supposed to bring?"

The Secretary was dumbfounded. "The reporters were not interested in coming, given that they had to leave their families on Christmas," he retorted. Then he just kept shaking his head. Finally he spoke again. "I guess I figured the bodyguards would be on the ground in Baghdad. I haven't seen them, period. Did you? I mean, when you got on, did you see them?"

The VP's face had drained of color. Something was wrong.

"Hello, gentlemen," the booming voice hailed from the cockpit. "I trust we are comfortable."

The two men looked at each other. The VP felt he recognized the voice but could not place it.

"I'll be with you in a minute to explain our descent, well, your descent," the booming voice exclaimed. And just then the man appeared.

"*You!*" the VP exclaimed. "*You!*"

George Bruce grinned. "You bet! How ya doin', old friends?" he asked, as he approached the two men with his hand outstretched for a shake.

The two men did not physically respond. The Secretary did notice, with alarm, that the man had a parachute on. He was sure this had not gone unnoticed by the VP.

"Okay," George Bruce said, retracting his hand, "here's the game plan."

"Who is this guy?" the Secretary blurted out finally to the VP.

"A coward. He's a coward who shamed his country, and now he's trying to embarrass me."

Bruce looked at the Secretary with a shift of his eyes only. "You must remember me," he said calmly. "The one who was accused of letting his troops down?"

It suddenly dawned on the Secretary. He knew who Bruce was. *Uh, oh,* he thought. *This man had definitely been scapegoated, and he knew they all knew it. It was not a speculation. And nonetheless, the VP was egging him on. He wished he'd just shut up. The ball was in Bruce's court at this very moment. Couldn't the VP tell? Was he just so arrogant as to think it didn't matter?*

"How are you doing, George?" the Secretary asked, hoping to find out what the man wanted before it was too late.

"Oh, well, let's see," Bruce said, sitting to face them a couple of rows up and clasping his hands behind his head. "How am I doing? Well, I'm divorced. I'm unemployable, except for the occasional substitution I provide for pilots who do not enjoy being separated at the last minute from their families on Christmas to take you," and he nodded in the direction of the VP, "to an unannounced destination, which I can do since I got my security clearance back to do nasty jobs for this guy. I guess that's about it. How are you doing?"

"Fine," the Secretary said, sighing.

"Good to hear it," Bruce said, standing up. "So, here's what's going to happen now. We're flying at about twelve thousand feet. The controls are set on autopilot, with coordinates preparing you to land in the Baghdad airport in . . . ah . . ." he looked at his watch, "approximately forty minutes. So hang tight, keep your head down with your arms in front, you know the drill I'm sure, and it should be okay. They'll see you coming. Then get out as quickly as possible, in case there's any fuel leakage, since we just filled up."

Both men were stone-faced.

"You'll never live if you parachute out of this jet," the VP said calmly. "The speed will kill you."

"I've slowed us down appropriately, don't worry about me." The confident grin was disconcerting.

"Is there anything we can do to dissuade you from doing this?" the Secretary asked. "It doesn't make sense. Why bother? I mean, why all of this effort just to have us land safely anyway?"

"I needed a free ride to get away from you bozos. I have some money and friends in the region, and I don't like being abused by my government anymore. Believe me, it's not about you. It's about me. It's for my peace of mind," he said convincingly, if not insultingly. And with that he headed toward the back exit, helmet in hand. "I'm outta here now, so hang onto your seats, this might get a little drafty," he said, looking over his shoulder. "And, oh . . ." he said, stopping and looking back at the VP, "if for any reason you feel lost upon landing, just check out your moral compass, you'll know where you are in a jiffy. So long." And with that, the rush of suction made both men grab their seats with all their might. It was over in the flash of a second, however, as the cabin pressure stabilized, due to Air Force 2's safety door automatically sliding in to replace the door that had literally been torn off its hinges.

"Do you know how to fly this thing?" the VP practically screamed.

"No. Absolutely not. I've never flown anything."

"Aren't you the Secretary of Defense?" he demanded.

"Of course. So what? Being a pilot is not a requirement."

"I know, I know. Well, can you at least go up there and see if you can make the radio work?"

"Oh, for God's sake. I'll go take a look, but I doubt I'll recognize anything," the Secretary said somberly, unlatching his seatbelt and standing up.

He got to the door to the cockpit and pushed on it gingerly, almost afraid to enter. It swung open easily. He ducked slightly and started toward the controls, only to see a big white sheet of paper taped to the front of the panel with five words on it, written large in black.

DON'T EVEN THINK ABOUT IT

The Secretary immediately backed out of the room, afraid that it might be booby-trapped.

"Well, do you know how to work it?" the VP demanded to know.

"Not a clue," the Secretary responded, sitting down and buckling his seatbelt again.

The VP sighed loudly. He tapped his fingers on his briefcase, which he had laid on his lap. "What's in that, anyway?" the Secretary asked rudely. "You act like it's filled with diamonds or something."

"Just plans," the VP responded smugly. "Just some plans."

Now it was the Secretary's turn to sigh. He looked at his watch. "It's about time. . . ." Just then the jet began to turn and bank to the west. The Secretary looked out his window. Because the aircraft was flying so low, he could see quite a lot below them. "Isn't that Baghdad?" he asked, alarmed as the jet continued over it.

The VP jumped up and came over to look. Indeed, the city was clearly directly below them. "I hope no one shoots us down," he said nervously, straining his eyes to see as much as possible.

"It's a distinct possibility, I'm sure," the Secretary said, rubbing his sweaty palms together and wondering if he'd ever see his family again. But as the two very powerful men waited and watched, the jet continued on, the engines droning, the city disappearing, and then it began its descent. The speed began to decrease. They heard the wheels come down next. It was not going to be long before they met the earth. The VP rushed back to his seat and buckled himself in. He placed the briefcase on his lap again, crossed his hands over his head, and leaned forward. The Secretary did the same. He heard the VP muttering, but he couldn't make out what he was saying. It almost sounded like "mommy."

And then the jet hit the ground. Nothing but blackness enveloped both men's minds as the impact ripped through their limbs and rattled their skulls. It took several hundred yards of skidding before the enormous machine finally came to a halt, but the engines still raced on. The fuselage was damaged immediately upon impact, torn as the jet hit a myriad of objects on the ground, including twisted metal from bombed-out cars, huge piles of garbage, and rocks and other natural debris. Once this happened, the fuel began to slowly spill out and pool. It created a small stream as it weaved its way down the body and onto the desert ground, where it obediently and deliberately soaked back to its origins. The Secretary tried to pry himself away from the seat where he had been pinned. He finally realized it was the seatbelt that was preventing him from rolling out into the aisle. He unclipped it and then was able to drop out and crawl along the plane's floor. He stopped when he got to the closest exit door. He read the directions for opening it and did so. It was quite a distance to the ground. He looked around for the VP and saw him huddled in a ball several feet from his seat. He hobbled back to him and tried to see if he was alive; he was, and he was moaning.

"Can you stand up?"

"I don't think so, the pain is too much."

"Where is the pain?"

"My ribs."

"Okay, but we've got to get out of here, I can smell fuel. It might blow up any second."

"Okay, help me or drag me, but get me out of here," the weakened man demanded.

As the two of them looked out the exit door, the ground seemed miles away. "I'll never survive this jump," the VP whispered, still holding onto his briefcase.

"Yes, we will, unfortunately," the Secretary said, looking out at the God-forsaken, hot, cloudless, desolate land where they had crashed. He wasn't sure, but he had a sneaking suspicion as to where they were.

"Let's go," he said, and he jumped, trying to remember to roll, but really not able to control anything. The pain seared through his leg as he collapsed not far from the aircraft. He tried to stand up but realized he must have broken his right leg. He dragged himself quickly away from the jet, hoping to avoid being burned up or worse, torpedoed by the VP himself. The man came hurling down a few seconds later, right after the briefcase. "Can you move?" the Secretary asked after a few minutes. He was sure the man would want to get away from the aircraft as well. There was no response.

Eventually, the heat from the engines ignited the liquid that was pooling. The flames leapt first to the cargo, where it in turn began to ignite the fireworks that the VP had insisted on bringing. The first one that exploded practically burst the Secretary's eardrums. It also brought the VP back to consciousness. On seeing the bright, glistening light, the VP first thought that he was in a hospital and the doctor was shining the light into his eye to determine if there was any damage. Instead, as he became more cognizant, he became aware of his dismal situation. His eyes focused more clearly on the bright light. It was caused by the reflection from the sun on a shiny, silvery, cylindrical object. What it was he did not know, but he began to notice many of them, all around him. Some were quite beautiful. He tried to move his legs, but he could not. The pain from his ribs was severe, but he eventually was able to sit up, to a degree. He looked over and saw the Secretary staring at him. Then the fireworks began to go off simultaneously, sounding as though twenty men were trying to shoot their way out of the belly of the jet. The Secretary continued to stare. Finally, the noise subsided enough to allow them to talk.

"Can you walk?" the VP asked.

"If I could, I would not be here," the Secretary said simply. He started to drag himself a little bit further away, but very carefully, the VP noted.

"Where are we?" the VP asked, trying to keep the man engaged. "Do you know where we are? Do you know if someone will look for us?"

The Secretary did not respond. Some more pop, pop, pops from the fireworks started again, but then they stopped.

"I'm talking to you," the VP yelled. "Where are we?"

"Fallujah."

The name did not compute. "Where are the people?"

"Dead, all dead, I imagine. If they didn't get away, then they're dead," the Secretary said, as he continued to crawl like a crab across the parched ground again, diverting here and there.

The VP was baffled. He couldn't think straight. "Fallujah . . . Fallujah," then it started to dawn on him. He looked again at the tiny cylindrical items surrounding him. "What are these?" he screamed. "What are these shiny colored things?"

"DU, depleted uranium," the Secretary said hoarsely, as he continued to move away. "I knew I should never have agreed with you to having the President sign off on the DU. I knew better. I should have had my head examined," the Defense Secretary added, looking back.

"Oh, quit griping," the VP retorted. "You liked the idea of its use even more than me. You said it was the perfect weapon. Your words exactly." The Secretary grimaced as he recalled saying precisely that. "Where are you going?" the VP asked nervously now, "Where are you . . ." and then he heard a loud explosion. It did not come from the jet. The Secretary dropped flat and began writhing on the ground. He moaned and cried, and then his body went limp.

The VP sat, alone; the briefcase was not far. He reached over for it and pulled it toward him. He opened it slowly. Then he tentatively reached in it and found the map. As he pulled it out, a burst from the plane created a powerful air current, which seemed to snatch the map right from his hand. It floated across the ground for a few yards and then landed flat against a rusted-out automobile hood, fluttering periodically in the windless air as though it were supernaturally suspended, taunting him.

No one came. No one could. The land was off limits. It had died a while back.

92

As news of the missing Air Force 2 came in, Lowell, the VP's Chief of Staff, was notified. It was the day after Christmas, so he was, of course, in his office. He was staring at a letter he had just received by priority mail from a George Bruce, when he got the call from CENTCOM. "The VP's jet is missing. It looks like it just disappeared. We're awaiting further information, and we will keep you posted," the man on the other end stated robotically. Then he added, "Don't mention this to anyone, I repeat, *no one!*"

Lowell began to feel the discomfort of cognitive dissonance, given the intrinsically conflicting information he had just received. He was looking at a message and map indicating exactly what had happened and where the jet was now. In the letter, George Bruce stated the following:

December

By the time you receive this message I will be dead, along with the official occupants of Air Force 2. All other staff departed from the aircraft in Riyadh. As the person piloting Air Force 2 during this trip, I take full responsibility for the downing of the jet in Fallujah and the death of its occupants. Their complicity in the use of depleted uranium on civilians as well as our own soldiers was the reason for my actions.

Sincerely,

George Bruce

George Bruce, Lieutenant General

ATTACHMENT: MAP, Fallujah, Iraq

While Lowell was debating what action to take, if any, the Pentagon was meeting with the Deputy Secretary of Defense to discuss what they were going to do about the crash and deaths. Unbeknownst to Lowell, the highest ranking general at the Pentagon, along with the Deputy, had also received a copy of the same letter. They had met briefly prior to the group meeting, to discuss its implications. Neither man was pleased with the arrival of the letter.

"The President has not yet been informed," the Deputy was stating to a somber group of men, all Caucasian, sitting around the table.

He glanced at the general, who said in response, "We'll need to decide how we're going to present the picture of the death of the VP and Secretary to him."

"Exactly," the Deputy said. The euphemism did not go unnoticed by the others. "In cases like these," the Deputy continued matter-of-factly, as though this kind of incident was not uncommon, "it is best to ensure that the country knows its high-ranking public servants died as heroes, that they did not die in vain."

"My sentiments, also," the general said, nodding. Others around the table began to nod in agreement as well, not knowing what was coming down, but not wanting to be on the wrong side of it, whatever it was going to be. Having said that, he got up and went over to the map of the Middle East on the far wall and picked up a laser pointer. He directed it at Fallujah and then tracked to the east toward Baghdad, where he held the light for a second and then continued further east to Iran. "I do not believe we can rule out that the plane was shot down," he mused, turning the light off and returning to his seat.

"I was thinking the exact same thing," the Deputy said thoughtfully, continuing to stare at the map.

The room became silent as everyone at the table digested this information.

Another Pentagon staff member spoke up. "If it was shot down, I believe we can identify the weapon and its origin within days," he said authoritatively.

"That is good to know," the general said, looking back at the Deputy.

Following another period of silence, the general and Deputy stood simultaneously. "This confidential meeting is now over," the general said. "We will be notifying all of you of our next steps and intentions momentarily. Please stand by." The men filed out and waited to be called back to hear their marching orders.

"I believe we need to inform the President immediately," the Deputy said.

"I agree one hundred percent," the general said.

"He will need to address the nation, by TV and radio, as soon as possible."

"Exactly," the general said again.

"Are you prepared to tell him what happened?" the Deputy asked.

"Yes. Absolutely. We have got to ensure that we maintain control of this situation and use it to our advantage."

"Agreed," the Deputy said, nodding. "Let's call the men back and let them know what to expect. Then please have your man call the VP's Chief of Staff again and have him meet us at the White House. I'll call there now."

"Right."

"One more thing," the Deputy said, as he paused before opening the door.

"What is it?" the general asked.

"Do you think anyone else received the letters we received?"

"You better pray day and night that the answer is no," was all he said, as he stepped through to call the men back in.

93

Elliot and Andie agreed that he should go alone to see what had become of his house. As intimated in all of the news reports, they suspected it was gone. But he needed to know. He had unfinished business there, and so he went. Charles loaned him one of their cars.

He provided his ID to the police guard and was allowed in. As he ducked under the yellow tape he had to laugh to himself, even though the scene was tragic. There was yellow tape around a bunch of ashes. That was it. Ashes mixed with snow. It did seem a bit absurd, but then Elliot had no idea that the "authorities" had been looking for teeth in the wreckage to match to dental records. By now, however, the Feds were pretty much finished. They had found nothing, absolutely nothing. Because the place had been torched so thoroughly, there was nothing there.

Elliot walked around the lot while the police guard kept watch, looking up and down an empty street. Elliot found this to be humorous as well. He shook his head sadly as the realization sunk in that he'd lost everything . . . just about. He went to where the door to the bunker was hidden and came to understand that fortunately they had not seen it. Charred material from the doors that had always covered it continued to lie on top of it, but now they were in the formation of a big ash heap. He was quite sure that the evidence he had so carefully protected in the suspended liquid was safe. He thanked the guard and returned to Charles Winsome's house, where Andie and Simon were still staying. Nathan and Deidre had left earlier. Nathan was going to take her to his home in West Virginia, and then the two of them planned to travel to Europe together. Nathan would help her find an apartment in Scotland, in a town of her choosing, and then he planned on returning to Iraq.

"It's there," Elliot said breathlessly, as he sat down next to Andie in the Winsome's living room. "I know it's there still. We'll just have to be patient. There's a guard there, so I can't go in."

Simon had been told that the DU was still in the underground. "That's good news, then," he said, smiling. Simon had pretty much returned to his old self, Andie noted with pleasure. He was such a good friend, and his commitment to get Claire's tribute, now above the fold, in next Sunday's edition simply thrilled Andie, even though she would not be cited as the author.

"Very good!" Elliot said, sighing with contentment.

"Well, Charles has called for a taxi to take me to the Metro," Simon said, getting up. "I don't want anyone to know I've been here, given the danger it might create for you, Andie. But it's time I get back to the station so I can take it back and make sure it's covering the truth," he said boastfully, standing as tall as he could. Andie jumped up to hug him good-bye.

"When will I see you again?" he asked affectionately. Charles had just walked into the room.

"I don't know, Simon. I don't know where I'll be for the next few weeks. I'll contact you as soon as I feel it's safe or, if possible, when I can clear my name. I just don't know what it's going to take."

"Okay," he said. "Stay safe." He looked at Elliot and shook his hand for a long time. "Thank you again for, well, for saving my life."

"Please don't think of it that way," Elliot said modestly.

"Anyway, please take care of Andie," Simon entreated.

A slight scowl crossed Andie's face upon hearing this. Elliot laughed. "I don't think I need to take care of Andie; it's more like the other way around."

Simon laughed sheepishly. "You're right of course," he said, and hugged Andie again. "Okay, I need to go, the taxi is here. I'll see you soon," he said, as he picked up his coat and what belongings he had left from the trek up the tunnel.

Wenona had joined them now. "Good-bye, Wenona and Charles. Thank you for a wonderful Christmas, your hospitality, and, most of all, for keeping us safe," Simon said, shaking both of their hands. Wenona grabbed him and hugged him. "You take care, ya hear?" she said. "We'll be watching your news from now on, knowin' we can get the facts from you. No more storytelling."

"No way," Simon said. "Okay. Good-bye, all," and with that he was gone.

Charles sat down in the lazy boy next to the fireplace. Wenona left to get some coffee for them, returning quickly with a pot and four cups and saucers. She poured for everyone and then sat down in the chair adjacent to the couch.

"We've been talking," Charles started, looking over at his wife. She smiled. "We know what kind of trouble you two have. Elliot, you have no house to go back to, and, Andie, you can't go back out, 'cause you're a dead criminal," he said, smiling. Andie and Elliot were very interested in finding out where this line of discussion was going.

"Oh, just hurry up and ask 'em," Wenona said impatiently.

"I'm getting there darlin'," Charles said. "So, we're wondering if you want to stay here for a while. I don't mean stay here, exactly, but I mean we've got lots of acreage, you could have your forty acres, I'm just kiddin' y'all, but you could build here, get your lives back together, even tend your own garden. Our kids only come for visits now, and we could use the company, and well, we want to thank you for stickin' up for our country. All those things."

Andie and Elliot looked at each other. There was no doubt that they were very fond of each other. They hadn't had a chance to talk about what they were going to do next, but this situation could provide a lot of opportunities. They could remain here indefinitely while they made new plans. Where else? They slowly nodded to each other.

"Charles, I don't know much about building, but we appreciate your offer and accept."

"Oh, joy," Wenona said. "Let's celebrate!" she said, as she clasped her hands together. "I have some leftover Christmas wine and cheese, I'll be right back."

Charles got up to put some wood on the fire. When he turned to return to his seat, he looked over at the TV, which had been on mute. "Why, look," he said, turning up the volume. "Something's up."

What the three of them saw was startling, disconcerting, and absolutely unfathomable.

The President was addressing the nation from the Oval Office. The twenty or so American flags behind him were at half-mast. The Pentagon's top general, the Deputy Secretary of Defense, and the VP's Chief of Staff surrounded him. The President himself was dressed in a black suit.

"It is with great sadness that I am here today to report a tragic incident," he said, looking down for what seemed like an unbelievably long time. Then he looked up again and continued.

"We have lost two great patriots today. Both the Vice President and the Secretary of Defense have been fatally wounded," the President said, choking and looking teary-eyed into the camera. Then he cleared his throat and continued. "They served their nation well, and their untiring commitment will never be forgotten. They awoke every day with you, the American people, in mind. They went through each and every day concentrating on how they could make life for you, the American people, better and more fulfilling," and here he paused, "and more safe," he added. "There is nothing we can do to bring them back. They are gone, but never to be forgotten."

"Oh, good Lord, what's happened now?" Wenona asked, as she bustled in with the wine and cheese, and what smelled like some very fresh bread. She poured everyone a glass while listening carefully, like the rest of them.

"What appears to have happened here is no less than a violent act against our truest of patriots," the President continued. Now his eyes had dried up and become steely. "I am going to ask the general to describe what we know so far," he said quietly, turning to the general.

The general, a tall man of broad stature, stepped forward. He started by stating again that the country had lost two great patriots. "We now have information indicating that the jet was shot down," the general commented, looking out at the assembled Americans. "We are not sure by whom, but it is becoming an undeniable truth that enemies from outside Iraq have committed this atrocity."

"Look at the VP's Chief of Staff," Andie said suddenly. The man was visibly uncomfortable. He shifted from foot to foot, keeping his head down the entire time.

"But the Deputy Secretary of Defense doesn't look too upset, does he?" Elliot asked. The man was standing by the general with his hands clasped in front of him and looking out into the audience.

"That's because he's got a big fat promotion comin'," Wenona said flatly, shaking her head and sipping her wine.

"Something else is up, though," Andie said, as the camera panned the audience. "You'd think everyone would be watching the men on the stage," she said, "but they're all looking at their Blackberries. Has yours recharged Elliot?" she asked him eagerly. She was afraid to use any of her communication technology.

"I'm sure it has," he said, getting up to retrieve it. He returned with a big grin on his face. "Ms. Aaberg, we have made it to the big time, well, Tim has blogged us into the big time. You are right. All those Congress people are totally perplexed right now. They're being told about heroes while reading factual data documenting the Pentagon's affront on the, well, on just about every minority here and in Iraq, the murders of investigative journalists, and the brainwashing. I'm sure they are totally confused. Some interesting days are ahead for sure," he said convincingly.

"Uh, oh," Charles said just then, "here come those stories."

The group looked back at the TV just as it was switching to the MSM "analysis" of the announcement. "What analysis? We don't need analysis," Wenona said. "I just witnessed what the men said. I don't need interpretation."

"You're going to get it anyway," Charles said in return.

John and Wendy from the RW&B had just popped up, with the background indicating *Presidential Speech Analysis*. "Well, folks, it looks like we have lost two of our best and our brightest," John said, peering into the camera. "What are you hearing, Wendy?" he asked. Wendy now appeared to be standing outside of the White House.

"She gets around doesn't she?" Elliot said.

Wendy started talking on cue. "John, yes. We understand that the crew tried desperately to avoid the oncoming missile, or whatever type of armament from the enemy killed them, but they were caught unawares, so time was not on their side," she said, smiling slightly. And just then, she scratched her upper arm.

"Uh, oh," Andie said.

"Yeah, I saw it," Elliot said.

"Wendy, have you heard yet what the plans are for any kind of retaliation to prevent this from occurring again?"

"Yes, John, they have set up an internal commission to review how this came to be and are planning on reporting back to the President within the next two days, prior to the New Year, as to next steps. Oh . . . that's it for now," she said, smiling largely and turning to run toward the Congressional crowd that was exiting the White House.

Elliot got up and took the remote off the shelf. "May I?" he asked.

"Knock yourself out," Charles said.

"May I have some more wine?" Andie asked Wenona.

"Sure. I think you're going to need more than wine by the end of this fiasco, though," she said.

New shiny faces had shown up on another MSM station. "Joan, what do you make of the fact that Iran was the perpetrator of these murders?" a man named Bob was asking his on-screen co-host.

"Well, as horrendous as it was, we've just learned that Iran had been planning the shooting of the VP's jet once it entered Iraqi airspace for several weeks now."

"So, now it's definitely Iran," Andie commented, obviously angry. "You wonder what happened to the other folks who must have been on that jet," she added. "Not only that, but why didn't we know the VP was going to Iraq?"

"Well, you never know that," Charles replied. "Those folks have got to *sneak* in," he said, emphasizing the word sneak.

"Oh, yeah," Andie said, "so . . . this is just another bogus story. Uh, oh," she added suddenly. Elliot had switched back to the RW&B. "There's Wendy again."

"Wendy, what are you hearing from the Congress?" John asked almost jovially.

"She don't look so good," Wenona said. "She doesn't know what to say. Look at that." Wendy was standing and staring at the camera. Tears were showing in her eyes.

"Wendy, we understand you're upset about these patriots' deaths, but . . . Wendy, yes?"

Wendy had composed herself now. "Uh, John," Wendy said, holding her arm. "I just spoke with two Congress people, and they are both under the impression that another, greater tragedy has occurred. I need to close now, John."

"Wendy, Wendy, you can't . . . shit!" John turned back to the camera, looking cross and apologetic, but then smiling suddenly. "Folks, sorry for that slip-up, we'll be back after a station break."

Elliot switched to WSSN. Their regular newscaster, Neal Kirkland, was back.

"Boy, Simon made good on his word and fast," Elliot said, smiling and looking over at Andie.

"Yes, he did," she said, smiling back at him. "Can you turn it up a bit?"

"Right now we're going to take you back to the White House," Neal said, with little emotion. "Apparently, the President would like to address the nation once again. I must say that we'll be back after his statements to provide you with other breaking news from the Hill, but, for now, let's listen."

"My fellow Americans, I am back to let you know that new information has just been provided to me that has allowed me to make an immediate decision. We are now convinced, without a doubt, as to who the perpetrators of this foul act are. I promise you, someone will pay, my fellow Americans. Mark my words, someone will pay."

Author Bio

P.J. Allen

P.J. Allen currently lives and writes from Madison, Wisconsin. The author earned a Doctorate in Communication from Florida State University and works to promote health and education in developing countries, including South and Central Asia, and West and Southern Africa. Allen also lived and worked in Washington D.C., advocating for these same issues. *Deadly Untruths,* the author's first novel, blends Allen's knowledge of communication and politics. A second novel is currently under way, *The Yeti Quotient,* that draws on Allen's knowledge of health and politics.

CPSIA information can be obtained at www.ICGtesting.com
Printed in the USA
LVOW070650210912

299580LV00002B/1/P